DOCTOR WHO

BYZANTIUM!

KEITH TOPPING

Published by BBC Worldwide Ltd
Woodlands, 80 Wood Lane
London W12 0TT

First published 2001

ISBN 0 563 53836 8

Printed and bound in Great Britain by Mackays of Chatham
Cover printed by Belmont Press Ltd, Northampton

Byzantium!
is dedicated to Shaun Lyon,
because I promised that I would

and

to Jon Miller and Jim Swallow,
for their valuable advice and friendship.

As it is written in the prophets,
Behold, I send my messenger before thy face,
which shall prepare thy way before thee.
Mark 1:2

Prologue
Once in a Lifetime

'And these signs shall follow them that believe.'
Mark 16:17

London, England: 1973

'... And what is your name then, young man?'

The little boy stopped pretending to be Tony Green (Newcastle United and Scotland) dribbling brilliantly around the static (and imaginary) Chelsea back-four, and looked up at the pretty lady and her bewitching smile. 'Hello,' he said, without a trace of inhibition. 'I'm John Alydon Ganatus Chesterton.' He held out a delicate child's hand which the woman took and shook, gently. 'And I'm six-and-a-half,' he continued, precociously. 'How do you do?'

'Bet you're only six-and-a-quarter, really?' she asked.

Johnny grinned with a gap-toothed smile.

'Those are unusual names,' the lady noted.

Johnny nodded, half of his attention on the lady's clear sea-green eyes, the other half drawn to the fabulous exhibits around him. 'They were friends of my mommy and daddy,' he replied in a well-rehearsed little speech. 'They live in a place a long way away.'

Barbara appeared from around a nearby corner with an irritated scowl on her face. 'There you are,' she scolded. 'What have I told you about running off like that?'

Johnny looked at his shoes and said nothing.

There was an embarrassed silence before anyone spoke. 'Don't be too hard on him,' said the woman, kindly. 'We were talking.'

Barbara shrugged her shoulders. 'He can be a bit of a handful,' she confided and then playfully ruffled Johnny's hair. 'Can't you?' she asked. Her son continued to cling, mutely, to his mother's dress with a contrite look on his face. 'He's at that age where everything's one big adventure. Which is just fine for *him*, but it's a right pain in the neck for everyone else.' She paused and looked down at her son. Her stern expression remained until the urchin holding her tightly melted her icy heart to slush.

The woman nodded. 'My youngest is exactly the same,' she replied. 'She's only three, but you wouldn't believe the kind of things that she can get up to... Well, actually, you probably *could*.' She held out her black-gloved hand. 'Julia,' she said brightly.

'Barbara. Chesterton,' replied Barbara. 'Pleasure to meet you.'

Julia looked down at the still-silent boy. 'And this little man, I've already met. What do you want to be when you grow up, Johnny?' she asked, kneeling down beside him.

Johnny unwrapped himself from his mother's side and grinned broadly. 'I want to be a top pop star like Julian Blake. Or Mr Big Hat out of Slade.'

'I'll buy all of your records,' said Julia, charmed by Johnny's cheeky, ragamuffin smile. 'He's so sweet. Can I take him back to Redborough with me?'

'Oh, don't encourage him, for goodness sake,' Barbara said, wryly. 'He's a dreamer, this one. Last week he wanted to be an astronaut. Next week it'll be something different.'

The miserable and overcast slate-grey November sky, seen through the British Museum windows, was full of drizzle and spit as Barbara and Julia sat on a hard wooden bench in the middle of the vast and virtually deserted hall.

'*An Exhibition of Roman and Early Christian Archaeology*', noted a sign next to an open-topped case containing fragments of broken Samian pottery and jagged-edged silver and bronze coins.

'One of my specialities when I was still teaching,' noted Barbara, gesturing towards the case. 'That's a piece from a first-century drinking goblet,' she continued, pointing to a curved fragment of a reddish-brown pot. 'It's probably from the Middle East. Antioch or Rhodes. Or maybe Byzantium.'

"Istanbul, not Constantinople?!"

'Was there once. A long time ago,' noted Barbara in passing.

'Oh *lovely*,' said Julia. 'It'd be pure joy to have a foreign holiday but the costs are so expensive. I must find Robert soon,' she added. 'He's up at New Scotland Yard. We always do this when we get a weekend in London. He swans off drinking with the Flying Squad and gets completely slaughtered and I have to amuse myself up and down Carnaby Street and then fish him out of the Bent Copper's Arms and drag him back home to the rolling pin. It's like a little ritual with us.'

Barbara was surprised at her new friend's acceptance of such a regimented lifestyle. 'I'm amazed you put up with it,' she said as they stared at another of the Roman empire exhibits, and shared tea from Barbara's thermos flask in a pair of dirty-yellow plastic cups. Ahead of them, Johnny happily ran in circles around the exhibit case.

'Haven't you ever been in love?' Julia asked.

'Yes,' replied Barbara cheerily. 'Like Byzantium, I was there once. But there are some places that you visit briefly and leave and then there are others where you stay all of your life.'

EPISODE ONE
LXIV, AND ALL THAT...

And Jesus said unto them, Come ye after me,
and I will make you to become fishers of men.
Mark 1:17

Chapter One
Direction, Reaction, Creation

And Pilate answered and said again unto them,
What will ye then that I shall do unto him whom
ye call the King of the Jews?
And they cried out again, Crucify him.
Mark 15:12–13

Sharp, like a needle.

As hot as burning coals, the spikes were hammered through flesh and muscle. Through sinew and bone. And finally through the gnarled wood of the flat-board, to the dirt beneath.

As sparks from the clashing metal danced in the air, blood spurted in a fine mosaic mist onto the arms and face of the legionnaire. The soldier winced and spat, though not at the touch and taste of the blood, for he was well used to them both after half a lifetime in the service of his emperor.

He wiped away the red specks with barely a second thought, leaving an ugly slash streaked across his cheek.

No, the blood didn't bother him too much.

It was the screaming that really annoyed him.

Why didn't these snivelling scum just die quietly, and with some dignity?

Like a Roman.

'They squeal and wrestle like a sticked-pig,' he told his watching comrades as he struggled with the tool in his hand. 'Keep him straight and still,' he continued, shouting at the hapless foot-soldier gripping the victim's shaking hands. 'Or you shall find yourself nailed up there with him.'

The hammer struck again and the hands were joined together at the wrist. At that very moment, when the sickening frenzy of pain was at its most intense, the victim lost all control of his bowels. It was something that the legionnaire had experienced on more than one occasion and the stink was, also, of no concern to him. But, again, he wished that this wretch would cease his infernal noise.

'Rot in Xhia's pit, you Roman bastard,' cried the victim in a hoarse and guttural voice, and through tightly gritted teeth. He would undoubtedly have enjoyed spitting in the legionnaire's face as an afterthought. But this wasn't an option as the prone victim's throat was bone-dry. A consequence of the blood-chilling pain in his wrists and at his feet.

'Stick him up there,' the legionnaire told his colleagues. 'Stick him up straight and hard and let him dangle. Let us see what an hour of that does to his opinion of his superiors.' Sycophantic laughter filled the air as a group of troops heaved the dead weight of the victim upright, and fixed him to the *stauros* on which he would die a horribly slow and painful death.

The judgement was read. 'Jacob bar Samuel. Having been accused by his own people of being a common and lying *thief*, and having been fairly tried and condemned by Thalius Maximus, representative in the free city of Byzantium of his most great and awesome emperor Lucius Nero, is, this day, crucified for his banditry and thievery. Let his just and righteous punishment serve as a rare example to all who would consider perpetrating crimes and treasons against the authority of the empire of Rome.'

Centurion Crispianus Dolavia turned his horse away from the crucified thief whose loud screaming had partially drowned out the reading of the sentence. But the way that Dolavia was now facing offered him no sanctuary either. A phalanx of black-clad women, their heads shrouded with funereal coverings, knelt in the dirt several feet away, wailing and crying out the name of the executed man and beating the ground with their fists. 'If you do not get these screeching whores from my sight with great haste, I shall take pleasure in having you put to the sword,' the centurion told a nearby soldier who instantly rushed forward and drew his own weapon, holding it threateningly above the women.

'Move yourselves,' the soldier shouted, kicking dust into the women's faces as they scattered and ran down the steep hillside with the soldier at their heels, growling at them like a crazed dog.

Crispianus admired such dedication, even in the face of his own terrible threat. 'Be advised that I wish for that soldier to be given extra pay for his efficiency,' he told the captain of the guard, who nodded and helped the centurion from his saddle. 'Five *denarii* at the least.'

Sore and skinned from the chafing leather, Crispianus landed on the ground with a wince and a curse to Jupiter. Then, a little unwillingly, he returned his attention to the condemned man. And the noise that he continued to make.

'What crime did the *dog* commit?' he asked the captain.

'Stole bread from the garrison,' replied the barrel-chested man. 'To feed its starving family, it said.'

'Crucifixion is a punishment far too good for the cur,' noted the centurion.

But that simply wasn't true.

The principle of this form of execution was sublimely simple. Yet it was about as undignified a death as it was possible to imagine, with the wrists and feet of the unfortunate victim nailed together in such a position that the prisoner slowly died of hyper-asphyxiation and hypovolemic shock whilst they jerked spasmodically with the last of their energy. Sometimes, if there was a lack of nails, the legions simply used rope bindings instead,that scarred and chafed the skin raw instead of piercing it cleanly. But the effect was much the same. The Romans were experts at this sublimely cruel manner of dispatch. they could keep a person alive for days on the *staurous* if they wanted to, dehydrated, exhausted, in terrible pain, but still clinging to life.

The only relief for the dying man was the ability to push himself up by his feet and so ease the vice-like pressure upon the chest and allow himself to breathe. But this required undergoing the agony of scraping the broken bones of his feet against the thick metal spike nailed through them. The usual custom was to let the executed man fight a cruel and hopeless struggle for air for an hour, or five, or ten, depending on the severity of his crimes. And, when the overseeing officer eventually got bored with the proceedings, or when darkness encroached, to break the man's legs and thus prevent him from relieving himself any longer.

Death would follow soon afterwards. If the executed man was lucky.

But the saddlesore centurion was, frankly, already bored. The heat of the day was beginning to take its toll, making him weary, and the shrill screaming was giving him a dull ache in his head.

'Captain. Have one of the men finish the job,' he ordered. 'Put this beast out of my misery.'

The captain had every intention of doing so, one did not disobey an order from the likes of Crispianus Dolavia. But he *was* curious. 'The condemned has been up there for less than an hour, sir. Should we not leave him longer as an example to others?'

'Do you wish to spend any more time than is absolutely necessary listening to *that*, Captain?' Crispianus moaned with resignation as the dying man let out another loud and pitiful cry. 'We require that this deed is done with. The three Jews responsible for the murder of a soldier in a market brawl have a date with gross justice and I want this one down and in the ground before we drag *them* to this place.'

'Very good, sir,' said the captain disinterestedly, turning to the closest legionnaire and barking a command to carry out the centurion's order. The legionnaire, Marinus Topignius, picked up his short *pilum* lance and, without ceremony, speared Jacob bar Samuel through the ribs like a hot knife sinking into butter. The victim's eyes bulged open fully and a final choking cry of pain and a prayer for vengeance from beyond the grave escaped his lips. And then his guts spilled onto the parched earth beneath him and he was dead.

'Agitators and terrorists. This land is *full* to bursting with such as they,' snapped Crispianus Dolavia bitterly, taking a mouthful of wine from his flask. He swilled it around his dry mouth and spat the wine onto the ground. 'If not the Zealot Jews that wickedly defy us, then it is the Greeks. And if not them, then the Macedonians, or the Samarians... A plethora of petty and vicious races who do not have the capacity to realise when they are well off. We bring them peace, bread, prosperity and a place in the empire and what do they present to us for our gifts in return?' He paused and gazed at the crucified man who was now being wrenched from the execution place by Marinus and his legionnaire brothers. 'Wonder you why these flea-ridden wretches seem so content to die for such a ridiculous cause, Captain?'

'Cause, sir?' asked the captain. 'He was just a thief...'

'Not the condemned, specifically,' the centurion replied, wearily. 'I mean, generally?'

The captain, Drusus Felinistius, shrugged. 'I am but a mere soldier, sir, and as a consequence of this, not paid to think.'

Crispianus Dolavia shook his head. 'Bury his bones, captain. Bury them deep and salt the earth.' He watched as the thief's broken body was thrown into a dirt pit at the side of the hill. One of the legionnaires began to shovel the blood away from the base of the *stauros* pole, but the centurion called for him to stop. 'There is no time for that now, soldier,' he said miserably. 'We have another three of these troublesome scum to exterminate before sunfall.'

By all of the gods in the heavens, Crispianus Dolavia *hated* Byzantium.

Chapter Two
There Are Seven Levels

How hardly shall they that have riches
enter into the Kingdom of God!
Mark 10:23

'All of the civilian executions have been carried forth this day.' Tribune Marcus Lanilla sat without being asked in the general's quarters and wore the look of someone who took great satisfaction in a job well done.

'Were there any incidents to report?'

'None to speak of,' Marcus told his superior, a smug and thoroughly-pleased-with-himself expression on his rounded and handsome face. 'Of course, I personally did not expect that there would be.'

General Gaius Calaphilus was not a man who took that kind of implied rebuke lightly. Not that Lanilla had actually said anything that could be construed as insubordination or misconduct. But both of the men were astute enough to know sarcasm when it presented itself. Calaphilus's eyes blazed beneath his battle-scarred, furrowed brow, topped with a thinning mat of grey hair. 'When you have been in as many occupied territories of the empire as I have, *boy*, you might be in a position to question my authority. Be that understood?'

The young tribune blanched at the general's reply for a moment, but Marcus Lanilla quickly recovered his composure. Far too quickly for Calaphilus's liking.

Once upon a time Gaius Calaphilus could have terrified the likes of Marcus with a mere glance, such was his reputation for swift, decisive and majestic retribution on those subordinates who tried his patience and questioned his authority.

But Marcus had the arrogance of youth on his side and, frankly, the general just didn't seem to frighten him in the slightest. Calaphilus's days were numbered, Marcus seemed to have decided that months ago along with every other ambitious young officer in the legion. Anyone with a basic understanding of politics knew what was happening in the Roman world. Claudius, the God, had been gone a decade and gradually his favourite sons were following him to the grave. Some of them willingly, others with a helping hand. The conservative military, as ever, had been slow to follow the new emperor's lead. But things were changing. Rapidly.

Now was the time for a new order to make a name for themselves across the breadth of the empire, and Marcus, and many like him, were determined to muscle their way to Nero's side when they and their brothers of the future swept away the last crumbling debris of the past.

Marcus Lanilla was not so much ambitious as *destined*.

'You believe that you know it all, do you not, *boy*?' Calaphilus asked with contempt. 'That is the kind of ignorance that almost lost us Britannia two years since. Leaving pups like you, fresh off their piss-pot, in charge of matters. I would not let you run the public whorehouses, much less anything bigger or more important.'

'You believe that Britannia is worth keeping?' sneered Marcus. He was clearly appalled that he should be spoken to like this by a man of most base and common birth. One who had merely risen through the army ranks rather than achieving his lofty station through a noble lineage, as Marcus and all of his friends had.

'Had you ventured to that land, boy, then you would know that it most certainly is.'

The old soldier paused, aware that his anger was making him say dangerous things. This insolent cur, Marcus Lanilla, had friends in some very high places. His father had been a senator, as had his grandfather before him. People with those sort of contacts could be hard enemies to fight, as Calaphilus knew from bitter experience. Gaius was a soldier who hated the deceitful two-faced conflict of politics more than he hated the Jewish wretches that he willingly slaughtered in the streets of Byzantium in his emperor's name. It did his soul good to know that Marcus would get his ripe comeuppance once day. Arrogant young thugs with delusions of grandeur like him always would.

And, Calaphilus hoped, he would be there to see it. That would truly satisfy the old soldier. But, for now, they had more pressing issues to worry about than Lanilla and his games of conquest. Like the increasing number of attacks on Roman property and citizens from a fanatical element of the Jews.

'By executing half a dozen, we have shown these Zealots that we are frightened of them. It was the same in Judaea. We grow lazy and decadent and think that they do not have the capability to hurt us in the great dominions. But we are *wrong*. We should do, this day, what was done in the emperor's name in Gaul and string them up, mercilessly, in their hundreds. One massive show of strength is all that is needed. Then we shall have a *pax Romanus* for decades. And we could, if the powers that be would let us.'

Though neither could quite believe it, Marcus found himself agreeing with the older man about their mutual enemy, a weak and flaccid, transient *praefectus* who had opposed and prevented plans for such a demonstration of Roman power and control.

'These Jews have clearly been inspired by the recent Zealot uprisings in Jerusalem. They seem intent on causing trouble. They should be put down with maximum force,' he noted. 'They are only, after all, a race of syphilitic scum. Wipe them from the face of the earth once and for all, that is what *I* say.'

'And that is your wise counsel is it, boy?' Calaphilus looked gravely at the young tribune. 'The Jews have faith as well as blood running through their veins,' he noted.

'I do not understand such views, personally.'

'Then *that* will get you killed,' continued a sneering Calaphilus. 'You, and a lot of good men who serve under you.' He sat down again and began to fan himself with his riding crop against the heat of the late afternoon. 'The Jews are waiting for a *messiah*.' He saw Marcus's baffled expression with considerable amusement. 'An "anointed one", if you prefer. Someone who will lead them out of their oppression and to the freedom of a promised land. If you want to defeat these people then you should try to understand their customs and culture. And about the ancient Hebrew chieftains like Joshua and Moses and Solomon whose prophecies they follow.'

'I am not interested in such tribal nonsense. Or in the demented ramblings of a race of cowards and traitors.'

Now Calaphilus lost his temper again, though more in sadness than in anger. 'You just do not listen, do you? The Jews are a people who celebrate the fact that they raised themselves from slavery. They have a tradition of forbearance going back to a time before Rome was even Rome as we know it.'

Marcus Lanilla seemed to have become bored with the lecture he was getting. He yawned, loudly, and picked up his tunic as he stood to leave.

'Fortunately for Rome,' continued Calaphilus, ignoring his subordinate's blatant rudeness, 'both the Zealots and the Pharisees are usually too busy fighting amongst themselves and with a new internal faction. A cult of nomadic insurrectionists called the Christians, whom I presume you will be unfamiliar with?'

'Should I know of these people?'

Calaphilus began to laugh. 'You will, *boy*, you will. They are a nuisance to Rome as of now but, seemingly, they are of more threat to the Jews. I am thoroughly content to see them tear each other apart if it means that we are left to police Byzantium as we have for the last 200 years. Many good men have fought and died protecting this outpost and I will not believe that they fought and died for nothing. Because, unlike you, my *sacramentum* means something to me.'

Enraged at the suggestion that he did not care about his sacred oath, Marcus turned on his general, a hand dramatically clutching the hilt of his sword. 'I fight as well as *any* man, beneath the *aquilia* of my legion, and I shall kill with great vengeance whomsoever suggests otherwise. I leave the machinations of politics to those who are too weak to fight and die,' he continued, dismissively. 'And history was never my strong point.'

The shadows of twilight were stretching across the city as Marcus reached his villa to find his wife, Agrinella, and their friend, Fabius Actium, already eating supper. He threw his tunic onto a marbled statue of the God Augustus with little ceremony and squatted down on a pillow beside them, kicking off his sandals and stuffing a handful of cold meat into his mouth before washing his hands in the flower-scented water bowl.

'I am *starved*. Wine,' he bellowed to a nearby serving girl as he splashed water onto his sunburnt face, and deeply inhaled the smell of jasmine. 'And make it quick or I shall have some haste beaten into you.' He smiled charmingly at his guest as the girl began to fill his goblet. 'Fabius, you old rascal. I apologise for my inhospitable late arrival. That ancient cretin Calaphilus wanted to give me a lesson in Jewish history that I could well have done without.'

'The man is such a vulgar bore,' noted Agrinella with a timely yawn, as she reached for a grape and slipped it into her mouth.

'Marcus is contemptuous of Calaphilus's handling of the current situation *vis-à-vis* the Jews, and he has every right to be,' Fabius explained. 'Instead of being asked his counsel, he is shunned or ignored publicly and treated shamefully in private.'

Marcus clearly agreed. 'With a *praefectus* keen to see the military powerless and castrated, what Byzantium needs is strength, not weak old fools. People like us, Fabius.'

'As one tribune to another,' confided Fabius in a low, conspiratorial whisper, 'what is needed here, I believe, is direct action.' His raucous laughter, and that of Agrinella, was halted by a sour look on Marcus's face as he swallowed his wine.

'Cartethus,' he roared. The tall and slightly stooping figure of the head of the household appeared instantly at Marcus's side, his face a passive mask. 'This wine is rank,' Marcus bellowed, throwing the goblet to the floor where the wine spilled onto the marbled tiles leaving an ugly red stain.

Cartethus bowed and then grabbed the wrist of the serving girl, twisting it and making her cry out in pain. 'Yes, Excellency,' he noted. 'A most unfortunate error. I shall deal with this incident personally,' he continued, dragging the slave with him through the doors.

Agrinella waited until he was gone and then propped herself up on one elbow and took a sip from her own cup. 'Tastes perfectly all right to me', she said, grabbing a chicken leg and hungrily biting into it. 'You are *so* impetuous, my heart. How many times have I cautioned you to consider the consequences of your deeds before you act with such rash impatience?'

'Do we speak of the chastisement of a slave girl for arrant insolence or of plots and schemes concerning the ridding from our sight of the worst general in all the empire?' asked Marcus, licking his lips into a wicked and lustful smile whilst Fabius raised his eyebrows quizzically.

Agrinella merely lay back and began to laugh. 'My brave soldiers,' she said at last, holding her stomach against the niggling pain of indigestion. 'So nakedly ambitious but, oh, so *obvious*!' She rolled onto her side and slipped from the couch to the cool marble floor. She walked, barefooted, across to Fabius and sat in his lap, stroking her hand down his chest all of the way to his groin. She kissed him full on the lips, and plunged her tongue deeply into his mouth, biting hard his bottom lip and drawing blood from it. 'Dear Fabius,' she said at last, casting a quick and knowing glance at her husband on the other side of the room. 'It is not that we do not seek your welcome company, our good and loving friend, but Marcus wishes to take me, now, to his bedchamber and roughly fill me with his seed. Do you understand why you must leave our home at once, my sweet?'

Fabius pushed Agrinella gently away, slapping her playfully on the buttock as she snaked her way back to the couch with a swish of eastern silk. He stood, straightening his uniform and reattaching his belt and sword to his full and sore stomach. 'You married a vixen!' Fabius told his friend. 'This one will take you and I all of the way to the Circus of Nero. If she does not have us dragged through the streets in chains and beheaded like common criminals first.'

'Then we can all forget about Byzantium forever,' Agrinella added, like a hungry child anticipating a lip-licking feast. Her husband, once again, seemed distracted. 'What say you, my love?' she asked.

'Before we can forget Byzantium,' Marcus offered, 'firstly, it must be ours...'

Chapter Three
Through the Past, Darkly

Why doth this man thus speak blasphemies?
Who can forgive sins but God only?
Mark 2:7

The bottomless chasm of time and space *did*, seemingly, have a bottom after all.

A strangely comforting thought, that.

Finally, after what seemed like an eternity (but was probably just seconds), the craft stopped falling. The TARDIS impacted with something solid and its inhabitants ceased to be tossed around the console room like tiny objects collected in a matchbox.

As his head thudded, hard, against the floor, Ian Chesterton felt only a momentary numb and warmish sensation, as though an off switch had been flicked in his central nervous system. It wasn't at all unpleasant, he decided. A bit like how he felt after three pints of Theakston's and a whisky chaser in Pages Bar.

For the merest fraction of a second there was utter blackness around him and then the emergency lighting kicked in. The only sound was the constant hum of the TARDIS instrumentation in the console room. Until, that is, Vicki began crying.

Ridiculously, in retrospect, Ian found himself back in the physics lab in Coal Hill school, talking to a class of 'O' level pupils about the mechanics of Newton's first law of motion. *A body will remain at rest or travelling in a straight line at constant speed unless it is acted upon by an external force*.

'The tendency of a body to remain at rest or moving with constant velocity is called "the inertia of the body". This is related to the mass, which is the total amount of substance,' Ian told the class. The thick and tangible smell of chalk dust, books, damp uniforms and of school dinners wafting through the corridors was almost enough to make him believe that he had travelled in time.

An *outrageous* concept.

NEWTON KNEW HIS ONIONS, had been scrawled in a child's handwriting on the blackboard behind Ian. He looked at the motto, shook his head, took the duster and removed the final word, replacing it with APPLES. 'Much better,' he noted.

'Therefore, the resultant force exerted on any given body (in this case, a Time and Space craft disguised as a 1952 London police telephone box by means of a science wholly beyond any explanation that I can give you) is directly proportional to the acceleration produced by the force. In this case, gravity. Kenneth Fazakerley, are you eating in class?'

The reply wasn't at all what he expected.

'Ian. Are you all right?'

First Barbara Wright's voice and then her face sliced into his hallucination. *That* wasn't especially unpleasant either. Just like that first time they had met, their eyes drawn to each other across a crowded room in that quaint little tea shop on Tottenham Court Road.

'Sir Isaac Newton told us why an apple falls down from the sky,' Ian mumbled and tried to stand, with the aid of Barbara. But he only succeeded in bruising his knees on the console room floor. 'Why didn't he just leave gravity alone? We were doing quite nicely before *he* came along...'

Barbara towered over him, elongated. Bent out of shape by gravity's pull and seemingly at an angle of 60 degrees. Don't get me started on Pythagoras, Ian thought angrily. Another right silly-sausage with his hypotenuse and his *theorem*. Barbara's hands rested on her hips and she had a concerned look on her face, of the sort that she normally reserved for tending to a second-former with a grazed knee in the playground. 'Have you hit your head?' she asked, maternally. Ian just smiled, stupidly, and tried to get back to *for every action there is always opposed an equal reaction*.

Somewhere nearby Vicki was still sobbing. 'Look to the girl, Miss Wright,' Ian murmured and then slumped into unconsciousness to dream, happily, of sitting in a tree and throwing apples at that clever-dick Newton's head.

'Good gracious, child, stop that snivelling. It's only a flesh wound.'

Ian had always found that particular phrase a little ludicrous. A flesh wound means, surely, that one's own flesh has been wounded? Which is, let's be fair, pretty painful. Therefore, he saw no reason to quantify this as somehow less dramatic than any other type of *non*-flesh wound. Considerably more than some, in fact. He opened his eyes and saw the Doctor and Barbara struggling to apply a cotton bandage to Vicki who had, seemingly, cut her arm on the rim of the console. Feeling dizzy and sluggish, Ian closed his eyes again and swam happily back to his warm and cosy dream-world until a sharp poking in his ribs brought him out again.

'...And as for you, Chetterton,' the Doctor said, prodding Ian with his stick, 'they would call this malingering in the army.'

A scowling face and a shock of white hair greeted Ian as he reopened his eyes.

'I did two years' national service in the RAF, Doctor,' Ian replied, pushing the walking stick away. 'You *know* that. Honourably discharged. I can still remember my rank and serial number if you want?'

The Doctor seemed to spend an age considering this before he chuckled and patted Ian on the back. 'You'll live, my boy,' he noted and returned his attention to the still-complaining Vicki. 'Oh, do stop making such a fuss...'

Barbara joined Ian and knelt beside the wicker chair in which he was resting. 'How do you feel?' she asked.

'How do I look?'

'Like you've just gone fifteen rounds with Henry Cooper,' she replied, truthfully, and held up a mirror to Ian. One side of his face was swollen and an ugly purple bruise was beginning to manifest itself around his right eye.

'Sort of feels like it too,' Ian admitted as he stood, gripping the arms of the chair for support. 'You ought to see the other fellah...'

'... but it hurts,' shouted Vicki from across the room.

'Of course it does,' replied the Doctor, in exasperation. 'It's *supposed* to.'

Barbara rolled her eyes. 'We'll have to get her toughened up a bit,' she said, glancing at their newest travelling companion. Ian followed her gaze at the girl who, with the bandage applied to her arm, was now discovering other bumps and bruises. And complaining, loudly, about them. 'She's got a chip on her shoulder the size of Big Ben,' continued Barbara. 'I told her to act her age and she asked how she was supposed to "act fourteen". You'd never have heard impertinence like that from Susan.'

'You've got a short memory!' Ian noted with a wry smile. 'Susan could be a right scallywag when the mood took her. Vicki's no different.'

'Perhaps,' Barbara replied, 'but I can't see the Doctor putting up with too many lead-swinging performances like this, look-alike replacement or whatsoever...'

Ian was amused by this. 'If she'd gone to Coal Hill, you'd have sent her to Mrs McGregor, no doubt?'

Barbara winced at the thought of the eighteen-stone Scottish form mistress who not only terrified all of the pupils, but a fair percentage of the staff as well. 'I can't see Vicki at Coal Hill, somehow,' she noted.

'Come to that, I can't see you or I returning to a life of registers, dinner money and log tables,' said Ian flatly. That he had given a lot of thought to the possibility of returning home didn't surprise Barbara in the slightest. She, herself, spent a portion of every day pondering on when and if it would ever happen.

'Do you think we ever will get back?' she asked. 'To our own time, I mean?'

'In the lap of the Gods,' Ian noted with a fatalistic shrug of his shoulders. 'Or, should I say, in the hands of the Doctor?'

'Is it always like this?' asked Vicki as she flexed her bandaged arm.

'No,' replied Ian. 'Now and again we actually arrive somewhere and don't get thrown headfirst into peril, danger and mayhem. Isn't that right, Doctor?'

The Doctor raised his head from a complex piece of TARDIS equipment, clasped the lapels of his Edwardian waistcoat and strode purposefully towards Ian who was standing by the console. 'What's that, eh? Had enough, have you, hmm? Care to get off? I'm sure that could be arranged.' He peered at the schoolteacher across the rim of the half-moon spectacles that rested on the bridge of his nose, his blue-grey eyes resembling a raging sea in the middle of a force-ten gale.

Vicki stared, aghast. This was to be her new home? A surrogate family of squabbling, loud, authority figures.

'Stop fighting, you two,' said Barbara, clearly embarrassed that their new companion was being introduced to such a confrontational aspect of TARDIS life. 'We're safe now... For the time being, anyway. Shouldn't we find out exactly where we've landed?'

The Doctor gave a muffled humph of bellicose indifference and moved to the console, edging Ian out of the way with a terse 'excuse me'.

'A vexed question, clearly,' Ian observed as he followed.

'Earth,' the Doctor said, grandly, pushing a few random buttons until the TARDIS scanner spluttered into life. He noted the joyous expressions on Ian and Barbara's face with clear disdain. There was an entire universe to explore out there. Whilst he waited for the picture to clear, the Doctor read from the gauges in front of him. 'The Yearometer tells us that the date is, using a calendar that you would be familiar with, 14 March. In the year 64.'

'AD or BC?' asked Ian.

'The former,' replied the Doctor. 'We appear to be somewhere close to the peninsular between the Bosphorus straits and the Black Sea.'

'Turkey?'

'Thrace during this period,' corrected Barbara. 'More of a Greek and Macedonian influence than Middle Eastern, though it's likely to be under Roman rule. It consisted of a series of free city-states until circa AD73. Before that they were all a Roman protectorate.' She seemed genuinely excited by the prospect of where they had landed. 'This is a real chance to have a close look at a fascinating collection of cultures.'

'You said that about the Aztecs once, remember?' replied Ian with a sly chuckle. The Doctor shot him a reproachful look.

'And I learned my lesson well,' added Barbara with barely a tinge of regret in her voice, as she continued to look at the clearing monochrome image on the scanner screen. The TARDIS had landed at an angle on an outcrop of sand and stone, beside a rock crevice and a steep incline. Beyond, in the shimmering middle-distance of a lengthy stretch of barren scrubland, was the glistening, pale azure majesty of the river meeting the sea. And beside it, a large settlement of towering domed roofs and spires and minarets - a town of white sandstone that rose vertically out of the desert like a mirage.

'Istanbul?' offered Vicki.

'Constantinople, not Istanbul!' replied Ian, reflecting that the girl's history could do with a bit of revision.

'*Byzantium*, actually,' concluded Barbara with a wink to a crest-fallen Ian. 'It won't be Constantinople for another two hundred-odd years. The Imperial City. Gateway to the East.'

'Very educational, I'm sure,' noted the Doctor with seeming disinterest. 'And now, I suppose, you want to go and have a look at it, do you, hmm?'

Barbara was suddenly thirteen again and trying to persuade her father to take her to the Tower of London. 'Oh Doctor,' she said, almost pleadingly, 'we must. When the Greeks talked about *stin polis*, Byzantium was the model on which all others were based, including Athens. There's so much history...'

The Doctor's face was a picture. 'It is always like this whenever we land in Earth's past. I am lectured on matters of which I am already aware.'

'I apologise,' said Barbara, genuinely, clasping her hands over the Doctor's own, 'I know I can be a bit academic at times, but...'

'Yes, we can go,' sighed the Doctor. 'And, no doubt, some terrible fate will befall us. It usually does.'

'Where's your spirit of adventure, Doctor?' asked Ian.

This brought a scowl to the old man's face. 'It seems to have suffered a rather severe dent from all of the trouble you two keep getting me into,' he growled. 'I don't know why I continually allow you to persuade me to blunder into such hair-brained adventures.'

And, with that, he shuffled out of the console room, muttering to himself.

'He is joking, isn't he?' asked Vicki.

'I think so,' replied Barbara. 'With the Doctor, you can never tell.'

Correctly dressed in suitable clothing for the period, Barbara stood beside the TARDIS food machine considering whether or not to give it a thump with the flat of her hand as the Doctor emerged from one of the numerous changing rooms adjusting his tunic and toga robe. 'I wish you would get this contraption fixed,' Barbara offered. 'This morning I wanted porridge and it gave me boiled eggs and toast.'

'Unreliability is a sincere virtue,' replied the Doctor, convivially. 'What would life be without a surprise every now and then?'

'I'll remember that the next time you get a curry instead of chicken soup,' noted Barbara. Then she returned her attention to the scanner and the city. 'I can't tell you how excited I am about this.'

'So I've noticed,' replied the Doctor, flatly. He wore a worried look and drew Barbara closer, as if what he was about to say was a secret never to be repeated. 'Please, be careful,' he said at last.

'Aren't I always?' asked Barbara, offended. 'I mean, since Mexico I've...'

The Doctor impatiently cut into her by now well-rehearsed mantra. 'Yes, yes. That is not the issue, don't you see?' he asked, strongly. 'I know how much first-hand knowledge means to you, my child. I know, too, that you would never willingly endanger the safety of any of us.'

Barbara was both touched and surprised by this revelation. 'Thank you,' she said, a little flustered. 'So, why the headmaster's lecture? Don't you think you should be giving Vicki a crash course in how time looks after itself? You've drummed that lesson into me often enough.'

'I shall take care of the girl,' the Doctor said quickly. 'Her destiny was mapped for her thousands of years before she was ever born.' He stopped, as if feeling that he had said too much. 'There will be grave danger during this stay,' he continued. 'I sense it.'

With a caring hand on the old man's shoulder, Barbara tried to look concerned as if she really meant, it while all the time her mind was screaming at her to just leave the Doctor to his paranoia and get out there and experience the moment. 'I've never seen you like this,' she said. Which was true. 'It's normally you that's desperate for us to explore whatever is on offer. We have a chance to see the glory of the Roman Empire...'

'Gracious,' said the Doctor with a really sarcastic sneer. 'I admire your intellect, Miss Wright, genuinely I do, but I never took you for a romantic fool.' The scorn in his voice was marbled with disbelief. 'Do you really believe everything you read in those history books of yours, child? Do you think it was all that simple?'

'No,' replied Barbara, shocked that the Doctor was being so deliberately offensive to her on all sorts of levels. 'The history of ancient Rome is the tale of a community of nomadic shepherds in central Italy growing into one of the most powerful empires the world has ever known. And then collapsing. That, in itself, is one of the greatest stories ever told. But I'm a complete realist when it comes to history.'

'Are you indeed?' asked the Doctor with a fatalistic shake of the head. 'There are none so deaf as those who will not hear...'

'And there are none so dumb as those that will not speak,' replied Barbara, angrily. 'What are you talking about? Please tell me what I've done wrong...'

The Doctor shook his head again. 'Your excitement at seeing a glimpse of the Romans, my dear – it's infectious. Chadderton and young Vicki are simply agog with all of your stories of the Caesars and the gladiators and the glorious battles. You expect to go out there and find bread and circuses and opulence in the streets, don't you?'

'Yes, frankly,' replied Barbara. 'I know it won't be Cecil B. DeMille, or *Spartacus* exactly, but I've a pretty good idea of what it *will* be like. Are you telling me it won't be that way? Because, historically...'

'I visited Rome with Susan,' the Doctor said quickly. 'And Antioch. And Jerusalem. All before we came to your time. I found them to be brutal and murderous places.' He stammered over the word 'murderous' and gave Barbara a grave look. 'Dear me, it was terrible. Slavery, crime in the streets, everybody stabbing everyone else in the back. You and Chesterton come from an era of political complexity, where saying the wrong thing does not automatically make you a target, or an outcast, my child. Things were much more black and white in these dark days.' The Doctor was aware that his voice was becoming raised and deliberately lowered his tone to a whisper. 'Added to which, the Roman Empire stands for all of the things that I left...' He stopped himself and sighed deeply. 'When I left my people, it was because of their ambivalence to just these kind of issues.'

Again, Barbara found it necessary to hold the Doctor's hands. She gave him a little smile as she squeezed them together. 'I'll go and get the others. They're just outside. We can depart immediately if you're not comfortable with our staying here.'

With another sigh, the Doctor opened the TARDIS doors and indicated that they should go outside. 'I am a foolish and tired old man,' he said simply. 'An adventure of some description awaits us.'

But suddenly, Barbara didn't seem nearly as enthusiastic for what was to come.

Chapter Four
Naming All the Stars

For even the Son of man came not to be ministered unto, but to minister, and to give his life a ransom for many.
Mark 10:45

High above Ian and Vicki, and also above the wispy, cotton-wool clouds, the stars of a milky twilight were beginning to settle into their familiar constellations. Reassuring patterns that spoke of being close to home in space, if not in time.

At least they did to Ian. 'They look different, somehow,' Vicki noted. 'The stars, I mean.'

'They will have moved to different positions in the next few thousand years,' Ian explained. 'Pegasus will be closer to Andromeda and the Seven Sisters get more spread out, if I remember my astronomy. A break-up in the family, if you like.' Ian chuckled at his witty pun, then realised that Vicki had not understood it and he cursed to himself that he hadn't saved that one for Barbara or the Doctor.

Vicki, in the meantime, seemed mesmerised by the soft-velvet indigo night spreading out before her. 'No, that isn't what I meant,' she continued, without taking her eyes from the star-filled heavens. 'They seem so much clearer. At home, when I used to look at the sky from the building I lived in, well - you could hardly see the stars at all. Except in winter, and even then, they were so faint...'

'Where was this?' Ian asked. It occurred to him that he knew so little about his young companion's past life on an Earth in his own far future.

'New London. Liddell Towers on the South Circular Road.' Vicki blinked what could have been a tear from her eye, but was probably just moisture from the chill of the oncoming night. 'Every evening, I went up to the roof and looked out into space. That seemed like the future to me. *A* future, anyway. An open road to the stars.'

Now Ian understood her question about the sky looking different. 'Ambient light,' he said. 'In towns, even in my time, the street lighting often made seeing anything in the sky difficult. When I was a boy...' He stopped, aware that his tenses were all gone to pot – a habitual problem for the unwary time traveller. 'When I *will be* a boy, I should say,' he noted with a broad grin. 'I used to go on holiday to a cottage in North Wales, out in the country where the nearest neighbour's house was about a mile away. My brother and sister and I used to fish in the river and play cricket in the fields and at night we'd take my father's telescope and try to name all of the stars.' He knelt down beside the teenager and pointed up. 'There, on the meridian. That's Orion, the hunter. In Greek mythology, Artemis, the goddess of the Moon, fell in love with Orion and neglected her duty of lighting the night sky. Her twin brother, Apollo, seeing Orion swimming, challenged his sister to shoot an arrow through a tiny dot in the ocean, which she did without realising that it was her lover that she was killing. When she discovered what she had done, she placed Orion's body in the sky for all eternity. Her grief explains why the Moon looks so sad and cold.'

'I see him,' said Vicki excitedly, her eyes transfixed on the patch of sky that Ian was pointing to. 'That's a beautiful story. Poor Artemis.'

Ian smiled at the girl, warmly. 'The big star at the top left is Betelgeuse. Bottom right is Rigel. In the middle, you see that little shiny thing that looks like a boy scout's badge? That's the Horse-head Nebula, a globular cluster of stars. The three stars in the belt are called Orionis Zeta, Epsilon and Delta. Now, trace a straight line up from Betelgeuse and you hit Polaris, the pole star. That's in Ursa Minor. Down and a little to the left, you'll find Castor and Pollux, the twins of Gemini. And those two bright lights just above the horizon, they are Venus and Jupiter. I can never remember which is which. In ancient times, astronomers didn't know the difference between planets and stars. Because the planets roam across the sky in their orbit around the sun, the sky watchers of olden times called them "wandering stars", thinking that they were lost and trying to get home. A bit like us, really.'

Vicki turned, a look of grim determination on her face. 'I want to visit all of them,' she said. 'With you and Barbara and the Doctor. I never ever want to go home.'

From behind, the sound of distant voices made them turn to see Barbara helping the Doctor struggle with considerable difficulty up the steep incline. It was Barbara who was speaking. 'Certainly the Romans were a fierce warrior culture who enslaved nations and ended in an orgy of decadence and decay,' she was saying. 'But their practical achievements, bringing civilisation to large chunks of the world, and their success in maintaining an empire of that size was pretty impressive, wouldn't you say? I mean, the aqueduct alone...'

Out of breath, the Doctor seemed to be both nodding and shaking his head at the same time. 'Enslavement,' he gasped at long last, as he stood with his hands on his knees and his chest heaving. 'It is a truly terrible thing to keep intelligent creatures in fear and bondage, my child. Your appreciation of the Roman face, I mean race, will be lessened, I should say, when you actually *see* some of the reality of everyday life.' He stumbled to a pause, then added, 'Tales of the glories of the Caesars are but one aspect of life in these times. The Romans didn't appreciate or understand either diplomacy or democracy, do you see? Those are Greek words and they had already *conquered* the Greeks, as you are about to find out. Look over there and you'll see what I mean.'

So Barbara and Ian and Vicki looked. And they marvelled at what they saw.

There is a shade of paint, a kind of burnt orange that the colour charts of hardware shops identify as Arabian Sunset. Barbara Wright once used it on the walls of the scullery of her little flat in Kensal Rise. It helped to give the place more light on the long evenings of an English winter when the television finished at 10:30 and she would read, by candlelight, some of the second-hand history books that she bought from shops on the Charing Cross Road, to save putting another shilling in the electric meter.

She had never quite understood why the colour was called what it was.

Until now.

The sky was a staggering rich shade of Arabian Sunset, stretching all the way to the horizon of the Black Sea; only it wasn't black at all, it was a rich, rolling aquamarine with silver streaks reflecting back the moonlight like a fractured, deep, dark and truthful mirror. Between themselves and the sea lay the city, lights from it twinkling through the twilight. A great sandstone vista in the middle distance, surrounded on three sides by water and on the fourth by rocky hills, it was laid out not in a haphazard and disorganised fashion as most towns are when viewed from a distance, but with perfect symmetry and co-ordination.

'It's utterly magnificent,' said Ian. 'When did you say it becomes Constantinople?'

'When the emperor Constantine gets here, fairly obviously!' There was a warmth to the sarcasm in Barbara's voice that Ian found both attractive and exciting.

'History's her strong point,' he explained hurriedly to Vicki. 'If we come across anything requiring an explanation on how the laws of physics have just been broken, or don't apply in this case, then I'm your man. Everything else, just ask the Doctor.'

The Doctor, meanwhile, had wandered a short distance from the group. Across the scrubland and into the city lay a destiny of sorts. The Doctor's acutely honed sense for trouble in the making was telling him (actually, it was screaming at him) that there was some on the way.

A whole wheelbarrow full of trouble.

A soft noise behind him caused the Doctor to spin around

quickly, which didn't do his vertigo any favours and he, once again, felt dizzy and disorientated.

Vicki helped to steady him. 'I'm sorry I startled you,' she said.

'Child,' replied the Doctor, 'I suspect that you will be having a similar effect on me quite frequently in our future travels.'

The girl wasn't entirely sure how to take this enigmatic statement. Before she could decide whether it was a reproach or a compliment, she found the Doctor asking her a question and turned her attention back to him.

'What do you think of it?' he asked, indicating towards the city.

'It's fab' replied Vicki.

'"Fab",' the Doctor noted with disdain. 'Now there is an example of the way in which computers have ruined the universe's most individualistic language. The youth of the future all speak in tautologies, malapropisms, migraine-inducing syntax, sentences without apparent subjects or verbs and metaphors so mixed they would do credit to a... a...' he paused, momentarily lost for a decent metaphor himself.

'A parliament of rooks?' asked Ian with a cheesy grin.

'I believe this illustrates a point, somewhat,' the Doctor added, testily.

There was a sulky streak in Vicki's justification. 'I don't know what it means,' she said. 'Is it a bad word? It's just something I picked up from somewhere.'

'It's *gear*, daddio,' mocked Ian as he moved to the edge of the incline and took a few careful steps down the bank. 'Come on,' he continued, breezily. 'It's high time we got this show on the road.'

So they headed off towards the city with the Doctor continuing to warn them that they must be very careful.

'I will say this once and once only, and then I shall refrain from any further comment on the subject,' he noted, as he reached the base of the hill with Barbara and Vicki's help. 'This is a very dangerous time.'

Across a mile of desert sand, Byzantium awaited them.

Chapter Five
Babylon's Burning

Then came together unto him the Pharisees, and certain of the scribes
Mark 7:1

'There are times when I almost feel an admiration for them.'

The confession shocked Titus. 'I cannot believe that you, of all people, would express any sympathies for blasphemers!' he said, with not a little outrage.

Hieronymous, the leader of the Byzantium Pharisees, merely nodded wisely and stood to walk around his chamber as he continued to formulate his thoughts. 'Be, then, assured that I seek the total and final obliteration of the followers of the false prophet.' He paused and turned to face his deputies, Titus and Phasaei. 'Say you otherwise, men?'

'Titus was merely voicing a legitimate concern...'

A single word from Hieronymous halted Phasaei's bold but useless show of self-defence. 'Silence,' he snapped. And there was. After a moment, the priest continued, his tone lower and yet in some ways even more menacing than before. He was a truly striking figure, much taller than both of his deputies, and with a handsome, weather-beaten face and a huge, bushy and slightly greying beard that was *de rigueur* amongst those in his position and with his status. 'As a younger man I had cause to study beneath the high priest of Jerusalem at the time that the Galilean impostor was about his most singular ministry. A man of great sagacity and sorrows whose mother named him Caiaphas.'

'I have heard of this righteous man,' noted Titus. 'His wisdom was oft likened unto that of Solomon the Wise,' he continued sycophantically.

Hieronymous gave Titus a withering look. 'Let us not over-exaggerate. Caiaphas was strange and troubled, but he understood the value of showing those who would follow the teachings of this upstart, who would call himself The Christ, that power is a stronger weapon than blind faith.'

The deputies both nodded, slowly, unsure about exactly what point Hieronymous was trying to make. If any. When the old man became silent while continuing to pace the room, his brow deeply furrowed, Titus and Phasaei exchanged worried glances.

'Wise master,' began Phasaei. 'The Christians...'

Hieronymous turned again, his face dark with anger. 'You would dare to use such a foul name in this *holy* place?' he shouted.

'A thousand humble apologies, good master. These followers of the Nazarene. You were of the opinion that you held a degree of admiration towards them?'

'Not so,' replied the priest. 'I admire the dignity with which those misguided souls that I have personally condemned have gone to their deaths. But that is all.' Hieronymous stopped pacing and sat with his deputies again. 'Is it not written that a father may have many children? And that some shall be in need of great chastisement whilst others walk the path of righteousness without aid? Ten years ago, one of my first acts as Pharisee of Byzantium was to judge upon the case of a girl, no more than a child, named Ruth. A holy name and a spiritual child, seduced by the lure of the Nazarene's sect. They filled her head with notions. Dangerous notions, about the wonders of the alleged Christ and thereafter she preached to the many. She was filled with the fire of her devotions and her faith. And many came to her cause. Because it is sometimes comforting to witness the passion of those who have belief.'

Hieronymous paused, his glassy eyes filling with undisguised regret. 'We took her from her family to the temple and tried to scourge the false teachings from her, but she was strong-willed and determined. She was tried and shamed, but still refused to denounce the other members of her church. So we took her to the market-place, broken and shaved, and stripped of whatever dignity she had once possessed. And then we stoned her until she was dead. Our sources tell me that her people now regard her as a martyr. It takes incredible courage to die for thy beliefs. Courage that I am not sure that I, myself, would possess in such circumstances.'

The deputies were clearly sceptical. 'I have heard similar stories,' noted Titus. 'But that is, largely, all that they are. Fables put about by desperate criminals to try and make their foolish beliefs acquire validity. They have little basis in reality.' He paused and turned to his colleague for support.

Phasaei seemed indecisive. 'Well,' he began. 'Some might say that...'

'We also have problems much closer to home to deal with,' Titus said, brutally changing the subject and giving his fellow deputy a pointed look of disgust. 'The crazed actions of Basellas and his band of fanatics. The followers of the Nazarene and their sinful ways are but a minor irritant compared to those black-hearted devils, the Zealots.'

At that moment, in a different part of the city, within a poor stone dwelling, the Zealots were deep into an emergency meeting.

'The systematic ethnic extermination of three of our brothers yesterday now brings the total dead this year to...' Matthew Basellas, a scarred and embittered veteran of the struggle against the Romans, turned to his comrade and ally, Ephraim. Basellas was rough-shaven and dirty, a clear sign of a life spent constantly dodging arrest and certain death. And yet he was a powerful figure – the leader of the Zealots, a group of fanatical religious bigots who opposed both the Roman occupation of their lands, and the spread of the Christianity based on the teaching of the false prophet Jesus of Nazareth. 'A lot,' he concluded.

'Nineteen,' Ephraim corrected. 'That is, of whom we are yet aware,' he continued, spitting phlegm onto the dirt floor and scuffing at the resulting damp stain with his sandal. 'They try to crush us as they continue to oppress our brothers in Judaea.'

'The Roman scum will never annihilate the tribes of Israel,' Basellas noted, and turned to the others in his group for comments. Hopefully supportive.

'Matthew speaks the truth,' said Yewhe in a harsh and angry voice. 'What have the Romans ever done for us?'

'Let us not travel down *that* road again,' a tired Ephraim said, wiping the sweat from his forehead with the sleeve of his black clothing. 'They give us water and bread and yet they murder us in our beds and defile our temples with their heathen ways. They violate our women and sodomise our boys, they plunder our goods and our cattle and they tell us that *we* are barbarians whilst they are civilised men. As it is written, surely, they shall be put unto death?'

Murmurs of agreement ricocheted around the room.

'I echo the beliefs of Ephraim,' said Yewhe, standing and punching his fist into the palm of his other hand. 'For too long the tyrants have despoiled our land with their wicked, godless ways. We need to plan a public vengeance upon the Romans for the execution of our brothers.' The murmuring became louder and more pointed.

A youth stood to join Yewhe, his large brown eyes ablaze with a fanatical fire. His name was Benjamin and he was sixteen. When he was twelve he had seen his father dragged through the streets to the execution place and put to the sword while his mother and sister wept in the dirt. From that day onwards his only thoughts had concerned the death of Roman soldiers and destruction of Roman property. 'The beast must die,' he said through gritted teeth. 'Matthew, show us the way, and we shall follow. An "inspired act of God" should happen. What say you?'

Basellas was silent, his hand stroking an unshaven chin. When he spoke, his voice was low and conspiratorial. 'For too long,' he began, 'we have suffered under the yoke of Roman occupation. Of the vile and base dogs which enslave us. Now is the time to strike against them.'

'No.'

A lone voice cut through the rising tide of hysteria within the room. All heads turned to the solitary figure at the back, sitting half in the shadows with his wife by his side. Simeon stood and moved into the light, revealing a handsome yet sad face. Instantly, the room parted for him to walk towards Basellas and the two hot-headed young agitators. 'Zealots we are, and Zealots we shall ever be,' Simeon continued, 'until we are Zealots no longer, and are united with all of the children of Israel.'

There was a look of amusement on Basellas's face. 'Wise words, my brother,' he told Simeon. 'Our father would have been proud of you this day. Would, if he had not been done to death two years past by those pigs of Rome.'

There were shouts of agreement from around the room. But not as many as there had been before. Simeon commanded just as much respect as his older brother amongst the group, if not more. He was a good and intelligent man and the others knew this. Simeon had always favoured uniting the disparate tribes amongst the Jews so that they could fight the Romans as one people with one voice. A calming influence on his brother and a brilliant strategist, his voice carried authority and commanded that it be heard.

Only a fool would argue with Simeon.

'I do not believe that a son of Jacob does not wish to see the land awash with the blood of the gentiles,' hissed Yewhe, bitterly. 'Your father was a great man, Simeon. And your brother *is* a great man. But you...' He paused, and gave Simeon a look of pure contempt. 'I know not what manner of man *you* are.'

There were gasps from some of those present, amid one or two voices of support and encouragement. Yet Basellas sat and said nothing, watching the protagonists like a man following the intricate plots and subplots of a chariot race.

'You may wade knee-deep in Roman blood if you wish, Yewhe,' said Simeon. 'You and your...' He looked at Benjamin with pity in his eyes. 'Your disciple. And you will die. And, upon this being so, there shall be no memorial for you after you have gone. No tributes save that "Here lies Yewhe, he was young and headstrong". The graveyards are full of those who are so inclined.'

'Your words are wise indeed, Simeon,' said Ephraim from the side of the room. 'Not least because they are so cowardly and self-serving.'

Benjamin took an aggressive pace towards Simeon. 'Meanwhile, you would stand aside and do nothing whilst your brothers are hunted and killed. How long, Simeon, how long before a Roman with a twitching sword comes to thy door at the dead of night and slits your gullet asunder before taking himself to Rebecca's chamber?'

'Enough,' interrupted the woman beside Simeon. Rebecca joined her husband and gave Benjamin a vicious cold stare. 'You are a child grown old before thy time, Benjamin,' she told the young man. 'The horrors visited upon your family made me weep for you all. But there my sympathy must end. For rage hath made you bitter and twisted and loosened your judgment. Listen you well to my husband, Benjamin, and all others that would follow your brash and ill-advised quest. For if we are not united then we are divided and shall all die. And in our death Rome shall have their undeserved victory.'

As those in the room were digesting this, Rebecca slapped Benjamin across the face. 'Thy mother should have curbed you thus, two years since, insolent child. If any Roman dog were to lay his filthy hand upon me, then he would die the death of a thousand cuts with his manhood removed.' She turned angrily to Basellas and rounded upon her brother-in-law. 'Why allow you this?' she asked, half-kneeling before him. 'Why will you not take thy brother's counsel and accept it with opened arms instead of listening first to the ranting of these children who crave nothing more than death and glory for its own sake?'

'My wife speaks the truth,' Simeon added, holding Rebecca's hand tenderly. 'We are strong only when we all stand together.'

'My own dear brother,' Basellas said, staring so closely at Simeon that he could see his own reflection in his brother's eyes. 'I remember the dying words of our father even if you have forgotten. "We fight and we fight until we die and then others will fight after us." That is how it is. That is how it always has been. And that is how it shall be hereafter.'

Simeon turned away, aghast, and ignored the gloating looks on the faces of Benjamin and Yewhe. 'Then we have nothing left to say to each other, my brother,' he said.

He and Rebecca began to walk slowly out of the room.

Behind him, Basellas shouted at the departing figure, his voice rising in manic tones. 'The gutters of Byzantium shall overflow with the blood of every last Roman within the city. Blessed be the men that ease our suffering and use their swords diligently and with no mercy, for they shall have a place in heaven awaiting them.'

'Byzantium shall be ours once more,' Yewhe added, his fist raised to the roof. Others joined his salute to Basellas who sat, smug, in victory.

Chapter Six
The People Who Grinned Themselves to Death

Woe to that man by whom the Son of man is betrayed!
Good were it for that man if he had never been born.
Mark 14:21

The *praefectus*, the governor protector of the *coloniae civium Romanorum* Byzantium, Thalius Maximus, strode into the domed vault of the atrium of his villa.

'I beseech the God Janus to stand watch at this door and protect the humble wretches that dwell within. And the virgin Goddess Minerva to grant wisdom to all of those who seek its pure embrace,' he muttered and he tugged at the fastening of his soiled and filthy purple-trimmed toga. He was tired and weary and his temper was frayed at the edges. 'Drusus,' he bellowed as three slaves approached to help him remove his clothing. A tall and imposing man with a bald head and piercing brown eyes strode from the direction of the kitchens. Despite his subservient position to the *praefectus* within the household, there was nothing remotely fawning or weak about the way in which this freedman carried himself or went about his, and his master's, business.

'Forgive me, master,' he said with complete sincerity and regret and yet also dignity. 'We did not expect you to return to this place until some days hence.'

'My bowels did give me a sudden desire to leave Rome far sooner than anticipated. I am weary and require that my bath be filled for me and fresh garments made ready. My head aches from the lack of food, so prepare a meal, which I shall take in the *peristyle* after I have bathed and rested. I should like Gemellus to join me there, also.'

Drusus ran the household of the *praefectus*, ruling it and those within it with a rod of iron. He bowed and within the space of no more than a dozen words, had effectively conveyed a series of sharp commands which made certain that everything that Thalius had asked for would be done. Quickly.

As the *praefectus* retired to his bath and sank deeply and gratefully into the soothing hot spa waters, he was thankful that he was surrounded by men like Drusus and Gemellus, and others within his house who did what they were told and also, frequently, what they were not, but should have been. And who protected him from his enemies and, more often than he would have liked, from himself.

Other *praefecti*, he reflected, were not so fortunate.

The governor was just finishing the first of several courses of dinner, vegetables and shellfish with black olives, when Gemellus Parthenor arrived. Thalius's advisor, Gemellus was a wise and clever little man, with piercing eyes. Studious, and with a sparkling infectious enthusiasm that made him popular amongst Roman society in Thrace and beyond, perhaps Gemellus's only major failing was that he was unable to see the worst in his enemies, believing that he was a man who had none.

But few men are so fortunate.

'My good friend,' said Thalius, half-standing and offering a seat to Gemellus in the peristyle, a secondary atrium courtyard with a wide, opened ceiling that allowed exterior light to flood in. The yard was surrounded by a garden shrouded in shrubs and bright and colourful flowers. Candles were lit around the *praefectus*'s table as sunset was approaching with the stealth of a fox. 'Please join me, we have much to discuss,' commanded Thalius.

Gemellus sat beside his friend and looked around the newly decorated yard. 'I approve of the changes here,' he said. 'Your absence has, at least, proved beneficial to the decor. If not to the political and social situation.'

Thalius winced. 'And not to my health, and strength,' he added with a wry smile, pausing while breaking some bread to mop up the juices on his plate. He belched, loudly, as he swallowed the bread and then returned his attention to the unasked question that Gemellus was obviously itching to hear answered. 'Woe to all Rome, my friend. It is in a sick and sorry state of crisis and depression.'

The little adviser nodded, sagely, having suspected such a tale of misery from occasional injudicious or wine-provoked comments made by visitors from the Imperial city. 'The boy emperor is, I suspect, proving to have fewer administrative abilities than was hoped.'

'Nero is a *fool*,' spat Thalius, bitterly. 'He always was a fool, he always will be a fool. His father was no idiot, no matter what the history books of our children will tell us, for history is written by the winning side and, make no mistake, my friend, but this arrogant pup has won it all.' He stopped, shook his head and then looked closely at his advisor. 'I tell you this, Gemellus. If this popinjay with his ludicrous notions of grandeur is not bridled and harnessed well by someone with integrity, and soon, then Rome shall drown in an ocean of its own vanity. But who shall this be? For all of the good men are now gone: Palas, Narcissus, Burrus. And now Seneca.'

Gemellus gasped. 'Seneca is dead?'

'So the rumours state. Last month, in Pompeii. The new praetorian *praefectus* is a deranged madman named Tigellinus who casually brings out the worst despotism in Nero's disposition. The energy and hope of the *quinquennium* has disappeared from the hearts of all true men. Instead, there is wilful narcissism and depravity abroad, even within the senate itself.'

Again, Gemellus said little, but cast a quick and nervous glance over his shoulder to make sure that they were not being overheard. 'Chose your words carefully, my friend. There is no sense in drowning yourself before the flood is upon us.'

'Oh but I am weary and lost, Gemellus,' replied Thalius, sadly. 'Sometimes I yearn for the simpler life. The people of this land, the growers of grapes and olives and wheat, and the herders of sheep and cattle. The merchants and craftworkers who practise their trades in the city. Do *they* have the troubles that I am party to? Do they spend half of every night doubled in the pain of indigestions and diarrhoeas caused by worries for my beloved Rome?'

'In their own way,' said Gemellus with a little smile, 'they probably do, my friend. What are the troubles of one man but dust in the wind to another? For he has troubles of his own and no one with whom to share them. The servant who breaks his master's vase shall have the skin whipped from his back, yet he cares not for Lucius Nero and his mismanagement of the great empire.'

Thalius Maximus seemed satisfied with this piece of beautiful philosophy. He was well aware of how others saw him – as a bored politician, who was thoroughly mistrusted by the military and who mistrusted them in return. He hated this part of the empire, cursing the very day that he had been sent by the emperor to this benighted land. He truly longed to return to somewhere closer to Rome. He was certainly a competent organiser, and for that reason had been entrusted with this key outpost. But Thalius was at a loss to understand the religious tensions of the region and he had never been keen to meddle in the internal affairs of the Greeks or the Jews, both of whom (and especially the latter) he struggled to understand as a people.

The chaos in Nero's capital was, if truth be told, a necessary diversion for him from the mundanities of Byzantium and its frustrating levels of society. 'Tell me of what has transpired here in my time of absence so that I may be apprised of any changes pertaining to this place and my role within it,' he asked.

'There have been the usual regretted outbreaks of lawlessness and debauchery. The latter, usually, amongst our own troops.'

Thalius rolled his eyes and clucked his tongue against the roof of his mouth. 'I suppose that I should make an example of the next legionnaire found on his knees in some Greek or Jew whore's bedchamber. One swift and merciless kill for all to see and reflect upon should help to keep the ill-educated vermin in line.'

'You may have trouble with our noble general if you attempt such a thing,' Gemellus added with a sigh. 'The Greek city-states have no important military or political role, as well Gaius knows, but he likes to think that he is still in Britannia, fighting the Trinovantes, or Boudica's wretched Iceni at the God Claudius's side.'

At that moment, as Thalius continued to discuss mundane household affairs with his friend, Gaius Calaphilus entered, announced from the peristyle exterior by Drusus in a loud and booming voice.

'My friend,' Gemellus whispered to Thalius as the old soldier laid his helmet and sword by the entrance, bowed, and strode into the peristyle. 'Do not make this any harder than it needs to be.'

Thalius Maximus nodded to the soldier and then, with some obvious relish, continued his conversation with Gemellus, ignoring the presence of general Calaphilus entirely.

Calaphilus stood by the table awaiting a request that he sit which never came. After a while he simply sat anyway and picked at the *praefectus*'s olive-bowl. Gemellus, meanwhile, a little embarrassed at his friend's rudeness, inadvertently stoked the fires of hatred between the two men by mentioning a Greek slave girl from Thalius's own household staff, Dorcas, who had expressed her Christian belief and wished to have her religion recognised.

'Her belief in what?' asked Thalius with a genuine puzzlement.

'She is a Christian, *praefectus*,' Gemellus explained. 'They are a legal if somewhat minor sub-sect of Judaism who believe that...'

'We all know of the Christians and of what nonsense they believe,' Calaphilus noted sharply. 'At least, those few amongst us with an ear cocked hard towards the ground. This girl? May I suggest that she be flogged until she begs for mercy? That would, perhaps, be an effective cure for her wanton and treacherous ways.'

Thalius tutted loudly, appalled at the very suggestion. 'I am not keen to meddle in the internal affairs of the Jews. You know that,' he told Gemellus, whilst continuing to ignore the general. 'I cannot say that I have ever heard of these "Christians", did you say? What manner of men are they? What do they believe in, exactly?'

'That is a very interesting question, *praefectus*,' replied the little adviser. 'All Jews believe that a messiah, a literal "King of the Jews", shall come unto earth from heaven and redeem the land of Israel and all of its tribes. This prophecy was first made by their ancient law-giver, the prophet Moses, shortly after the Jews had first been led out of Egypt, during the reign of Rameses II, which the Jews refer to as the *exodus*.'

The *praefectus* nodded. 'I know my Egyptian history even if I am seemingly ignorant of that of the Jewish peoples,' he noted. 'Please do go on.'

'Many Jewish scholars, prophets and holy men have written of the coming of this messiah. He is said to be born of the lineage of their King David who, as you know, built the great temple in Jerusalem between five and six hundred years ago. And that of his son, King Solomon the wise. They believe that this messiah will be born in a village named Bethlehem, which is a real place in Judaea. That he will gather together the tribes of Israel and cleanse them of their sins and free them from their bondage for eternity. These scriptures are not always consistent about this messiah. He is sometimes described as a great warrior and leader of men. Yet at other times he is cast as a meek and sorrowful outsider, disowned even by his own people. Some Jewish scholars regard the entire concept as nothing more than a metaphor for their perpetual struggles. But most Jews of my acquaintance *do* actually believe that the messiah is, or was, or shall be hereafter, a real person.'

An impatient Calaphilus gave a harsh laugh which caused both Gemellus and Thalius to turn their heads in his direction. 'Superstitious nonsense,' said the solider with great sarcasm.

'What do you expect from a race that only believes in one God?'

Gemellus continued, undeterred, with his precise little essay on the Roman perception of the Christian cult. 'Over the centuries there have been numerous men who have claimed to be this messiah. Indeed, thirty or forty years ago, during the reigns of the God Augustus and of his son, Tiberius, there were a positive slew of them cropping up all over Judaea and Syria. The authorities in the region used to have a saying: "every week, a new messiah". The Christians, as I am given to understand, basically believe that one of these men who claimed to be the messiah was, indeed, the Christ from whom their name derives.'

'By Jove,' said Thalius with a fascinated amusement. 'Was this Christ known to us?'

'Indeed he was, *praefectus*. He was a maverick rabbi named Joshua-bar-Joseph, also more popularly known to his followers as Jesus of Nazareth, his name meaning, literally, "saviour" in Greek. He was the son of a poor carpenter and a native of the province of Galilee. He had a considerable following amongst the uneducated masses in that area and preached to some very large crowds. He was, by all accounts, a man of striking appearance, extremely handsome, charismatic and persuasive. As a boy, he had been something of an infant prodigy, which is quite common amongst the children of the region, preaching at the temple from an early age. He is said to have found Judaism intellectually limited and to have openly criticised its inadequacies for use in everyday living.'

'That sounds like many of the Jews that I know,' interjected an irritated Calaphilus.

Gemellus laughed, and nodded his approval to the general, who seemed to take the compliment in the spirit in which it was intended. 'This Jesus,' continued Gemellus, 'gathered around him a sizeable group of fanatical followers from amongst the fishermen and farming communities along the shores of Lake Galilee. They were a kind of personal bodyguard and set about spreading his teachings. Delivering his *gospel*, that is, "good news", in the form of simple parables, most of which had a nice moral twist at the end. He was good. *Very good.*'

'Not so good that he could avoid ending his days nailed to a *stauros*,' said Calaphilus, chuckling to himself.

'Ah, I see that you are aware of his story?' Gemellus asked.

Thalius Maximus was merely intrigued. 'What happened to this messiah?' he asked.

'The Jewish religious authorities of the area grew suspicious of this man and of his teachings,' noted Gemellus. 'He became a threat to their authority. They questioned him repeatedly on obscure aspects of the law of Moses, but he was a clever man and always had an answer for them, chapter and verse from their holy texts. Eventually, however, he was betrayed by one of his inner circle of followers to the Pharisee, who had the procurator of the region, Pontius Pilate, arrest the man as a heretic.'

'Pontius Pilate,' said Calaphilus wistfully. 'Now *there* was an official one could so easily respect.'

Thalius gave Gemellus an unimpressed smile. 'He was an acquaintance of my father,' he said. 'A man of somewhat limited intellect and many disturbing ways. So, this *messiah* was executed, yes?'

'Crucified near to Jerusalem, in the twenty-first year of the reign of Tiberius Caesar. But it is what happened next that is even more interesting. Just about all of the ancient prophecies about the messiah from the Torah, pertaining to his betrayal and his death, did seem to come true. After his internment, his body vanished. It was probably taken away by his followers, but a macabre rumour was circulated thereafter that he had actually been raised from his grave by the Jewish God. *Resurrection*, they called it.'

'These Christians believe that their saviour is a ghost?' asked Thalius, incredulously. 'What a pathetic bunch of ignorant peasants, to base a religion on such a superstition.'

'There is a little more substance to the cult than simply that, *praefectus*,' noted Gemellus. 'It is said that this Jesus performed many miracles. Raised a number of people from the dead and often healed the lame and the wretched. Could turn water into wine and base metal into gold, that kind of thing. Most of it is errant nonsense, of course, as our noble general rightly points out. But there are a lot of witnesses to some of these alleged events.'

'Mere conjuring tricks,' Calaphilus noted. 'Friends of mine were within Palestine, where all of this furore was happening. They told me that this character was nothing more than a charlatan peddling his mumbo-jumbo to the masses. No man with common sense in his brain believes a word of this *Christos*.'

'Perhaps,' said Gemellus. 'But as for the Christians themselves, essentially they seem to be relatively harmless. Their creed dictates passive resistance to that which they do not regard as the word of their God and, otherwise, non-aggression. And, at least, they pay their taxes. In both of these regards, they are infinitely preferable to such as the Zealots.'

By now Calaphilus was outraged that he had been kept waiting whilst such trivialities were discussed. 'If I may make a brief observation,' he said loudly, 'I learned long ago, in Britannia, that pandering to the beliefs of indigenous savages is as sure a way as any to the path of ultimate destruction.' He paused, aware that he was on the verge of ranting, and drew in a deep breath. 'Perhaps the *praefectus* would like to hear another children's story. A senator with whom I was acquainted had a wife who could not get what she wanted from him. So she slept with a sergeant of the praetorian guard and became the talk of all Rome. That is a story with much more *relevance* to the *praefectus*, I would have said.'

The implied threat to Maximus was brutally clear. 'I know of this story,' replied the *praefectus*. 'Both the man and his woman were beheaded and spent their days on the end of spikes on the city walls. I believe our business is concluded, general.'

'So it would seem,' replied Calaphilus turning on his heels and marching noisily out of the peristyle.

'Oh dear,' noted Gemellus. Calaphilus had clearly been referring to the problem of Maximus's own former wife. 'A number of events occurred whilst you have been away, which you should perhaps be made aware of,' he told his friend.

Elsewhere within the city, in a slightly smaller (but equally opulent) home, Antonia Vinicius was in the process of discussing her former husband, and his hatred of the military, with an interested friend.

'Sometimes I so envy your life, Agrinella,' she told Marcus Lanilla's wife, as the pair of women lay on stone tables having their backs massaged by their respective handmaidens. 'I often wish *I* had but one man to think of all the time.'

'Really?' asked Agrinella, astonished.

'No,' replied Antonia. 'I am afraid to say that I lied.'

The women laughed, a long and bawdy chuckle that culminated with the pair raising themselves from the tables, wrapping their clothing around themselves and simultaneously dismissing their handmaidens. When they were alone, Agrinella came and sat beside Antonia, looking at the slender neck and shoulders of the woman peeking out from the loose-fitting *palla*. Antonia was beautiful, Agrinella decided. Far, far too beautiful for the overweight and long-past-his-prime Thalius whom she had divorced less than a year ago.

Maximus's former wife was now remarried to a usually absent local senator, Germanicus. Not that the long and frequent periods when the master was not about his house seemed to have dulled Antonia's insatiable appetite for the company of men. Any men. A hugely promiscuous woman even when she was married to the *praefectus,* Antonia was, even now, boasting about her latest dalliance.

'Centurion Castus Pilaigus is a handsome man, do you not think so?'

'Oh Antonia,' said a shocked Agrinella, 'you haven't?'

Antonia nodded, like a dog eager to please its owner. 'Five times. He rode me like he would ride to the moon and back in a flying chariot.'

'Antonia, you are so wicked,' Agrinella giggled like a schoolgirl as her friend dismissed the adventure with a shrug of the shoulders.

'I was starved of true affection for so long. A woman has many and certain needs. Speaking of which, have you seen that new slave whom Germanicus picked up in Egypt? The black one?'

Though it was difficult, Agrinella ignored the question and turned her attention to the real reason for her visit, as if the prospect of sharing sexual secrets was not cause enough. 'Antonia,' she said quickly. 'What can you tell me about any history between Maximus and that vulgarian general Gaius Calaphilus?'

If Antonia was surprised by the question she was asked then she did not show it. 'Byzantium is not, and shall ne'er be, a space enough to hold both these men,' she noted.

Chapter Seven
Cephalic Symbol

What therefore God hath joined together,
let not man put asunder.
Mark 10:9

'I still don't fully understand how we're able to converse with everyone so fluently. I don't speak Latin, and I've only got a very basic smattering of Greek,' Barbara noted. 'I took it at school, but I used to get my diphthongs mixed up with my past participles...'

This was something that had bothered Ian on several occasions too but, as so often on their travels, the Doctor had casually dismissed such trivialities with a neo-gobbledygook explanation that left neither of his companions any the wiser. 'I was taught Latin,' replied Ian with a half-remembered look of horror on his face. 'Now *that* was all Greek to me! My teacher was called Mr Dumbie, I remember, which was a name positively crying out for a bit of *Boys Own* innuendo. It's funny the daft things that stick in your mind about school, isn't it? My form tutor was a man named Quibbs and there was a Jewish lad in my class called Goldfinkle. I picked on him mercilessly.'

'Bad boy,' Barbara said, wagging a finger at him.

'I was thirteen, what can I say? I was discovering all sorts of things. Irony, sarcasm, the fact that the world didn't revolve around rugby... Hormones: now that was shocking, the day I woke up and found the world had girls in it. With breasts and everything...'

Barbara Wright tried hard not to laugh. Which only made things worse.

'I can still remember a few phrases,' Ian continued. 'Mainly disgusting. *Foetorum extremae latrinae* was a good one.'

'What does that mean?' asked Barbara.

'"You stink like the worst toilet".'

Barbara looked disgusted. 'Anything more useful?'

'*Puella meretrix*,' Ian replied. '"Nymphomaniac whore",' he informed Barbara before she could ask. 'And *deformis anusque oblatratrix* means "ugly old bag who can't keep her trap shut". Came in handy quite a few times, that one. Now there's a funny thing. How come when I just spoke Latin to you, it sounded Latin, but when someone else speaks in Latin to us, we understand it like it was English? And how about the fact that whatever it is that translates all of this for us uses words and phrases that are anachronistic to this time?'

Barbara shrugged. 'One of life's great mysteries, I suppose,' she said.

Several days had passed and the Doctor and his companions had spent their time living close to the market-place in the centre of Byzantium in rented accommodation. They had enjoyed themselves greatly, observing the plethora of different races and cultures within the city, while posing as a travelling family from Britannia. However, all good things must come to an end and the time was fast approaching for them to leave.

'I'll be sorry to go,' Ian said. Barbara nodded in agreement. She picked up a clay ornament that she had bought in the market the day before. It was a simple, home-made representation of a Greek woman carrying water. 'Just think,' Barbara noted, 'if I buried this where it wouldn't be found and then came back in two thousand years and dug it up, I'd be rich.'

'Not to mention, of course, *home*,' Ian added, helpfully. 'What is it, anyway?'

'A Greek urn,' replied Barbara. 'And if you say, "What's a Greek earn? Ten drachmas a week", I'll give you such a thumping...' she threatened.

'Wouldn't dream of it,' replied Ian with a broad grin. 'Besides, everybody seems to get paid in Roman currency. *Quadrans* and *dupondius* and *denarii*. I've only seen a couple of Greek and

Jewish coins since we've been here. And none of them look anything like half-a-crown, or a threepenny piece.'

'This place is so magical,' Barbara continued, changing the subject away from the often upsetting thoughts of London and 1963. 'Just seeing everyday life for these people, the practical, ordinary things that you'd never find in any history book. That's always the true revelation for me.' She paused and looked out of the window of their first-storey room to the sun rising above of the dome of the synagogue. On the roof was a single figure, stark and silhouetted against the shimmering early morning light. The man was chanting in Hebrew, calling his people to prayer.

'How can you not be affected by something like that?' Barbara asked, pointing to the man. 'Isn't it amazing?'

'He's certainly got a good head for heights!' noted Ian sarcastically.

At breakfast they ate the last of their food and talked excitedly about where they might end up next. It had been a happy and relaxing week; a stimulating experience for Barbara and, much to her own surprise, for Vicki, and a nice, quiet holiday for Ian. As for the Doctor... well, who knew?

However, today, even he was ready to admit that he was glad that they had come to Byzantium, though his reply to a question from Barbara about whether they should announce their departure to the several people whom they had come to know locally during their time in the city was a firm negative.

'Goodbyes will not be necessary,' he noted, bringing the subject to a close. 'They get in the way of just.... going. Chedderton and myself shall buy some food while you can take young Vicki to visit that temple to Jupiter for one last look.'

'Sounds like a plan,' noted Ian, standing hurriedly and tripping over his own feet.

'Oh, do stop larking about like a child, Chestington,' the Doctor groaned.

'Don't I get any say in where we go?' asked Vicki, before cracking into a broad smile. 'Only joking. I'd love to have another look at that temple.' She found herself looking at three scowling faces. 'What?'

Barbara pointedly ignored her. 'Highlight of the visit?' she asked the Doctor.

There was a long pause. 'Discovering,' replied the Doctor at last, 'that things are never quite as bad as you expect them to be.'

Ian and the Doctor walked the short distance to the market to buy bread for the journey back to the TARDIS which, they expected, would take them most of the day. The fresh and crisp early morning was beginning to give way to the sultry and oppressive heat of the day as the Doctor again confessed that his misgivings about the Romans and their ways had largely proved unfounded. Ian was amused that the Doctor could actually admit to being wrong.

'I have been wrong before, my boy,' the Doctor said, wounded by his companion finding humour in his shortcomings. 'Not often, it's true, but occasionally... It is not a sin to admit that you have made a mistake.'

'No, indeed,' Ian replied, trying to hide the smirk on his face. 'It's just that it is something you so rarely see. From you.'

They arrived at the bread stall in the already-bustling market. The stall was a rough wooden bench covered in thick muslin cloth and protected from the searing heat by a canopy of reeds. The Greek owner, Nikos, greeted them with a friendly smile, commented on the weather, and asked them about their plans for today.

He was a small and delicately boned man with a handsome, if puffy, face and a nervous and hesitant laugh which he seemed to lapse into at the end of everything he said.

Ian liked him enormously, probably because he reminded the schoolteacher of a man he had once met who sold second-hand jewellery on the Portobello Road. He was a Greek as well, Ian remembered.

'We have a long journey ahead of us,' Ian said, casting a quick glance at the Doctor who merely blinked his eyes like a cat sitting contentedly in the sun.

'Travel is the greatest thing in the world,' Nikos added, handing four flat pitta bread pieces to Ian. 'It makes a wise man of the fool. And a great man of the wise man. That will be three *obols*, or half of one *drachma*, or one *sestertius*, or one half *shekel*, or a knife to my throat if you prefer. For I am just a poor and humble shopkeeper...' He shrugged his shoulders in mock-surrender as Ian fumbled in the pocket of his tunic and brought out a battered and dirty silver Roman coin, a *sestertius*, that he had found on the roadside two days earlier.

'Blessings be always upon you, good traveller,' said Nikos with a smile as wide as the Bosphorus estuary, flashing two rows of gleaming white teeth. 'I wish you and your fellow companions good fortune and fair weather for your travels. And may your Gods go with you.'

'Thank you, good patron,' replied the Doctor. 'And may you always find the world in need of... bread. Or whatever.'

As he finished speaking, a group of ten rough-shaven and aggressive-looking men barged past the Doctor and Ian and strode towards the centre of the market-place, pushing out of their path any hapless locals that had dared to get in their way. 'Trouble,' the stall owner noted nervously, picking up his money and leaving his bread without another word.

'I knew it was too good to last,' the Doctor said regretfully. 'We should have left yesterday, I had a feeling in my bones.'

'Doctor,' Ian said. 'Don't be so paranoid. They're probably just out to do their weekly shopping. Come on, let's find Barbara and Vicki.'

They walked into the central square of the forum. In front of them was the massive frontage of the synagogue whilst to the right were the more architecturally staggering Roman temple buildings, their Ionic columns and arches a wonder in an age where most other cultures were still building houses out of mud and straw.

'They certainly knew a bit about construction,' Ian said, as the Doctor and he reached the base of the sweeping granite steps leading up to the temple. 'Must have taken a thousand labourers to throw up this little beauty.'

'Mostly slaves,' the Doctor said, absent-mindedly. 'Coerced into building these triumphalist monuments. It's sickening.'

Ian craned his neck to look up to the temple's high, arched roof. 'I agree, but it's impressively sickening, wouldn't you say?'

At that moment, they spotted Barbara and Vicki emerging from a smaller building on their left across the crowded market square. Ian waved his hand and Vicki responded. 'There they are,' Ian could lip-read the girl telling Barbara.

And then all hell broke loose.

The violence erupted, terrifyingly, without warning. One moment the square was packed with thronging, jostling crowds, the next a shout went up and fists were flying everywhere. Just like Saturday night down the Old Kent Road, reflected Ian Chesterton. Men wrestled each other to the ground. Ian and the Doctor looked on aghast as, around them, knives were produced and a Roman soldier standing mere feet from them had his throat slit from ear to ear by a grinning man in Jewish garb.

The man shouted something unintelligible at the collapsed corpse and then spat at it, gleefully. The meaning was clear enough. He turned with livid madness in his eyes and stared at Ian, the bloodied knife still clenched in his hand. 'The insurrection is come among us, brother,' he shouted. 'Kill, kill, kill.'

And then he was gone, leaving the Doctor and Ian to stare, open-mouthed, at each other. 'Let's get...' began Ian, but before he could finish what he was saying, the pair were swept away in the tidal wave of humanity that came running down the steps of the temple to flee whatever was taking place inside.

The Zealots, led by Basellas, had begun their indiscriminate attack on various Roman stalls. Chaos ensued, with people fleeing in panic. Basellas himself stood amid the carnage, laughing a dangerous and crazed laugh of triumph as, around him, his followers attacked anything that moved. A Roman legionnaire lay dead at his feet, his throat crushed by Basellas's vice-like grip. Now the crowd was moving towards side-streets and outlets from the square. Anywhere, in fact, but where the action was.

The Doctor cautiously tried to follow Ian towards the terrified Vicki and Barbara on the far side of the market-place but, five steps into the crowd, he was knocked to the ground. As Ian turned and tried to help him, he was attacked from behind by a Roman soldier who had clearly mistaken him for one of the Zealots. Ian was pulled back around and found himself fighting for his life against a big and powerful opponent.

He struck a blow under the man's heart and then another, lower down his abdomen, pushing him backwards and trying to wrestle the man's sword from his hands. A head-butt to the bridge of the soldier's nose, and Ian had the weapon. He thrust forward, twisted instinctively as he had with a bayonet during national service and withdrew as the man collapsed, dead, at his feet.

Ian looked, horrified, at the sword in his hand, momentarily distracted from the life-and-death struggles taking place around him. There was an eerie silence in Chesterton's mind, and a small clearing in which he stood. At the heart of the battle, Ian Chesterton was utterly alone. Then, something kicked in within him and he held the sword high above his head and bellowed a vicious, terrifying scream that came from the pit of his stomach. Sunlight glinted on the sword and was reflected around the crowd. Other swords were raised.

It was a carnival of swords.

Chesterton looked to his left and to his right. The Doctor was gone. Barbara was gone. He briefly imagined that he saw Vicki, her pale, screaming face standing out from the crowd around her, haloed in the sunlight. Then she, too, was gone and Ian was truly alone.

And then, some blunt and hard implement hit him squarely at

the base of the skull. Dazed, he saw the sword spill from his hands and he found himself toppling forward.

Slipping.

Falling.

He was drowning in a sea of bodies.

Blackness came upon him and he was swallowed by it, whole.

Vicki thought she saw Ian fall, but she couldn't be certain of anything. She was rooted to the spot, too terrified to run or to throw herself back against the stone walls behind her which, at least, offered some protection against the crush. She had seen Barbara swept away by a surge in the crowd that had missed Vicki herself by mere inches. Now she cowered amid the shouting, chanting, excited hordes. She was pushed with them several feet forward and then thrown back as, somewhere above her head, someone was screaming that the Romans were coming. The shout was repeated and the entire crowd, as one, panicked.

Vicki had no option but to allow herself to be carried along by the crowd's momentum, her feet barely touching the ground and she was thrown first this way and then that.

'Kill them all,' shouted one mouth-frothing agitator. 'Cut off their heads and stick 'em up high on poles for all the world to see.'

Vicki tried to turn, to find a way from the madness, but her route was blocked in every direction. She couldn't see anything but bodies in front of her, bodies behind her, bodies to the left and right of her. She felt herself about to faint and her knees buckled.

Terror seized her by the throat. 'Help me someone, please, help me,' she cried out. 'I'm being suffocated. Help.'

For a second, Vicki believed that she saw Barbara trying to fight her way through the crowd towards her. The girl reached out her hand towards Barbara's and they almost touched across the heads of the surging crowd. But then she was gone – the last image that Vicki had of Barbara was of her friend falling to the ground, her face frozen in terror, amid a stampede.

Vicki began to lose consciousness, fully aware of how ridiculous it was that she was going to die two-and-a-half thousand years before she was even born. But just as she was about to collapse to the floor, she was grabbed by strong hands and hauled out of the crowd and into a twisting series of back alleys.

'Keep moving,' said a male voice, holding onto her hand and literally dragging her away from the dense centre of the crowd. 'If you want to live, keep moving.'

Chapter Eight
Right Here, Right Now

And if a kingdom be divided against itself,
that kingdom cannot stand.
Mark 3: 24

It did not take the arriving Roman soldiers long to put down the insurrection.

They were experienced and tough. Hard men, battle-scarred and terrifying to look at. They had fought across the length of the empire against conspiracies and revolutionaries of all shades, creeds and persuasions. In Britannia. In Gaul. In Germania, Dalmatia, Macedonia, Judaea, Syria, Galatia and Assyria. Through all of the lands of the known world and into the barren wastes beyond. They were a superior race of men and they feared absolutely no one. For they fought with mayhem and violence in their hearts and the promise of the emperor's money uppermost in their minds. What place had true faith and the bleating of sheep against such power as this?

With crimson cloaks, dull-grey body armour and plumed helmets, their black-and-gold shields glinting in the sun and their eagle standards held high, the legion charged into the square and panic rippled across the face of the crowd in a visible wave. They came rushing in a fearsome, shouting, terrifying volley of shields and swords, javelins and nets, separating the crowd with a pincer movement that sliced straight through the heart of the packed market-place. Everyone was pushed back until those at the edges of the crowd were forced into the narrow passages that surrounded the square. And, once a few had begun to dissipate, like a cork from a wine bottle, this freed the route for others to follow.

The air was filled with dust, whipped up by thousands of scampering feet.

Plus screams and cries for help. And for blood.

Some of the desperate crowd were crushed as they tried to flee the advancing Romans, but many found an exit eventually, tearing their way past those weaker and less mobile than themselves. They fled for their lives from the men with glinting swords, hot on their heels, their stinking breath on the necks of those they pursued.

After an hour of almost operatic violence, the market-place was littered with hundreds of broken bodies. From the vantage point of a turret overlooking the market-place, Basellas and some of his followers were jubilant at the sight.

'Look upon that,' Basellas noted with pride at a job well done. 'Look upon that, you Roman dogs, and despair.' He turned, jubilantly to his men. 'See you what has come to pass within this place?' he asked. 'We have spoken. And they have been forced to listen, and listen well.'

'Your good brother should have been here upon this day and witnessed with his own eyes the carnage that we have brought down upon their noble heads,' Ephraim shouted in a sarcastic voice above the noise from below them.

The moaning and wailing of the dying.

'For we have given the Romans a merry thing to think on, this day, have we not?'

Basellas said nothing. He merely watched the comings and goings beneath him, like a general observing movements on a battlefield.

Instead it was Ephraim who spoke for him. And for all of the Zealots watching the activities in the market-place. 'This is a great day for Byzantium,' he noted. 'A great day. The brutish and damnable actions of these Roman swine will bring the freedom of our people closer. Byzantium shall be free.'

The door burst open and Simeon turned to find himself facing a trio of armed adversaries stepping from the shadows.

'What business have you men within my house?' he asked without raising his voice. Yewhe ignored him, instead reaching behind the sackcloth curtain that separated the main room from a bedchamber to the right. He dragged Rebecca, spitting and kicking, from her hiding place behind the curtain and forced her to drop to the floor the scythe that she held in her hand.

'There shall be no good sport for you this day, my pretty,' Yewhe said, kicking her viciously in the stomach and throwing her down.

Simeon flung himself at Yewhe but a blow to the side of his head from Benjamin sent Simeon sprawling to the ground beside his wife.

Benjamin stood over Simeon's prone body and drew back his foot. It impacted with the side of Simeon's head which juddered under the power of the blow. Benjamin did it again and this time, there was no movement at all from Basellas's brother.

'Simeon,' screamed Rebecca. She scrambled towards her husband, but Yewhe's arm around her throat dragged her backwards.

'Silence, you piteous and mewling sow,' he spat. 'So endeth the lesson, and so perish all of those who oppose the will of our leader, thy brother,' Yewhe continued as he withdrew a knife from his belt and slit the woman's throat in one casual movement before letting her slide from her knees to the floor. He turned to Benjamin and the third man, Dimodis, who were about to ransack the house. Yewhe grabbed the ear of his young fellow freedom-fighter and twisted it, causing Benjamin to cry out in pain and, like Rebecca, drop to his knees.

'What do you think we are, Benjamin?' asked Yewhe angrily as Dimodis looked on, terrified. 'Are we thieves? Do we covet what is within our neighbour's house?'

'No,' screamed Benjamin as the pressure on his skin tightened. 'Stop it!'

Yewhe put his blood-soaked and razor-sharp knife to Benjamin's throat. 'Know you the substance of the ten commandments handed down to Moses from God?' asked Yehwe.

Benjamin didn't reply quickly enough and Yewhe moved the knife away and struck him, viciously, across the face with the back of his hand. 'What say you, Benjamin?'

'Yes,' the boy replied, as the knife returned to its threatening position. 'Yes. I know them all. For strong is my devotion to them.'

Yewhe released his tight grip. 'Tell them to me...'

Benjamin stared at him, open-mouthed. Another blow to the face brought a swift response. 'Take not the name of the Lord thy God in vein. Honour thy father and thy mother. Thou shalt not kill. Thou shalt not commit adultery. Thou shalt not steal. Thou shalt not...'

'Yes,' said Yewhe, quickly. '*Thou shalt not...*' He stopped and bid Benjamin rise up. Yewhe pointed to the two dead bodies on the floor next to each other. 'They did not observe the word of the Lord,' he said. 'And behold what sorry and infamous fate befell these wretched sinners.'

Benjamin looked, firstly, at the bodies of Simeon and Rebecca, and then at Dimodis. And finally at Yewhe, who had the madness of killing within his eyes.

'We do the Lord's work,' Benjamin said, flatly. 'And nothing else.'

'Good,' said Yehwe, heading for the door. 'Let us return from whence we came and tell Matthew the good news of that which has been done here in his name.'

Meanwhile, within the market-place itself in the aftermath of the riot, Gaius Calaphilus and his tribunes, including Marcus Lanilla and Fabius Actium, and various ranking centurions, were surveying the carnage about them.

There was a furious, if mute, atmosphere about the Roman party as they stared at the bodies of their soldiers amongst the trampled remains of dead townspeople.

The Romans knew, of course, exactly who was responsible. A branch of the revolutionary Zealots, known as the *sicarii*, the 'knife-men', had been using tactics just such as this for more than twenty years. They would mingle in a crowd on festival occasions with daggers hidden in their garments. After striking down prominent collaborators with Roman officials, they would disappear back into the crowd from where they had come. These terrorists greatly contributed to the unbearable atmosphere of tension the region.

And now, they were amok in Byzantium. A chilling thought.

Things like this were not supposed to happen to Roman soldiers. Anywhere, but least of all in a free city.

One stiff-backed and regal-looking centurion, walking amongst the dead and the dying, turned over the fallen corpse of a crimson-clad soldier and, upon seeing who it was, let out a wail of despair, turning to his colleagues with a disbelieving look on his face. 'Sergeant Gatalius,' he shouted angrily. 'Dead and accounted for. Tell the surgeons they will not be needed here, this day.'

'What a sad and sorry mess,' Calaphilus said at last. Then he let his subordinates know, in no uncertain terms, that he blamed the *praefectus*'s weakness for the catastrophe. 'If that indolent full-of-himself clown in the *Villa Praefectus* would have allowed me to deal with these Jews in a right and proper manner, we could have stamped on these maggot-ridden scum and squashed them flat beneath our feet like slithering things. Instead we watch mute and bewildered as they waste the lives of a generation of Romans. I will not allow this to happen again.' He paused and shook his head at the silence around him. 'I want the Zealots infiltrated, weeded out, dragged from their homes, publicly tried and shamed as an example to all others and then executed whilst they beg for mercy. What say you? Does any man here have reasons why this should not be done?'

Again, there was silence until Marcus Lanilla loudly proclaimed, 'We all stand behind you with our swords at the ready, general.'

Gaius gave his tribune a withering look of contempt and turned his back on him, as if offering the young officer a first stab. 'Mark you well,' he told the rest, 'this day has seen the beginning of the end for organised resistance to the might of Rome. The sub-human things whose acts of wanton violence and mayhem have produced this sight, abhorrent in our eyes, shall rue the day that they sought to usurp the power of the empire. Let an awesome vengeance begin.'

He climbed onto his horse and was through the market gates and riding back to the barracks with a flank of the guards before anyone could speak.

'You heard the general,' shouted an eager junior tribune. 'He wishes vigilante justice upon these dogs. Let us start with the burning of a few Jewish homes and see if that loosens their tongues as to the whereabouts of Basellas.'

As most of the soldiers left, Lanilla and Fabius stood to one side, by the towering steps of the temple, looking at the littered market-place with undisguised glee.

'Another stitch in Thalius Maximus's funeral shroud, I should have said,' noted Marcus eagerly.

'Of that there is little doubt,' Fabius added. 'Calaphilus has a few uses and one of them is the way in which he will report this outrage to Rome. We have a state of martial law declared without the *praefectus*'s knowledge or permission. In my opinion, I should be surprised if Thalius survives with his reputation any higher than a snake's gut.'

Marcus clearly agreed. His laughter filled the almost-deserted market-place and caused the few of the Roman soldiers still involved in the clearing up of the bodies to look at him sharply. And then to quickly turn away when they realised who it was that was laughing. 'But the old man is losing his grip. He thinks that Byzantium needs no one save him. He is *wrong*.'

Just as they, too, were about to leave, a captain leading the body-clearance detail strode across the square and informed the two tribunes that one of those presumed dead was actually still alive.

'He looks Roman,' said the captain, turning Ian Chesterton's bloodied face towards them.

EPISODE TWO
FOUR SIDES TO THE CIRCLE

Jesus answering said unto them, Render to Caesar the things that are Caesar's, and to God the things that are God's.
Mark 12:17

Chapter Nine
The Culture Bunker, Part One – Heliocentric

And he took the damsel by the hand,
and said unto her, Tâl-Î-thã cû-mï;
which is, being interpreted, Damsel,
I say unto thee, arise.
Mark 5:41

The house was carved from the living rock; bare and gnarled sandstone hewn into habitable shapes by the combined efforts of man and nature. Two medium-sized square holes in the wall, covered by a gauze-like substance, were the only sources of light besides the roaring fire that danced and crackled merrily in the centre of the spartan and undecorated room. Behind the fire was a small wooden table at which sat three curious people whose eyes were glued onto the new arrival into their home.

Vicki, meanwhile, feeling as if she were an insect being observed under a microscope, was sitting in the opposite corner, her knees drawn up to her chin, literally shaking with fear and trying hard not to cry.

Finally, one of her rescuers spoke.

It was the man.

'Be not afraid, child,' he said in a deep voice. Every kidnapper in every bad video film that Vicki had ever seen had used that as an opening line. She wasn't buying it in the slightest.

'Sorry but that's, like, pure dead easy for you to say,' she stammered in reply.

'I mean thee no harm.'

'I don't believe you. You're a liar.'

The man stood up from the table. He was in his late thirties, unshaven and with the dark, olive-skinned complexion of a

Greek. Vicki had seen many of the indigenous population during her time in Byzantium and she was, she thought, getting fairly good at spotting the differences between Thracian Greeks and other cultures in the town, like Palestinian Jews, Mesopotamians, Macedonians, Nomadic Turks, Bedouin Arabs, as well as the Romans who, with their uniforms, all looked so different to everyone else.

Still, the fact that these people were from the civilised race that built the acropolis and produced (so Barbara Wright had told her) Socrates, Plato and Archimedes (whoever they were) cut no ice with young Vicki. Her present predicament was looking 'a bit iffy', to use one of Ian Chesterton's favourite phrases. Decidedly iffy.

'What do you want from me?' Vicki asked nervously.

'Want? I saved your life, little one. You were crying out for the help of anyone with ears to listen to your pleas,' the man replied.

'Thank you,' said Vicki, and she genuinely meant it. 'Much appreciated, I'm sure. Now, how do I get out of here?'

'No, no, no.'

It was the woman, still sitting at the table with a girl of roughly Vicki's age by her side, who answered. Well built and with arm muscles that looked as thought they could sink a battleship, the woman's head was wrapped in a grey shawl whilst she wore the clothes of poverty. Her face betrayed a strange mixture of curiosity and apoplectic anger. 'You are not going anywhere to tell them that we were the hapless ones who helped you. What, and see us end up in terrible trouble all because of you?'

'Who is them?' asked Vicki, but her question was ignored as the woman turned to the standing man and began to berate him in their own language for bringing this, whatever she was, into their home and endangering them all.

'I can understand every word you're saying,' Vicki noted when the woman paused for breath. 'I speak many languages. Apparently.'

All three heads in the room turned in her direction, including the still silent girl whose deep brown eyes betrayed a fear equal and opposite to Vicki's own. And Vicki's revelation had the effect of making the older woman not just angry but frightened as well. 'Get her out of here,' she told the man. 'Get her out, now. And make sure that she speaks to no living soul about us.'

'That sounds peachy-fine to me,' Vicki replied. Then the full implications of what the woman was suggesting sank in and she realised that this was not meant as a solution to everyone's problems, merely those of her rescuers. She shuffled backwards, scraping her hands and legs on the rough stone floor, until her back collided with the bare rock of the wall. She hugged her knees to her chest again. 'Oh God,' said Vicki, quickly. 'Look, you really don't have to do anything rash. I wouldn't tell on you, miss. All I want to do is find the people I was with, my family, if you like, and go home.'

'And where is your "home"?' asked the man, taking a pace towards Vicki, his hand outstretched in a conciliatory gesture.

Vicki thought about telling the truth, but then decided that a cover story would save a lot of head-scratching and accusations of witchcraft. Probably. 'England. Britain. I'm not sure what you people call it,' she said. 'A place called... TARDIS. You won't have heard of it. It's a small fishing village on the Thames. I was travelling the empire with...' Now came an inspired piece of lying. 'My uncle and aunt. And my grandfather. I'm an orphan, do you see...?' Wonderfully instantaneous tears appeared in Vicki's eyes and she let out a wail of misery. 'I just want to see them all again.'

The man gave the woman an ominous look, then turned to face Vicki wearing a mask of pity. 'I am so sorry,' he said. 'If they were in that crowd with you then the chances are that they are dead.'

'No,' shouted Vicki. 'They can't be.'

The man tried to smile. 'Perhaps not,' he said, with a horribly false optimism. 'But it is certainly not safe for anyone to be on the streets tonight. The Romans will seek out anyone that ventures abroad this night and do them a terrible vengeance. We can search for your family once the curfew hours are lifted.'

Vicki nodded and wiped a crocodile tear from her eye. 'Thank you,' she gulped, between sobs.

'I am Georgiadis, the shopkeeper,' said the man. 'This is my wife, Evangeline, and our daughter, Iola.'

'Hello,' said the girl, with the first words she had uttered since Vicki's sudden arrival. 'Welcome to our home.' There was a shy embarrassment in her voice that reminded Vicki of a childhood friend who, likewise, had difficulty in speaking unless it was absolutely necessary. From Iola, Vicki looked again at her mother. The frown on Evangeline's face was gradually beginning to seep away and be replaced by something less hostile and industrial. Not kitten-soft and fluffy, exactly, but at least a bit less abrasive. And then there was Georgiadis. Handsome and dignified, a thin and wiry frame that spoke of many meals missed so that others could eat instead.

A watery grin appeared on Vicki's face. 'Thank you. Thank you all. I'll try not to get in the way, really I will. Just please don't kill me.'

Chapter Ten
The Culture Bunker, Part Two – Spies Like Us

And as he went out of the temple,
one of his disciples saith unto him,
Master, see what manner of stones
and what buildings are here!
Mark 13:1

A temple can be made to assume many roles. A house of worship. A thing of beauty, or divinity, or hope. Or, to the cynical, it is merely bricks and mortar. A shell into which spiritual belief is poured in the mistaken assumption that this makes the husk, by definition, a holy thing, in itself.

And then there are those to whom a temple offers sanctuary in a literal, as well as a metaphorical, way.

Somewhere to hide.

Barbara Wright had a phrase in her mind as she staggered, her head bloodied and sore, towards the temple door. It had taken the last of her strength to reach this far, through a maze of doorways, winding alleys, cul-de-sacs and dead ends. 'My body is a temple'.

She was trying, in vain, to remember where the quotation was actually from. What the context was. Who had said it, and why. The situation was similar to her first year at university when she had become drunk for the first (and so far only) time and had needed to negotiate a lengthy mile-and-a-half trek through darkest Cricklewood with only the most basic of directional and sensory equipment still functioning in her brain. She had invented a little game attempting to read, out loud, road signs and car number plates. Anything, in fact, that would help her to stay alert while simultaneously cursing the very name of the spotty, immature legal student who had introduced her to the satanic qualities of gin and tonic.

Herbert Effemy.

Well, *that* was impressive from a distance of fifteen years and at least a couple of cases of probable concussion.

Herbert Effemy.

Spotty Herbert.

Probably an MP, or a judge or something similar, these days.

Except that 'these days' is nineteen hundred years from now, give or take a few months, she told herself.

'My body is a temple'.

Temple Gate. That's where the Law Society in London is based.

Was based?

What tense is this?

Past tense? Present tense? Future tense?

I was. I am. I will be...

She had visited the Temple Gate building in the dim and distant past (or future) and knew that it had been built (or would be built) by the Knights Templars.

Looming out of the darkness, the temple door was within reach. Barbara limped the last few painful paces and pushed at it.

Mercifully, it creaked open.

Barbara found herself at the back of a huge and imposing tabernacle interior. At the far end of the massive central chamber were several dozen people who had gathered around a space lit by many candles. Hurriedly Barbara covered the lower part of her face with the shawl that had miraculously clung to her shoulders during the madness in the square.

Cautiously, she moved towards the group, happy to have found a refuge, but wary that her presence might be unwelcome here. As she grew closer, she recognised that the people were listening to a prayer to Jehovah, spoken in a rich and deep voice by the impressively bearded man standing amidst the candles. A rabbi or Pharisee, clearly. A man of power and influence. Unfortunately, Barbara chose that exact moment, when the murmur of voices in front of her had all but died, to stand on a loose stone on the synagogue floor.

She winced as the slab grated loudly against its neighbour and every head in the building turned in her direction.

'Sorry,' she said, quietly, moving the shawl a fraction to allow her words to be heard and then pulling it back into place.

The holy man began to say something but his words struggled to reach Barbara as others within the group moved slowly towards her. There was an old woman at the front of the congregation, small and squat, with a sore-looking red growth on the side of her neck and several blackened stumps for teeth. Suspiciously, the woman approached Barbara, who found herself rooted to the spot and, as she attempted to say something to calm the atmosphere, the woman reached up an arthritic claw of a hand and pulled away the shawl from Barbara's face, revealing it to everyone present.

'I know not this woman. She is a spy,' spat the old woman, her words tripping over themselves for release. 'A dirty, filthy, infidel Roman spy.'

The Jews behind her, already furious at the Roman soldiers' murder of their people, seemed ready to take any scapegoat presented to them at a time like this. Someone shouted, 'Stone her!' and there were other horrifying and unintelligible screams. Barbara tried to speak but found herself tongue-tied. Her legs had turned to jelly. She felt as though she would surely faint.

And then, from a distance, there came the booming voice of the holy man, silencing everyone within the temple.

'Cease this unsavoury clamour in the house of the Lord.'

Barbara closed her eyes, swallowed hard, and then opened them again in the hope that she had been magically transported back to Coal Hill. Or Cricklewood. Or Skaro, for that matter. Anywhere, in fact, but here.

Instead, what she found herself looking at was the holy man walking towards her as the crowd parted for him. Like Moses and the Red Sea, Barbara thought, before deciding that this wasn't, perhaps, the most tactful of moments to be using biblical metaphors.

'What are you, woman?' asked the priest.

Barbara opened and closed her mouth rapidly but again nothing emerged. She stared into the holy man's marine-blue eyes and found a glint, a sparkle. He was amused.

'You have no need to be afraid, good daughter. For I am Hieronymous, by my mother's name. This is my tabernacle and there shall be no word or deed of violence spoken against or by any man nor woman within this house of Jehovah.'

Still Barbara stammered, trying to make herself understood to him.

'She is a simpleton, perhaps?' asked one of Hieronymous's group.

'No, she is a spy,' shouted the old woman, leaping up and down with spittle drooling from her lips. Her red-scabbed and misshapen mouth formed itself into an obscene parody of a smile. 'It is plain to see. She is no Jew.'

Hieronymous turned and scowled at the woman. 'There shall be no more sacrilege within my sight, Löruhämah. Be at peace and let this poor woman speak.'

'But...'

'Silence, thou aged and haggard and bent old crone,' Hieronymous shouted. 'There shall be no more talk of spies and deceit.' He turned to Barbara. 'From whence come thee, woman?'

'Britannia,' said Barbara, happy that she had finally recovered some powers of speech.

'And by what name did thy mother bear thee?'

'Barbara,' she replied quickly. 'Barbara Wright.'

Hieronymous nodded, wisely, and then returned his attention to the rest of the people within the temple. 'Know this,' he said in a deep and authoritative voice. 'Be it understood that from this hour forward, Barbara Wright of Britannia is a guest of the Temple of Jared bar Abraham, of the house of David and Solomon, in the city of Byzantium. And of its leader and law-giver, Hieronymous bar Jehoiachin, let his name be revered. That Barbara Wright, of Britannia, is under our sacred and divine protection and that any man, or woman, who harms her shall answer unto the laws of God and man.'

Trying not to look as smug or relieved as she felt, Barbara mouthed a quick 'Thank you' to Hieronymous and then looked defiantly at the hostile, grimacing faces of the people surrounding her.

If you're going to get any ally in a place like Byzantium, she thought to herself, might as well go to the top man himself.

Chapter Eleven
The Culture Bunker, Part Three – Going Underground

And he answered, saying, My name is Legion: for we are many.
Mark 5:9

A dim half-circle of clear white light in the distance beckoned lovingly to the Doctor.

He felt brain-numbed and sluggish as he tried to move towards it. Inert, like wading through a lake of thick, sticky treacle.

His movements were slow and painful.

And then, as suddenly as if a rope and anchor had been cut from his feet, he threw himself into the light and rose from the cloth matting that he was lying on.

Sitting upright, he looked around, trying to focus on any movement within the near-darkness that surrounded him. A candle flame flickered, briefly, somewhere to his right and the Doctor followed the source, aware, for the first time, of the tight bandage wrapped around his head. A dull and nagging ache throbbed in his temple. Quite without warning, his vision began to swim and wobble before him, his eyes rolling around in their sockets. The Doctor slumped back onto his temporary bedding and moaned out loud.

That got their attention. Who ever *they* were.

Strong yet gentle hands held him and laid him back on the matting. 'Be still, old one,' said a spectral female voice. 'You are safe. Rest, and you shall recover, fully.'

'My head...' the Doctor managed to say. His throat was dry

and hoarse. He could feel a damp cloth being pressed onto his lips and, after a moment of spitting and spluttering, he sucked, greedily, on the liquid. It tasted peculiar.

Gradually, the Doctor recovered his wits and found himself in a cave outside of the city walls. Besides the gentle woman, tending to his wounds, there were also a man and two younger women present. The man was standing at the mouth of the cave, naturally formed from the wind-ravaged rock, looking down on the city below, which was beautifully silhouetted against the skyline. It was an outstanding view and, for a moment, all the Doctor could do was to take it in and be grateful that he had lived to see it.

Then a pertinent question cut through the fog in his mind.

'How did we get to this place?'

The man and the woman looked at each other. This was clearly esoteric knowledge. Eventually, the man shrugged his shoulders and came across and knelt by the Doctor. 'Passages,' he said. 'Hidden entrances and exits. For is it not written that "judgment also will I lay to the line and righteousness to the plummet; and the hail shall sweep away the refuge of lies, and the waters shall overflow the hiding place"?'

'Was that the weather forecast, hmm?' the Doctor asked, still feeling sluggish and numb.

The man shook his head, sadly. 'No,' he said. 'A prophecy that has become all too true in these dark days and times. I am Daniel,' he continued. 'My wife is Rachel, and her sisters are Miriam and Xanthe.'

'You forget another,' came a voice from the darkness. 'And if introductions are to be so given then, surely, they should also be reciprocal, yes?' An older man stepped from the deep shadows. Dressed in rough haircloth and with a head of white hair that matched the Doctor's own, he moved over to the cave entrance and gave the municipality below them a cursory glance. 'My mother named me James, that I might tell the world this fact wheresoever I wander. And what of you, old stranger?'

The Doctor, still groggy from the blow to his head, muttered something incoherent and the older man came closer. 'Say again?' he queried.

'Doctor,' came the reply. 'It means, in the language of my people, a creator.'

James nodded, satisfied. 'Rachel,' he said quickly, 'this place shall not be safe for long. We must prepare to leave at once. Send thy good sisters on ahead to warn the others that we are coming and that we shall have with us a guest.'

'Is that wise?' Daniel asked.

'It is better if the two travel together. They are quick and nimble and will not be seen.'

Daniel nodded and turned to the girls. 'Go. And God's speed be with you.'

'We shall run like the wind,' said Xanthe, giving a circular signal with the thumb and forefinger of her right hand.

'... And also with you, my cherished one,' Rachel said, returning the gesture, and kissing both of her sisters. Then the men did likewise.

'Hurry through the wilderness, sisters,' James continued. 'We shall follow presently.'

The Doctor propped himself up on one elbow and looked at James, Daniel and Rachel curiously. 'The sign of the fish?' he asked. 'You are Christians, yes? Followers of the church of Jesus of Nazareth?'

'You know of our ways?' asked Daniel, clearly surprised.

'I *am* aware of your work,' the Doctor noted.

'From whence?'

The Doctor gave a dismissive gesture. 'Oh, here and there, my boy. I've been around, don't you know?'

Daniel turned to James with a gleeful look on his face. 'Hear you this? The Word has spread even to the outlands of the empire.'

James nodded and again turned to look out over the city as the sun set below the distant horizon. As the last rays of twilight rippled across the dark waters of the Black Sea, the old man's eyes were misty and full of emotion.

'It has come to pass, as He always said it would. Just as Paul and Barnabas, Mark and Peter and Luke all said it would. Secrets can not be kept hidden forever.'

'It is not safe for us to be so near the city,' Daniel said, looking down at the glowing torches of the first of the Roman columns leaving the city to search for those breaking the curfew. 'We must go, or they will be upon us and we shall be undone.'

'Can you stand, good father?' asked Rachel. The Doctor nodded, and struggled to his feet.

'I didn't think I would be leaving Byzantium alone,' he noted.

'You are not alone,' James replied.

'No, that's not what I meant.' Fresh in the Doctor's memory was seeing young Chesterton bludgeoned to the ground and trampled underfoot, just before he, himself, was knocked into unconsciousness by a stray blow to the head. Not only had the Doctor seen Ian struck down, but he believed that he had also seen Vicki being plucked from the crowd and carried away as he was falling to the ground and fighting for his very life.

The poor child had been abducted, to who knew what terrible fate?

And as for Barbara...?

'I arrived with friends,' the Doctor told his rescuers. 'Three of them. A man, a woman and a young girl. I must find out what became of them in that chaos.' Woefully, in his mind, he was already speculating on what could have happened to his companions. And he didn't like what he was imagining at all.

'We shall endeavour to find out when the sun is risen anew,' James told him. 'For now, Byzantium is not safe for anyone, except the legions of Rome.'

Chapter Twelve
The Culture Bunker, Part Four – Everybody's Been Burned Before

And when the centurion, which stood
over against him, saw that he so cried out,
and gave up the ghost, he said,
Truly this man was the Son of God.
Mark 15:39

Indignant at his harsh treatment, Ian Chesterton's patience finally snapped. 'I *am* telling the truth. I *keep* telling the truth. Why the hell is it that no one will believe me? I mean, am I speaking a foreign language here or something?'

The Roman sergeant grabbed Ian by the collar of his tunic and thrust him up against the wall of the barrack dungeon, wrapping a piece of rusted chain around his prisoner's neck. 'Spy,' he spat. 'Filthy, conspiring insurgent.'

'*Not so*,' Ian shouted, ignoring the constriction at his throat. 'I am from Britannia. That's part of the empire, right?'

The sergeant relaxed his grip and let the chain fall away. Then, as Ian relaxed and sank to his knees, gasping in grateful lungfuls of air, the sergeant brought the chain down, hard, across Ian's back, making the Doctor's companion cry out.

He spilled to the floor, amid the dung and straw, and for several moments found himself unable to move. Finally he spun onto his back and stared up at the leering face of his torturer. He looked, Ian was forced to concede, pretty damn hard. 'If you live in a vacuum, chum, you die. Don't you know that?' he asked.

'What say you?'

'Oh, just something that'll be discovered in about eighteen hundred years time,' Ian said, sardonically. 'Do you mind awfully if I get up, only it pen and inks a bit down here?'

Chesterton had become the subject of much attention at the cadet guards' barracks. Through an observation hole in the roof of the dungeon, Erastus, the cadet trainer, gave the new arrival another look.

'No,' he said at last. 'I do not recognise that man. If he is a Roman solider, he must be a deserter. Or perhaps he is a slave.'

Marcus Lanilla nodded. 'Then we should put this slave to death for such infamy.'

Erastus shrugged. 'Perchance he speaks the truth,' he noted.

Marcus gave the prisoner one last, cursory look and strode away. 'You decide,' he said, abdicating all responsibility for Ian Chesterton's life.

A moment later, Erastus was in the dungeon with the sergeant towering over Ian, who was again lying on the ground, his lip bloodied by a savage punch from the soldier. Again, and with commendable if foolhardy determination, Ian tried to stand, but was thrown back. Erastus placed his foot on Ian's hand and began to apply his full weight to crushing the bones in it to dust.

'Stop it,' shouted Ian with what seemed to be the last of his strength. 'Stop it, you big bully.'

Erastus removed the foot. He was a huge bear of a man, incredibly hairy and muscled. 'They say you are an escaped slave. Or a deserter. Or a spy,' he told Ian. 'Spies are traitors. Traitors are to be crucified unto death.'

'Then they are wrong, whoever they are.' Ian said angrily. 'I am not a slave. I am not a deserter. I am not a spy. I am not a traitor. I am none of those things. What I *am* is a free-born man of the British Isles. Part of the Roman empire. Is this any way to treat a Roman citizen?'

This made Erastus pause. As the Roman world had expanded over the last hundred years, a new social class had become important within the empire, consisting of prosperous land-owners and business people who were called *equites*. Citizenship for all peoples of the empire meant equal protection under Roman law. The privilege of citizenship helped to promote loyalty to the empire and gave peoples of all classes and all nationalities a greater stake in its success.

'Roman law permits the torture of slaves and people considered dishonourable,' he told his prisoner. But, he had to consider the possibility that if this man was neither.

'I am neither,' Ian confirmed. 'I'm a Roman citizen.'

For many years, Romans and non-Romans within the empire had been governed under different sets of laws. Roman citizens lived under the *ius civile*, while a separate set of laws known as the *ius genitum*, the law of the nations, was devised for those from conquered lands. However, it was now generally accepted that all citizens within the empire had equal rights under the law which was based on common-sense notions of fairness, taking into account local customs and practices.

Erastus reached out a hand and dragged Ian roughly to his feet. As Ian stood there, flinching against the expected torrent of physical abuse, the trainer grabbed him by both forearms and looked closely at his hands.

'You have certainly never done an honest day's work in your life with these delicate palms, freeman.'

Ian didn't know whether to be relieved or offended. 'I'm a teacher,' he said, betraying a modicum of outrage at the suggestion that he didn't work damned hard for his meagre salary. 'Science, English and, occasionally, P.E., and you have absolutely no idea what I'm blathering on about, do you?'

'You say that you are a Briton?' asked Erastus.

Chesterton nodded.

'Then we shall soon know the truth, or otherwise, of your tale, freeman.'

Summoned by the potentially serious injury to one of his men, general Calaphilus arrived at the barracks soon afterwards. He strode into the dungeon along with Drusus, who had also been called to assert whether the unknown man was an escaped slave or not. Calaphilus gave the *praefectus*'s freedman a cursory glance as they both saw Ian for the first time. Drusus shook his head.

'Not one of ours,' he said.

'He is clearly no soldier, either,' Erastus confirmed. 'He claims...' he continued but Calaphilus merely scowled, as though several minutes of his valuable time had just been wasted. He turned and was about to leave when Ian Chesterton decided that, just as when he was a wing-three quarter for Harlequins Third XV, attack was the best form of defence and shouted angrily after him.

'Are you in charge here?' he asked. 'Because if you are then you should know what a pretty shoddy operation you're running. I've been in some toilets in my time, right, but this takes the biscuit.'

The general turned, wearily and ignored Ian's outburst. 'What is he blathering about?' he asked Erastus.

'He says...' began the big man.

'Why don't you try asking me, you very rude man?' Ian continued.

Calaphilus walked over, slowly, to where the sergeant was still holding Ian upright and looked him squarely in the eyes. 'And who, exactly, might you be, little man?' asked the general with a dismissive tone that made Ian both vexed and very scared at the same moment.

'Ian Chesterton. Who are you?'

'I have the dubious honour of being general Gaius Augustus Calaphilus, commander of the forces of his most divine and awesome majesty Emperor Lucius Nero. That is, if this be any of your business, slave.'

If Ian was impressed by the general's little proclamation of his power, he didn't show it. 'I am not a slave. I am not a deserter. I am not a spy. I am not a traitor. I am none of those things. What I am is a free-born man of the British Isles. Part of the

Roman empire. Is this any way to treat a Roman citizen?' he said, repeating what he had told Erastus earlier. Ian placed his still-chained hands on his hips and then, considering this to be a somewhat effeminate gesture, let them drop to his sides with a rusty clank. 'And I demand that justice be done, and be seen to be done!'

'You say you are from Britannia?' asked Calaphilus, the merest trace of curiosity in his voice. 'I, myself, served in fair Britannia for many years.'

Oh, well you *would have*, wouldn't you? thought Ian miserably.

'Fine,' he said. 'Then ask me what the weather is like in Londinium. It's wet and cold, by the way, except that we normally get four or five decent days in July. A month, incidentally, named after the divine Julius. How am I doing so far?'

Calaphilus gave little away with a bland and expressionless poker-style face that stared back at Ian Chesterton. 'You allege that you are from Londinium?' he asked.

'Yes,' Ian replied quickly. 'Well, at least, I live there now. I am a teacher... A scribe, if you like. I was actually born in Reading, know it at all?'

'I was with the God Claudius and Aulus Plautius when he took the wild and barren land, twenty years since. I saw the savage king Caratacus of the Catuvellauni defeated. I was but a mere legionnaire in those far off and troubled days and, as my rank progressed I saw much of that beautiful and harsh land from whence you say you come. Segedunem and the bridgehead at Pons Aelii where we could smell the breath of the Caledonian scum...'

'Well, I've never been too keen on the Scots myself,' Ian noted. 'You won't get any argument from me. You want to try building a great big wall from Carlisle to Newcastle and keep the blighters out.'

Time always looks after itself, Ian thought. That was one positive thing that the Doctor had taught him.

Maybe it was the casualness of Ian's reply that impressed

Calaphilus, but Ian could certainly sense a change in the general's attitude towards him. Perhaps only a fraction, but when the general began to speak again, his voice was lower and noticeably softer in tone. 'I was garrisoned at Eboracum. And then Aquae Sulis, Corinium and Camulodunon,' continued the soldier. Ian recognised the second Latin place name as the ancient Roman designation for Bath on Avon, a place he knew little about except that it had some impressive Roman baths, and that he'd once got drunk in the rugby club there. Nice beer, he remembered.

However, the last name...

Ian shuddered. 'Colchester,' he said. 'A perfectly horrible town. I spent one of the worst weekends of my life there with a girl from Guildford. It rained, and it rained...'

'Yes,' noted Calaphilus. 'That sounds like Camulodunon all right.' Now, for the first time, there was a glint of shared experience within the soldier's eye. He had clearly loved the land of Ian's birth and if Ian was to be his only link to it then he was, seemingly, better than nothing at all. He half-turned away from Ian and indicated to the other men in the dungeon that there was at least some truth in the stranger's story.

'So, you believe me then?' asked Ian, relief etched into his voice.

But still, Calaphilus's eyes were like those of a snake as it hypnotises its prey. 'You and I shall talk further on this matter at another time, *alleged* Briton,' he said.

Ian seized a possible opportunity. 'My companions. A woman, an old man and a young girl. They were in the square with me when all hell broke lose. We lost each other in the panic. I have to know if they're all right.'

The general shouted to Drusus, still standing by the door. 'Find a place for this guest of Byzantium within the *Villa Praefectus* until we can ascertain whether his family survived the terrible massacre.'

Drusus bowed to the general's authority.

Ian, too, was impressed. 'You have my thanks, general,' he said.

Calaphilus nodded and then told Erastus, the sergeant and

Drusus to leave them for a moment. When they were alone in the dungeon, the general drew Ian to one side and, in a conspiratorial whisper said, 'I would appreciate that you keep open and wide your eyes and ears within the *Villa Praefectus*.'

Ian understood. 'Politics,' he said, 'is not my area of expertise.'

'In Byzantium,' the general noted, 'politics is *everyone*'s area of expertise. Only the dead are free of it.'

Chapter Thirteen
The Enemy of My Enemy Is My Friend

Forbid him not: for there is no man
which shall do a miracle in my name,
that can lightly speak evil of me. For he
that is not against us is on our part.
Mark 9:39-40

Sunrise over the desert. It was something of an anticlimax, Barbara was forced to admit.

This was her first proper look at the phenomenon. She couldn't sleep - there was simply no point in trying. Instead she had spent the small hours of the night pacing the guest room in Hieronymous's spacious three-storey home. Under more normal circumstances, Barbara could have found hours of amusement and enlightenment from simply observing all of the everyday household items, the decorations, the way the house was built. Learning about the past from first-hand experience.

But these were not normal circumstances.

The Doctor and Ian and Vicki were missing. Presumed dead.

She was completely alone.

As the rather washed-out and pale-looking sun came above the distant horizon and the sky began to lighten in jagged streaks, Barbara observed it from her window. Somewhere nearby, people were being called to prayer. Had it only been a day since she and Ian had observed the same process with the detached curiosity of travellers about to embark on their way, never to see such a thing again?

It had.

The wailing cry of the priest reminded her of a dog in considerable pain.

She shook her head. Life is too cynical, too critical, she thought angrily to herself. Get over your prejudices and your stupid, outdated twentieth-century ideas of right and wrong and make the best of what you've got.

Now.

'Things must change,' she said in a whisper.

She looked again at the sunrise and found it not to be disappointing, but rather miraculous. Get used to that, too, she noted. It might be the view that you wake to every day for the rest of your life.

From somewhere downstairs she heard voices. Raised and agitated. The Barbara Wright who had taught at Coal Hill School would have cowered under her bedclothes rather than face whatever potentially embarrassing situation she was about to walk into, but Barbara had already changed in the year or more that she and Ian had travelled with the Doctor. She had grown more assertive, more willing to face whatever life had to offer head-on, and confront its delicious ironies and capricious dangers. So she trooped down the stairs to Hieronymous's living room and found herself in a scene from a particularly melodramatic episode of *The Grove Family*.

Hieronymous was in the middle of a heated argument with a strikingly beautiful young woman in her early twenties with lengthy jet-black hair and skin like porcelain. The pair seemed not to have seen Barbara who froze at the foot of the stone steps, hardly daring to breathe.

'What treasons can be committed?' Hieronymous asked. 'No wrong-doing shall come to pass within this my house.'

The woman threw up her hands in exasperation. 'You are blinded by a pretty face, good father. And by loneliness. I do not trust this *gentile* woman. You are breaking each and every one of the very rules that you always instilled in me.'

The priest laughed. 'You were reticent to learn them, my heart. You only accepted them at the point of a stick.'

'That is as maybe,' said the young woman, with a half-hearted smile. She moved forward and grabbed the old man's hands in her own. Standing next to him, they were almost a comical sight with the woman dwarfed by her father's bulky frame. 'Trust no one except family,' she said pointedly. 'Those were the words that you always intoned. And after a hundred beatings, I firmly believed them. And now, this...'

'I sense no evil ways in the woman,' Hieronymous noted.

At this point, Barbara decided that valour was the better part of dissection and coughed, loudly. Two heads snapped simultaneously in her direction. 'Good morning,' she said with a practised and charming smile. 'I think it would be better for all concerned if I leave this house immediately.'

A long silence followed as Barbara waited for some reaction to her dramatic little piece of good manners.

It was broken only by the continued and distant call to prayers.

Finally, it was the woman who spoke. 'No,' she said in a flat, monotonous, almost-rehearsed voice. 'It is I who shall leave. Immediately.'

She turned and headed for the door.

'Gabrielle,' said Hieronymous in a small, cracked, slightly pathetic voice. 'You will return this evening?'

'Perhaps,' she said enigmatically, closing the door behind her.

'Oh dear,' Barbara noted. 'This is bad, bad, bad...'

Hieronymous didn't say anything. Barbara noticed that the old man was crying. Resisting every urge in her body, Barbara turned her back on the priest and began to walk up the stairs. She got halfway before her heart broke in two and she ran back down to him.

'Walk with me in the garden,' Hieronymous asked.

Barbara nodded and gently led the priest, his shoulders hunched with pain and guilt, to the door. 'I'm a good listener,' she said, then instantly regretted it as Hieronymous gave her a look of infinite displeasure. That was like a pick-up line used by every good-time girl in every sleazy bar in Soho, she reflected. 'I'm sorry,' she continued. 'I simply meant that if you need a sympathetic ear...'

'My daughter has never recovered from the death of her mother,' Hieronymous said as they entered the oasis of the temple gardens. Rich, green and verdant, life seemed to abound and flourish here, within five miles of a dust-bowl, bone-dry desert. The magical colours of the flowers and shrubs briefly startled Barbara. Hieronymous said something but she wasn't concentrating on him. So much for being a sympathetic ear, she berated herself, and said, 'I'm desperately sorry, what was that?'

Hieronymous looked sheepish and embarrassed, as though what he had just said had required a great deal of courage to get it out first time around and he wasn't looking forward to a repeat performance. 'It is about your friends,' he stammered. He stopped, turned and held Barbara by the shoulders. 'Be strong, woman, and have faith in the Lord when I tell you that over one hundred and sixty men, women and children died in the midst of the massacre in the market-place yesterday. The overwhelming evidence suggests that your friends were among them.'

He stopped and looked crestfallen.

Barbara accepted this news stoically. 'Life goes on,' she said, reflecting that now was not the time to grieve. 'And we, however reluctantly, have to go on with it.'

When Georgiadis and Evangeline awoke a sleepy Vicki to give her similar news, she was distraught.

'Well, thanks for sharing *that*,' she said tearfully and got back into bed, pulling the rough hessian blanket over her head.

Gently Evangeline pulled the blanket back down and Vicki emerged, blinking, into the light like a small animal after hibernation. 'Let your tears flow like the river, little one,' said the woman, putting an arm around Vicki's trembling shoulders. 'The pain will get so much worse before it, eventually, gets better. Embrace the pain; for a while it may be your only friend.'

Strange advice, reflected Vicki in a moment of clarity amidst the horror of her situation. The Doctor was dead. Ian was dead. Barbara... Poor Barbara.

'I have nothing left to live for,' Vicki said with a eye for the heightened drama of the situation. Curiously, what she really felt was utterly hollow. She was sad, of course. Her companions were the nearest thing that she'd had to a family since her father's death on Dido. But she was used to being alone. It wasn't the end of the world.

It was only the enormity of her own personal predicament that truly upset her. Without the TARDIS, she was stuck.

Here.

'Life is bigger than you, little one,' Evangeline said in a voice that reminded Vicki of her dead mother.

The association set off a chain reaction, like a dam being breached. As Vicki began to cry, huge choking sobs of regret and sorrow, a free-form melange of imagery and memories came flooding out with it. 'I was eleven when my mother died,' she said. 'She was going to call me Tanni, she always said, but daddy preferred the name Vicki so I was stuck with it... It's a stupid name, don't you think?'

Georgiadis gave his wife a look of concern, but Evangeline shook her head. 'Go on, angel, tell me what your heart feels.'

'Alone,' said Vicki, tearfully. 'Alone and afraid. I'm so scared.'

The Greek woman nodded wisely and sat on the bed, hugging Vicki close to her. 'My own parents were murdered when I was no more than a girl. Younger than you. I survived by my wits and the true kindness of others. And because you have to. Life is bigger than you, and you are not me. We are all unique, individual.'

Vicki clung to Evangeline as the woman gently rocked her back and forth. 'Ask for a shoulder to cry on, you get a philosopher,' she muttered.

'Your aunt and uncle meant the world to you?'

'Yes,' said Vicki, fighting back the tears. 'Literally. And the Doctor... They saved me from certain death.'

'Family does that,' Georgiadis said quickly, feeling somewhat left out. 'We shall be your family now.'

Evangeline brushed the wet hair from Vicki's eyes. 'Hush,

little one. You have learned a harsh lesson this day. But you shall survive it.'

Some hours later, Vicki emerged sleepily from her bed to the smell of cooking. She found Evangeline up to her elbows in a huge stone pot mixing some sort of vegetable stew. It didn't look particularly appetising to Vicki, but the aroma, after a day of having eaten nothing at all, was enticing enough.

'Smells nice,' she said in a croaky whisper. Her throat felt salty and tasted of the pain of loss.

Evangeline nodded and tapped the side of the pot with the wooden spoon she was using to stir the brew. 'I had to find the biggest one that we possess. I am cooking for four mouths now.'

Suddenly, the vastness of the change in this family's life hit Vicki. There they were, perfectly balanced and static in their own narrow lives and along comes a helpless orphan who...

'Thank you,' she said, as the tears started again. 'Thank you for taking me into your home. I really appreciate it. Sometimes, it might not seem like I do, but I do.'

Vicki ran to the door and stood, crying, on the threshold, looking out at the cobbled curved street where the Greek family lived. This was her new world and, grateful as she was to have shelter and food and a good chance of survival, she silently cursed that they had ever come to Byzantium.

Ian Chesterton had hardly slept either, though for vastly different reasons. Finding himself escorted to the *Villa Praefectus* by Drusus and having been given impressively lavish quarters, Ian was just settling down for the night when there was a soft but impatient knock on his chamber door. And, before he had a chance to offer entrance, he was treated to the arrival of a middle-aged woman in a white silken dress with her hair piled up on her head in a towering bouffant. She saw Ian lying naked in bed and her eyes widened.

'So, you are the Briton?' she asked, lustfully. 'Your arrival has caused something of a stir within this house.'

'Bad news travels fast,' Ian noted. 'Madam, it would seem that you have me at something of a disadvantage...'

The woman seemed to consider this for an age. 'I am the lady Jocelyn, the wife of the *praefectus*,' she said at last. 'And I am here for the sole purpose of seducing you.'

'Oh,' said Ian, matter-of-factly. 'That's nice.' He paused as the directness of her approach sank deeper. 'It's not that I'm ungrateful, or anything, I'm truly flattered, but...'

Joceyln inclined her head to one side, smiled, and then threw herself onto the bed at Ian's feet and began to crawl towards him.

Chesterton leapt from the bed like a scalded cat, almost falling as his legs entangled themselves in the bedding. He grabbed a robe as he freed himself and cowered in the corner, dressing, whilst the woman watched him with a look that was touching the torrid. 'It would,' Ian said, covering his dignity with some haste, 'be unseemly for a guest to take advantage of his host's hospitality before proper introductions had even been made. You understand, of course?'

'Humph.' Jocelyn seemed to have become bored by the chase. She rolled off the bed and moved towards the door before looking over her shoulder and giving Ian an ice-cold stare. 'I usually get what I want,' she said, flatly.

'Oh, I'll bet you do, missus,' Chesterton muttered as he scuttled after her and closed the door, standing with his back pressed against it for several moments before he finally went back to bed. He sat upright, shivering despite the balmy night heat. 'This place is worse than Notting Hill Gate,' he noted before drifting into a fitful sleep.

He awoke shortly before dawn and lay for a while, stroking his memories. 'I've got all sleep's secrets hidden in my bag,' he muttered, smiling at the pleasant, warm touch of the slowly rising sun on his arm, banishing the gooseflesh. Then the bedroom door opened again and Ian closed his eyes with a groan of disappointment. Would this awful woman never take a simple no for an answer?

Thinking lurid thoughts, he opened his eyes to find not the expected, unattractive noblewoman looking for a bit of rough, but a girl in her late teens, dressed in a short, white, and delightful one-piece dress and carrying a bowl of scented fruit.

'Smells like a tart's boudoir,' Ian offered, sitting up and exposing his bare chest again. The girl's eyes widened just as the lady Jocelyn's had earlier. 'Good morning,' Ian said brightly, covering himself with a silken sheet. 'I'm Ian, how do you do?'

The girl giggled, flirtatiously, and laid the fruit on a small table at the foot of the bed.

'I am Felicia, handmaiden to my lady Jocelyn.'

'We've met,' Ian noted, bluntly, and the girl had to place a hand over her mouth to stifle the giggles that followed. Ian didn't like the nuances of Felicia's amusement one little bit. Too coquettish, by half. Good gracious, did nobody in this household think about anything other than sex? 'Could you possibly inform housemaster Drusus that I'm awake? I have a few questions that I'd like answered.'

Felicia nodded, though she hovered for a long and lingering moment, tugging at the hem of her skirt in an act of open provocation that Ian had seen a thousand times in a thousand crush-driven schoolgirls.

'*Now*, please,' he continued with a slow-and-measured voice that tried not to give away how unnerved he was by the whole encounter. 'I'd hate you to get into trouble.'

Almost comically, Felicia seemed torn between throwing herself onto Ian, pinning him to the bed with her shapely thighs and making wild and passionate love to him until he begged her for more, and obeying his commands without question. Ian felt a bit sorry for her, but rejection was rejection, probably not something that the women of this villa had encountered a great deal of. Even the slaves, seemingly, got what they were after. 'Hurry,' he shouted, and Felicia ran from the room, her face a picture of scowling disappointment.

Briefly, Ian wondered why he had suddenly become a magnet

for every woman in Byzantium. 'Looked in the mirror lately, pal?' he asked aloud, as he puffed out his chest and let his pride swell significantly. 'Nice work if you can get it,' he mused as he dressed, ready to face whatever else this place had to offer.

Drusus and Erastus were eating a breakfast of bread and cheese when Ian was shown into the servants' mezzanine, overlooking the main hallway of the *Villa Praefectus*. It was clear that both men had been discussing Ian, from the sudden silence that accompanied his arrival.

'Thank you,' Ian told the young serving boy who had brought him to Drusus. He sat, without being asked, beside the house-master and the cadet trainer and smiled at both men. 'Lovely morning for it,' he noted.

'For what?' asked Erastus with an irritated snarl.

'Oh, a bit of this and that, you know? Ducking and diving.'

Drusus attempted to change the subject but Ian brought him to a juddering halt.

'You both think I'm a Jew spy, don't you?' he asked casually, taking a small bite of cheese as they digested this.

Erastus looked uncomfortable, Drusus merely curious. 'Well...?'

'I'm not,' said Ian, as if that would be enough. 'Any chance of a little wine to go with this? It's somewhat dry.'

Two hours later, after a drinking session of which Ian hadn't seen the like since Friday nights in the West End with his friends from teaching college, everyone's position was much clearer. Drusus, he freely admitted, naturally distrusted everyone, it wasn't anything personal. In his position it always helped to keep an open mind about the allegiances of those who claimed to be one thing. 'Because they are frequently something else,' he noted as he stood from the table and excused himself, staggering off in search of the lavatory.

'I'll tell you something,' Ian noted, raising his goblet to his lips.

Erastus watched him closely. 'Where I come from, wine as good as this would cost a pretty penny.'

'And where, exactly, do you come from, freeman?' asked Erastus.

'Britannia. Londinium. I've told you all the complete truth,' Ian said, tapping the side of his nose. 'Of course, my method of arrival was a sky chariot from the stars and I come from the far future where we have television sets and aeroplanes and computers that fit into a room half this size.' He laughed, aware that the wine had dangerously loosened his tongue. 'I offer you a toast of reconciliation,' he said, half-standing and then slumping into his seat again, drunk. 'To the nights of Byzantium, and the rise and fall of the Roman empire. God bless her and all who will *sink* in her.'

For a moment there was a complete silence. And then Erastus burst into spontaneous laughter. 'You are either a simpleton or a clown,' he said, draining his wine and standing to leave. 'Whichsoever applies, you are of no concern to me. But I thank you, Briton, for the entertainment which was appreciated.'

Ian watched him leave and finished off his own wine. 'Nice fellah,' he said as he stood, knocking over the table as he did so. 'Leave that,' he said, apologetically, to the empty room. 'I'll wipe it up in the morning.'

After a siesta to sleep off the effects of this most potent of wines, Ian awoke with a sore head and determined to walk off his hangover by exploring as much of the house as he could.

Soon, he found himself inside an enormous library in the west wing. Picking a scroll at random from the numerous neatly stacked shelves, he looked at the opening line which seemed to concern a great sea battle. Ian didn't feel in the mood for war stories that hadn't been written by Alistair MacLean and slipped it back into its place.

'Ah,' noted a soft voice behind him. 'Marcus Agrippa's account of the great battle of Actium. A most excellent and wise choice.'

Ian turned. 'History's not really my field,' he said, noting the presence of a studious-looking man with a kindly face. 'I'm a scientist, I deal in the present rather than the past.'

'But without the past, there can be no present. Or future,' noted the librarian.

'Good point,' muttered Ian, reflecting on how Barbara would have loved it here.

'Of course, it is perfectly possible that one day all of my books will be nothing more than dust in the wind,' continued the librarian sadly. 'But the knowledge of what is contained within them will live on in the minds of scholarly men. All things must pass into the pure light of knowledge.'

Ian found this a curiously narrow view for a man of such obvious intellect. 'Entropy,' he said at last. 'That is what will destroy your books. It's an inevitable process.'

'I do not follow.'

Ian picked up another scroll and drew his fingernail along the edge of the paper, flaking off a fine dust onto his thumb. 'See. Entropy. It's a thermodynamic constant that changes in a reversible process by an amount equal to the heat absorbed or emitted, divided by the thermodynamic temperature. It is measured in joules per kelvin. It also means a lack of pattern or organisation.'

The librarian shrugged. 'Which means...?'

'That everything gets old, decays and dies.'

'Except knowledge,' noted the old man. 'You are our recently arrived guest from far and distant shores, yes?'

Ian couldn't believe how infamous he was becoming in this place. 'Don't you people have anything *else* to talk about?' he asked.

'Not in Byzantium,' the librarian replied with a rueful smile. 'I am Fabulous, the keeper of the master's library. Erastus believes that you are a wandering fool.'

'I have been called one often enough,' Ian noted sullenly.

'I take a less parochial view than our noble cadet trainer,' said Fabulous. 'My passion is for stories. I have a feeling that you have many a fascinating tale to tell.'

An ally, perhaps, in this house of secrets and sin and danger.

'I have travelled far and wide through many distant lands,' Ian said, truthfully.

'What did you do there?'

'I survived.'

This brought a broad smile to the librarian's face. 'Then, my friend, you will find Byzantium a challenge. But I have a feeling that you will rise to the tests that are to come.'

Chapter Fourteen
He Not Busy Being Born Is Busy Dying

If any man have ears to hear, let him hear.
Mark 4:23

It did not take Ian long to find another ally within the massive household. Fabulous introduced the school teacher to Gemellus later that day when the advisor came to the library to do some research for the *praefectus*.

Ian could tell, instantly, that here was another man whom he could trust.

Gemellus smiled genially and asked Ian a few cursory questions about Britannia, seemingly to satisfy himself, as others had before him, that Ian was not a spy of some kind.

'One can never be too careful in these times, my friend,' Gemellus said, almost apologetically, as Ian successfully passed the authenticity test by rattling off a few half-remembered facts about the invasions of Julius and Claudius, and a couple of timeless stories about London. He didn't mention sky chariots and was thankful that Fabulous didn't either.

'I feel a little out of my depth in Byzantine society,' Ian admitted, acknowledging that he could trust his new friends with such a statement. 'Even within these four walls, I'm ignorant of so much. And I haven't even met my gracious host yet.'

There was something to be said, clearly, for showing but not telling.

Gemellus sympathised. 'It is as well to know the whys and wherefores of every man, and woman, and slave hereabouts,' he offered. 'Starting with the *praefectus*.'

'This is undoubtedly true,' Fabulous added. 'For on such knowledge can a man's need for alliances depend.'

Ian understood. 'So,' he said, 'tell me about the boss.'

'Thalius Maximus,' began Gemellus. '*Praefectus* of Byzantium, executive to his most awesome and imperial majesty, this-that-and-the-other, the Emperor Lucius Nero Caesar.' He paused. 'You have heard of *him*, I take it?'

Ian gave Gemellus a keenly sarcastic stare. 'I'm an outsider, not a numbskull,' he said.

'Your point is well made,' noted Gemellus.

'The master is a politician,' continued Fabulous. 'A good one.'

'Though often a *bored* one,' added Gemellus. 'And I speak as a friend of the man, as well as his counsellor. He is hugely mistrusted by the military, which some may regard as a sign of his considerable worth.' Gemellus paused and asked the librarian if he thought this was a fair summation of Thalius.

'I should say so,' Fabulous agreed. 'Of course, you did leave out the damsel in this tale of woe.'

Ian's eyebrows raised. 'Ah, the distaff side?' he asked. 'I should have guessed there'd be a Judy in there somewhere. Do tell.'

'Antonia Vinicius,' Gemellus almost spat the name out. 'Thalius's former wife, now married to a usually absent and ambitious senator called Germanicus. Be very careful of her.' As he said it, he cast a nervous glance behind to assure himself that this observation had not been overheard.

Fabulous instantly poured oil on troubled waters. 'A woman for whom the purpose of life is the pleasure which can be gained from that portion of her body beneath her navel and above her knees,' he said, bitterly.

Chesterton got the message. 'I know the type,' he said.

'Oh, but I do not think you do, young Briton,' Gemellus countered, still clearly angry to be talking about a woman such as this. 'You have had the dubious pleasure of meeting the *praefectus*'s new wife, the vivacious lady Jocelyn, yes?'

Ian shuddered and nodded his head.

'And, you will also, no doubt, have encountered the deliciously flirtatious Felicia who can produce a momentary awakening even in these tired and bent old bones.'

Fabulous winked broadly at Ian in agreement.

'I have been made aware of her, yes,' Ian admitted.

'The whole of the barracks and half of the city besides are aware of Felicia and Jocelyn,' Gemellus said. 'Now, put the twix of them together and you would still be a dozen Roman miles and more besides behind the minx Antonia and her wild and frivolous ways. She is hugely promiscuous and enjoys, so it is said, the company of soldiers. And even slaves.'

There was a shock in Gemellus's voice as it dropped to a whisper for the final accusation.

'Okay, so the former lady of the house goes like the netty door when the plague's in town?' Ian asked. 'I can dash a mean hundred yards if there's a reason for it. What about that general I met last night? The one who's been to Britain? He seemed relatively sane.'

'Gaius Calaphilus,' Fabulous said. 'A much underrated fellow. Now *there* is a man worth having on your side.'

Gemellus seemed unsure of whether he should be saying what he was about to. After a moment's hesitation he pressed on. 'It is no secret that Thalius and the general do not agree upon most issues. And their mutual dislike is sometimes justified...'

'But...?' asked Ian.

'They are the only two truly honest men in Byzantium, present company excepted. In a city of thieves and whores and ruffians, they are both too proud to be the friends that they should be. Fabulous knows the general better than I.'

Fabulous accepted this as a compliment. 'He is a dedicated career soldier,' he noted. 'He served under Claudius during the conquest of Britain, as you know. He is a man of common blood who fought his way up through the ranks. I have talked with him often and I know that he holds some enlightened views. And some dangerous ones. He loathes the excesses of the imperial family. Like all good leaders of men he is popular with his legions but is a ripe target for his ambitious junior officers.'

Chesterton got the general picture that the two men were painting. 'You think he has enemies?' he asked.

'I *know* he has enemies,' replied Fabulous. 'Marcus Lanilla for one. A devious and sly individual. Marcus forms, with his wife Agrinella, a deadly duo in the internal politics of the Roman establishment in Byzantium.'

'A man of moderately noble birth, married into his wife's powerful family, Marcus has his eyes on Calaphilus's job,' added Gemellus. 'His best friend and closest ally is Fabius Actium, another tribune. Fabius is not nearly as clever as Lanilla, but equally as ambitious and much less subtle in his methods.'

The two men shook their heads at the terrible viper's nest of corruption and decadence they had just described.

'Oh well,' said Ian, breaking the silence that had settled over the library. 'It has most of the things that a decent soap opera requires. Power, corruption, lies, sex. I think I'm going to like it here.'

Thalius Maximus was reading the reports of the military concerning the impressively co-ordinated quashing of the attempted rebellion of the Zealots in the market square. It was a mundane task, the language was stale and couched in bloodthirsty euphemisms.

'No, no, no,' he said angrily, throwing down the parchment scrolls and kicking them away in disgust. 'It will not do.'

Gemellus bowed, deeply. 'The *praefectus* is, of course, expressing what many within the community in this state feel. I should caution the *praefectus*, however, that there are an equal, if not a greater number who do not share the *praefectus*'s concerns.'

'You are saying that the civilians want this kind of... bloodshed?'

That was an interesting question, thought Gemellus, and one that deserved a considered answer. 'Many believe that the alternative to such aggressive and brutal tactics is that they run the risk of having their throats cut in their own beds by Zealot gangsters,' Gemellus offered. 'In such a climate, then I should say that yes, this is the view of the majority.'

'But do *you* agree with it?' asked the *praefectus* quickly.

The advisor never had the chance to answer. The doors behind him crashed open and Drusus entered and cast the governor a wearied and apologetic glance. 'The lady Antonia Vinicius, wife of senator Germanicus of Byzantium, humbly entreats an immediate audience with his most high excellency,' he said, rolling his eyes heavenward.

At his heels, Antonia strode into the room without waiting for an invitation. She gave Gemellus a look of unadulterated contempt. 'You may go, *little man*,' she announced. 'You too, Drusus. The *praefectus* and I have matters of great import to discuss. And we shall not wish to be disturbed.'

Both men stayed exactly where they were and looked at the *praefectus* who waited for a few seconds before casually dismissing them with a wave of his hand.

When the door was closed, Thalius rounded on his former wife.

'I will not have good and loyal members of my staff spoken to in such a manner by the likes of you, Antonia. You have no power or position within this household anymore, no matter whose bed you are currently occupying. And when you march in here as if you still own the place with your demands and your outrages, I would ask you to remember that .'

There was a look of amusement on Antonia's face. 'Marriage to that vapid creature, Jocelyn, has made you bold, Thalius. Can it be that you have finally found a woman who can satisfy your unique needs?'

If Thalius felt belittled by such outrageous innuendo, he chose to hide it under a blanket of moral disgust. 'You are nothing but a common whore, Antonia,' he chided. 'A pathetic *moecha* of alleged maturity trying to recapture the splendour of her youth in ever more desperate ways.'

Antonia gave a short, harsh laugh and threw back her head, shaking her mane of rich, brown hair. 'You weak and flaccid fool,

Thalius,' she berated him. '*Lingua faciosi, inertes opera*. I have heard about the ways in which that old idiot Gaius Calaphilus is making you look like the half-man you truly are. And always were.' She turned and flounced towards the door. She had simply come to insult Thalius and, this having been done, she was leaving.

'Goodbye Antonia,' Thalius called. 'And may all of the afflictions that blight you be major and painful ones.'

At the door, Antonia threw it open to be confronted by Gemellus and Ian, whom the counsellor was waiting to introduce to the *praefectus* once he had finished his audience with his former wife. 'Lady Antonia,' Gemellus said flatly. 'I have the honour of introducing to you Ian Chesterton, a guest of the *praefectus* and of the city, from Britannia.'

'Charmed,' said Ian, remembering what Gemellus had said earlier but with enough home counties breeding to take the lady's offered hand and kiss it.

'A Briton?' asked Antonia with a scorpion-like speed that startled both Gemellus and Ian. 'I have heard reliable information that all of the men of the Isles are brutes and savages.'

'You were, therefore, clearly misinformed, my lady,' said Ian who felt wonderful after he'd said it.

'A pity,' noted Antonia, wiping the snigger from his lips, as she continued to stare at Ian for several lustful seconds before patting him on the cheek. 'We shall meet again, in less formal circumstances, Briton. Be sure of it.'

Somewhere on the other side of the Roman barracks that surrounded the *Villa Praefectus*, a furtive meeting was taking place.

When the door was locked and bolted to prevent sudden interruption or discovery, the conspirators removed their cloaks and hoods.

'I hate this subterfuge,' said Marcus Lanilla, angrily casting his cowl aside. 'Sneaking around like rats in the gutters of Rome.

We are noble men, soldiers, pure of body and heart and mind, we should not be skulking in the shadows.'

The others nodded their agreement.

'Sadly,' continued Marcus, 'circumstances force us not to reveal ourselves too early in the game, lest the hunters become the hunted.' He paused, making sure that his three acolytes were following his grandiose pronouncements.

'We should use stealth instead of ignorant haste?' asked Fabius Actium, very pleased with his own cleverness.

'Yes,' noted Marcus. 'We must plan for the time when we shall be ready to act.'

The two other tribunes with Marcus and Fabius were Honorius Annora and Edius Flavia. Part of the same social group, they were slightly younger but from the same cadet academy as their more illustrious companions, equally ambitious with a lust for power that made them dangerous men. They were calculating and knew that their route to leadership and, ultimately, to Rome lay initially in the death of their general.

'The *praefectus*,' spat Marcus with disgust, 'has taken issue with the way in which the insurrection was put down. Politics, gentlemen. The business of compromise. Of weakness in the face of aggression. I should sooner deal with the Zealot leader, one-on-one, face-to-face, with my sword at his throat than trust the ditherings of a transient governor at the eleventh hour of his reign.'

'We shall have Basellas's head on a pike soon enough,' noted Edius.

Fabius sensed that Marcus might have other plans for Basellas and motioned his young comrade to silence. 'The plan is not so simple,' he suggested. 'Is this not so, Marcus?'

'All in good and ample time, my fine friends. For are we not Roman? Do we not reveal our hand until it is the one that carries the sword to make the striking blow, and seals our victory in all things?'

Again, there were nods of agreement and echoed shouts of 'Victory'.

'The *praefectus* and Calaphilus are mutual thorns in our side. And to remove the one without the other will bring neither satisfaction nor the redress that we seek for all of the wrongs that both have done upon us, and our men, and our people.'

What followed was a strange and mesmerising silence, as though the full implications of what Marcus was proposing had failed to penetrate the closed minds of his ambitious but short-sighted colleagues. After a moment of waiting for a reaction, Marcus added a punchline in the hope that this would provoke some sense of what they could achieve.

'We are the knights of Byzantium. And Byzantium shall be ours,' he said with a gesture of solidarity and strength.

That went down very well indeed with his three friends.

EPISODE THREE
WINDOW SHOPPING FOR A NEW CROWN OF THORNS

Whatsoever thou shalt ask of me,
I will give it unto thee, the half of my kingdom.
Mark 6:23

Chapter Fifteen
Pale Shelter

For it is written, I will smite the shepherd,
and the sheep shall be scattered.
Mark 14:27

It took Vicki approximately a day to become used to the idea that in all probability she would never see Ian, Barbara or the Doctor again. That part of her dilemma, in truth, didn't take a lot of accepting. She was, after all, well used to losing those people close to her. She was grateful that the TARDIS crew had saved her life on Dido from the madman Bennett and his deranged schemes. After that, she swore that she would never trust anyone other than her rescuers again. But circumstances change all the time.

The concept of Byzantium being her permanent home, with Georgiadis and Evangeline and Iola, took a little more effort for her to become enthusiastic about, however.

Certainly the Greek shopkeeper and his family were nice enough people, and she was genuinely obliged to them for saving her life yet again. But, she reflected, she was now stuck in a time two-and-a-half thousand years before she had even been born. She came from an age of computers, electronics, space travel, interactive learning, virtual reality, chemical stimulation, instant maturity. She was fourteen, going on 108, yet to these people, for whom all of the things of her world that she took for granted were greater and more astonishing than all of the seven wonders of their own put together, she was what she appeared to be to the naked eye: a mere *child*.

There would be trouble somewhere along the line, Vicki was sure of it.

Iola didn't talk very much. Vicki had to literally drag out the first few conversations that she had with the girl.

'Let's be friends,' Vicki said, considering that a young ally in this place, as opposed to adults who merely tolerated her eccentricities, could be really useful. Someone with whom she would share secrets and hopes and aspirations. Someone whom she could use as a barrier, a protective shield against the outside world. More importantly, someone to keep her right on etiquette, laws and required behaviour.

Gradually, after two or three stilted and embarrassing attempts at striking up a conversation, a rapport of sorts had developed. Iola, younger than Vicki by six months, but in reality by about a lifetime, was a shy and introverted girl, who clung to her mother's skirts quite literally. Though one or two of the things that she said made Vicki sense that beneath the opaque exterior was an imaginative and playful soulmate just waiting to burst out.

On the morning of her second day with the Georgiadis family, Vicki began to explore the world of the Greeks into which she had been so unwillingly thrust. Iola offered, in the spirit of their new-found friendship, to take Vicki around the local market streets. Actually, Vicki suspected, her parents had told Iola to do this. Whatever, at least it meant that she would see a little of Iola's world, and that could only be a good thing.

In reality, it wasn't. Within minutes Vicki was bored to tears with a seemingly endless round of 'this is the butcher, and this is the baker'. She nodded and smiled whenever Iola looked in her direction, but she longed for something exciting to happen. Vicki was also introduced to Dorothea and Damian, the immediate neighbours of the family. They were, as with most of the people she met, seemingly good-natured and friendly. Damien, she learned, made pottery whilst his wife was a bookbinder.

They chatted about trivialities for several moments, and both of the neighbours were interested in Vicki telling them about Britannia. So Vicki lied through her teeth, using a mixture of outrageous stories and the few facts that she remembered from her studies about the Romans in Britain or that she had learned from

Barbara's frequent verbal essays on the culture that surrounded them.

Poor Barbara.

Vicki kept coming back to that...

The girls left the house of their neighbours just as a rank of Roman soldiers marched by on the other side of the cobbled street. Iola froze, her hand gripping Vicki's arm tightly and making Vicki yell out in surprise and pain. One or two of the soldiers gave the girls an ominous glance, but they were obviously on their way to do something important that would most likely involve arresting or killing someone, so they moved off whilst Vicki and Iola watched them go.

'Whenever you see the Romans coming,' Iola hissed, despite the fact that the men were, by now, well out of earshot, 'get away if you can. Run for all you are worth. There are alleys and passages that can be used. Learn them, well. If you have no obvious means of escape, then stand still, do not move, never avoid looking directly at them because that will make them suspicious. Above all, act as you would normally.' There was a terror in Iola's voice as she spoke what seemed to be a well-learned litany of rules. What she was telling Vicki wasn't a suggestion or an advisement, it was The Law.

Vicki was nonplussed. She knew that the Roman soldiers were a nasty bunch of black-hearted rapscallions. Quasi-Nazis with a sadistic streak a mile wide (at least according to Ian Chesterton on day one of their stay in Byzantium), they had bullied their way across most of Europe and large chunks of the Middle East. But surely their idea of suspected terrorists and insurgents didn't include a couple of teenage girls? 'Why, what will they do to us?' Vicki asked, expecting anything but the answer that she got.

'If the luck of the Gods is with us, and I mean by that, *real luck*,' Iola said softly looking at her shoes and visibly shaking at the thought, 'four or five of them will take us into a side-yard and take their pleasure upon us. If we are not so fortunate, they shall probably kill us for mere sport.'

Vicki began to laugh. Then she saw that Iola was completely serious and was appalled. 'They do that?' she almost screamed.

'I have seen such things happen with my own eyes,' the girl confirmed. 'Many, many times. To friends of mine. To Greeks. To Jews. To the Bedouin. Life is cheap in Byzantium. Life is cheap everywhere that the Romans are.'

Vicki didn't know what to say. After a moment, the jaw-dropping horror of what she had just been told fully sank in. 'Come on,' she said. 'Let's go home.' Suddenly, the boring streets of Byzantium didn't seem nearly so dull after all.

During the evening, several of Georgiadis's friends and acquaintances called at the house. Word had clearly circulated within the Greek community that the Georgiadis home now had a new and interesting attraction to be viewed. So they came to stare at the girl of Iola's age with the pale skin and the strange accent – chattering women, who talked to Evangeline in hushed bursts of whispering, and men who would give Vicki a cursory glance and then talk to Georgiadis about the cost of living in these most difficult of times.

Vicki was thankful that they didn't want to prod her as well, but she smiled and made all of the right noises as a succession of Greeks to whom she was introduced asked her some banal questions about where she was from, commented upon how good her language skills were, complimented her on her beauty and her good manners, and then left. Several of the visitors also had news for Georgiadis. Though they could not be certain, enquiries about the three Britons with whom the girl had been travelling had given rise to a series of shaken heads. Certainly the old man of whom Vicki had spoken as her grandfather had been seen to collapse in the crowd. There were also rumours that a man who fitted the description of Vicki's Uncle Ian had attempted to fight with a Roman soldier and had been skewered for his pains. Of the aunt, Barbara, there was no news at all.

Vicki was crestfallen.

As the sun set, and darkness fell across the house, Evangeline lit a fire and a new arrival came. Papavasilliou was an aged friend of Georgiadis whom Iola had mentioned earlier in the day. He was a wise and ancient man who acted as a genial giver of advice to many members of the Greek community.

Following a gentle tap on the door, Georgiadis admitted him and he seated himself beside the fire with a groan of discomfort. 'These old bones ache so in the chill of night,' he said.

'It is good that you honour us with a visit to this humble abode, good father,' said Evangeline. 'You will take bread with us?' Papavasilliou indicated that he would as Iola happily skipped across the room and sat herself beside the old man.

'And how is my angel of the stars?' he asked. Iola giggled and rested her head on the old man's shoulders.

Vicki, feeling rather left out of all of this, coughed from her uncomfortable corner seat, hoping to attract a smidgen of the attention that everyone else was getting except her.

Old eyes turned towards her. 'And this, presumably, is your gift from the Gods?'

Vicki didn't quite see herself as that, but she was flattered by the suggestion.

'Her name is Vicki,' said Evangeline with an amused scowl. 'A strange child.'

'Another from the stars,' said the old man with a bewitching smile. 'Good daughter, I am usually to be found at the base of the foothills, where the lambs gamble and frolic in the water meadows,' he continued. Vicki wondered why he was telling her this. 'There may come a time when you are in need of a friendship. Of an ear for whatever woes that you may have. Remember me at these times and whence I can be found.'

There was something about the way in which he said it that made Vicki certain that one day (perhaps quite soon) she would, indeed, be sitting in the water meadows with this gentle soul pouring out all of her as-yet-unknown troubles to him. 'I will remember,' she whispered. Papavasilliou stood and hobbled towards the door.

'Be tolerant of her,' Vicki heard him tell Georgiadis. 'Her ways are not our ways, but they are no less valid for all that. There may be many misunderstandings and clashes ahead in the relationship between this girl and the family, but you must strive to overcome all of them. She is a child of the universe. Treasure her.'

He turned to Evangeline. 'Good daughter,' he said, with a nod of the head. 'May the Gods look kindly upon all of those who dwell within this good house.'

Iola let out a long sigh after the old man had left. 'I wish he could stay here, with us, always,' she said.

'I should like that also, but Papavasilliou has his own roads to travel,' replied Georgiadis. The little exchange confirmed what Vicki had already suspected. Georgiadis was a kindly, sensible man whom it was easy to trust.

A few moments after the old man had departed, there was yet another knock on the door, this one louder and more insistent. Vicki sighed, expecting someone else ready to view her. 'Why don't you just poke me with a stick and see if I squeal?' she muttered.

'Tax collector. A rare and dubious honour,' said Georgiadis as he opened the door to a tall and serious-looking man who had to stoop to get through the door frame.

'Good evening, shopkeeper,' said the new arrival. 'Thank you for allowing me into your home.'

Georgiadis gave his visitor a look of utter contempt which indicated to Vicki that, if he had the slightest excuse to do so, he would have thrown the tall man bodily into the streets and kicked him while he was down. Then Georgiadis indicated towards Vicki. 'There she is, tax collector. Another mouth to feed. I should have known that within hours of her arrival, you would be knocking upon my door for your share of her.' He crossed the room to the wall opposite Vicki and withdrew from a hole in the rock a small wooden box that rattled as he opened it. Removing a handful of coins, Georgiadis threw them onto the stone floor at the tax collector's feet. 'Your tribute, Luke Panathaikos. Count it all. Employed by the Romans and mistrusted by everyone else, not least your own people.'

This was something that Vicki had not heard before in the voice of Georgiadis - a weary yet bitter hatred of the man standing before him. The tax collector bent to the floor and retrieved the coins from the dusty cobbles, pocketing them after first counting them, slowly, from one hand to another.

'Render unto Caesar that which is Caesar's,' he said when he had finished. 'That is The Law, shopkeeper. You know this. And you know what fate shall befall you, or anyone, who fails to abide wholly by it. You have given me too much.' He held out his hand with a single copper coin in it.

'A penny for your thoughts, tax collector. You may keep the change,' said Georgiadis dryly.

'Get out,' continued Evangeline. 'And take your Roman law with you, parasite.'

The tax collector did so, without another word, and Georgiadis slammed the door after him, turning to his wife and shaking with anger. 'I might have known that such a horse-leech as that man would not be long in claiming his flesh of our flesh.'

'This would probably be a bad time for me to say something, right?' asked Vicki, about to make an equally unkind observation about the recently departed tax collector. Three heads turned in her direction. Iola seemed astonished that Vicki had spoken at such a moment. She shook her head and found something interesting on the floor to look at.

'You are correct,' said Georgiadis through gritted teeth. 'It assuredly would.'

Vicki nodded silently, rolled over and pretended to go to sleep in her corner while she felt the stares behind her back.

Chapter Sixteen
True Faith and Brotherhood

Take heed lest any man deceive you:
For many shall come in my name
Mark 13:5-6

As Ian Chesterton walked the corridors of the *Villa Praefectus* lost in his own thoughts and memories, a woman's voice cut through the mind-fog. Startled, like a rabbit caught in the headlights of his Hillman Imp on the North Circular Road, Ian snapped to attention and sought out the direction from which her voice had come.

'What would a rabbit be doing on the North Circular Road? Come to that, what would *I* be doing on the North Circular Road?' Ian asked out loud. It brought a curious expression to the face of Antonia Vinicius.

'I know not of that which you speak,' she replied, genuinely puzzled.

'The question was rhetorical,' Ian mumbled and turned to resume his lonely circumnavigation of the villa.

But he wasn't getting away that easily.

'You are a very complicated man, Briton,' said Antonia. 'So different from the other men of Byzantium.'

'I should say that I am a man of Byzantium now,' Ian noted with a tinge of regret in his voice. 'There are worse places to be, I suppose.'

'Do you think so?' the noble woman asked with a haughty laugh as she moved closer to him. 'I would suggest that of all of the benighted, godforsaken and depressing holes in the backwaters of the great empire, this is by far the worst. And I have seen Antioch.'

Ian suspected that this should mean something to him and he nodded accordingly. 'At least the weather's better than London,' he mitigated. He felt Antonia place her hand on his bicep and pulled away from her, sharply. 'If you want to talk geography, darlin', then fine,' he said as his face flushed with embarrassment. 'Not my subject, but I'll give it my best shot. But if you're looking for somebody to warm your bed for you then you can think again.'

Antonia was either amused or outraged, Ian genuinely couldn't tell which. 'Do you not find me pleasing to look at?' she asked.

Actually, and considering that he had been told she was in her early forties, he did. But that was not the point. 'That is not the point,' he confirmed. 'It would be impolite of me to take advantage of the *praefectus*'s hospitality...'

'And yet you seem to have no qualms about bedding his wife's handmaiden?' shouted Antonia accusingly.

'Felicia?' Ian asked, bemused. 'Who on earth told you that?'

'It is the talk of the city,' Antonia announced grandly. 'Everyone knows it.'

'Then everyone is wrong,' Ian said as though he were explaining some complex physics theory to a class of fourteen-year-olds. 'I'm sorry, but I'm not really in the mood right now. I've got a headache...'

He turned, walked a few paces and then broke into a sprint down the corridor. He could hear for a dozen paces the clip-clop of Antonia's sandals on the floor tiles behind him until she gave up the chase. At the corner he glanced back and saw the woman, her shoulders hunched in defeat, walking angrily away in the opposite direction. 'That was hard work,' he decided, as he walked straight into Felicia coming out of one of the servants' rooms.

'Ah, I want a word with you,' said Ian, grabbing the girl by her arm and dragging her into a quiet and poorly lit corner of the corridor.

'Sir,' said the wide-eyed slave girl with a saucy and eager grin. 'Not here. It would not be proper.'

'Not anywhere,' Ian announced. 'I'm just about sick to death of getting offers of casual hanky-panky. Do me a favour and put the word out, will you? I am not interested.'

Felicia struggled free of Ian's clamp-like grip and backed off from him into the light. 'Uncircumcised *eunoukhos*,' she shouted. '*Stultissime maialis*. Are you a man, or...?'

'A mouse?' Ian asked, smiling. 'Give me a bit of cheese and I'll give you a definitive answer on that one.' He was glad that at least one of them was finding humour in this bizarre situation. 'There is absolutely no need to get all discombobulated about it,' he said. 'Now, do you want me to ask the *praefectus* for protection from you and his wife? And his ex-wife, come to that?'

'The *praefectus*?' Felicia asked anxiously. 'You wouldn't!'

'Mice can do amazing things when they are cornered, my girl,' Ian remarked. 'Survival of the sneakiest. It's a well-known fact. Now, get off with you, and make sure you tell your mistress and your ex-mistress and anyone else that's interested about what I've said.'

When he was finally alone, Ian reflected on what his friends back home would be making of all this. 'They'd probably be calling me a stupid twerp,' he noted as he went off in search of something to eat.

Vicki awoke late in the morning, hungry and alone in the Georgiadis house. The fire was cold and the Greek family were nowhere to be seen.

On the otherwise-bare table there was half of a loaf of stale bread which Vicki broke and began to gnaw at, easing her hunger slightly. When she had finished she looked around to see if she could find anything else. In the base of the still-warm clay oven she found another small loaf, just cooked.

'Man cannot live by bread alone,' she muttered. But, she reasoned, the famous quotation hadn't mentioned teenage girls specifically. Besides, if there wasn't anything else...

As she picked up the bread, she felt a presence behind her and turned to find Evangeline entering, carrying two water jugs.

'I thought you'd all run off and left me,' said Vicki. 'Have you been to the well?'

Evangeline ignored the question. 'What do you think you are doing?' she asked, angry at seeing the bread Vicki was holding. She put the pots down beside the door and advanced into the room.

'I was hungry,' Vicki answered, as if that explained everything.

'I left you food on the table.'

'Wasn't enough,' Vicki noted.

Evangeline strode across the room and inflicted a neck-snapping back-handed slap across Vicki's face. See, I knew she had the strength to sink ships with those muscles, Vicki thought in the micro-second before the impact knocked her to her knees. This hurt, too, the stone floor grazing the skin. But she didn't have time to dwell on the pain as Evangeline hauled her roughly to her feet, shook her by the shoulders and slapped her across the other cheek.

Too shocked by the first blow to speak, the second produced a suitably indignant response from the girl. 'Cut it *out*,' said Vicki, her voice raising to a crescendo on the final word. 'What've I done to deserve that?'

'Theft,' shouted Evangeline, shaking with anger. 'And insolence when caught in the act. I know not what the customs of your land dictate when a child steals, but in this house, the rules are clear and distinct. The child is disciplined that she shall steal no more. It is the way that Iola was taught and, if you are to live amongst us, then it is the way that you shall be also. Go, and fetch me a stick with which to beat you.'

Vicki blinked back at Evangeline in mute astonishment. Then she began to giggle at the stupidity of the command, as though the entire episode was some big practical joke. 'You are not serious?' she asked. Her skeptical reply was answered with yet another flesh-rattling blow to the cheek. 'Ow,' cried Vicki, shrinking away. 'You have got absolutely no right to impose your outdated ideas of child psychology on me. I'm not your daughter.'

Red-faced with anger, Evangeline grabbed Vicki by the scruff of the neck and shook her with a terrifying strength. 'You are a stubborn and wilful girl and your lack of respect for your elders is a disgrace,' she snarled. 'Your family have clearly let you run wild. I intend to cure you of that independent streak.'

This was getting out of hand. Vicki tried a more common-sense approach. 'I though the Greeks were supposed to be a civilised race,' she argued. 'Where I come from no one would dream of beating a child. It just isn't done,' she stammered.

'Then that explains much about your barbarous and backward nation, and why it is regarded as the most vile and heinous in the whole of the empire,' Evangeline said, releasing Vicki from her grip. 'Wait here whilst I find a suitable rod. And not another word or you shall rue the day that your mother bore you.'

'Well, this is just great,' Vicki shouted as Evangeline left her alone. 'Orphaned again, starved, an object of curiosity and subjected to brutality. I *am* a character from Dickens.'

Woefully, she sat at the table and rested her chin on her fists, feeling very sorry for herself as she waited pensively for Evangeline's return.

The Doctor's two days with the Christians had passed in a blur of constantly changing locations as the small group of thirty or so shuttled about from cave to cave in the foothills just beyond Byzantium's city limits. They needed to move with such regularity to avoid the persecutions of the Romans *and* the Zealots, he was told.

'We are vulnerable to attack from all sides,' Daniel advised him as they made their latest hasty evacuation of a cave at Byzantium's outskirts and travelled up a narrow passage to another, more hidden cave, further into the rock. 'The Word terrifies those too blind to see and too deaf to hear.' He handed the Doctor his torch as he led the small group into a wider area of the tunnel.

They were a curious bunch and, despite his usual reservations about enthusiasts of all varieties, the Doctor had grown to quite like them. They were mostly gentle and serene, afraid of the forces arrayed against them but had a calmness about living under the threat of death that the Doctor found impressive, if a little disquieting. But, despite enjoying the warm hospitality of Daniel and his family, of James and his wife, Judith, and of their aged friend Hebron, among the others in the group, he was keen to see the back of them and leave them to their faith and their destiny.

No information had been forthcoming about his companions as the Christians had few friends within the city itself once they, themselves, had fled to the hills surrounding it. They said that they would try to find out what they could when they had re-established some lines of communication, but things were moving far too slowly for the Doctor's liking. He had no idea if young Vicki, or Chesterton, or Miss Wright was even still alive, but he did know one thing for certain - if they *were* and they had half a chance, they would make for the TARDIS and try to stay as close to it as possible until he was able to join them. That thought maintained him through the many frustrating hours as he waited for his strength to return.

He also used the time while he was with the Christians to get to know as much as he could about them. And he was very surprised by what he discovered.

James, for instance, was a second-generation Greek Christian, whose extensive family background in Judaea provided a direct link for many of the newly converted Christians with the actual teachings of Christ himself. James's uncle, he said, had witnessed the sermon on the mount, whilst other family friends had included Mary of Jerusalem, the mother of the apostle Mark, in whose house Jesus and his first disciples had met and worshipped.

The Doctor had many interesting conversations with the man, who told him that he had met several of those major figures in the early church left alive after the Jewish and Roman purges of the previous twenty-five years. James had travelled the empire widely, across the Mediterranean area, to Antioch, Cyprus and

Caesarea and into North Africa spreading the gospels. He recently settled in Byzantium with a series of secret parchments which, he said, contained the memoirs of his old friend Mark and Mark's cousin, the priest Barnabas, and included numerous stories given to them by their travelling companion, Paul of Tarsus.

The writings, James said, had been compiled whilst they were all under arrest in Rome and had also contained portions gained from interviews with the first apostle, Peter the fisherman, with whom Mark was currently hiding in or around Babylon.

Although Christianity itself was conceptually alien to the Doctor, he had always found in his studies of the basic principles of the religion, a lot of ideological trappings that he considered to be worthy of considerable investigation, particularly its similarities to Greek philosophy. In his lengthy conversations with James and his friend Hebron by the light of a glowing, crackling fire, the Doctor enjoyed the healthy debates that cut through the rhetoric of the faith's dry language and got to the actual personalities involved - something that the Doctor found much more interesting than moral and ethical questions.

Hebron, fascinatingly, was another former travelling companion of Paul and his group of followers who included the physician Luke and also Barnabas and Timothy. Luke had, similarly, been compiling a testament to the miracles that they believed had been performed by Jesus, the carpenter of Nazareth. Both he and Mark had, seemingly, been influenced by an earlier set of spiritual histories written by one of Jesus's original disciples, a Galilean tax official known as Matthew. But there were subtle differences in the three sets of stories told that interested the Doctor somewhat more than the actual stories themselves.

Lessons could be learned here in semantics, perspective and contextualisation. 'It's known as Chinese Whispers,' the Doctor told James, when his version of one of the stories conflicted with the sample of another text read by Hebron. 'A man tells something to two people, who tell it to others. Somewhere along the line what the man originally said is distorted in some subtle yet important ways. If I tell you that I have three oxen and a box that travels through space, by the time you have imparted this information to, say, young Daniel, and he has told it to his brother, and the brother had told a friend, and the friend had told his friend, and his friend has told a Roman soldier he meets in the market-place...'

James nodded, understanding perfectly well the example that the Doctor was making. 'Then you would have ten oxen and a box that travels through time?' he asked.

'Uncannily accurate,' the Doctor replied with a little smile. 'But do you see the danger of placing all of your faith in mere words on a page?'

'But we are not,' Hebron told him. The old man's voice was rough and coarse from an illness which had recently prevented him from continuing his travels. 'The Word is the Living Word. It is divine and, therefore, infallible.'

'Perhaps,' the Doctor said, enjoying his jousting with these two honest and likeable men. Towards Daniel, on the other hand, he was cooler. Daniel was an idealistic young Christian who had fled persecutions in Damascus with his wife Rachel, their infant son and his equally headstrong brother, Aaron. They were all pleasant enough, but they had the fire of fanaticism within them that time had not yet dulled with a liberal dose of common-sense. The main conversation that the Doctor had shared with Daniel had been about the young man's belief that the Jewish establishment in Jerusalem was engaged in a concerted and active conspiracy to discredit Christianity.

'There was a man named Lazarus,' he told the Doctor, 'risen by the Christ from the dead.'

'I have heard the story,' the Doctor said. 'I always found it rather unlikely, personally. A man being regenerated... Whatever next?'

'After Jesus himself rose and ascended to heaven,' Daniel said, unperturbed, 'the Pharisee tried to murder Lazarus and other members of his family to cover up the resurrection that had transpired in that place. And there was a systematic policy of extermination of anyone who had ever been in direct contact with the Christ himself.'

'I have no doubt that they, the Jews that is, consider Christianity to be a danger to them,' said the Doctor, trying not to sound dubious. 'The problem of one system of belief replacing another is a regular occurrence through history. And fear accompanies such a change.'

Finally, on the third day, the Doctor felt well enough to move outside of the caves for the first time since he had returned to consciousness after the market square massacre. The fresh air of a fine Thracian morning engulfed him and for a moment his senses were almost overcome. Dizzily, and with emotion in his voice, the Doctor turned back to his new friends in the cave and grandly announced, 'I have been renewed.'

James nodded wisely. 'It is the will of the Lord,' he said.

The Doctor's exuberant mood was slightly pricked by this. 'Hmm, yes, perhaps,' he blustered. 'Now, the question that I have asked you so many times during these last days - will you allow me to return to my carriage?'

James thought for a moment. He turned to Hebron, whose old eyes were filled with tears. 'It would be selfish to keep the Doctor from his quest to find his friends any longer than is absolutely necessary,' Hebron noted.

'I agree,' said James, turning back to the Doctor. 'Daniel and Aaron will guide you to the place from whence you came,' he continued, rising and joining the Doctor at the cave mouth. 'May you go with peace in your heart and the will of the Lord in your soul.'

'Thank you,' said the Doctor. 'I shall not be sorry to say goodbye to Byzantium, but I shall regret a farewell to you and your people.'

Daniel and his brother Aaron guided the Doctor through the twisting rocky paths of the hills behind Byzantium, and then through the long stretch of wasteland towards the place where the TARDIS had crash-landed. The journey took them most of the day, with the Doctor frequently having to stop to catch his breath. If truth be told, he was not feeling at all well, the concussion in his head having yet to clear fully, despite what he had told James earlier.

At last, the small outcrop of rocks where the TARDIS had come to rest a week earlier came into sight. The Doctor's mood visibly brightened and he pointed towards the incline behind which his salvation lay. 'Over there,' he told Daniel. 'That is where my carriage rests.'

The Christian nodded and then turned to his brother. 'Run on ahead and make sure that an ambush has not been prepared for the unwary,' he said.

Aaron raced off into the distance.

'Can I just say,' the Doctor said, shaking the hand of Daniel, 'that I hope everything works out for you and your people. And I don't think I would be breaking any great laws of time if I were to tell you that your religion will continue to flourish and grow over the coming years. Eventually, every man, woman and child on Earth will know of Jesus of Nazareth and what he did and said.'

Of course, whether they believe it or not is a different matter, the Doctor thought as Daniel digested this. A shout from the distance caused both the Doctor and Daniel to look up suddenly. Aaron was running back towards them, his arms pin-wheeling as he dashed across the dry lake bed, a cloud of dust trailing behind him.

Panting and out of breath, he took a moment to recover, doubled-up, hands on knees.

'Is everything all right?' asked Daniel, fearing that a trap had been sprung, but he could see no other sign of the approach of hostile forces.

'What does this carriage of yours resemble unto?' Aaron asked the Doctor.

'Blue,' the Doctor replied. 'Slightly taller and broader than the height of a man.'

Aaron shook his head. 'There is nothing of such a description in that place. Lots of tracks and footprints. If your carriage was there, it is now gone.'

A cold chill ripped through the Doctor. Suddenly, he felt very old and very tired.

And very alone.

Stranded, in Byzantium.

Chapter Seventeen
The Culture Bunker, Part Five – How Soon Is Now?

And he began to speak unto them by parables.
Mark 12:1

'Well, this is a fine kettle o' fish, isn't it?' Ian asked Fabulous as the old man poked his head out of the library door and then returned with the news that the coast outside was clear.

Ian emerged from his hiding place in the space between two rows of shelves and looked nervously around. 'Are you sure?' he asked, ready to spring back into concealment at the slightest hint that any of his numerous female pursuers were in evidence.

'As certain as it is possible to be,' noted Fabulous with a bemused smile. 'The ladies of the household seldom venture into this unworthy vessel of knowledge.'

'I could make a comment about that,' Ian replied, 'but I'm in enough trouble with every woman I seem to come into contact with. I don't want any more of them after me.' Chesterton sat down and put his head in his hands. 'This is ridiculous,' he said, in an anguished comedy-voice. 'I feel like a character in a Whitehall farce, rushing around trying to *avoid* nookie.' He looked up to find his friend laughing. 'And you're not helping any, I'm sad to say.'

Fabulous was puzzled as well as amused. 'Why do you not simply surrender to the arms of your admirers and let them have their way with you? There are worse situations to be in, surely?'

'Because,' Ian said, 'that would be the worst thing I could possibly do. I'm not here to make enemies and get my end away as often as possible.' He shook his head at the continued puzzlement on Fabulous's face. 'Never mind, let's just say that I don't want to do anything that would give anybody who wishes me harm any possible ammunition.'

Fabulous saw the wisdom of Ian's reticence. 'There are those who would see you compromised, my friend,' he confirmed. 'They hide themselves in the shadows and say little, but they are getting bolder in their submersibility. Soon, they will act. You must be ready for them.'

'Great,' Ian said fatalistically. 'I mean, that's just great, isn't it? Every time my life seems on the verge of being sorted out, these animals come crawling out of the woodwork and start messing things up with their plans and their plots and their sneakiness. Why won't they just leave me alone?'

'Because they fear you, young Ian Chesterton. They fear the intelligence and the honesty that you have brought with you as your baggage to Byzantium.'

'That's logical,' Ian noted sadly. The intrigue of the *praefectus*'s household did both fascinate and repulse Chesterton, it was true. It hadn't taken Ian long to develop for himself a reputation around the villa as a great entertainer and orator who had a wealth of folk tales previously unheard. He was spending as much time in the company of Fabulous, Drusus and Gemellus as he could, while attempting to fight off the advances of Jocelyn, Antonia and (to a lesser extent, since their talk the day before) Felicia.

And that was where the real hard work started.

As he continued to bemoan his lack of fortune to Fabulous, the door to the library opened and Ian threw himself dramatically to the floor, instinctively crawling under the table fearing, after Fabulous's revelations, that the new entrant was either an armed assassin or a spurned potential lover. He didn't particularly want to face either right now.

When there was no reaction after a few seconds, he popped his head out from beneath the table to find Gemellus looking at him quizzically.

'Sorry,' said Ian. 'I'm just having a *very* bad day.'

'Then now would, perhaps, be an inopportune moment to carry out the task that I am commanded to do by my *praefectus*?' asked Gemellus.

'That depends,' replied Ian.

'Thalius Maximus wishes an audience with his guest.'

Ian nodded and emerged from the dusty floor.

The day before, on their first meeting, Ian had told the *praefectus* a few stories from his travels, reducing the tale of the Daleks and the Thals to a parable about fear of the unknown. A couple of pieces of cod Shakespeare from his repertoire, singing an *a cappella* Irish folk song and one or two knock-knock jokes had completed the act and, to Ian's immense relief, Thalius had been extremely taken with the young scribe from Londinium.

These were people, Ian mused, who had never heard *Carmina Burana*, or Fauré's *Requiem*, or *Bolero*... Or 'Brand New Cadillac' for that matter. Who had never been exposed to Shelley, Byron or Tennyson. Who had never seen *The Morecambe and Wise Show*.

He had a whole lifetime of important things to teach the *praefectus* of Byzantium and his minions.

'He wants to give you something,' Gemellus added. 'I do not know what it is, he would not tell me.'

'I hope it's different to what his wife wants to give me,' Ian added, cynically.

The *praefectus* was reading from a lengthy scroll when Ian and Gemellus entered his atrium. For several seconds he was, seemingly, too engrossed in its contents to look up and acknowledge their presence. Then he paused, rolled up the scroll and handed it to the young legionnaire standing beside him. 'Tell the general...' There was a long pause before he concluded, 'there *is* no message. Just thank the general for his most perceptive comments.'

The soldier clicked his heels together and said 'Hail!' which reminded Ian of exactly how much Nazi Germany owed to the

Roman *Reich*. Thalius, meanwhile, with his other business concluded, wore a beaming smile and was ushering Gemellus and Ian in to join him.

'My good and dear friends,' he said convivially. 'Gemellus, I am pleased to see that you have brought our cousin from Britannia to us once again. May the Gods look kindly upon you, Ian Chesterton.'

Ian nodded as he and Gemellus sat besides the *praefectus*. Thalius clapped his hands together and Drusus swept majestically into the room as if attached to the *praefectus*'s throne by a piece of elastic. 'Bring wine, Drusus,' Thalius announced grandly. 'Our guest must think us impolite savages.'

'Nothing could be further from the truth,' Ian quickly countered. 'The hospitality I have received from everyone within this household has been... pretty unique.'

Thalius seemed pleased to hear this. 'One always worries that cultural differences may lead to mistakes being made,' he said. 'My motives for seeing you, however, are slightly ulterior. I have something which I should like you to have.'

The *praefectus* reached down beside his opulent silver-trimmed throne and produced one of the short stabbing swords, the *gladii*, carried by Roman legionnaires and centurions. He held it up to the light and looked along its razor-sharp cutting blade like a craftsman inspecting his finest tool. 'The *gladius*,' he said proudly. 'This is the weapon of an artist. I am no soldier, though I suspect you are, or have been at one time in your life.'

'I was trained as a fighter, it's true,' Ian agreed, wondering whether six months spent whitewashing doorsteps at RAF Lynham truly counted as such. 'I studied some oriental disciplines; karate, ju jitsu and unagi.'

'Then you will know that military might depends upon possessing the weapons of power. I am a historian and I know that the Assyrian king, Shalmaneser II, boasted that he could raise an army of 120,000 men and charioteers. These men wore coats of iron scales and chain-mail and carried nine-foot-long spears that could stop an enemy dead at fifty paces. But their weakness was in the wicker shields that they used with which to defend themselves.'

'Most shields are pathetic and useless against the might of a sword,' Gemellus added. 'Particularly small and weak ones. They are of no use to man nor beast.'

'Roman soldiers have no such weaknesses and the *gladius*,' Thalius banged the sword on the arm of his chair, 'the *gladius* is our way of ruling the world.'

Thalius handed the weapon to Ian. 'I should like you to have this,' he said, turning the sword over in his hands and revealing the initials 'IC' carved into the hilt. 'I have had the weapon inscribed for you, lest anyone hereabouts should fail to realise to whom it belongs.'

'The *praefectus* is a generous man,' Ian said simply, taking the sword and weighing it in his hand. 'It is a fine weapon and I am honoured to accept it.'

'Use it wisely, and with prudence,' the *praefectus* told Ian, 'but keep yourself alive with it. Life is the most precious thing that a free man can possess.'

The wine arrived and the talk turned to move trivial matters, Ian telling the governor of his adventures in the land of the Aztecs. However, just as he was beginning to relax in the atmosphere of power politics around the *praefectus* himself, a question was sprung on him that threatened to change everything.

'What know you, good Briton, of these Christians?'

Gemellus seems as surprised by the question as Ian. 'I *am* aware of them,' Ian noted. 'I am not a believer myself,' he added quickly, remembering where he was. 'I've always found their views to be rather narrow and inflexible. I am a rationalist and a humanist, personally. I don't feel that divinity is necessary in an ordered and scientific world.'

'Find you not that position to be a little... sad?' asked Gemellus.

Ian considered the question for a long time. 'There are many religions in the world, and, I dare say, many more yet to be born.

They can't *all* be right,' he said eventually. 'A man of reason must ask himself whether he believes that free will is an illusion, which is what having Gods who direct our every move would suggest? I cannot allow myself to believe in a world like that so I retain a healthy dose of scepticism about all religions.'

Thalius nodded, slowly. 'And the Christians?'

'As good a creed as any, I suppose,' Ian suggested. 'Far better than some. They believe in many laudable things, but some of my experience often have an intolerance for those who do not share their views...' Ian paused, suddenly aware that he was speaking with his own prejudices of the twentieth century. Of cosy village churches and bigoted people who learned the Bible parrot-fashion without actually understanding its meaning. Who used the words of a man of peace as the justification for horrible acts of warfare, judicial murder, anti-Semitism and the oppression of women without bothering to know the context in which these statements were written. Or, refused to acknowledge the inherent contradictions within a work as large as the Bible. People who, when they came knocking on your door and asked if you would like to let Jesus into your house, deserved a reply like, 'Yes, He can come in. But you'll have to wait outside.' 'Perhaps I am being too hard on *your* Christians,' he said quickly. 'Are they making a nuisance of themselves?'

'Not specifically,' answered Thalius. He turned to his adviser. 'You tell him,' he ordered. 'I find the complexities of the matter too much of a bore.'

'Two Christians who live within Byzantium, Obadiah and Malaci by name, are to be crucified upon this afternoon,' began Gemellus. 'They were arrested by the Pharisee and accused of gross heresy and sacrilege several days past. Ridiculously trumped-up charges, of course, but they have been handed over to the *praefectus* after judgment for execution.' Gemellus paused. 'We have something of a dilemma on our hands.'

Ian gave Gemellus a curious glance. 'You *support* this?' he asked, his voice raising in anger. Then he turned to the *praefectus*. 'You *both* support this *outrage*?'

'Not at all. If there were any way to save these men, then I should be suggesting it most strongly,' replied Gemellus. 'But, unfortunately...'

'Well, here's a thought,' Ian suggested. 'How about you just *don't do it*? You tell the Jews that their ideas are utterly nonsensical and that you won't kill two innocent men, simply because they don't believe what *they* believe.'

Thalius was taken aback by Ian's impassioned horror at the situation. 'I do not understand, my friend, why this offends you so,' he noted. 'You do not know these two unfortunates, do you?'

'*Any* needless death should offend *anyone* with an ounce of morality in them,' Ian replied, shocked at the callous Roman attitudes to life and death. 'These men have *done you no wrong*.'

'They are *Christians*,' said Gemellus defensively. 'By the very nature of their religion, they deny the true divinity of Caesar.'

'As do the Jews,' admitted Thalius, 'although they are a little less, shall we say, "strident" about it?'

'That still doesn't give you the right to kill someone simply for their beliefs.'

Again, Thalius Maximus was surprised by such an argument. 'But does not both the Jewish and Christian holy text support the taking of life?' he asked. '"An eye for an eye, a tooth for a tooth". I am told this is a very popular chant when Roman soldiers are those upon the receiving end of summary justice.'

'The Christians also have a doctrine that states that let he that is without sin cast the first stone,' Ian added. 'I am aware of the contradictions, even if they are not.'

A lengthy silence followed, Ian finding himself breathing heavily. He knew how red-faced with anger he was, and how harsh his voice must have sounded to his allies. One part of his conscience was cursing him for putting his future in danger over the lives of two men whom he had never met. And in all probability never would. But another part of Ian Chesterton was standing on a soapbox at Speaker's Corner in Hyde Park, being loudly applauded by a crowd of concerned citizens.

'You provide wise and unexpected counsel, young Briton,' said Thalius at last.'Your compassion and integrity do you great credit. Unfortunately...'

At that point Ian actively stopped listening to what Thalius was saying. There was a lot of stuff about how the Pharisees were a powerful force within Byzantium and that Thalius needed a fight with the Jewish community far less than he needed the antipathy of the small Christian sect. He went on to say that the lives of two men were but a small price to pay for the continued peace of the city and that if their deaths saved the lives of dozens of others in rioting and mayhem then, surely, that was a price worth paying.

All the while, Ian simply shook his head.'The end justifies the means,' he muttered.'Horrible, just horrible.'

'I am forced to wash my hands of the entire affair,' Thalius concluded.'I will not interfere in a predominantly Jewish matter. The executions will go ahead.'

Both he and Gemellus were clearly embarrassed by the whole business. Ian thought about adding something, then decided that it wouldn't do any good. He stood and bowed to the *praefectus* and his counsellor.

'Gentlemen,' he said. 'It is, in my experience, easier to regret something that you haven't done, than something that you have.'

And with that enigmatic thought, he left them.

Barbara was also learning about the forthcoming executions. Hieronymous, contrary to her expectations, was showing neither a squeamishness when discussing such terrible events in front of his female guest, nor a bloodthirsty and vengeful delight at the prospect of nailing two heretics to a pole and watching them suffer and die. Instead, he talked about the death of the Christians in a chillingly matter-of-fact way. Barbara suddenly understood just how cheap life was in Byzantium. Just as the Doctor had predicted when they had arrived here. Death was a daily companion for these people. Physical and capital punishments were factors not to be dreaded but actually looked forward to as a release from the constant *threat* of pain and torture and death.

The rules were simple. Obey *all* the rules. If you don't, you get whipped. Or stoned. Or crucified. Or have your head chopped off. Or any one of a hundred other ways in which the Romans and the Jews and the Greeks amused themselves with methods of dispatch.

'Don't you find the idea of killing someone purely for their beliefs at all troublesome?' she asked Hieronymous in all seriousness.

'No,' the priest replied simply. 'For it is written, "whomsoever shall disobey the commandments of the Lord, surely he shall be put unto death".'

'Written on the wall of the local public lavatory, no doubt,' said Barbara through gritted teeth. 'I mean, can't you see how downright barbaric the concept is?'

Again, Hieronymous replied with a certainty that Barbara might have admired under different circumstances, but now just found sinister. 'An Arab woman, a Bedouin, stole into the temple one night to exact her vengeance upon one of the priests whom she had accused of terrible wrongdoing. She did it with no mercy, or pity. When found, and tried, she offered no mitigation for her dastardly and terrible crimes.'

'Was there any point?' asked Barbara. 'You'd already made up your mind she was guilty, surely?'

'Such things as guilt and innocence,' Hieronymous replied, 'can only be decided by the Lord God, in heaven. The Pharisees merely arbitrate on the execution of His law. Now, the issue of the death of the two Christians comes before us. I should attend, to be certain that the Romans have complied with our requests.'

Barbara shook her head. 'Oh, I'm sure you'll find them very efficient in such matters,' she noted. 'I don't think you should go.'

'Why?'

The real reason? Barbara managed not to say. Because I can't share a roof with someone who attends public executions without remorse. 'Such spectacles merely incite violence,' she noted, persuasively.

Before the debate could continue, a knock on Hieronymous's door brought the conversation to a halt. Phasaei and Titus, Hieronymous's deputies, entered into the priest's home, bowing respectfully to Barbara. She took an instant dislike to the pair of them, both of whom, Hieronymous had assured her, were usually involved in separate (though occasionally linked) power struggles against the old man.

'We were unaware that you were occupied in your private matters, Hieronymous,' noted Titus with a cunning glance at Barbara. 'Had we known you were so busy...'

Hieronymous failed to rise to the offered bait. 'You are to attend the execution this afternoon in my place,' he ordered.

'You will not be overseeing the spectacle yourself?' asked Titus, eager for any scrap of information that would explain such a surprising development.

'No,' said Hieronymous, simply. 'I have more important matters to attend to.'

Titus and Phasaei exchanged corner-of-the-eye glances. 'More important than the death of heretics?' asked Phasaei with none of the subtlety of Titus's questions. 'Be you sure of this course?' Without waiting for Hieronymous to answer, Phasaei continued. 'Is it not written in the law of Moses, "he that offendeth the sacrifice unto the Lord shall bring about his own destruction"?' With a satisfied smile, Phasaei folded his arms and awaited Hieronymous's reply.

'The Lord also commands that his work should take the precedence over all other things, does he not?' asked Barbara, her sudden interjection surprising all of the three men. 'For do not the commandments also order that thou shalt not take the name of the Lord thy God in vain. For the Lord thy God is a jealous God, visiting the iniquities of the father upon the children unto the third and fourth generations of those that wrong him in such times.'

Phasaei turned with a most startled expression on his face. 'I certainly did not mean to suggest...'

'Answer me this: the Lord who commanded that Moses say unto the Pharaoh, "Let my people go", demands also that the sin of ignorance be punished, yes?'

'The female guest of Hieronymous is wise and fair,' said Titus with a cruel sneer that Barbara ignored.

'To err is human, to forgive is divine,' Barbara continued. 'And I am sure that Hieronymous forgives you your trespasses, as you forgive those that trespass against you, is that not so?' It was New Testament, not Old, but Barbara didn't care. She knew that she had won a great victory against ignorance and hate.

Phasaei and Titus again exchanged glances. Glances that seemed to say, 'Oh, but she's good!'

'The twin pillars of the Pharisaic system are Torah and Tradition; the application of the laws of Moses to everyday life. I can see that such a noble approach is alive and well in the hands of you both, rabbis. The advisers of Hieronymous do this humble traveller great honour with your words,' Barbara continued, on the assumption that a little bit of flattery can usually get a girl a long way. 'Hieronymous thanks you both for the interest you have taken and asks that you represent him at the forthcoming...' She struggled to say the word 'executions'. 'At the forthcoming judgments.'

With a smile, she guided the two men towards the door. 'Gentlemen,' she concluded. 'It was the will of the Lord that we met this day. Go with my, and with the Lord's, blessing.'

She closed the door behind Titus and Phasaei's bemused faces and turned away, putting a hand to her mouth to stifle her involuntary laughter. Then she saw Hieronymous's furious expression. 'I'm sorry,' she said. 'That was wrong of me.'

'No it was not,' replied Hieronymous. 'But it was foolish. You have made two very dangerous enemies for yourself. And for me. It is not difficult to run circles around Phasaei and his childish attempts at entrapment by the scriptures, but Titus will not be dealt with so easily.'

Iola had been searching for Vicki most of the morning when she found her friend standing on the banks of the Bosphorus, staring into the distance. Vicki flinched as Iola tapped her on the shoulder and she spun around quickly.

'What?' Vicki snapped.

'Hello,' said Iola. 'I've been looking for you everywhere. What are you doing?'

'Thinking,' replied Vicki sullenly.

'You seem upset. Do you want to sit down and talk?'

'I'd sooner stand if it's all the same to you,' answered Vicki. 'What's so urgent?'

Iola was almost hopping up and down with excitement as she told Vicki about what she had learned. 'There's going to be a crucifixion,' she said, brightly. 'Soon, at Beylerbey Mount, beside the golden gates. That's where they always do it.'

Vicki was somewhat disturbed to find Iola had an intimate knowledge of such barbaric spectacles as public executions. 'Do they happen often?'

'Yes, yes,' said Iola, grabbing her friend's arm and literally dragging her along the road by the sea walls. The pungent smell of fish and sea salt filled the air. Vicki almost stumbled as she shook herself free from Iola's grasp.

'Hang on, slow down,' she said, but Iola was hurrying ahead. 'What's the hurry?'

'Come *on*,' said the girl, eagerly. 'We shall be late and miss it.'

Vicki had to run to keep up. 'Who's going to die?' she asked, hoping she didn't sound as morbidly curious as she felt.

But Iola seemed not to mind. 'Two Christians, apparently. Heretics.'

'Oh,' replied Vicki as they reached the base of the rising ground. 'Well, I'm sure they deserved it.'

The two girls ran to the dry-stone wall that surrounded the

hillock and Iola pulled Vicki with her. They crouched down and peered over the wall at the hive of activity taking place fifty feet higher up the rolling grassland.

'Are you sure this is wise?' Vicki asked, her voice cracking as she said it. 'The Romans might...'

Iola gave her a sharp look. 'The Romans want people to see,' she replied. 'That's why they do it out here.'

'Well, what about your mother?' Vicki hissed. 'I'm sure she doesn't approve.'

'She does not have to know,' Iola replied. 'Unless you were thinking of telling her?'

Vicki shrugged and turned her attention to what was taking place on the hillside. There were muffled shouts from the Roman legionnaires as two men dressed in filthy rags and chained together were pushed towards two vertical stakes which stood erect and stark against the gathering gloom of the afternoon sky behind.

'It appears as though it is going to rain,' Iola noted. 'I hope not, we shall get wet.'

Vicki gave her friend a horrified look. 'Do you realise what...?'

A scream from the knot of people on the hill silenced Vicki. She turned to see one of the men being thrown to the ground and having something large and shiny hammered into his hands.

'Oh my God,' she said, as the screaming continued.

'They're called *cruciamentum stauros*,' Iola noted, matter-of-factly. 'Torture stakes.'

The man was dragged to one of the torture stakes and attached to it by ropes around his arms whilst, simultaneously, a nail was driven into his feet.

Meanwhile, other soldiers were beginning the execution process on his companion.

'I think I'm going to be sick,' Vicki told her friend, who was watching the horror on the hill with undisguised glee.

Vicki put her hands over her ears to block out the screaming.

To block out *everything* that Byzantium had to offer.

Chapter Eighteen
Searching for the Young Soul Rebels

But when Jesus saw it, he was
much displeased, and said unto them,
Suffer the little children to come
unto me, and forbid them not
Mark 10:14

'Cease that infernal wailing, you ignorant, flea-ridden peasants,' tribune Edius Flavia told the assembled crowd as the Christian heretic Malachi was hoisted upright to join Obediah on the *stauros*. Flavia pointed his riding crop towards the group and told the sergeant of the guards that he should 'watch this rabble closely. I smell trouble at the heart of them.'

'Yes sir,' said the sergeant, clutching his *gladius* threateningly in his hand. In his eyes, Flavia could see an obvious desire to use his sword if the opportunity presented itself. Or even if it didn't.

On the other side of the hill, Flavia spotted the two senior Pharisees who had requested an isolated spot from which to observe the crucifixion. They, at least, seemed satisfied. But now they were ready to leave.

Flavia rode across to them on his sea-grey horse.'Going so soon, gentlemen?' he asked. 'We have yet hours of fine entertainment and revelry to endure before this thing that you requested is done.' So typical of the Jews, he thought angrily. They get us to do their dirty work for them but they have not the stomach to see it through.

'We are merely here to observe that the judgment of the court of the law of Moses, as ratified by his most gracious excellence, the *praefectus* Thalius Maximus, has been carried out,' said Titus with a rather watery smile.

Edius Flavia did not like this man at all. Too cunning by half.

The other one, Phasaei, was more thuggish and easy to manipulate into compromise. He said little that wasn't a quotation from their holy texts. A man who speaks in riddles and verses, Flavia decided, presents no threat to those who favour more direct action at the point of a *gladius* or a javelin.

'What crimes did these men commit, exactly?' he asked.

'They *defiled* the word of the Lord,' Phasaei told him.

'The Jewish equivalent,' Titus explained, 'of calling the emperor of Rome a bloated, pox-riddled, worthless son of a whore.' Again, he smiled. 'Not that any Jew would utter such damnable slander, of course.'

Flavia turned his horse away from the men without further comment and rode back towards the execution, leaving them to go on their way.

Back on the hill, the situation was in the process of turning ugly. The crowd was in a restless and feverish mood. 'Something bad is going to happen here this day,' Flavia told the captain who offered to help him down from his horse. 'No, I shall remain saddled in the event that we have need of urgent retreat.'

From out of the crowd, suddenly and surprisingly, a group of fifteen or so young men burst forward carrying a variety of homemade weapons. Aaron was leading them and he strode confidently towards Flavia, his group behind him, shouting angrily. Others in the crowd were joining them.

'This obscenity is wrong,' shouted Aaron. 'We demand that it be stopped in the name of our Lord, Jesus Christ.'

'Demand?' asked Flavia, nervously, as the staggered column of Roman legionnaires took an ominous pace towards the rebels.

'Request, if you wish to play with words. I shall not banter semantics with the likes of you, Roman. Get those men down now, or you shall be smitten by the vengeance of the Lord.'

For a moment Flavia was genuinely unsure of what to do next. There was no chance whatsoever that he would order the executions to stop, and there were enough Roman guards on the hill to put down this little insurrection eventually. But the numbers and their proximity to him, personally, worried him greatly.

Before he could say anything, however, from out of the crowd a young Jew sprang at Aaron, a knife in his hand. Flavia recognised the boy as Yewhe, one of Basellas's men. Suddenly there were Zealots everywhere, as Yewhe slid his knife easily and quickly between Aaron's ribs, screaming for the Christian to 'die like the pig that you are'.

From somewhere further down the hill, a young girl was screaming.

'Come, my hearts,' Yewhe continued, blood covering him from the fallen Christian. 'Let us have our sport upon these heretics.' The Zealots outnumbered the Christians two to one and began to pick off the terrified men as they scattered, broke ranks and fell back down the hill.

'Orders, sir?' asked the captain.

Flavia briefly considered sending in the soldiers behind the Zealots to massacre both sides. Then he made his decision.

'Our task is to see that this judgment is addressed and applied,' he said, watching the hand-to-hand fighting continue. 'No Roman blood need be spilled. If these dogs wish to wipe each other out, then so much the better. Let them have their rebellion, Captain, they hurt no one of any consequence.'

As the raging fight continued, behind the wall at the base of the hill, Iola finally removed her hand from Vicki's mouth.

'Be quiet,' she whispered.

'But they're killing each other,' Vicki replied at a more sensible volume. 'It's... it's unbelievable.'

A shadow passed across the pair and they looked up to find a Roman legionnaire towering above them with a thin and cruel smirk on his face. Two hands reached down and grabbed their arms, hoisting them up.

'Shouldn't you two be somewhere else?' he asked.

Iola began to stammer a reply, but Vicki shook herself free of the man.

'We'd be perfectly delighted to be somewhere else,' she said, angrily. 'So let us go and we will be.'

The soldier ran his hand down her cheek and cupped her chin between two enormous fingers. 'But you are a feisty one, my kitten,' he said.

Again Iola tried to say something but all that would emerge was a few isolated noises.

'What manner of talk is that?' the legionnaire asked both of them. 'Cat got your tongues?'

'Leave her alone, you big bully,' continued Vicki. 'Pick on some-one your own size.'

The legionnaire was rendered momentarily speechless himself before grabbing Vicki by the arm again and pulling her closer to him. 'Your tongue will have you hanged, girl,' he said. As his hand clasped her back, Vicki shouted with pain and tried to get away from him. Instantly the legionnaire dropped her like a piece of hot coal. 'I have not touched you. Yet,' he said.

'Nor shall you,' Vicki replied, looking him directly in the eyes. 'I'd sooner die first.'

Behind them, on the hill, the Zealots had routed the Christians, several of whom lay bleeding to death. The Romans, meanwhile, continued to hold a casual disinterest in the entire battle. The legionnaire cast a nervous glance towards the crucifixion. Vicki followed it and understood.

'Deserting your post for a quick rape?' she suggested. 'What will they give you for that? Public castration? Broken on a wheel? Hung, drawn and quartered?'

The soldier looked worried, but said nothing.

'One decent scream from me,' Vicki noted, 'and I'll bet half a dozen of them come running. That's if the Zealots don't get to you first. And I'd hate to think what they'd do to you if there aren't any of your Roman mates around to save your life.' She clutched her back, and winced with pain. 'See, the thing is, I got the beating of a lifetime this morning from my new mummy. One false move and I could be in the most terrible agony.'

'Why did she beat you?' the soldier asked, backing away.

'Why? Oh, obviously a criminal desperado who has nothing to lose. So, what do you say then, you and me behind the wall?'

The legionnaire took a final glance at Vicki. 'You and I shall have a date one day at the gallows pole, my kitten,' he said before breaking into a run, leaping over the dry-stone wall and sprinting up the hill.

'Men,' Vicki told an astonished Iola. 'Predictable in any age. Come on, we'd better get back to your mother before she decides I've corrupted you enough.'

He had faced the fifty-eight terrors of the universe with bravery and a philosophical shrug that suggested that beneath his exterior of befuddled compassion was one of nature's true fatalists.

The Doctor watched the sun setting over Byzantium and the sea beyond from yet another cave mouth overlooking the city. He could feel nothing but a numb indifference to everything.

The TARDIS was gone. Nothing else mattered.

Memories flooded back to the Doctor. In the sixty years since he had hurriedly abandoned his home and fled in terror into the universe, he had stared death in the face on numerous occasions. In France and Mexico. On Skaro and Mondas and Cassuragi. After a while, the adventures tended to merge into a giant conglomeration of escape-capture-escape-capture-escape. How many metallic corridors had he run down, dragging startled and bemused companions with him? How many times had he blundered into history's minefield of brutality and aggression and, by sheer luck, blundered his way out again?

'I am an old fool,' he had told Barbara and, for once, he had been absolutely right.

Strangely, the memory that was staying with him as he watched the orange-tinged sky fade to black was of a tavern on Rigel during the early years of the Draconian Purges. The first movement of Satie's *Trois Gymnopédies* was being played by a green-skinned, three-armed creature on a keyboard-type instrument that the Doctor had not seen the like of before or since. It made a change from the usual scratchbeat Vivaldi or Venusian opera of the place. The Doctor was recovering from bruised ribs inflicted upon him by the Mountain Mauler of Montana. Susan was asking him a question, and...

He looked up to find James standing beside him holding a torch and a concerned expression. 'Now, good sir,' he asked. 'What *are* you?'

The Doctor couldn't help but be amused by the irony of the question. '"A most poor man, made tame to fortune's blows,"' he said, remembering that he had witnessed *King Lear*'s debut performance, fifteen hundred years in the future. Richard Burbage was a good actor, the Doctor reflected, but rubbish at portraying old men crushed by the delicious uncertainties of life. 'Oh, but I am tired, my friend,' the Doctor said, wistfully, looking into the half-distance at the lights of the town. 'And horrified at the thought of spending the rest of my days stuck in your Byzantium.'

James seemed unsure of how to reply. 'There are worse places to be, surely?'

'I'm struggling to think of one just at this particular moment.'

'I am sorry that your carriage has disappeared,' James continued, sensing the cause of the Doctor's misery. 'Perhaps it will turn up.'

'Perhaps,' the Doctor noted. 'Though I doubt it.'

'You must have faith,' said James. Then he saw the thoroughly grumpy expression on the Doctor's face and decided to change the subject. 'Hebron is worse,' he said.

The Doctor stood up and followed James back into the cave, to a quiet corner where Hebron lay propped up on one elbow, his face twisted in pain. Seeing the Doctor approach, Hebron instantly switched on a beaming smile and lay back. 'You have come at last, my friend,' he said.

The old Christian was clearly ill, the Doctor had seen that

in Hebron's pale face, the sagging skin that was evidence of a dramatic weight loss and those sudden moments when he could no longer hide the excruciating pain that he was suffering. The Doctor seldom befriended anyone, but in Hebron, with his fascinating tales of his travels, the Doctor had sensed a kindred spirit. Someone to whom the cause of adventure was not lost or hidden, but which had been embraced.

The Doctor knelt beside Hebron and gave him a clay pot to drink from. It was painful to watch as the old man coughed and struggled to swallow the water in his throat.

'Do you know what ails him thus?' asked Judith, resting a hand on Hebron's fevered brow. Her palm came away slick and wet and she gave the Doctor and James a grave look.

'I have some very unpleasant suspicions,' the Doctor noted.

Hebron's eye opened and he seemed suddenly alert again. 'Then you will share your knowledge with me, perhaps?' he asked.

The Doctor shook his head. 'I am only guessing.'

'Then make it a good guess, my friend,' Herbon replied.

Placing his hand on Hebron's chest and using his fingers and the heel of his wrist as two pressure points, the Doctor rocked his hand back and forth around Hebron's breastbone. 'The pain,' he asked. 'When you swallow, particularly. Is it here and here?' He indicated two small lumps on Hebron's chest.

'Yes,' choked Hebron as the pressure of the Doctor threatened to squeeze the life out of him. The Doctor removed his hand just before James had the chance to grab his arm and remove it for him.

'Do you know what it is?' asked James.

The Doctor nodded, sadly. 'A blockage in the oesophagus, the part of the alimentary canal between the pharynx and the stomach. It could be something very basic like a hernia or a stricture of some kind, but...' He paused and looked at Hebron with a sadness in his eyes. 'I'm sorry, but I believe it to be a cancerous growth.'

'Can it be cured?' asked Judith.

'No,' said Hebron before the Doctor could speak. 'Not even the Lord himself can choke the thirst of a cancer.'

'I am very sorry,' the Doctor repeated. 'I wish there was something I could do apart from giving you a diagnosis.'

'You have given me the greatest gift of all,' Hebron said brightly, the pain lessening from his face. 'The knowledge of the future.'

The Doctor had never felt so helpless, in more ways than one. 'Your fortitude in the face of such news is commendable,' he managed to say, standing, and wiping the dust from his toga. 'You are a good and brave man, Hebron.'

'And you, my friend, are a braver and better one,' Hebron noted as he closed his eyes and fell into a light sleep.

'Let him rest now,' the Doctor said as Hebron's final words played around in his mind. 'I am not usually so selfish,' he told James. 'It seems I must mend my ways.'

James gave the Doctor a casually dismissive gesture. 'We must *all* do that before the judgment of God,' he said. 'It is what is contained within our hearts that truly counts.'

Just then, there was a commotion at the entrance to the cave. 'Someone is coming,' said one of the Christians keeping watch on the approaches. A moment later, Daniel burst into the cave. Even in the dim light it was obvious that he was exhausted and very upset.

'What is wrong?' Judith asked instinctively.

'I tried to stop them,' Daniel said, pitifully. 'But they would not listen to me.'

'Who?' asked James.

'Aaron. Jacob. John the weaver and his brother Samuel. They're all dead.'

The cave was plunged into total silence by this revelation. 'How?' asked James at last.

'They tried to stop the executions. As though the Romans would have had any intention of allowing them so to do.' He stopped and wiped the tears from his eyes. 'The Zealots attacked them and the Romans stood by and did nothing.'

Again, it took time for this information to register within the shocked and stunned group. Finally James picked up a handful of dust and poured it on to the fire, extinguishing it.

'We must make ready to flee this place,' he said as the flames died and the cave became a dark and cold place. 'Pack up your belongings and make Hebron as comfortable as possible. Byzantium is no longer safe for Christians. We leave within the hour.'

Vicki and Iola ran through the streets of Byzantium as the gathering gloom turned to the velvet black of night. The rain came as they ran, hard and slanted, splattering on their faces, set grim by the foul weather, and soaking their clothes to the skin.

'Hurry,' called Iola who was fitter and more sprightly than Vicki as they reached the corner of the market square and hurried towards the Greek quarter. 'The curfew is enacted. If they catch us, you will not be able to talk your way out like you did back at the hill.'

'That never happened,' Vicki said, catching up with her friend, grabbing her shoulders and shaking her so that rainwater cascaded from her bobbing head and fell to the puddles already forming on the cobbled streets. 'Do you hear me? We were never there. We've just been walking around and we lost track of the time.'

'My mother will flog the skin from our backs with no mercy if she discovers that we have lied to her,' Iola said in a terrified voice. 'I am not going to do that.'

'That's nothing to what she'll do if she finds out how close we were to being deflowered by that Roman. Now say it, Iola, tell me where we've been.'

Iola shook her head. 'I can not...'

'Yes you can, tell me where we've been.'

'Just walking around the city,' said Iola in a staccato burst. 'We lost track of the time and we are very, very, very sorry and we shall never do it again.'

Vicki nodded, approvingly. 'Good, let's go.'

They reached the door just as Evangeline emerged from the

Georgiadis house; she seemed more frightened than angry. 'Where have you been?' she screamed as the girls threw themselves into the house and Georgiadis himself, standing behind the door, shut it, and placed a wooden pole over the door frame to prevent any further entrances or exits.

Vicki gave Iola a sympathetic look. 'It's all my fault,' she said. 'We were just walking around the city, down by the sea walls, and in the Jewish quarter. We didn't realise how late it was. Well, Iola kept on telling me that we should get back home but I dillied and dallied. So, I'm totally to blame, and I'm very, very sorry.'

Georgiadis joined his wife and the pair looked at Vicki closely. 'Do you believe her?' he asked.

'Not a solitary word of it,' replied Evangeline. 'Iola,' she snapped. 'Is this story true?'

There was a long and terrible silence, during which Vicki's entire life seemed to flash before her eyes. Her pony, Saracen. Learning her lessons for an hour a day wearing a virtual reality headset. Her mother dying shortly before she and her father left Earth for a new life in 2493. Dido and Koquillion. The Doctor.

'Iola,' shouted Evangeline.

'Yes, Mother,' said Iola quickly. 'It is all true, every word of it. We were just walking about, by the sea walls. I told Vicki that we should get back home but she said we had plenty of time...' Iola's voice trailed away and she began to cry. 'Father, you believe me, do you not?'

Oh, *excellent*, thought Vicki, cynically. Set your parents against each other, why don't you?

Georgiadis clearly wanted nothing to do with this argument and ignored his daughter's plea, going to sit in the corner and stoke the fire instead.

It was then that Evangeline placed a maternal arm around her daughter's shoulder and hugged her tenderly. 'Be not upset, my lamb. I believe you. Set the places for supper.' Iola sniffed, nodded, kissed her mother and scuttled over to the table trying hard not to look at Vicki.

'As for you,' Evangeline told Vicki, clearly blaming their interloper for coming perilously close to leading her daughter astray with her alien ways, 'after supper, you and I shall speak again about your conduct within this house.'

'Oh good,' said Vicki with an innocent smile. 'I'll look forward to that.'

Chapter Nineteen
Some Call It God-Core

And all the city was gathered together at the door.
Mark 1: 33

So long as unwanted visitors like Titus and Phasaei were absent, then life was quiet and peaceful for Barbara in Hieronymous's home. She found time to recover her shattered nerves in the beautiful gardens, and read some of the scrolls in the priest's library. They were mainly obscure Jewish religious texts, but no less interesting for all that.

Barbara had decided that if she was going to be spending the rest of her life in Byzantium, then she wanted to be armed with as much knowledge as to the beliefs of those who lived there as she could.

A further encounter with Titus and Phasaei after the execution of the two Christians had helped to cement her initial impressions of the pair. One was clearly a clever and dangerous man. Titus said little, smiled a lot, and could viciously press home a point or change the subject in the bat of an eyelid without the unwary even being aware that they had just made a mistake.

Phasaei, on the other hand, Barbara continued to twist around her little finger. Even a basic knowledge of the contradictions contained within the Old Testament was all that was needed to destroy any of the arguments that he attempted.

And, what was even more amusing, he didn't even seem to be aware that he was being manipulated and thoroughly set up. Titus was, though.

After the meeting, once again Hieronymous warned Barbara to be careful when dealing with the men, particularly Titus, but this time he was more encouraging with the way in which she had used chapter and verse against Phasaei's bombast.

In fact, Barbara had the uncomfortable feeling that everything she was doing, from the simplest of household tasks, was impressing Hieronymous more and more.

Too much, in fact.

She had asked Hieronymous if he harboured any desires towards her and the priest had blustered and squirmed his way out of the question with clear embarrassment.

So, she went back to thinking about how it might be nice, for once, not to be spending New Year's Eve alone this year, with a small box of Quality Street and a bottle of Babycham and endless turkey sandwiches.

She had seen nothing of Gabrielle, Hieronymous's daughter since their brief and tense meeting almost a week ago. So she was quite surprised to hear a female voice drifting up the spiral stone stairwell to her bedroom early one morning.

Cautiously, and not wishing to announce her presence, Barbara crept to the top of the stairs and eavesdropped on the conversation taking place.

'I have been worried about you,' Hieronymous was saying. 'I was not certain of whereinsoever you were.'

'You made no significant effort to find out,' Gabrielle replied, harshly.

'Not so.'

'I was abiding but five minutes away, Father. At the dwelling of Esther, the widow of Joachim the carpenter. You could have discovered that with just a few simple questions. But you did not.'

Barbara knelt down, pressing her ear close to the stone so that it amplified the voices.

'It was your decision to leave, not mine to command you to leave.'

'Command?' Gabrielle shrieked. 'You would have me share a roof with *that woman*?'

Barbara winced. Clearly Gabrielle hadn't got used to the idea of Barbara remaining as a house guest. In a roundabout way, Barbara understood her feelings. It cannot have been easy having your home life disrupted in such a way and by an outsider. Barbara decided that she would go downstairs immediately, apologise for her intrusion but assure Gabrielle that she harboured no wish to break up her family, and that if Hieronymous was agreeable, she would leave as soon as a safe place within the city could be found for her.

'I intend to make *that woman* my wife,' Hieronymous said.

'What?' Gabrielle asked, a fraction of a second before this was echoed by Barbara herself.

'She is a good and wise woman with numerous qualities that I greatly admire. She will make a good wife.'

Gabrielle's reply was predictably myopic. 'She is a spy,' she cried, as Barbara scurried down the stairs and stood at the bottom with her hands on her hips and a look of disgust on her face.

'Now just one blinking minute,' she said quickly. 'It is traditional even in your culture, I believe, to tell somebody that you have intentions towards them before announcing it to the whole world?'

'Barbara,' Hieronymous said with an embarrassed gulp. 'You heard nothing but speculative words.'

'Indeed,' said Barbara, cutting off Gabrielle who was about to say something spiteful and vindictive. 'And that is all they shall remain. I have no wish to marry you, Hieronymous. I am grateful for your kindness and hospitality, and for protecting me from ignorance when it would have been easier for you to have thrown me to the wolves. But I have no desire for you. I am not your cuckold, and neither am I your slave.' She turned to Gabrielle, still angry and confused. 'And as for you, young lady, your father is a decent man and deserves better than the treatment that you have seen fit to shower him with. For your information, I have no desire to remain in this house for a single second longer than is necessary for my own safety. I will not be used as an excuse for either of you to shatter the harmony of this home. If it ain't broke, don't fix it. A blessing be upon all of those who dwell within this house,' she concluded sarcastically.

Barbara turned her back on the silenced pair and walked slowly back to the staircase with an unseen yet rueful smile on her face.

That's been and gone and torn it, she told herself.

At the stairs she stopped and turned back to the still-silent Hieronymous and Gabrielle. 'I am disgusted and annoyed with you both,' she said. 'I feel betrayed by you,' she continued, pointing to Hieronymous. 'And you, madam, belittle me with your suspicions. I am what I am. A woman of a strange land trying to keep her head while others all around are losing theirs. You both wrong me in different ways. I have said my last word on this matter.'

She hurried upstairs, listening intently for a break in the silence. At long last Gabrielle began to speak but Hieronymous stopped her with an almighty roar of anger and pain. 'Return you to your widow woman, for that is where I wish you to remain. If you see Phasaei or Titus, inform them that I wish to see them.'

'Very well, Father,' Gabrielle replied, tearfully. 'Goodbye.'

For a long time afterwards, there was an eerie and tangible quiet about the house. Barbara was almost afraid to breathe. And she certainly didn't wish to face Hieronymous again for a while until his emotions had been calmed by the passage of time.

Some time later, she heard Titus and Phasaei's unmistakable voices at the door and, again, listened closely at the head of the stairs.

'Come in,' said Hieronymous with a mean-spirited and harsh voice that made the hair of Barbara's neck stand on end. Here was a man who had suffered a brutal and humiliatingly public rejection. Oh dear, thought Barbara, perhaps I should have cushioned the blow a little.

'I have decided that my policy towards the Christians has been both too passive and weak. I have treated those base heretics with too much kindness. No more.' There was a terrifying pause, during which Barbara wanted to run downstairs, hug Hieronymous and tell him to forget what she said earlier and that true love could conquer all obstacles.

Truth is always the victor, Barbara told herself, and bit her tongue.

'I wish to persecute the Christians to extinction,' Hieronymous told his gathered deputies.

Something human within the heart of Barbara Wright died.

Another day, another move of location. The cave that the Doctor and the Christians now occupied was set so deep into the hills that Byzantium was now a mere speck on the horizon, straddling a river the colour of the TARDIS.

Like a distant and shimmering mirage, almost as if it were trying to convince the Doctor that it had never really existed at all.

Everything the Doctor looked at, or thought about, reminded him of what he had lost. Of the life that was now over for him. He would live and regenerate and live and regenerate and live and regenerate and, maybe, in two thousand years he would be in the right place at the right time to find an escape route from this alluring, yet primitive, world.

With this thought making him feel a little bit more positive, the Doctor found himself a corner of the new cave, rolled down his straw-mat bedding and fell into a deep and untroubled sleep.

Silhouetted in the entrance to the cave, one hand groping along the moist walls and into the dark interior, the visitor was suddenly assaulted by the light of five torches springing at him through the blackness.

'My God,' he said. It was an exclamation of alarm, rather than worship.

Luke Panathaikos, the hated Greek tax collector, stood at the mouth of the cave, a hand clutching his fast-beating heart and a look of shock on his face.

'If your intention was to have me defecate myself,' he said, sullenly, 'then you have almost succeeded.'

'What manner of ignorance is this, tax collector?' asked Daniel.

Luke gave the young man a contemptuous stare. 'If you had posted sentries in those locations where they would be of some use then my arrival would not have been so stealthy.'

James pushed Daniel away from the Greek and placed a welcoming arm around his shoulders. 'But it is good to see you, my friend. We did not know if you were still at liberty within Byzantium. You are our only ally now within those walls.'

Luke relaxed, sat cross-legged by the fire and warmed his hands. 'It would be wise for that to remain so for a while longer,' he told Daniel and James. 'For even now, as I speak, Zealot aggressors roam the streets to sate their thirst for vengeance.' He paused and looked around hopefully. 'Any food, hereabouts?'

'We have little,' James replied. 'But what we have is yours.'

The tax collector nodded. Briefly, he looked at the sleeping figure of the Doctor. 'Another convert to the cause?' he asked, somewhat cynically.

'None are disbarred from our ranks, Luke,' James said, sitting by the fire. 'Not even the likes of you.'

It was a perfect cover, of course. No one would suspect someone hated by his own community and trusted implicitly by the Romans of being a secret sympathiser with the Christians. But that was what made Luke Panathaikos such an important part of the Christians' organisation. He could go (and was welcomed) in all of the places that they could not. He could hear what was restricted to them. Like the night itself, he could slip unnoticed around the city, collecting snatches of conversation that might have some effect on the Christians.

'What news do you bring us today?' asked James, handing Luke a piece of cold chicken which the Greek ate hungrily.

'Many things,' he said, clearing his mouth and wiping the grease from his lips with the back of his hand. 'Basellas's thugs are on the rampage everywhere that the Romans are not. They loot and pillage each house where they believe a Christian might be, and leave them burning into the night when they have taken what they want. They defile their women and girls in ways that even the Romans would find base and depraved. Everyone is scared. The Arab quarter is off-limits to all but the Romans and the Bedouin have announced that they intend to leave the city soon.

I also heard from a Mesopotamian in the market-place that others, too, are considering a tactical withdrawl.'

James shook his head, sadly. 'My beautiful city shall lie in ruins at the hands of these Jewish extremists.' He paused. 'Do the Pharisees have nothing to say on the matter?'

'Much,' replied Luke. 'But they are weak and powerless to come up with so much as a contingency plan. Phasaei wanders the streets muttering from the scriptures and becoming an object of ridicule to most while Titus plots and schemes his way further and further up his own anus. He is twisted, that one. He thinks too much.'

'And Hieronymous?' asked Daniel.

'Ah, the ways of love have made Hieronymous blind to the goings-on of Byzantium. He spends his days in his flower garden, skipping and humming to himself like a girl.'

This amused James greatly. 'I dread to think what manner of woman could bring the great Hieronymous to his knees,' he said. 'What else?'

'This and that,' replied Luke, aware that the old man in the corner was stirring in his sleep. But it lasted only a moment. 'Nothing of any great consequence,' continued the tax collector. 'The Romans have officially blamed the riot in the square on Zealotry. There are some ubiquitous rumours circulating about the way in which they intend to prosecute the crimes. There is a fair-skinned girl living with a family known to me in the Greek quarter who seems to have come from nowhere though I think she is a little young to be a spy.'

'You are always looking for spies, Luke,' Daniel interjected as the snoring from the Doctor intensified.

'And I have survived thus far because of it.' Panathaikos replied. 'This apart, life is quiet and as slow as ever. Things will change but only in their own time.'

Chapter Twenty
What Did Your Last Slave Die Of?

If thy hand offend thee, cut it off: it is
better for thee to enter into life maimed
than having two hands to go into hell,
into the fire that never shall be quenched:
Where their worm dieth not
Mark 9:43-44

The pale and wan light of dawn had barely broken through the clouds of an overcast sky as Vicki slipped silently from her bedding, padded her way, shoeless, across the cold stone floor and, with a melancholy glance over her shoulders, opened the door and fled.

Freedom tasted bitter, frankly. She felt nauseous and afraid. Without the vaguest clue as to where she was going, Vicki put on her shoes and jogged out of the Greek quarter and down towards the sea walls. Perhaps, she had thought, she could stow away on a fishing boat and find a safe harbour somewhere. But the dawn brought with it heavy clouds and the threat of rain. The fishermen would not be venturing out to sea today.

For some reason, Vicki turned north, heading through the twisting and interlocking streets of the Arab quarter and making for the city walls. Soon, the towering sandstone building gave way to the water meadows of Byzantium's outskirts. It was here that, for the first time, Vicki paused and actually considered the ramifications of what she was doing. Leaving the Georgiadis family behind was the biggest gamble of her life. She was completely alone in a world where she did not belong. More scared now than at any stage since she had first arrived in Byzantium, Vicki sat on a cold jagged rock and watched the sun rise across the river in the east. With a deep sigh she looked down at her feet and wondered how much walking she could do before they were raw and blistered. How far could she get before somebody started to ask questions about who she was and where her family were?

She would lie, that was the easy part.

But how long would it be before she met the wrong person?

Her encounter with the Roman legionnaire the previous day had given her a horribly prophetic view of the rest of her life. Constantly running, using her wits to talk her way out of awkward situations. Constantly looking back over her shoulder until finally, one day, she ran out of places to hide.

'It is a beautiful morning, yes?'

Vicki spun around, and slipped from her rock perch, landing in the mud on one knee.

'Oh well, that's just the bloody limit,' she shouted angrily, looking down at her filth-splattered toga. 'As if I haven't got enough to worry about...'

She glanced up to find the somewhat bemused face of Papavasilliou, the genial old man that she had met at the Georgiadis house some nights earlier.

It seemed a lifetime ago.

'I'm not going back,' she said flatly. 'You can tell them that the next time you see them. Thank them very much for their hospitality. I'm grateful, I truly am. But I've had enough of trying to fit in like a square peg in a round hole. I don't belong here.'

'I know that,' said Papavasilliou, sitting on the rock that Vicki had recently vacated. 'None of us truly belong anywhere.'

Vicki sighed loudly. 'Look, don't trade any of that philosophical babble with me, old man, I'm really not in the mood.' Then she saw the look of hurt on Papavasilliou's face and felt like a shoplifter. 'I'm sorry,' she said, feeling very upset. 'I didn't mean to take it out on you. But there's a lot going on in my life that you don't know about.'

'You mean that your new guardian regards you as a headstrong and naughty little girl. That she punishes you for things that you do not deserve. That no one hereabouts understands you or your needs. That you feel threatened, alone, betrayed. That you wish you could be with those who would treat you as an equal...?'

Vicki was impressed at this remarkable piece of insight. 'Something not wholly dissimilar to that,' she said, trying not to sound too blasé. 'And about a million more things that I could mention, but we'd be here all day.'

Papavasilliou's aged and lined face cracked into a broad smile. 'I have no pressing engagements,' he said. 'That is the beauty of being old. I have nothing but time on my hands.' He patted one hand on his knee. 'Come, little one. Sit by me and tell me of your troubles.'

Ian Chesterton was beginning to enjoy the luxurious breakfasts within the *Villa Praefectus*. Here, even the slaves ate like kings, as Ian found out by taking many of his meals with Drusus and his staff.

This morning, he had woken early and arrived in the mezzanine vestibule to find only a lone serving girl drinking a bowl of milk. Ian smiled at her and the girl averted her eyes from him.

He had seen her around the villa on several occasions; sometimes with Felicia waiting upon the lady Jocelyn, sometimes undertaking the tasks that Drusus had given her with fellow male slaves. And sometimes, like now, on her own, her head bowed in silent contemplation.

It was a well-known fact (which Barbara Wright had spotted some time ago) that it was the quiet birds that always got Ian Chesterton's attention. She was peach, this slave girl, her dark brown eyes and dusky Mediterranean complexion reminding Ian of the kind of women you see on the cover of twentieth-century travel magazines advertising holidays in exotic locations the likes of which he could never afford.

'Hello,' he said brightly. 'I'm Ian.'

'I know who you are and from whence you have come,' the girl said, her eyes still fixed to the floor. 'I have heard much about you.'

'None of it good, I hope,' Ian said with a cheeky grin.

'Oh no, sir,' the girl said, raising her head and looking horrified at the prospect. '*All* of it good.'

Ian was as embarrassed as she was, his joke having spectacularly backfired. 'And you are...?' he asked, trying to wrestle the initiative back from complete defeat.

'My name is Dorcas,' the girl replied.

'Ah,' said Ian, remembering a snatch of conversation with Fabulous some days before. 'You're the Christian, right? You and another of Thalius's slaves have asked to have your religion recognised?'

'Yes, sir,' she said, and returned to looking at the floor in a mixture of subservience and fear. 'I am sorry, sir.'

Ian tried hard not to laugh. 'Don't apologise for what you believe in, Dorcas,' he said. 'We are what we are, we should never have to be sorry for it.'

The girl seemed suitably encouraged by this, and brightened considerably. 'Myself and Tobias, that is another of the *praefectus*'s slaves, we were converted by The Word when a man named James told us of the teachings of the good news.'

'Where do you come from?' Ian asked.

'I was born on the island of Crete and lived there with my family until the mariners came through the surf and carried us all into bondage.'

'And now you want your freedom?'

Dorcas giggled and placed a hand to her mouth. 'Gracious no, sir. I am better fed under this regime that I ever should be, living the life of a fisherman's wife.'

'But you are not free?'

'Freedom is an illusion,' the girl replied with a philosophical flourish. 'At night we all dream of being locked in cages; of running down never-ending corridors. We are *all* prisoners of some power greater than ourselves. Only through The Word shall we know freedom.'

Ian found this view strangely unsettling. 'And the Romans approve of your faith?'

'They...' Dorcas paused and searched for the right word. 'Tolerate it,' she concluded. 'Some of them punish us for our insolence in daring to believe in anything other than the *de facto* aspects of life. Others are amused by our whims and caprices. The *praefectus*, though, is a man of compassion and tolerance. As long as we practise our faith in private and do not let it affect our work or subservience, we are indulged.'

'Do you fear that one day the Romans may look upon the *Christians* as their problem rather than that of the Jews?' Ian asked, already knowing the answer.

'That would be... unfortunate,' said a voice from the back of the mezzanine. Dorcas stood and sighed heavily as a tall and elegant, well-muscled African man joined them at the table.

'Tobias,' Dorcas said. 'Another believer.'

Chesterton introduced himself as the black man broke bread and nodded to his new acquaintance. 'You are from Britannia, I understand?' he asked.

'Londinium,' replied Ian.

'A cold land, I am told. I, myself, am Egyptian. I find the Thracian winter to be a savage ordeal.'

'Oh, my friend, you'd hate England,' Ian said flatly.

'In answer to your question,' Tobias offered, 'it is likely that the Romans may, soon, regard our brothers as a direct threat to their authority. And as word of the Christ's message is spread, we shall without doubt face persecution and death.'

'There is much truth in what you say,' Ian noted. 'But I have a feeling that Christianity will survive its brush with whatever Rome can throw at it.'

The sound of someone clapping his hands stopped Ian in his tracks. He turned to find Drusus giving both Dorcas and Tobias severe looks of displeasure.

'There are people hereabout who should be working instead of being involved in the idle chatter of good-for-nothing dogsbodies,' he said angrily. Both slaves hurriedly finished their breakfasts and left the vestibule without another word.

'That was my fault,' said Ian quickly. 'We were talking about how Christianity is spreading, and...'

Drusus shook his head. 'Christianity,' he scolded. 'It comes between those two and their wits. You should not be encouraging them in their strange and abnormal beliefs. You are an outsider in this land and still have much to learn about the internal affairs of the empire.'

'I know exactly how Pete Best felt,' Ian said sarcastically. 'I'm a superfluous item here, clearly.'

The master of the house shrugged his shoulders defensively. 'This is the way that things are,' he continued. 'Tobias and Dorcas should not be encouraged.'

'That's terrible,' Ian replied. 'Even slaves have the right to be treated as equals.'

Vicki finally finished her woeful story. 'And, you know,' she concluded, 'the worst of it all is that I actually like it here. Apart from the fact that I seem to be completely clueless as to the right and wrong thing to say at any given moment.'

She stopped and hoped that she did not sound as pathetic as she felt. 'I'm being rather childish, aren't I?' she asked. And, when she said out loud all of the things that were troubling her, she was forced to admit that it didn't sound like very much at all.

'That is because you *are* a child, my angel,' Papavasilliou told her. 'Oh, you try to obscure that. You like to think that you are old before your time. That you have had your childhood stolen by tragedy and circumstance. You have seen much that the likes of I shall never see. But, at heart, you are still blessed with the vigour of youth and the freedom that goes with it. To try and kick against the thorns of that eventuality is a betrayal of your own life. Do you understand?'

'Probably,' said Vicki with a wry smile. 'But that doesn't make living my life any easier, does it?'

Papavasilliou agreed that it didn't. 'Try to be objective about situations,' he said.

'Objectivity is subjective,' Vicki replied with a rather smug expression on her face. 'Checkmate,' she continued; then a realisation seemed to dawn upon her and her face fell to the floor where it shattered into a million pieces. 'That's an example of why I get everything that's coming to me and more besides, isn't it?' she asked.

The old man said nothing. He didn't need to. He merely smiled and stared up at the rising sun.

'I don't mean to be such a smarty-pants,' Vicki bemoaned. 'I try my best, really I do, but I can't help it if I'm in a world of simple-minded peasants!'

'Simple minds are closed minds,' Papavasilliou told her. 'What I am about to tell you is good advice. The differences between many people are mainly due to fear. Fear makes a slave of us all. Fear makes a whore out of woman and a thief out of man. Fear is why Rome occupies the world - because the Romans are afraid of how different the world would be if they didn't.'

Vicki almost started to applaud him. 'You *know*,' she said. 'So why don't they?'

'Because they are afraid,' replied Papavasilliou.

'But that's so unfair,' Vicki continued.

The old man tried to give Vicki a reassuring look. 'No one said that life is fair, little one. Only that it is life. Come, my angel,' he said, standing up. 'You and I should return to Georgiadis and Evangeline.'

For a moment, Vicki said nothing. Then she nodded.

'I cannot promise that your return will be smooth or easy. But at least I know, and you know, that you will understand them a little better, even if they do not understand you.'

'I can live with that,' said Vicki and she helped the old man to wade through the mud as they set off for home.

The library was deserted as Ian searched for some companionship. He felt alone and in need of someone to talk to. Perhaps the realities of Byzantium were finally beginning to become clear to him.

Protect yourself with friends, or you're dead. Watch what you say and to whom you say it, or you're dead. Guard your privacy, or you're dead.

First rule: don't die.

'You look lost and afraid, Briton,' Antonia Vinicius told him.

Ian spun around and did an impressively comedic slip and pratfall onto his bottom. Feeling like Tommy Cooper at the London Palladium, Ian stood, his face flushing bright red, brushed himself down.

'Sneaking up on unsuspecting people is a cruel trick,' he said, wounded. 'I'm sure you find it greatly amusing, but it isn't.'

'Your boldness is intriguing,' said Antonia, 'but it could become such a bore. *Pedicabo ego vos et irrumabo*.'

Now, having played the sad clown for far longer than he would have chosen, Ian turned into Ian Chesterton, schoolmaster again. 'You most certainly will not have me upstairs and downstairs, missus,' he replied to Antonia's lewd suggestion. 'Stop this nonsense, Antonia,' he continued angrily. 'You're used to people giving you what you want, and playing your devious games with the *praefectus*. Well, I'm sorry but I'm not inclined to join in.' Ian started to walk towards the door but Antonia caught him by the arm and he turned around, frothing with rage.

'You really are a selfish and stupid woman, aren't you?' he asked the dumbfounded senator's wife. 'You just click your fingers and every man in Byzantium comes running?'

'Yes,' she replied with a slight pout. 'That is the way that things work around here.'

Ian laughed. 'Well, not with me, sweetheart. I'm my own man with my own needs. And one of them isn't to end up with my head stuck on a pole for committing indiscretions with you. Understand?'

For a moment she said nothing, then she allowed her hand to fall away from Ian's shoulder. There was regret in her big brown eyes, but also something else. Something hard and nasty floating beneath the surface.

'You should know that I have many powerful friends both in this city and in Rome itself, Briton. I can make life very difficult for you whereinsoever you may wander.'

Ian had just about had enough. 'I'm sure you can, darlin', and frankly, I don't give a damn,' he said as dismissively as he could. 'It's nothing personal, but I'm nobody's toy. I stand alone.'

As Antonia left, a red velvet curtain behind Ian rippled and Gaius Calaphilus stepped out, grinning like a Cheshire cat.

'That was,' he said with a painful slap on Ian's back, '*the* funniest jape that I have e'er witnessed in all of my life to this date. It is high and proper time that such a deceitful bitch as the lady Antonia were to be given a taste of her own bitter medicine.'

'Does everybody in this city spy on everyone else?' Ian asked, genuinely interested.

'Yes,' replied the general, in all seriousness, 'although this was, in actual fact, a bonus. I was about this place to see Fabulous and I thought it wise that anyone entering be unaware of my presence within the villa. You have made a bad enemy there, Briton, for everything that the *moecha* Antonia says is highly true. I would not wish to be her enemy for she has many dangerous friends. But you have made a friend in me and I admire your bravery. I salute you.'

Calaphilus strode towards the door, then stopped and turned to give Ian a parting thought.

'Watch your back, Briton. But if you need anything, then come to me. I shall not fail you as others within this household would.'

EPISODE FOUR
INFAMY, INFAMY, THEY'VE ALL GOT IT IN FOR ME

And he taught them many things by parables,
and said unto them in his doctrine
Mark 4:2

Chapter Twenty-One
Perfume (All on You)

Arise, and take up thy bed,
and go thy way into thine house.
Mark 2:11

The depression that had seized the Doctor in its stranglehold after the discovery that the TARDIS was missing took several days to lift, despite his determination in the face of Hebron's illness not to wallow in the depths of self-pity. The Doctor knew that life could have dealt him a much worse fate; knew that there were worse places to be stranded and alone than first-century Earth in a tropical climate.

But, as ever, the wanderer in him champed at the bit of freedom. His feet itched and he longed to have the ability to travel to far and distant worlds and increase his knowledge of the universe and how it worked. If he had wanted to locate in one place, a mute observer of the passage of time, then he could have stayed on his home planet where time had less meaning and revolved at its own pace.

They had little time for revolutions in the realm of the Lords of Time.

That idea, in itself, had depressed the Doctor enough to flee his roots.

And now, he found himself in a situation of stunning similarity. Only, this time, he had nowhere to run to.

After a further burst of switching locations, the Christians finally settled for a longer period in a cave close to the peak of one of the Byheomentalah hills. Byzantium, in the distance, still glistened like a jewel, but now the Doctor had to strain his eyes to see the city's details. It was fading, like the passing of a memory, first into a half-remembered dream state and then, finally, into oblivion.

In the cave next to the one in which James and his followers now found themselves, the Doctor was introduced to three earnest young Christian scribes who lived in this most desolate and isolated of places for much of the year. The normal peace and quiet, now rudely interrupted, aided their task which was to translate into Greek the mostly Aramaic and Hebrew, and occasional Latin, scrolls and parchments of holy texts that were arriving by the day in Byzantium. They came from Palestine, Antioch and Babylon, in the form of letters from various prophets, sages and priests around the region and beyond.

This was a very new church and, as such, had little in the way of written lore to work from. Thus, anything, even letters from nomadic priests like Peter the fisherman or Paul the gentile were regarded as quasi-sacred texts.

James took the Doctor into the cave where three candles were the only illumination. Spread around the cave floor, in a seemingly haphazard fashion, were dozens of parchments; the trio of scholars sat, their heads bowed, studying with great concentration, the words of the various pages. Occasionally, one would stop, stand up to stretch his cramped and aching limbs, and walk to the mouth of the cave, blinking in the light like a small rodent emerging from underground. Their skin, as a result of their seclusion, was pale and chalky. They all looked, the Doctor thought, like they could do with some exercise.

'Good scribes,' James announced as they entered the cave. The three men looked up, cross at having been interrupted in their most important of works. When they saw it was James who addressed them, they all stood and bowed their heads in deference. 'I should like to introduce to you the Doctor, a man of great knowledge and learning from overseas.'

The Doctor didn't reply to the half-hearted grunts of acknowledgement that came from the three men.

Reuben, seemingly the eldest and most senior of the group, was also the tallest and easily the most approachable. Thin, almost to the point of emaciation, he, like the others, had thick black hair and a straggly, unkempt beard. Rayhab was smaller and more docile with dull eyes, the colour of mud on a river-bed. Amos, the third scribe, was short and stout, a roly-poly figure with blotchy skin and a squint from working long and tedious hours in near darkness.

'The Doctor may, perhaps, be of some use in your studies,' said James, who seemed to be hurrying towards the cave exit. The Doctor thought briefly about begging James to take him with him, away from these terminally studious young men and their nasty-looking skin, but he decided that it wouldn't do any harm to stay here for a while and annoy them further.

'So,' said the Doctor as they were left alone, 'tell me what you are working on.'

For a moment, all of the men were silent, as though they had simultaneously lost the power of speech. Then they answered in a rapid series of short and to-the-point replies, one picking up the sentence wherever one of the others had left it. It was, thought the Doctor, almost as if they shared one gestalt-like mind.

'We are attempting,' Reuben began, 'to translate...'

'The rough notes, in Hebrew and Aramaic,' continued Amos.

'Of the prophet and scribe Mark of Jerusalem,' added Rayhab. 'As told to him by God, and through the mouths of the divine apostles Paul of Tarsus and Peter of Galilee.'

'And,' said Amos, 'brought back from Babylon by James months past.'

'Into a Greek *gospel*, that will complement the work of the disciple Matthew the tax-gatherer,' concluded Reuben.

Amos, however, added one final thought. 'Only *we* have the knowledge to do this.'

The others give him a sly and rather pleased corner-of-the-eye glance.

If there was one thing that really annoyed the Doctor it was hubris in all its forms. 'Knowledge is not the province of arrogance, gentlemen,' he said dismissively. 'It is a gift, a wonder of enlightenment.' He paused and gave the three scribes his most charming smile. 'May I be permitted to have a look at your work thus far?'

Marcus Lanilla arrived back at his villa following a particularly long and tedious day, spent firstly in the company of a group of pathetic and whining centurions who could all, Marcus had decided, have done with a good flogging to settle their grievances. This was followed by an hour torturing several Zealot prisoners, including one who had offered (before he died, screaming) a likely location as to the whereabouts of Basellas and his gang of murdering savages. However, when Marcus and a heavily armed retinue of guards had arrived at the house mentioned, it had been occupied only by an aged couple and their young grandson. And, despite applying much painful coercion to all three, no information had been forthcoming about Basellas, Ephraim, Yewhe and the rest.

With a dull ache in his head, Marcus had returned to the barracks and signed some execution orders to calm himself. He had tried to find one of the other tribunes, to assuage the doubts in his mind about the plots and schemes that had come to the attention of Calaphilus, a nagging and persuasive voice that he could not shake.

But Fabius and Honorius Annora and Edius Flavia were all engaged on different matters and it was impossible to talk to any of them. Finally, with his mind and his stomach in a turmoil, Marcus had left the barracks and headed for home.

The villa was in virtual darkness, the only light coming from candles in the Atrium. Marcus strode into the central courtyard and looked around, sniffing the perfumes and oils in the air eagerly. 'Come out, she-devil, and take that which is coming to you,' he shouted into the darkness.

Agrinella emerged, naked, bathed in the soft glow of the candlelight.

'I've been waiting for you for so long, my heart,' she said, sullenly. 'I thought that you would never come.'

'Get on your knees before me,' Marcus commanded, sneeringly.

Agrinella, willingly, complied.

Stroking her hair, Marcus took a long look at his wife's delicate body. His hand brushed against her cheek and he felt her shiver at his touch.

'You are cold, my heart,' she said, cradling his hand in her own. 'You require warmth to take the chill from your bones.'

The tribune said nothing. But actions spoke louder than words as the back of his hand rubbed the skin of Agrinella's face. She moved to stand and Marcus helped her up until their eyes were level. Lips met, skin on skin, tongue on tongue.

Marcus moved his head to the right and his mouth slid down Agrinella's throat to her neck. His teeth sank into the bare flesh, drawing blood. Agrinella moaned, softly, and grabbed the hair at the back of Marcus's head in both hands, tugging at it.

They dropped to the floor, bodies flailing, limbs entwined. Marcus licked the blood from Agrinella as it dripped down her neck to her breast. Her hands went to his side, and then further, clawing at his garments, and pushing them from his back.

As they rolled across the floor, Marcus's leg struck the base of one of the bronze candle-holders and the contraption swayed and fell to the floor, hot wax splattering across bare limbs.

Agrinella sat bolt upright, flicking the wax from the skin of her legs.

'I am burning,' she told Marcus, but her husband didn't seem interested.

Kneeling astride her, Marcus looked at the now-solidified candle wax, and then at his wife's flushed face.

'When I have finished with this city, many will drown in boiling wax,' he said.

Agrinella believed him.

Despite himself, the Doctor was becoming fascinated with the opportunity to see the gospel of Mark in such an unedited state.

And, despite the unbearable temptation to make fun of the scholarly and serious trio of Reuben, Rayhab and Amos, the Doctor had begun to look upon his presence here as a chance to observe history (and important history at that) in the making. Forget the Aztecs, or the French Revolution, or Marco Polo. Or the terrible events of the Passchendaele. The Doctor had been at Dunkirk, sailed around the Caribbean in a pirate galleon and had watched the assassination of President McKinley, but they were nothing compared to this - the writing of one of the most significant and well-known pieces of literature in the history of mankind.

It was the equivalent of collaborating with Shakespeare between draft one and draft two of *Hamlet*.

The Doctor was almost humbled by the thought.

Almost, but not quite.

Because he *had* collaborated with Shakespeare between draft one and draft two of *Hamlet*.

'These notes are very rough and ready,' he said after a brief scan of some of the scrolls that the scribes had yet to look at. 'The handwriting is almost illegible.'

'They were mostly written in Rome while Mark and Paul were under house arrest,' noted Amos. 'It is hardly surprising. The rest of the scrolls were completed last year in Babylon, when Mark finally found Peter.'

The Doctor knew he would probably regret asking, but one question kept nagging away at him. 'Who, exactly, was ... sorry, *is* this scribe Mark?'

'A cousin of the prophet Barnabas,' replied Amos. 'He was just a boy when the disciples held meetings with the Christ at the home of Mark's mother in Jerusalem. He tried to save the Christ's life when they were all betrayed by Judas and Jesus was arrested at Gethsemene. Mark escaped from the gardens and hid in the family home for many months. Eventually, with the disciples scattered across Judaea and in hiding, Barnabas, who was teaching in Antioch, was sent as an emissary to Tarsus, to the home of the recently converted Paul, he that was Saul. Barnabas brought

Paul back to Jerusalem because the church needed a figurehead around whom it could spread the word.'

'After a brief time in Jerusalem, they coaxed Mark from hiding and set out on the first of their missionary journeys,' Rayhab added, helpfully. 'But there was friction between them during this time. That was when Barnabas and Mark went to Cyprus. It was all a nonsense and was later settled to the satisfaction of all parties.'

'Oh good,' said the Doctor, sarcastically. 'I do so love a happy ending.'

'They received a very mixed reception whereinsoever they went,' continued Reuben. 'On such occasions as, with the will of the Christ, they were seen to perform miraculous cures, they were treated as avatars-incarnate.'

'But,' added Amos, 'such teachings as they offered caused great offence to the Hellenistic Jews and, especially, to the hated Zealots.'

'They were often chased out of town and survived only by the skin of their teeth,' Rayhab added.

'They founded churches in Galatia, Corinth and the Areopagus in Athens,' continued Reuben. 'They stayed for more than two years at Ephesus, building a Christian community, and it was there that Mark started his writings, based on his personal knowledge of the early days, and on the stories he was hearing from Paul and Barnabas.'

'He was a journalist, in other words,' noted the Doctor, approvingly. He had read accounts of the cross-empire journeys of Paul, Mark, Timothy and the rest. He had always considered them to be a collection of quasi-fairy tales with only the most narrow basis in reality. Now, he wasn't so sure. 'And this would be, what, about ten years ago? Hmm?'

'Yes,' confirmed Amos. 'Then they returned to Jerusalem, but Paul's enemies provoked a riot when he tried to preach at the temple and he was arrested and tried before a Roman court in Caesarea.'

'But,' the Doctor added, 'because he was a Roman citizen, he could appeal directly to the emperor. So they sailed to Rome, surviving a shipwreck near Malta. And Paul, while still under house arrest, continued to preach until last year when he was either freed and now resides in Miletus, or executed in the Circus of Nero, depending on which version you believe.'

Rayhab was surprised by the Doctor's apparent cynicism. 'Paul *is* alive. We believe in the truth,' he said. 'In the word of the Christ, and of God himself.'

'I find the origins of the Christian church fascinating,' the Doctor said defensively. 'How a minor sub-cult of Judaism could spread so quickly. Jesus of Nazareth only died thirty years ago and already you have churches in most of the major population centres. In an age where mass communications involve somebody shouting from up a mountain, or writing a letter, that's quite impressive, even I am willing to admit.'

'That was why Paul was needed,' Reuben admitted. 'Peter and the rest could preach to the Jews and converted many. And there were others within the movement who had free access into other territories like Thrace. But which Roman or other gentile would listen to Peter, or Philip, or John? Paul was essential to the mission.'

'An intercontinental public relations official,' the Doctor noted. 'The Damascus conversion was needed to turn Christianity from a Jewish cult into something altogether more complicated.'

'We needed to speak unto the nations,' Amos noted. 'Because of what was being done to us by the Jews in our own land. You have heard tell of Stephen, perhaps?' asked Amos.

'Yes. Stoned to death for blasphemy, poor chap. Your first martyr.'

'Would that there was another way,' Reuben continued. 'He was a friend of mine. And of James and Daniel. After *that*, Jerusalem was no longer safe for any of us. The only way in which we could survive was by taking our church out into the nations.'

'The prophets, John and Peter and Philip and the rest, all preached in Samaria. A *very* dangerous place,' Rayhab said. 'They all healed and resurrected, as the Christ had before them. The Jewish Christians eventually dispersed northwards to escape the oppression in Jerusalem from the Zealots. They followed the apostles into areas in which they had begun to make conversions. Hence, we are here in Byzantium.'

The Doctor nodded, wisely. 'Your people have suffered many hardships and trials in your quest to spread your good news. You have my sympathy if not my devotions.'

'Sympathy does us little good, Doctor,' Amos noted.

'Nevertheless,' the Doctor replied. 'I *will* help you with this,' he concluded, waving one of the scrolls in his hand.

Edius Flavia arrived at the *Villa Praefectus* and strutted, arrogantly, like a peacock with delusions of grandeur, into the great hall.

Once there, he headed up the sweeping marbled staircase to the servants' quarters on the mezzanine. At the top of the stairs, he was approached by a nervous slave boy who asked if he required any help.

'No,' said Edius, flatly, 'unless you want to throw yourself onto the end of my sword for sport, yes?'

The slave, Gravus, mutely shook his head, bowed and hurried away without turning his back on the Roman tribune, who stared after him with a gloating sneer on his face.

Halfway along the corridor, he met another obstacle. This one was more formidable.

'The tribune requires directions, perhaps?' asked Drusus in a heavy and sarcastic tone.

Edius turned and stared Drusus up and down for a long and considered moment. 'Be advised, freedman,' he said, 'that I come upon this house exactly on the hour, on the strict and sole orders of Gaius Calaphilus. I have business with one that is within and not with the likes of you. Now be off with you before I have you flayed across a wheel until you *die*.'

Drusus bowed so low that his head almost touched the ground. He stood upright, turned and slowly walked in the opposite direction with Edius staring hatefully after him.

The young soldier finally tore his eyes away from the departing figure and found the door that he was looking for. Without knocking, he threw it open to discover Felicia lying on her bed covered only by a thin sheet. She looked up at Edius and a smile grew on her lips. 'You came,' she said. 'I thought you might.'

Edius sat on the bed, roughly, and swung his feet around to kick Felicia in the back. 'Get on the floor and take off my boots, harlot,' he said with a cruel snarl. The handmaiden instantly complied.

She shook the sand from his leather sandals as she removed them and flung them into a corner as her vampire eyes looked up at him, hungrily.

'Now,' he said, 'my belt and sword need removing, unless you want me to fillet you.'

Felicia undid the silver belt-buckle and let the heavy scabbard fall away behind Edius onto the floor with a clatter. Edius slipped out of his own tunic and knelt on the bed.

'Stand up,' he ordered. The handmaiden did so.

'Come here,' he continued.

Felicia did as she was told.

'Lie down and don't make a sound or you shall suffer for it,' he concluded.

The sex, when it happened, was cold and impersonal, Edius clawing at the skin on Felicia's back as she moaned softly and bit into her pillow.

Then, as Edius cried out in triumph at the climax, the door burst open once more and he turned, naked and embarrassed, to find a dozen soldiers silhouetted in the doorway, most of them with wicked smirks on their faces.

Despite the circumstances, Edius felt powerful enough to scream an obscenity at them. Exhausted and drained, Felicia continued to lie on the bed, face down, sobbing into her sheets.

'What is the meaning of this?' demanded Edius in a shrill, almost feminine voice. Red-faced, he stood from the bed and began to walk towards the door, but stopped in his tracks when the guards parted to let Gaius Calaphilus through.

'Caught in a somewhat injudicious moment, seemingly, tribune?' asked the general.

Edius stared back defiantly and ridiculously, stark naked. But he still saluted in the presence of a superior officer. 'Hail Caesar,' he said flatly, before adding, 'Do you think that this is an appropriate moment to invade someone's privacy, sir?' he asked casually. 'As you can see, I'm busy giving this slave a moment that she will not forget in a long time.' He turned and poked Felicia in the side with his finger. 'Face the general when you address him, slave,' he ordered.

But the tribune's amusement turned to horror as his paramour spun around, her face lined with tears, and screamed loudly. 'That beast raped me,' she said with a mixture of pain and guilt. 'I said no but he would not stop.'

'She is *lying*,' shouted Edius, aiming an open-fisted blow to the handmaiden's face before anyone could stop him. 'You deceitful she-bitch, I shall have you dragged through the streets for your insolence.' He turned back towards the general, but as he swung around he was himself knocked back by a hard punch to the jaw. He skittered backwards, falling head over heels and lay in a crumpled heap at the foot of the bed.

'Seize him,' said Calaphilus, as the guards poured into the room and pulled up their naked tribune, still shouting and protesting his innocence. 'Take him to the dungeons,' continued the general. 'I shall be down to make an example of him later this day.'

As the screaming Edius was manhandled from the room, Calaphilus dropped a bag of coins on to the handmaiden's bed. 'Excellent,' he told the girl, who was dressing herself quickly and drying her tear-stained cheeks. She picked up the bag, weighed it in her hand, opened it and tumbled the coins onto the bed where they lay, glittering in the dim candlelight.

'Thank you,' she said, her face cracking into a smile. 'And kindly thank Caesar for his generous bounty.'

Without another word, Calaphilus turned and left her alone with her money.

Chapter Twenty-Two
The Culture Bunker, Part Six — Jehovahkill

For false Christs and false prophets shall rise,
and shall shew signs and wonders,
to seduce . . . But take ye heed: behold,
I have foretold you all things.
Mark 13:22-23

'This is wrong,' the Doctor said, loudly, catching the attention of the scribes.

'I beg your pardon?' asked Amos, haughtily. 'What are you saying?'

'This translation is wrong,' repeated the Doctor. 'Inaccurate. Incorrect. Substandard. Would you like me to elucidate further?'

Reuben took the manuscript from the Doctor's hand and read the passage to which the Doctor was pointing. 'He is referring to the story of Jesus curing the apostle Peter's mother-in-law from a fever,' he told his colleagues. 'And what, please tell us, is wrong with it?'

The Doctor waved the two scrolls in Reuben's face, angrily. 'Don't take that tone with me, young man, I've been translating ancient languages into other ancient languages since before you were born. And long after you've died as well!' He paused, and pointed again to the Greek translation. 'This is all nonsense. "Immediately he left the synagogue, and then he entered into the house of Simon and Andrew along with James and John. When he got there he found that Simon's mother-in-law lay sick with a nasty fever, and immediately they told him about this. So, he lifted her up, and the fever left her; and she, being better, served them food." Utter nonsense!'

'That is exactly what it says,' countered Rayhab, defensively. 'Word for word.'

'No, it doesn't!' spluttered the Doctor, laughing at their foolishness.

'It says, "And forthwith when they were come out of the synagogue, they entered into the house of Simon and Andrew, with James and John. But Simon's wife's mother lay sick of a fever, and anon they told him of her. And he came and took her by the hand, and lifted her up; and immediately the fever left her, and she ministered unto them".'

'What is the difference?' asked Reuben.

'*What is the difference?*' repeated the Doctor, with a girlish shriek. 'There's a whole world of difference. Dear, dear, dear, I can see I'm going to have to go back through all of the work you've already done and double-check it.'

Amos, Rayhab and Reuben stared at the Doctor, unable to believe that their carefully translated texts were being ridiculed in such a way. And by such a strange person.

'But, but...' stammered Amos. 'We translated it accurately.'

'Perhaps,' said the Doctor, testily, 'but your version is as dry as stale bread. It is a chartered accountant's version of the scripture. It ignores the nuances and the flair for language and poetry of the author. The flow of the sentences. The brilliance and sparkling energy of the piece. "*And she served them food*"! I ask you, who on Earth is going to get inspired enough to join your religion with phrases like that?! This,' he said rattling the recently translated piece, 'is soulless.'

'So you are suggesting what, exactly?' asked Rayhab.

'That you follow your inspiration, not your sense of accuracy,' the Doctor told them.

It had taken Barbara over a day to pluck up the courage to finally confront Hieronymous again. And in that time she had done a lot of thinking as to exactly how she was going to phrase what she needed to say.

What it was necessary for her to say.

She had practised and practised until her little speech was word-perfect. But all of that fell flat on its back the moment that she saw the hurt in Hieronymous's face.

'I think we really need to have a chat,' she spluttered, completely destroying her carefully worded opening gambit about how time can be a great healer.

'Say whatsoever you have to say, woman,' spat Hieronymous.

'I have decided that it would be best for all concerned, myself included, if I simply left. Not just your home, but also Byzantium,' she said, flatly, ignoring a multitude of ways of cushioning of her dramatic announcement.

Barbara didn't have to be a mind-reader to know that Hieronymous was bitter and furious at her rejection of him. 'Without my intervention,' he snarled, facing away from her, 'you would have been denounced as a spy and stoned unto your death.'

It was impossible for Barbara to do anything else but agree with this. 'That is certainly true,' she began, 'but do you expect that I should spend the rest of my life grovelling on my knees, thanking you for one act of kindness? I am grateful, as I've already told you. But you seem to require that I am something more...'

Her voice trailed away and she shook her head sadly as Hieronymous continued to ignore her. 'Although destiny brought us together,' Barbara added quickly, 'it will also be destiny that tears us apart. We were and are not meant to be so, Hieronymous.'

What tense is this? Past tense? Present tense? Future tense?

'And we shall continue not to be meant for each other. You surely must see the logic of that?'

Finally, Hieronymous turned to face Barbara, and she could see that the priest was crying. His dignity was in grave danger of being swept away and shipwrecked, lost in a swelling sea-storm of emotions.

'I am sorry, Hieronymous,' Barbara said softly. 'I did not mean to hurt you. That is the last thing that I would have wished for.'

'Go,' said Hieronymous in an barely audible whisper. 'No Jew will molest or mistreat you within the limits of this city. I will personally make certain of this eventuality.'

'Thank you,' Barbara said and she brushed past Hieronymous

and made for the door. She didn't pause there, even when he called out her name, nor did she look back once she was outside as he continued to wail after her.

She just kept walking into the Byzantium sunlight.

It had been the first time since that day in the market square that Ian had either been allowed, or had allowed himself, to leave the sanctuary of the *Villa Praefectus*. Ian had wished that his reintroduction into whatever passed for society in Byzantium could have occurred more at his own choosing but the command (when it came) had left little room for manoeuvre.

Come to the barracks, the note that had been passed to him by Tobias had said. *And come alone.*

Ian found the meeting place easily enough and then had to endure a torturous twenty minutes waiting around for whoever had written the note to make themselves known to him.

He felt like a spare groom at a wedding as numerous soldiers passed him, going in and out of the barracks.

When general Calaphilus finally arrived, his appearance didn't surprise Ian in the slightest. 'I'd figured that it was probably you who sent the note,' Chesterton said flatly. 'Less of a request, more of a command. It smelled of the military a mile away.'

'You came alone, as I asked?' the general queried.

'No,' replied Ian, sarcastically. 'I brought the household cavalry with me.'

'Your ways and words are strange and baffling to me, Briton,' continued the general when he was certain that they were alone. 'One should have thought that a soldier such as myself would prove to be a useful ally to one such as yourself? That you would do all that is within your power to cultivate such a liaison...'

'No offence,' Ian noted, 'but I still don't know if I can trust you yet,' he continued.

'I see that to which you allude,' the general noted, slipping behind Ian and drawing the schoolteacher's sword from its scabbard. Calaphilus held the *gladius*, dramatically, across Ian's chest, inches from slitting his throat. Then, after a moment he withdrew the sword and looked at it. 'A finely forged weapon.'

'A gift,' said Ian. 'From the *praefectus*.'

All of a sudden, Calaphilus didn't seem nearly so impressed. 'Get it out of my sight,' he said, handing the sword back, hilt-first, to Ian.

'You will be wondering why I was so anxious to see you, this day, Briton?'

Ian shrugged. 'Intrigue?' he asked. 'Nefarious skulduggery of some description? Isn't that what it's all about?'

'I see that you are a man who keeps his ear close to the ground,' the general noted in complete seriousness. 'This place is rife with both. But I have started a fire that will bring the whole rank and rotten corpse of Byzantium crashing down around the ears of those who would pollute it with their decadent ways. Last night, I arrested Edius Flavia, a young and hot-headed tribune-elect whose libido carries more influence within him than common sense. The charges will not stand to close examination, but I now have him under guard where I can attempt to loosen his tongue. And loosen it I shall, Briton, for there are plots and schemes afoot. Tangled webs like those of a spider that must be delicately unpicked before they can be ruthlessly torn apart.'

'You like tearing things down, don't you?' Ian asked, his trust in the general rapidly draining away.

It took Gaius Calaphilus a long time to answer the question. He seemed surprised by it. 'No,' he said finally, and honestly. 'If truth be told, I do not. Oh, I am jubilant this day that I have uncovered the first of the conspiring insurgents who attempt to destroy all that I have worked so hard to achieve. With luck, and with your help, I may be able to expose the trail all the way to the door of the *praefectus*.'

'These are dangerous sentiments to be voicing in the open,' Ian noted, casting an ominous glance at a group of soldiers in the middle distance. 'Perhaps we should be holding this conversation somewhere a little less exposed?' He paused, and directed the general towards a small outbuilding close to the barrack gates.

They slipped in, unobserved by the bored-looking guards and found themselves in the armoury.

Calaphilus took a javelin from a rack by the door and weighed the spear in his hand. 'I was once able to put out a man's eye at forty paces with one of these,' he said, as if it was a cherished memory. 'In Britannia, that was. Have you ever been to Corinium Dobunnorum?'

A memory cog rotated and clicked into gear in the back of Ian's mind. 'Cirencester?' he asked.

'Yes.'

'Sadly, I have not,' Ian replied, thankful that he had at least remembered the place's English name. 'I know where it is, though.'

'Whensoever you return to the land of your birth, Briton, do me a favour and go there. Go to the fort and the *vicus* settlement by the river. You will find a beautiful and unspoiled piece of Heaven on Earth. I long for the simple if harsh life that I enjoyed in your land.'

'You're not the only one there, squire,' noted Ian.

'So much more preferable to the corruption and decadence of Rome and all of its *civitas* replicas, say you not?'

It was a rhetorical question and, when he received no reply, Calaphilus threw the spear to the ground and sat down at a rough wooden table. He was clearly upset. 'How could so much go wrong in so little time?'

'With Rome, do you mean?' asked Ian.

The general nodded. 'Yes, with Rome, and with the Romans. We have grown soft and weak and depraved. We gorge ourselves at banquets and on gladiatorial sports and grow drunk on the power of being just who we are. And all the while, the republic grows a further and more distant memory.'

'The republic? Isn't that a rather dangerous view for a general of Caesar to hold?' asked Ian curiously.

'All of the best Romans have been republicans. Including at least two *great* Emperors. The divine Claudius spent most of his time in Britannia lecturing the troops about how one day, the republic would return to Rome. Of course, there are reasons why it cannot happen at this precise moment...'

'Like, losing the empire overnight?' Ian asked.

'And would that really be such a bad thing?' Calaphilus noted as he slumped in his seat.

Ian Chesterton genuinely didn't know the answer to that one. 'Listen,' he said at last. 'I know that you told me to come alone, but I didn't. I'm sorry, but I thought it was important that someone else hear all of this.'

The general raised his head and half-stood, snarling angrily at Ian as, with as little intrusion as possible, Gemellus slipped quietly from the shadows.

'You brought the advisor of the *praefectus* here?' Calaphilus yelled. 'Are you insane, Briton? This meeting, regardless of its contents, could in itself be regarded as treason.'

Gemellus shook his head quickly. 'I know you are suspicious, Gaius Calaphilus,' he said. 'That point of view has served you well in a long, distinguished career, but it has also kept men who could have been your allies at arms length when they should have been much closer. The *praefectus* and you are more alike than either of you would care to admit, particularly on such subjects as I have just heard you discussing with our mutual friend.'

Calaphilus began to laugh. 'Thalius Maximus is a republican, say you?' he asked, sarcastically. 'I have heard it all now.'

'Not a republican as such,' acknowledged Gemellus, 'but he is a man whose views on the monarchy closely resemble your own. I have talked with him on such matters upon many, many occasions.'

'The reason I asked Gemellus to come with me,' Ian explained, 'is because of an old proverb from my homeland that seems to be particularly applicable in Byzantium: "The enemy of my enemy is my friend".'

'The *praefectus* and the general are on the same side, even if they do not realise it yet,' Gemellus continued. 'The real enemies of both are within their own forces. And if something is not done about those enemies, then we all could perish under a mountain of deceit. And Byzantium shall be lost to the forces of darkness.'

The silence of the cave was shattered by a sudden thought that occurred to the Doctor. 'Mark's writing style is interesting, is it not?' he asked, as he wearily cast aside another parchment and yawned, stretching his tired and aching limbs.

Despite the long and tedious hours spent poring over the hundreds of pages of text, the Doctor was in no way bored with his task. On the contrary, he was fascinated.

'In which way?' asked Rayhab.

'He writes like a novelist,' noted the Doctor. 'There is a haste in the narrative. A rapid-moving flow to the words, as though the writer was describing the events from the perspective of someone within the eye of a hurricane. He uses "immediately" and "at once" an awful lot. His Christ was a man in a hurry, clearly.'

Reuben shrugged. 'Mark was there,' he noted. 'In the midst of all of the madness that surrounded the Messiah. He saw these things occur.'

'I would really have enjoying meeting *his* Jesus,' said the Doctor in a reflective moment. 'And Mark himself, where did you say he is now?'

'He was last heard of with Peter in Babylon,' said Reuben. 'Perhaps he is back in Rome, now.'

Amos stirred the fire and added, 'It is said that he hides from Zealot death squads who roam the empire attempting to silence him and others like him. That is the fate of many of the prophets of Christ's church.'

'Zealotry is a curse,' the Doctor noted sadly. 'In this or any other age.'

Vicki was trying hard to fit in. Really, she was.

It was an effort at times, having to constantly bite her tongue instead of giving her opinion where it clearly wasn't wanted. But two or three days of being seen but not heard had an impressive effect. Particularly on Evangeline, who had seemingly taken it upon herself to help Vicki understand the culture of the Greeks better than she had managed so far.

'Now add the flour,' Evangeline told Vicki as the girl continued to knead the sticky yellow dough that glued itself to her fingers.

'How long do I have to keep doing this?' Vicki asked impatiently. 'It feels like I'm handling brains. I'm sure I'm doing it all wrong.'

Evangeline shook her head. 'No, you are not. You live life in far too much of a hurry, little one,' she said. 'Carry on until you have pushed all of the air out of the dough. You will know when the time is right.'

Well, that explains everything, thought Vicki, but she kept her silence. 'I can't believe you get bread from this,' she said at last. For Vicki, bread was something that either came out of an oven, hot, or out of a food machine in the TARDIS corridor just outside the console room, sort of lukewarm and tasting ever so slightly of almonds. The Doctor was always telling her that he would get it fixed one day...

With difficulty, Vicki cleared thoughts of the Doctor from her mind. All in the past.

All long in the past.

Meanwhile, next door to where Vicki and Evangeline made their bread, the seemingly friendly neighbours of the Georgiadis family, Dorothea and Damien, were at that precise moment entertaining a recently arrived guest.

'It had better be worth my while coming all of the way to this place, Greek,' said centurion Crispianus Dolavia, removing the black cloak from his head and shoulders. 'I am a busy man, and my time is money.'

'Have I ever let you down before?' asked Damien quickly. 'I am the best spy you have, centurion, and you know it.'

'Keep your voice down,' Dorothea shrieked. 'Do you want the whole neighbourhood to know of these matters?'

The Roman soldier gave the couple the kind of look that he

normally reserved for something that had just crawled out from under a stone. 'Can you voice your objections a little louder, woman?' he asked Dorothea. 'For it is my belief that there is a deaf man in Antioch who did not quite hear your shrillness.'

Bitterly, Dorothea turned away from the men and sloped off into a corner to brood on the insult. The centurion considered, briefly, threatening her with a savage whipping for her insolence towards him, but decided that this could prove counter-productive.

'I am still waiting, potter, to know what information you have that was so urgent it could wait no longer before I heard it?'

Damien paused. 'A payment, for the risks that I take on your behalf, is always much appreciated, centurion. For I am but a simple craftsman earning a poor living amongst the impoverished of this quarter.'

Centurion Crispianus Dolavia sighed deeply, felt into the pocket of his tunic and removed a small bag of coins which he dropped, with a clank, onto the table. 'I am not an ungrateful man, potter. Unless, of course, my time is wasted in which case my gratitude has been known to extend even unto death. Speak and quickly, or forever hold your peace...'

So Damien spoke. 'The next house, whereupon lives Georgiadis the shopkeeper and his fat wife and their mewling brat. I have evidence that they are involved with the schemes of anti-Roman elements and insurrectionists.'

'I am listening,' said the centurion. 'Continue and present your evidence that I may make a decision upon it.'

'They have a new arrival,' said Damien. 'A girl.'

'A Briton,' interjected Dorothea, coming to her husband's side, her wounded feelings seemingly healed by the money on the table.

'A Briton in Byzantium is certainly strange,' noted the Roman, 'but it is hardly proof conclusive of any wrong-doing by these people. Perhaps I should ask them to their face what is their business...'

He reached out for his bag of coins but Damien's hand stopped him.

'Forgive me, centurion,' he said quickly, as Crispianus Dolavia reached for his sword. 'But there is more. The girl asks many curious questions. She very seems interested in the activities of the Roman legions. She has been seen in the Jewish quarter.'

'She is a spy,' Dorothea announced grandly. 'Why else would a Briton be sharing a roof with a Greek family?'

Centurion Crispianus Dolavia considered this for a moment. 'This matter would seem to require further investigation. Thank you for betraying the presence of this girl. I bid you both good night. A blessing be upon your house.'

Chapter Twenty-Three
You're History

And he cometh to the house of
the ruler of the synagogue,
and seeeth the tumult, and them
that wept and wailed greatly.
Mark 5:38

Having left the comparative sanctuary of Hieronymous's home, Barbara Wright didn't have the faintest idea of where she would, or could, go next.

Or, wherever that was, whether she would be safe from persecution there, because of her nationality and pale skin. By the Jews, or the Romans, or the Arabs, or anyone else for that matter.

She wasn't even sure whether, if she looked at someone in a way that they took exception to, whether she would find herself with her throat slashed, bleeding to death and gasping her final breath in the gutter of some Byzantine backstreet, cursing the dark November evening in London that she and Ian Chesterton had decided to investigate their mysterious and unearthly child.

Which is a wonderfully paranoid notion to have constantly in the back of your mind, she thought, as you wander through the streets of a strange and glittering metropolis. In a complex political and social landscape where you are a total outsider and with many inexplicable peoples, cultures and creeds. And in a brutal time of troubles and inhumanities.

A time of great sorrows.

And, to think, Barbara had been the one who had been excited by the prospect of coming to Byzantium in the first place.

That was a good idea.

Silly, silly girl, she reproached herself. Next time you want to go exploring the annals of history, stick to the British Library. At least you normally don't get stabbed in the back while in the reading rooms.

Uncertainty was a key word for Barbara just at the moment. More so than usual. The only thing that she knew for certain was that her future lay somewhere other than sharing a house with the old Pharisee, Hieronymous, however painful for both of them that fact was.

As she walked along the cobbled and narrow streets of the Jewish quarter, she began to formulate a plan in her mind that would at least point the way towards whatever the future held in store for her. Firstly, she decided, she would need to return to the market square, the scene of the apocalyptic horror that had taken her friends from her and destroyed the one constant thread in her life.

It would be painful and hard, but it *was* necessary.

While Hieronymous had been discouraging about the chances of her companions surviving the terrible atrocity of almost two weeks before, there had still been no definitive word from anyone as to whether Ian and Vicki and the Doctor had been among the casualties. Unlikely as it was that any or all of them may have survived, it was, Barbara had decided, time to find out one way or another.

Only once that question had been settled within her own mind could Barbara face the prospect of what was to come.

She felt a little like someone walking towards their own execution.

In the way that only a moment of clarity amid clouds of confusion can produce a line from Steinbeck, an image of Tyburn Hill and the beheading of Mary, Queen of Scots shared sudden and equal prominence within Barbara's mind.

And then they were all gone and she felt hollow, sad and alone.

Yet there was so much going on around her that she could have stopped and observed for hours and days. If she'd been interested in them any longer.

Dionysiac *House of Mysteries* artwork surrounded the approaches to the market-place. These depicted devotees of the Bacchae, and other Euripidian forms of pleasure, performing wild and ecstatic dancing to the accompaniment of the *aulos* and working themselves into a delirium while watched by Diké, the Greek goddess of justice.

Just waiting to administer the pain that must go hand-in-hand with the joy.

Much to her discomfort, this upset Barbara greatly. She had always found masochism (religious, or otherwise) really tacky.

At the entrance to the market was a temple to Isis and Osiris, Egyptian gods drawn into the Hellenistic-Roman spheres of influence, like Byzantium, by those who travelled through the empire and brought back with them to Greco-Roman shores these strange and exotic foreign ideas. The incorporation of the pagan goddess Isis into Roman society was, Barbara remembered, largely due to the mad, bad, and dangerous-to-know Emperor Caligula, who had erected a temple to her on the Campus Martius.

Was that before or after he'd made his horse a senator, Barbara briefly wondered? Then she let the thought pass and moved to the edge of the square itself.

She paused, frozen to the spot by a fear that had no rationality, but was there just the same.

The bloodstains that still marked the spots where so many had been crushed and trampled to untimely deaths made her wince.

For a moment she almost turned and ran from the market-place.

But, just as the fear was present, so also a strange fascination held her steady.

The colours were *brilliant*.

Simply breathtaking.

Blues and purples and reds and yellows of every shade of the rainbow. And beyond.

The mosaic-tiled floor of the market square was chiefly what caught Barbara's attention, despite the dust, the footprints, the blood and the horse manure - a representation of Zeus at the top of Mount Olympus, looking down upon the world.

His world.

The Romans had, of course, replaced an original Greek inscription, renaming the portrait as that of their own Father of the Gods, Jupiter, the centre of family life, of authority and discipline. The God of the Gods themselves.

All around, she noticed statues of Greek deities that had become Roman, like a series of irregular fractions changed beyond all recognition, simply by being rechristened. A beautiful metaphor for the way in which the Romans had simply stretched themselves across the template of Greek culture and had *become* it. Poseidon into Neptune. Artemis into Diana. Hermes into Mercury. Aphrodite into Venus. Prometheus into Vulcan.

Re-Christ-ened... The word, and all of its connotations, amused Barbara greatly.

Just as the bustling, thronging masses of plebeians, freedmen, citizens and slaves, of Greeks, Mesopotamians, Jews, Arabs and Romans excited her. A melting-pot of civilisation. Where the east meets the west and produces something neither one thing nor the other, but all things to all men (and women).

But, at the end of the day, the Doctor had been right when he said that these were not the glorious times that they were often made out to be. For some of the population, anyway. Many features of the social organisation of both the empire in general, and Byzantium in particular, had contributed to the debasing of any existing morality. That was what Barbara had always been led to believe, and here it was before her very eyes. Slavery gave occasion to cruelty and sexual licence. The punishment of alleged criminals through torture, public humiliation and execution by crucifixion showed the casual, almost dismissive brutality of these times. Combined with gladiatorial contests of which Byzantium seemed, thankfully, for the most part free, this reflected a cruel, barbarous outlook on life. The Roman policy of bread and circuses to keep the fickle populace content had prevented any great intellectual and social advances and emphasised, instead, simple sensual pleasures.

Which was all very well if you *liked* that sort of thing, but it wasn't really Barbara's cup of tea. At least, not with any old Tomus, Dickus or Harryus.

Many subsequent Christian writers had argued that the Greco-Roman world was characterised by moral and physical corruption. Some Jewish apologists suggested that the mortality rate sprang from idolatry, but anyone with eyes in their head could see the reality of life in the Roman empire.

And then there was the place of women within the order of things. Although the picture of classical Greek women kept in seclusion and bondage all of their lives had been long since disproved, historically, the average Greek woman's sphere was still definitely within the home. The Romans, on the other hand, were happy for their women to pass from the subjection of the father to the husband. And as for the Jews, a wife might be the mistress of the home, but nowhere else.

Oh, the Byzantines had their entertainments, to be sure. If not bread and circuses, then, at least, bread and spectacles. The lack of an arena within the city was more than made up for by other pleasures, as Barbara had discovered. There were several amphitheatres built into the hillsides that surrounded the city, with richly decorated tiers of colonnaded niches filled with statuary, at which lascivious masques, dramas and tragedies were performed by talented *hypokrites* and amusing comedians. There were the *pankration* athletic contests that accompanied Greek and Roman festivals, which began with a sacrifice and a prayer and, more often than not, ended in bloodshed of a different kind. And there were gymnasia and public baths and widespread social banquets.

All of it fascinating, and yet in its own way as trivial and uninteresting to Barbara as the football matches, Odeon cinemas and fashionable Knightsbridge dinner parties of 1960s London. Dear God, Barbara reflected. It was coming to a pretty pass when the complexities and intrigues of history (and, especially, as unique a historical time as this) didn't excite her any more. Maybe she was just getting jaded by her proximity to it all.

Loose morality, sexual perversion and an unhealthy disregard for the sanctity of human life were not (by any stretch of the imagination) attitudes only to be found here. Barbara resolved that, whatever else happened to her, and wherever she ended up, that she would experience every moment from now on with a spring in her step.

So, with this in mind, she conquered her sudden claustrophobic terror and stepped into the market-place of Byzantium, where her friends and companions from the future had (probably) died.

And, on standing on the Zeus mosaic, a question raised a moment before was fully answered. How, she had wondered several times in the days she spent with Hieronymous, would she feel when she stood where Vicki, Ian and the Doctor had breathed their last breath?

Now, she knew.

She felt nothing. Nothing, but a vague sense of outrage that they had died here, of all places.

Byzantium. A terrible place to die.

Chapter Twenty-Four
Rust Never Sleeps

And she went and told them that had been with him, as they mourned and wept.
Mark 16:10

The *triclinium* dining room of Marcus and Agrinella's villa home was an opulent homage to all of the riches that Marcus's life had brought them. A statue of Ceres, the Goddess of the harvest, in finest Athenian marble (imported at great expense), rested within a tiny fountain in the room's centre. It was surrounded by oil lamps and candles that reflected the trickling flow of water across the arched ceiling in mutated shards like moving pictures.

Agrinella entered the room, hitched up the hem of her *palla* dress and reclined, lazily, on the couch, drinking her wine as she kicked off her sandals and watched with a drunken amusement as they fell to the floor with a hard slap.

She inclined her head to one side, observing the richly coloured painting that decorated the far wall of the *triclinium* from such an angle as she had never seen before. It was a spectacular (and only mildly pornographic) depiction of a Dionysian scene, a baroque representation of the *Villa Item* outside Pompeii. A mostly naked woman was kneeling at the feet of the emperor, her head resting in his lap whilst the demonic figure of Diké, the personification of pleasure and pain, stood behind her. And, all the while, other women (wearing masks to hide their shamed faces) and mythical satyrs and maenads danced in joyous and total abandon, cymbals crashing, scarves whirling aimlessly. 'Glad *someone* is having a good time,' pouted Agrinella as she fell from the couch into a crumpled heap, spilling the wine over her *palla*.

As she struggled to stand and banged noisily on the floor for a slave to come and help her, Marcus entered the room. When he saw Agrinella sprawling on the floor, drunk, a look of disgust and contempt crossed his face.

'My sweet,' Agrinella stammered, 'I have been waiting here for you.'

'Get up,' Marcus snapped. 'You are drunk, madam. And, therefore of no use to man nor beast of the field.'

Agrinella began to cry, hot and shameful tears. 'But you were so long...' she wailed.

'Get up, you drunken mare,' Marcus repeated as he picked Agrinella's fallen cup from the floor, took aim and threw it at her as he would a *pilum* lance at a staked-out prisoner. Agrinella flung up her hands to deflect the impact, but the goblet still caught her a glancing blow on the side of the head and then skittered away across the floor.

The tribune's wife raised her head, her face tear-stained and a thin trickle of blood seeping from her temple where the cup had broken the skin. '*Prolapsus ab alvo*. Bastard son of a whore,' she screamed, suddenly finding the ability to stand that had been denied to her seconds earlier. 'Limp and tiny man of great infamy,' she continued as she advanced on Marcus who was rooted to the spot, unblinking. 'How dare you treat me like some chattel, some thing from the gutters of Rome? My father will have you tied to a horse and dragged through the streets for what you do to me...'

Her voice trailed away and she fell to her knees, weeping, her fists bunched tightly in front of her face to hold in her wracked sobs.

Marcus put a hand on her shoulder. 'Woman, arise,' he said, with a gentle softness that belied the situation. 'Is this any way for the daughter of a legate to behave?' he asked.

Agrinella stared at him and did not reply. 'Whimpering and crawling like a whelped babe. Your father would have *you* dragged through the streets before me for such a show of weakness and self-pity.'

Still Agrinella said nothing. She wiped her eyes without taking them from Marcus's calm and handsome face.

'Is that any way for the wife of a future *praefectus* to behave? For the wife of a future senator?'

'For the wife of a future emperor?' she asked, at last.

'All things in the world are possible,' said Marcus, taking a handful of his wife's golden hair between his fingers and using it to dry a tear on her cheek. 'Without you, I am but *nothing*.'

'And I, you, my wonderful soldier.'

Marcus swept Agrinella off her feet and cradled her in his arms, lifting her to his chest and carrying her towards the door. 'The world is ours for the taking, my heart,' he said as she clung to him, tightly. 'We alone shall inherit the gifts of the Gods.'

The door burst open and a terrified slave stood silhouetted in its frame.

Marcus allowed Agrinella to swing back to the floor. Both heads turned in the direction of the interloper.

'What is the meaning of this loud intrusion?' bellowed Marcus.

'Forgive me, master,' replied the slave, 'Cartethus is nowhere to be found and an important visitor beseeches an audience with you.'

'Get out of my way,' said Antonia Vinicus, pushing the slave away from the door and looking closely at Marcus and Agrinella, their arms still wrapped around each other. 'I pray to all of the Gods that I am not interrupting anything too interesting,' she said with a calculated sneer.

'Antonia,' Marcus replied, with a sigh. 'This is not a particularly good time for social intercourse.'

Agrinella giggled at Marcus's deliberately coital double entendre, but Antonia wiped the smile from her friend's face in an instant.

'Edius Flavia has been arrested,' she said flatly. 'As far as I can ascertain, he was caught *in flagrante delicto* in the chamber of that simpering worm, Felicia.'

'Arrested for what?' asked Marcus, angrily. 'Since when is the taking of a slave to your bed a crime of any description?'

Antonia laughed at Marcus's nativity. 'Since the manipulative, and no doubt by now much richer, *puella meretrix* in question screamed "rape" with ten praetorian guards stationed just outside of her door.'

Now Marcus understood. 'He was tricked by cruel chicanery?'

'Yes, yes, he was a fool unto himself and all others,' Antonia replied. 'And he will pay a heavy and deadly price for his rashness. But now we have a bigger problem to deal with than Edius's damnable libido.'

The shock of these revelations had quickly sobered Agrinella. 'Sweet merciful gods, what are we to do?' she asked in a panic.

'That is very much for your husband to decide,' Antonia told her. 'But whatever it is, make it quick. Calaphilus will not wait for long before he acts.'

Finally Barbara plucked up the courage to take another step into the market-place. And then another. And then another...

Before she knew it she was in the heart of the crowd. Walking steadily and without fear in the very place where Vicki, Ian and the Doctor had last been seen.

Now, what to do?

Suddenly, the reality of the situation struck her. What had she been thinking?

She couldn't simply start asking people if they'd seen a young girl, a handsome man and an old man wandering about the city, could she? Those descriptions alone would make up half of the population of Byzantium.

Just face it, she told herself, they're dead. Let them rest in peace.

At the heart of any Roman city lay the forum, a large open space surrounded by markets, government buildings, baths, arenas and temples. Rich and poor of all of the nationalities of the Roman empire mingled in the bustling forum without barriers or distinctions between the various social classes. Even slaves were free within the forum.

That was something Barbara Wright, of Form 2A at Cricklewood

Grammar School, aged twelve, had written in an exam almost twenty years ago. The teacher, Mr Dolphin, was an otherwise good-natured and likeable man, who had only used the cane on anyoney once (that was when Robert Smedley sang *While shepherds washed their socks by night, all seated on the ground*, during a Christmas assembly). But he had not been at all impressed with Barbara's efforts. 'Simplistic and banal,' he had said, dismissively, in front of the whole class. 'You are capable of much better work than *this* buffoonery, Miss Wright,' he added.

Well, that's one in the eye for you, Mr Dolphin, thought Barbara. Wherever you are.

History, for many like Dolphin, and other dry and stuffy men that she had met throughout her academic life, was not something to be touched and tasted, but rather a series of empty and vacuous facts; a kind of checklist for the mind. Barbara wanted to bring history alive in the hearts of those she taught, as it had been for her when, aged ten, she read a Ladybird book on Captain Cook while confined to bed with whooping cough. She wanted to replace dry and stale accounts of Runnymede and Tilbury docks with real pages from history, torn with the ink still wet from the fabric of time; from Wat Tyler's revolting peasants at Blackheath; Lilburne's Levellers army; the soldiers in their squares at Waterloo with French horses inches from their faces; the sailors clinging to the heaving decks of the Victory at Trafalgar as cannonballs exploded around them.

History that made people want to go out and create history of their own.

That thought cheered Barbara as much as her love of irking the purists always did.

Barbara turned, and started to make her way through the crowd full of a bewildering variety of races, with half a tear struggling for release. She fought to keep it inside herself and seemed to be winning the fight when she felt a tap on her shoulder.

She spun around quickly and found herself facing a Jewish couple, both of whom she was absolutely certain that she had never met before.

'Hello,' she said, trying to smile in a *please don't kill me* way. 'I'm sorry, do we know each other?'

The couple looked at one other for a moment and then returned the smile to Barbara. 'We have not been introduced, but we were within the temple when rabbi Hieronymous saved you from our madness during *Taanith*,' said the man in a friendly and cordial manner. 'We simply wished to apologise to you for this occurrence.'

'Oh,' said Barbara with a mixture of relief and surprise. 'That's all right, I imagine most people were very scared at that time, what with the terrible events in this square and everything.'

The man nodded. 'My mother named me Elisha, so that all the world would know it. And this is my wife, Rebecca.'

'I'm Barbara,' said Barbara, before she remembered that she had introduced herself to Hieronymous at the temple.

'Yes,' said Rebecca. 'Your fame has gone before thee.'

'Really?' Barbara replied, cautiously. 'I wasn't aware of that.'

Elisha laughed, reassuringly. 'Every Jewish man, woman and child in Byzantium knows of you. Hieronymous has blessed thee with his protection, Barbara Wright. You are in an enviable position.'

Barbara wasn't certain whether her position was really that enviable but at least this indicated to her that Hieronymous's influence was continuing to act in her favour. She thanked the couple with a simple blessing from the Torah and hurried away from their slightly unnerving, simultaneous smiles.

'I have heard it said of me that I am one who takes the responsibility of torturing a man under my command, even unto death, either lightly or casually.'

General Gaius Calaphilus picked up a lethal-looking *flagellum*, a wooden-handled whip with several thongs of leather, each weighted with metal balls to make the scourging of prisoners more painful and effective. Gaius swished the instrument through the air where it gave a satisfying rush of noise. 'Requirements and circumstances make such an abhorrence to me a necessity,' the general told Edius Flavia. 'But I want you to know, before I flay you to a bloodied pulp, that this need not be. Not so as to assuage my own conscience, you must understand, for I have none where you are concerned, tribune. But, rather, to save you from your own blind stupidity.'

Despite a reputation that sometimes suggested otherwise, Gaius Calaphilus was neither a cruel nor an unnecessarily violent man. It was true that, under him, the lower ranks were regularly beaten, but no more so than under any other Roman general, and considerably less than many. Executions among Calaphilus's legions, too, were far less common than in those of his numerous contemporaries. Gaius Calaphilus only used force against Roman soldiers when he considered that there was no alternative. He flogged the odd man, here and there, and even the odd legion, as an example to others to do what they were told and do it quickly and well. But he always felt badly about it afterwards.

Which mightn't have meant much to his men, but it allowed Gaius Calaphilus to sleep soundly in his bed at night.

Torture of a Roman citizen was, technically, illegal under the Porcian and Sempronian laws. However it was a permitted way of extracting confessions or of 'examining' the testimony of those suspected of crimes of treason against the state and the empire. For that reason, and that reason alone, Edius Flavia now found himself stripped to his waist and tied with tightly bound leather thongs to the *cruciamentum stauros*, a thick and gnarled wooden stake in the centre of the largest dungeon in the barracks.

The one that the soldiers avoided looking at as they passed.

The one from which *the screams* came.

'It is a very simple principle, Flavia,' Gaius told his tribune. 'Either you inform me of the details of those plots and insurgencies that you have been party to and the names of those that you conspired with or, if you remain silent on these matters, you shall suffer *cruciamentum*.'

With the tribune's back turned to Calaphilus, the general could see Edius Flavia's shoulder twitch at the prospect of a severe and possibly deadly scourging.

Calaphilus had often thought that, when put to the ultimate test, most of the young tribunes who served under him were cowardly and insolent curs who could not stand up to the rigours of physical pain. Now was his chance to find out if he was mistaken in his beliefs. He handed the *flagellum* to the heavily muscled sergeant standing beside him. 'Give him a goodly taste of *this*,' he said. 'But mark you to listen well to whatsoever words he speaks whilst this occurs. And if he reveals his treasons, stop instantly.'

The sergeant indicated that he understood his instructions and took up his position behind Edius Flavia.

'Hold,' continued the general as he walked around the *stauros* and faced Flavia. 'Your choice, tribune,' he continued. 'An ignoble and harsh torment until you talk, which you will. And then the ultimate indignity of public execution. Or, simply name the names.'

Edius Flavia gritted his teeth and said nothing. 'Proceed,' said Calaphilus.

The first stroke cut deep into the flesh of the tribune and Gaius heard the terrible gasp of pain from him as the scourge was withdrawn and the metal balls were sucked from the skin into which they had fixed themselves.

'Speak,' commanded Calaphilus. But there was no reply.

On the fifth blow, Edius's knees sagged and he cried out for mercy and for his mother.

On the eleventh, he called on Jupiter to spare him from the pricks of torment.

By eighteen, Flavia was screaming out the intricate details of the plot against Calaphilus. But still, he would not name the names.

'I tire so of these games, tribune,' Gaius told Flavia after twenty-five blows, with the tribune half-slumped against the *stauros*, his back-flesh caked with smears of blood. 'Stubbornness is not a sign of strength, it is a display of weakness.'

The general turned to the sergeant. 'Salt the wounds and return him to this place tomorrow for a second dose.'

Calaphilus stored the sneaking admiration that he had suddenly acquired for Flavia somewhere dark and hidden. Tomorrow, tongues would be loosened, and the world would seem a much less troublesome place.

Until then, the general would sleep fitfully, if at all, tonight.

Chapter Twenty-Five
Give 'Em Enough Rope

And when he had looked round about
on them with anger, being grieved for
the hardness of their hearts
Mark 3:5

'Are you able to translate this passage, Doctor? I, myself, am having abominable difficulties with the inflections and the tense.'

Rayhab handed the Doctor a fragment of frayed and torn papyrus written in a scratchy and indistinct hand that the Doctor recognised instantly as that of the prophet Mark himself.

'It seems to be something about sending a message to someone,' added Amos, helpfully. 'It's probably part of one of the letters from Paul to the churches of the nations.'

The Doctor ran his finger along the first ink-line of the words, as though the grooves left in the papyrus by the pen of the prophet had stored something solid and tangible within them. Like a vinyl record, or a photograph.

He began to read the words aloud, haltingly at first, but with increased confidence as he understood the context and form of the language. As he did so, Reuben dipped his stylus nib into the thick black ink and wrote in a beautiful copperplate script the translated words into a bound codex that he had reserved for definitive versions of the text.

'It's not Aramaic. Or Hebrew,' the Doctor noted. 'I think it is a form of early Greek. How *very* unusual. It says... "ΑΡΧΗ ΤΟΥ ΕΥΑΓΓΕΛΙΟΥ ΙΗΣΟΥ ΧΡΙΣΤΟΥ [ΥΙΟΨ ΘΕΟΥ.] ΚΑΘΩΦ ΓΕΓΡΑΠΤΑΙ ΕΝ Τς ΗΣΑΙΑ ΤΩ ΠΡΟϑΗΤΗ, ΙΔΟΥ ΑΠΟΣΤΕΛΛΩ ΤΟΝ ΑΓΓΕΛΟΝ ΜΡΝ Oς ΚΑΤΑΟΣΚΕΥΑΣΕΙ ΤΗΝ ΟΔΟΝ ΣΟΨ",' he continued.

'"This being the good word and sacred of the sun prophet, sending out a preference message to his face for them all"?' asked Rayhab, scratching his beard.

'No, no, no. "This is the beginning of the gospel of Jesus Christ, the Son of God. As it is written in the prophets, behold, I send forth my messenger before thy face, who shall prepare the way for thee",' the Doctor replied, without looking up from the text.

For a moment there was silence within the cave. And then Reuben began to laugh hysterically. 'My God,' he said. In praise, as opposed to blasphemy. 'It is the missing piece. The opening verses. This is what we have been searching for.'

'And now you've found it,' asked the Doctor, still with little apparent interest in his momentous discovery, 'what, exactly, are you going to do with it, hmm?'

In the spartan surroundings of general Gaius Calaphilus's quarters, a meeting took place that mere hours earlier would have been unthinkable.

The summit reminded Ian of Roosevelt, Churchill and Stalin sitting side by side at Yalta, smiling falsely for the official photographs before getting out the maps to partition up Europe.

Ian rose to his feet as Gemellus entered with Thalius Maximus behind him, casting furtive glances all around, still wary of plots and treachery.

It was noticeable that Calaphilus did not stand in the presence of his *praefectus*, but rather remained seated, fanning himself against the dry and oppressive heat of midday.

'*Praefectus*,' he said in a flat monotone. 'Welcome to my humble abode. May the gods look kindly upon those who enter this house with liberty in their hearts.'

'Oh, for God's sake, knock it off you two,' Ian said, which cut through the rhetoric. 'You both know full well why Gemellus and I have arranged this meeting. It's in both of your interests that you find some common ground, so get on with it and stop procrastinating or I'll give the pair of you a ruddy good biff on the conk.'

Neither man looked entirely sure of the exact nature of Ian's threats, but the outburst itself was seemingly enough for them both to sit opposite each other at a table in the centre of the room. Ian and Gemellus joined then, Ian beside the general, Gemellus at the elbow of the *praefectus*.

Gaius and Thalius eyed each other suspiciously, neither wishing to be the man who spoke first. So Ian did it for them. 'You know,' he began, 'where I come from, men of honour, of real integrity, are astonishingly rare. Oh, you meet the odd one every now and then, but you remember such occasions because they don't happen very often. Counting Gemellus, I'm sitting in a room with three of them. That should be the kind of memory I carry to my grave. But, you see, the thing is, if you two don't realise that you're on the same side then it's likely that my grave is a damn-sight closer to me than I, nor either of you two, I suspect, would like.'

Still neither the general nor the politician spoke. 'Our young Briton's sentiments are words of wisdom that belie his tender years,' continued Gemellus. 'But words of wisdom can also be lies. His words are the truth. You owe it to him to make his vision occur.'

Thalius Maximus began to say something. Stopped. Started again, then ground to a halt for a second time, shaking his head. 'Wise counsel is always appreciated,' he finally noted. 'Gemellus gives it to me until I am ready to drown in it. But...' He paused and looked directly at Ian. 'By what right do you presume to tell the general and I how to conduct the emperor's business?'

'Good question,' chorused Calaphilus.

Ian threw up his hands in exasperation. 'Stop talking like men divorced from reality,' he demanded. 'You are not ostriches, either of you, but unless you get your head out of the sand, you're going to die, and Byzantium will belong to those who would see it drown in an ocean of blood. Is that what you want? Because that's what will happen.'

'Do you take me for a squint-eyed dunderhead? For that would be folly in the extreme, young Briton, and our friendship would be at an end,' said Calaphilus, harshly.

'You are nobody's fool, Gaius,' Ian assured him. 'And this is the only way, believe me.'

An uneasy silence settled over the group.

'Come on,' Ian bellowed, breaking the hush. 'Talk to each other before we all croak.'

'We could, I suppose, discuss areas of mutual interest,' Thalius said at last.

'Such as?' bullied Calaphilus.

'Not dying a horrible and needless death, for one,' Ian interrupted. 'That would seem to be mutually beneficial, wouldn't you say?'

The *praefectus* nodded, slowly, while the general said nothing. 'Wake up, gentlemen. The assassins are at the palace gates; both of your lives are in dire peril. We have to do something.'

'I am doing something,' Calaphilus countered. 'Already I have, under close arrest, one of the men I suspect to be involved in the outrages.' he looked closely at Maximus. 'Edius Flavia, *praefectus*, a tribune of most high rank whom you, yourself, were instrumental in helping to obtain his posting.'

Thalius ignored the general's accusing stare and shook his head, sadly. 'I knew his father. A *great* man. Be you certain of Flavia's involvement in these hideous crimes?'

'Intelligence informs me thus,' replied Calaphilus. 'And I believe that I know the identities of several others who also conspire against me. As yet, however, Flavia has not been forthcoming with confirmation of these names and, thus, I am obliged not to act upon my numerous suspicions.'

The *praefectus* seemed to find this amusing. 'We all know Marcus Lanilla and Fabius Actium seek both of our deaths with relish, Gaius; one does not have to be the wisest man in the Pantheon to see such a blindingly obvious conceit. I shall go further and suggest that such plots also involve Lanilla's wife, the viperous Agrinella. Add in a plethora of local officials, bruised by perceived blockages to their political prospects, a few middle-ranking army officers, ambitious to crawl up the greasy pole of field promotion, one or two slaves promised their freedom, and yes, Gaius, perhaps even the former wife of a weak and tired *praefectus*, and you have a ripe and merry band of conspirators, poised for their moment in the sun.'

'Proof, however, is another matter, *praefectus*,' the general replied sarcastically. 'For some of us still believe in the tenets of Roman law.'

'A law including impunity from *cruciamentum* which you have, presumably, broken in the attempt to extract a damning confession and a conspirator's list from Flavia,' Thalius argued. 'Have you whipped him near unto death, or is there still something left that *I* may question as the prosecutor of this city?'

'Stop bickering like children,' Ian said, rolling his eyes. 'Gemellus, what have we done?' he asked.

'Begun a process. A dialogue,' the adviser replied. 'Gentlemen, we have begun to discuss mutual interests; surely maintaining order amid the anarchy of this part of the empire would fall into such a category?'

'Of course,' snapped Calaphilus. 'Every good Roman wishes to see the empire strong and well managed.' He gave Thalius a positively lethal glance. 'Is that not so, *praefectus*?'

'I want nothing more than to serve the empire and maintain its position.'

'You are two proud men,' Ian said. 'And perhaps we can make you realise that you have a lot more in common than may, at first, appear to be so.'

The room was plunged, again, into an eerie silence, broken only by the sound of Gaius's fan swishing through the air.

'I am ready to listen to reason,' Thalius said at last. 'And I suspect that the general is also willing.'

The row of twelve guards lined up in the cobbled street of the Greek quarter, stood rigidly to attention and then, at the barked command of their sergeant, shouldered their arms. Captain Drusus Felinistius walked along the row of plume-helmeted soldiers, their gleaming silver breastplates reflecting his own face back at him. He stopped next to legionnaire Marinus Topignius and tapped him on the arm with his *gladius*.

'Stand by the door, legionnaire,' he said, quickly. 'Move on my instructions.'

'Aye, sir,' said the soldier from the side of his mouth, so tight was the chinstrap that clamped his helmet to his head. 'Just like old times, sir.'

Felinistius was thinking exactly that. Just like fifteen years ago in Judaea when he and his men had formed the most feared and respected murder squad in all of Rome's legions. After such days as those, Byzantium had little to offer by way of comparison.

'Remember,' the captain told his remaining soldiers, 'this action should not require casualties. Straight in, seek out the objective, secure it and straight out. Any local resistance, you are authorised to use force, but make sure it is only so much as is necessary. If anyone goes in swinging their sword indiscriminately, I shall have you publicly flogged, is that understood?'

There were grunts of acknowledgement from the men.

'Is that understood?' bellowed Felinistius.

'Aye, sir,' they chorused, loudly.

In the window of one of the houses nearby, a curtain flickered, and a stray shard of candlelight briefly illuminated a portion of the street.

'Go,' shouted the captain, turning towards Marinus Topignius. 'Go, go, go.'

Two swift blows from the legionnaire's foot and the door to the house burst open, light flooding into the street from inside.

The soldiers poured into the house and Felinistius brought up the rear, arriving to the sound of a woman's high-pitched scream.

'Silence,' he cried as he stooped to enter through the low-framed door. 'Where is the girl?'

In the room, Felinistius saw a man pinned to the floor by two of the soldiers, a look of anguish and pain on his face as one of them tied his hands together with coarse rope. Beside the fire, a large woman, her face reddened by a single, stinging blow to the cheek, was also sprawled on the floor, a legionnaire towering over her, ready to repeat the dose if she gave him any cause. 'Where is the girl?' repeated the captain angrily.

'Here, sir,' said Marinus Topignius, throwing back a rough blanket under which cowered two pairs of terrified eyes.

Felinistius marched across the room to the two young girls and demanded, 'Which, amongst you, is the Briton?'

'Neither of us,' said Vicki, quickly. 'We're both as Greek as...' She stumbled to a pause. 'As Greek can be,' she concluded.

'This one,' the captain noted, and the rough arms of two soldiers hauled Vicki from beneath the blanket. 'She is the one. No Greek child would be so forward. Bring her.' He turned to Georgiadis, struggling against his bonds. 'Our business is concluded in this place, Greek,' he said, sweeping out of the door without another word, followed by his troops, dragging the terrified Vicki with them.

Chapter Twenty-Six
Jigsaw Feeling (A Poem for Byzantium)

And they watched him, whether he would
heal him on the sabbath day;
that they might accuse him.
Mark 3:2

Byzantium. The imperial city.

Approached from the sea, as most travellers would do, their ships passed from the Aegean through the Hellespont and then crossed the foaming, brilliant Sea of Marmara, the *Pontus Euxinus* of antiquity.

From there, the city dramatically rose as if by a trick of the light from the peninsular between the pale-blue sky and the hazy waters of the Golden Horn, the scimitar-shaped estuary of the Bosphorus. The domes and minarets and towers of Byzantium rose from the hills on either side of the deeply cleft mouth of the river, straddling the entrance to it like a colossus.

Twin wooden bridges linked the muddy banks of the Golden Horn. To the east lay Asia, where could be glimpsed the oldest part of the city, the Bedouin and Mesopotamian quarters at the foot of the Galata hills and amid sundry archeological ruins of earlier settlements that had been swept clean from the face of the land by the desert winds. And the wrath of a vengeful God.

But Byzantium was unique in that it was the only city on the planet to span two continents. On the western shore, at the very tip of Europe, stood the sea walls leading to the Greek and Jewish quarters and the Hellenic-Roman city centre; the Theodosian forum, the temples, the pavilions, the public baths and several curved amphitheatres. In the far west, where the outside city walls met the sea was the *Porta Aurea*, the golden gate. The walls were so thick and strong that on several occasions before the Romans came, they had withstood invaders like the Gauls and the Seleucid king Antiochus II, who had captured Chalcedon and other towns in the region.

Behind these walls began the seven hills of Byzantium. The first settlers in this place had been shepherds, Dorian Greeks who had come from these hills during the winter to shelter their flocks. Later came the Spartans, who fortified the peninsular and made it into the stronghold that it was now. Along with other Greek colonies, Byzantium was a *polis*, a city-state, its government usually democratic, though there had been occasions when it was controlled by oppressive oligarchies and despotic tyrants. The Romans had come to Thrace 170 years before, organising their empire in Asia and taking new lands. Byzantium, unconquered in a millennia, fell in a bloodless surrender and entered into a formal alliance with Rome, in which it enjoyed the protection of the empire and, though paying an annual tribute, was able to retain its free-city status. The Romans linked the new province to Italy with the Via Egnatia, a chariot road leading from the Adriatic coast to Thrace, with Byzantium lying at its eastern terminus.

The city had maintained excellent relations with Rome until early in the reign of the emperor Augustus who had, for reasons best known to himself, stripped it of its possessions in Bithynia and stationed a garrison within the town itself, instead of at its outskirts as previously. Although it was still, technically, an independent city-state, few of its inhabitants were under any illusions as to who the real rulers of Byzantium were.

Sweeping down the narrow streets that ran at right angles to the northern city walls, the traveller would exit into the circular Amphitheatre Cordelius which led directly into the *Villa Praefectus* and the barracks of the Byzantine army. If any such metaphorical traveller had been in Byzantium on this particular day, and possessed wings with which to fly through the window of the *Villa Praefectus* and into the atrium chamber, then he or she or it would have seen the *praefectus*'s wife frothing at the mouth in a furious rage.

'You had no right,' the lady Jocelyn told Felicia, her trembling handmaiden, as the contrite girl knelt before her and wept at her feet. 'To condemn a man of noble birth to the brutal and loathsome attentions of such as Gaius Calaphilus can have no justification of any form.'

Jocelyn slumped like an exhausted mother into her husband's throne, shaking her head sadly. 'What is to be done with you?'

'He forced himself upon me, lady,' Felicia said between anguished tears.

'And?' demanded Jocelyn angrily, gripping the sides of the throne until her knuckles bled white. 'You are nothing but a ministrant, *jade*. The only reason for your existence is the unquestioning service of your betters. And Edius Flavia, despite his peculiarities, is most assuredly better than the likes of you.'

Emboldened by a foolishly sincere belief in her own innocence, Felicia prostrated herself before Jocelyn, placing her head on the feet of the wife of the *praefectus*. 'Begging your most gracious pardon, lady, but general Gaius Calaphilus took a different view.'

Although muffled, the words carried perfectly well to Jocelyn, who lashed out a foot and kicked the handmaiden painfully in the ribs. 'I am thy mistress, *jade*, and your conniving knavery will not save thee from my wrath. I should have been told of what occurred beneath my own roof. Get thee hence to the slave quarters and await the manifestation of my displeasure against you, thou most wicked child.'

Felicia stood, her eyes downcast. Woefully, she began to speak but was hushed to silence by Jocelyn as she nodded to Drusus, who stood behind the handmaiden.

'Have this wretch of a girl taken from my sight,' Jocelyn announced as Drusus hustled Felicia away.

The significance of this little scene may have been lost on any casual spectator, even one with wings. But it is certain that, had they also been party to a meeting taking place less than a mile across the city, at the edge of the Jewish quarter at Haghia near the bejewelled synagogue and the copper market, they would not have been so confused.

The house was innocuous, like a hundred others, completely anonymous to anyone as a hotbed of rebellion and plots. That, presumably, was why Matthew Basellas, Ephraim and Yewhe and their Zealot brothers were within the house, living in the shadows of the city. Stealth was their watchword as they moved about Byzantium's nooks and crannies, scheming and searching for the opportunities to create mayhem and destruction.

As was the Zealot way.

Basellas was a changed man since the murder, at his own orders, of his brother. Simeon had been a strategist of considerable brilliance and Basellas had leaned on his brother's wisdom and expertise on more occasions than he had chosen not to. Now the true and brutal nature of Matthew Basellas was beginning to emerge with no one to hold it in check any longer. Ephraim was nothing but a glorified 'yes' man, agreeing, with ever-increasing sycophancy to each and every one of Basellas's outrageous schemes. Yewhe and Benjamin and others like them within the Zealots such as the miller, Saul Acunes, were willing lieutenants, perfectly happy and willing to die in the pursuance of any of the hair-brained situations that Basellas dreamed up next.

Today, however, more mundane matters were being discussed. Simple, yet deadly, assassination. 'Benjamin has been given his target,' Acunes told the assembled *kananaios* council.

'And his *sicarii* knife?' asked Ephraim who roared with laughter at his own cleverness until he realised that no one else was laughing with him. 'And I say unto you, good luck and fortune to that most blessed of our sons of Zealotry, that he may strike quickly, like the scorpion, and with much secrecy.'

Though he was stating the obvious, Ephraim's rousing wishes were met with a murmured chorus of approval. 'What say you, Matthew?' he asked, seeking the support of his leader.

'Knives into black hearts,' said Basellas in a slow, almost painful drawl. 'Black Roman hearts. Yes. Black. Like their eyes, mirrors to their black souls...'

Ephraim and Yewhe exchanged nervous glances and then, almost simultaneously, offered their verbal support.

'Fine words, Matthew,' noted Ephraim.

'I shall follow you to the ends of the earth, my leader,' noted Yewhe.

And both, despite the livid madness bubbling in the eyes of their commander, meant every word.

An aerial view of the city would only be possible for birds and angels but let us suppose, for the briefest of moments, that our winged traveller existed outside of the realms of fantasy.

High above the rooftops of the Jewish quarter, the highest point within the city was the tower of Nebuchadnezzar, named after the Babylonian king whose dreams the prophet Daniel had successfully interpreted. At its very apex, the Pharisees Titus and Phasaei stood against the stone ramparts, hundreds of feet above the ant-like people milling around below them. It was, both men simultaneously decided, like a vision of hell from the heights of heaven.

Zeus's face stared back at them from the forum mosaic below, mocking the Jews for their disbelief in Greece and its gods.

But Greece, like the Jews, had found itself enslaved.

'Hieronymous is fatally weakened by the choices that he makes, particularly those with regard to the gentile woman,' Phasaei noted. 'For, is it not written...?'

'Probably,' interrupted Titus before Phasaei had the chance to trot out another of his stock clichés. 'He is weakened, certainly, although whether it shall prove to be his downfall, I myself have doubts upon this matter. I like not this woman, so clever and wily in her ways. Nevertheless, Hieronymous has made his choice. And he must live by it. Or otherwise.' Titus turned to face out across the city and shielded his eyes from the harsh reflection of the sun. He looked across the central market square, and towards the city limits and beyond. 'This is a unique place and a unique time, Phasaei,' he noted absent-mindedly. 'Hieronymous once asked me whether I could live within any of history's pages, whence would it be? I ask you the same question.'

'In the olden days of yore,' said Phasaei instinctively. 'The time of Moses and Aaron and Joshua. When the law was the law, and there was no petitioning of the Lord with prayer. And you, my good brother, whence shall be your time?'

'My time is now,' Titus said simply. 'And it shall be, hereafter.'

Down within the forum, the bustle and rush of the day was beginning to drain the energies of those exposed to the ravages of the afternoon heat.

Even the hyperactive juggler who spent each and every day nimbly dancing in a perpetual motion seemed to have surrendered to the sun and gone for a nice lie-down.

Nikos, the bread-stall owner, sat on an upturned log behind his table of breads, his legs sticking out from the stump and keeping it upright with a feat of balancing that would have been impressive to anyone watching. If it were not so abominably hot.

He removed a piece of cloth from his toga and wiped the sweat from his eyes.

Business was slow on a day that gave slothfulness a good name.

'Thirteen loaves, good patron,' said a voice from under the shadow of the stall's canopy. Nikos leaned forward and then stood up, excitedly, as Daniel allowed a handful of battered coins to fall onto the stall.

'Thirteen, say you?' asked Nikos, calculating that such a purchase would almost double his sales for the day. 'You have many mouths to feed, stranger?'

Daniel said nothing, looking casually around him as crowds briefly mingled and then dispersed in an ebb and flow like the turning of the tide. 'I come from a very large family,' Daniel noted, finally. 'And it is growing all the time.'

'Wait a moment,' Nikos said as he began to wrap the loaves. 'I know you. Your mother had cause to name you Daniel, yes? You are a friend of James, the Christian?'

'No, I am not,' said Daniel flatly.

'Yes, you are,' replied a convinced Nikos.

'No, I am not,' repeated Daniel.

'I am sure of it.'

'You are mistaken,' Daniel said, denying his allegiances for the third time before breakfast. Then he hissed, 'What are you saying?' at the Greek.

Nikos looked nervously around, although he wasn't certain why. 'I know what you are, impatient youth, but I fail to understand your fear in everyone else knowing of it. Your faith is perfectly legal, is it not?'

'The law of man is corrupt and open to barter,' Daniel said in a harsh whisper. 'We are persecuted for what we are and what we believe, and no law can put asunder such persecutions,' he continued, hurriedly picking up the bread and turning away from the stall-owner.

'Wait,' called Nikos. For a moment, he thought that Daniel would break into a sprint away from the stall, as though he had the devil at his heels. Then, almost as an afterthought, the young man turned back to the stall, wearily.

'Yes?'

'In your haste you neglected to take the coinage to which you are due.'

Daniel snatched up a drachma that Nikos offered to him and, again, began to move away. 'You are *so* paranoid, my friend,' Nikos shouted after him. 'Who would wish to persecute you?'

As he said this, both his eyes, and those of Daniel, moved to the trio of Roman soldiers sitting in the shade of the temple, a dozen paces to the right of Nikos's stall. One of the Roman legionnaires raised his head at the sound of heightened voices but, after a second of seeking out the source of the brief commotion, he lowered it again and returned his attention to his wine and his comrades. Too tired, and too hot, to be bothered with such trivialities.

Run, Nikos silently mouthed under his breath, as he looked back towards Daniel, only to find the young man rooted to the spot in sheer terror. 'Run like the wind, Christian,' he whispered, knowing that his words would not be heard by anyone, least of all those for whom they were intended.

For a second, there was complete and awesome silence within the market-place. An unnatural calm as though time itself had become trapped in amber. The three legionnaires were all staring into the half-distance, their thoughts on good wine and cheap women to bed. Nikos looked at them and, for an instant, he seemed to leave his own body, looking down on the market-place from above as if he were a bird. Or an angel.

And it was in this curious and unnatural state that he saw, clearly, the young man with the *sicarii* knife slip into position behind Luke Panathaikos, the *publicani* tax collector of great infamy who was pausing as he crossed the square to straighten his robes.

Despite the contemptuous reputation that Panathaikos had acquired amongst his own people, Nikos quite liked the *publicani* and certainly didn't wish to see any harm come to him. 'No,' he cried in a disembodied wail and, in the blinking of an eye, he was back staring across the square from his own vantage point as the knife sank between Panathaikos's ribs and was then removed, cleaned and pocketed in one slick and rapid movement.

'Stop! Murder!' he cried, pointing an accusing finger at the Jewish youth of seemingly no more than sixteen years, who turned, startled, and with hatred in his eyes stared at Nikos as, behind him, Luke Panathaikos slumped to the ground.

'Murder! Murder!' shrieked Nikos. From the corner of his eye, he could see Daniel, still glued to the ground, looking at the fallen body of the tax collector with horror on his face. But then any attention to the Christian was lost as the square erupted in blur of noise and movement.

Somewhere, a woman screamed and, at exactly the same time, a small clay jar was dropped at the pottery stall next to Nikos and smashed on the mosaic tiles of the forum floor. The murderer was turning and running, pushing those too slow to move out of his way. Someone made a grab for him and the thick-bladed knife flashed through the air again.

A second later, there was much blood and a cry of pain.

As this occurred, all across the square, those in authority began to react. The three legionnaires sprang to their feet and were sprinting across the forum like Olympian runners. Other Romans and citizens were joining in the pursuit. Nikos, in a moment of madness, found himself leaping over his bread-stall and taking a couple of half-hearted paces in the direction in which the assassin had fled.

Then he looked at the slain body of Luke Panathaikos, encircled in a rapidly widening pool of red, and came to his senses, turned around and went back to his stall, his thoughts of heroics rudely shattered by a sudden vision of his own mortality.

The chase was on, the quarry scampering towards the mazy labyrinth of the Jewish quarter and, if he was lucky, sanctuary.

Behind him closed running, shouting, armed men, their breathless cries gibberish to the assassin's ears. A *pilum*, the short-armed spear of the Roman infantryman, flew past the assassin's head and thudded into a wooden door where it shuddered with a satisfying burr of vibration. Another followed, again narrowly missing the young man.

Benjamin, the Zealot, his hatred of Romans undimmed by time or experience, almost turned and gloated at his pursuers' poor marksmanship. He wished that he could; wished that he could stop to taunt the murderous and draconian dictators at his back. To leave them purple-faced and hopping mad at the fleet-footed assassin who had crept into the heart of their citadel and slain their collaborating ally.

Many of the Zealots objected to the Roman descriptions

of them as *terrorists*. They were freedom-fighters, they argued, a resistance movement dedicated to the freedom of their people and their adopted city from the oppression of any occupying force.

Benjamin, on the other hand, admired the term. If the terror being felt was by Romans, then he was proud to be the instrument of that terror.

He spun quickly around the next corner, his feet slipping on a patch of half-dried mud. His arms pinwheeled as he fought to maintain his balance and, with the grace of Jehovah, he staggered on for five or ten paces and was then back running again at his fastest.

The chasing group was led by the three Roman legionnaires from the forum, Cecius Corvectionious, Octavius Hamhabisu and Marinus Topignius, all veteran members of the elite, premier-division squad of captain Drusus Felinistius. The heart-bursting chase left many trailing in its wake, but not these three. For they could run all day and all night, up and down mountains with back-packs full of rocks, if it was required of them by their captain, or their general, or their emperor.

These were hard men who had seen service and wars across the empire. In Judaea. In Britain. In Germanicus. Different colours, different shades, in each land mistakes were made, but not by them. As each new dawn faded, they fought the indigenous tribes with their primitive weapons and tactics, never fearing for one second that they, or their legions could lose.

Romans *didn't* lose.

At the corner, as the Jewish boy almost came crashing to the ground, Marinus, leading the pursuers, came within inches of the assassin's back. But then with lightning speed, the boy slipped away again from the Roman's grasping hands, increasing his lead by three yards, four, five, six...

Leather-soled sandals created a rapid pitter-patter on the bare, impacted dirt of the twisting streets. More of the chasing group were dropped until there were only Roman soldiers, and fewer of them than before, left running.

Roman soldiers, and the boy.

And then, from the shadows of yet another corner, a shape emerged and collided with Benjamin, sending him spinning and sprawling to the ground. The impact was bone-crunching and, for a second, everyone chasing stopped dead in their tracks. Then, despite the ache in his side, Benjamin the Zealot raised himself from the ground and held out his knife before him.

'Come ye, and taste this mighty weapon, Roman dogs. You sons of mother-whores. Whom shall be first to feel her bittersweet kiss?'

Marinus Topignius held out his arms to stop any of his offended colleagues from rushing past him and tackling the child-assassin alone. 'Be not foolish now, lad, we mean you no harm,' he said feeling idiotic at talking to the boy in such a hackneyed way. The Jew had killed in plain sight. His life was done and he knew that. The only alternative now to a date with the *stauros* and the javelin on Beylerbey hill, was to be hacked to pieces here and now by Marinus and his brother warriors, at least one or two of whom he would, in all probability, take with him.

Marinus didn't particularly like the idea of that and, judging from the lack of those rushing to get past him, neither did many of his fellow legionnaires.

The stand-off was broken suddenly, and with little ceremony.

Marinus felt a pressure behind him and turned his head to find the bear-like figure of Erastus, the cadet trainer, moving through the crowd of static soldiers.

'Leave this child to me,' he grunted as he moved towards Benjamin.

'I shall slay you,' shouted the Zealot, juggling his knife from hand to hand.

'You shall try. Of that I have no possible doubt,' Erastus noted, sadly. 'One life ends here, Jew, and it shall not be mine.'

A heavily-booted foot lashed out and caught Benjamin on the point of his elbow, throwing the knife from his hand as he tried to bring it down on Erastus's trunk-like thigh.

With the speed and grace of a panther, the trainer was behind Benjamin and a thick length of cord was wrapped around the boy's neck.

Expertly, Erastus held the two ends of the cord in one giant hand and tightened them, as the boy's eyes bulged large and white in their sockets and his tongue drooped from his mouth, gagging and flapping like a stranded bird.

With his other hand Erastus grasped the back of Benjamin's head and, with a minimum of fuss, snapped his neck at the top of the vertebrae, killing him instantly before the garrotte could tighten and strangle the boy to a slow and painful death.

'I made it quick,' Erastus told the corpse as it dropped to the ground. 'Just as you made it quick for your victim. Be thankful that he did not linger or you, assuredly, would still be suffering.'

Marinus Topignius approached the dead boy. 'He is a Zealot,' he told Erastus. 'He is known to us, as are his affiliations with the criminal Basellas.'

Erastus nodded, still staring at the body.

'Give him a decent burial,' he noted. 'And tell his mother that he died quickly and well.'

In the market-place rumour quickly reached Nikos that the killer had been dealt with before the body of the tax collector had even been removed and the blood cleaned up.

It was a relief to the little stall owner, for he did not appreciate the thought of the murderer returning in the night to silence the loudest witness to his crimes.

He looked again at young Daniel, still staring with a terrified fascination at the corpse of Luke Panathaikos which was even at this moment being picked up by a number of Roman auxiliaries and carried from the square. Nikos followed their progress, reflecting that Luke was now free of all earthly worries. Was he happier now, or in Hades suffering the opening stages of an eternity of torments? Or, as some believe, was Luke now merely dead and gone, his body to be food for worms, with no better (or worse) place awaiting his spirit?

Nikos would like to have debated the philosophical questions concerned with such matters, particularly as, to everyone still around, buying bread seemed to be the furthest thing from their minds. But, when he looked back to the place where Daniel had stood seconds before, the young Christian was gone, having slipped into the forum crowd like a thief into the night.

And thus life and death in Byzantium, to the neutral observer, continued much as it had always done.

People lived, slaves were treated as slaves and accepted their lot accordingly, the Romans ruled to the disgust of some and the acceptance of others. Some people got rich, some people remained poor. And life went on.

Until death ended it.

In the Greek quarter, as the savage heat of the day finally began to exhaust itself, Crispianus Dolavia arrived at the home of the potter, Damien, and his wife, Dorothea, with a view to paying them further for information rendered.

He had been pleased with the last morsel that they had given him - the revelation about the young Briton girl whose presence in the Greek quarter had been a mystery. Last evening, the home of the family with whom she was living had been raided and the girl was now under the protectorate of the forces of Rome.

Soon they would know who she was and from whence she came. And, more importantly, what she was doing in Byzantium.

So Damien and his wife had proved useful, as they had on many occasions past. And Crispianus was grateful to them. He arrived at the door, his pockets full of coins for them if they could provide him with more of the same.

But something was wrong, the centurion knew that the

moment that he rapped on their door and found that it creaked open by itself.

In the bedroom of the Greek house, he found the blood-splattered bodies of the potter and his wife, murdered in their beds.

As he put a hand to his mouth to stop himself from vomiting, Crispianus reflected that such a reaction was most surprising. He had seen death in all of its shades and forms across the empire. Perhaps it was the knowledge that he, and his bargain with Damien and Dorothea, was responsible for their murders that upset the centurion.

But the feeling didn't last long.

After all, this was the inevitable fate of all who spy in Byzantium.

It was simply a question of when.

EPISODE FIVE
FOUR LANE ENDS

Have ye not read in the book of Moses, how
in the bush God spake unto him, saying,
I am the God of Abraham, and the God
of Isaac, and the God of Jacob?
He is not the God of the dead,
but the God of the living
Mark 13:26–27

Chapter Twenty-Seven
The Culture Bunker, Part Seven — Losing My Religion

And the veil of the temple was rent
in twain from the top to the bottom
Mark 15:38

It was all very strange for Vicki after her two weeks spent in the loving, yet impoverished, home of the Georgiadis family.

After she had been manhandled from the Greek quarter the previous evening and frog-marched back to the Roman barracks, each of her questions about where they were taking her, and why, had been met with a stony silence, then irritated looks from the legionnaires and finally a stinging mouthful of Latin swearing from the sergeant, who hauled her into the Roman compound, dragged her up a steep flight of stairs and pushed her into a bedroom that, although poorly decorated and unfurnished, was still the lap of luxury compared to what she'd been used to recently.

The atmosphere, however, was sterile and dowdy compared to Evangeline's fireside and Vicki quickly climbed into bed, pulled the blankets around her and didn't sleep at all, listening instead to the sounds of activity within the compound.

The next morning, they came for her early and she found herself in a military office facing the captain who had led the raid on the Georgiadis home.

'Good morning,' he said, without looking up from a scroll that he was reading, as the gruff and snarling sergeant pointed to the seat opposite the captain and made it clear that Vicki should sit in it and speak when she was spoken to.

So she did.

'I apologise for any unnecessary roughness yesterday evening,' the captain said, finally raising his head and giving Vicki a little half-smile that, she imagined, he reserved for people that he wasn't about to torture. 'We knew not with whom we were dealing. My name is Drusus Felinistius, tell me yours please.'

'Vicki. That's, erm, short for Vickius Pallister... us.' She returned the half-smile and then sat back, swinging her legs beneath the chair. The captain gave his sergeant an odd look and signalled that he should leave.

'And you are a Briton, yes?'

'Uh-huh,' affirmed Vicki, proudly. 'I'm from Londinium.'

'Your Latin is most excellent, Vickius.'

For a fraction of a second, Vicki tittered coyly, flattered that so handsome a man was giving her a compliment. Then, just as quickly, her indignity rose towards her Roman captor and she demanded to know what he wanted with her.

Captain Drusus Felinistius seemed surprised. 'You were being held captive against your will by those Greek *people*.' He pronounced the last word as though it were something vile. 'They will, incidentally, be dealt with most severely.'

'No, you've got it all wrong,' cried Vicki quickly. 'They were kind to me. Georgiadis rescued me when there was all that fuss and bother in the forum, and I lost my family. They've been looking after me.'

'And you were not abused, or forced into slavery by them...?'

Vicki considered mentioning the work that Evangeline made her do around the house, but then decided that wasn't really what the captain had meant. 'Not at all. I should hate for them to be badly treated for an act of kindness.'

'Very well,' said Drusus Felinistius, 'your loyalty to them does you great credit. Nevertheless, it is unbecoming for a citizen of the Roman empire such as yourself to be living with subhuman scum like the Greeks. We will find a place for you within Roman society.'

Vicki snorted with derision. 'The Greeks are a million times more civilised than the Romans,' she said, standing up. 'I know the drill, I'll be in my room when you want me.'

'So, you think that word of the general and the *praefectus* forming an alliance might have leaked out?' Ian asked Fabulous as they walked along the corridor towards the library.

Events since the previous day had excited Ian as, though still mutually suspicious, Gaius and Thalius did (finally) seem to be pulling in the same direction, spending over an hour together in the *Villa Praefectus* with Gemellus the previous evening, discussing tactics against their mutual enemies. Not just the Zealots and the other terrorist insurgents, but also within their own forces.

However, both Gemellus, and now Fabulous, were quick to warn Ian that as events were moving, so the conspirators were bound to be moving with them.

'I should say such a thing would be inevitable,' Fabulous noted. 'For whensoever great men are to be found, there shall be, not many steps behind, lesser men. Is that not so?'

As he asked the question, both spotted Erastus heading in the opposite direction.

'I hear you had a bit of an adventure today,' Ian said brightly, and the trainer nodded, though his look was one of regret rather than pride.

'Such events are a necessary part of life in this place,' Erastus added, with a melancholy edge that Ian found surprising.

As they talked, Ian was vaguely aware of a fourth presence in the corridor and he raised his head and turned it to his left just as a guardsman, wearing the uniform of the praetorian staff, raced towards him with a knife clasped firmly in his hand.

It wasn't the first time that Ian Chesterton had found himself the focus of an assassination attempt. In fact he was getting heartily sick of such things. He turned at just the right moment, catching the onrushing villain a glancing blow on the side of the head with his elbow; stunned, the man dropped to one knee and

Erastus fell on him just as the assassin threw the knife at Ian from close range.

Chesterton closed his eyes and waited for the searing pain of impact, but it never came. Instead he opened them to find Erastus lying prostrate over the struggling guard and Fabulous slumped against the wall, the knife in his stomach. Ian instantly forgot about the assassin and knelt beside his friend who was staring at his own hands, covered in blood.

'I have never been a man for whom luck has had a lot of time,' Fabulous noted with a dry chuckle. 'A poor throw, to be sure. Perhaps our friend Erastus could spend some time training this fellow to do better in future.'

Erastus raised his head and yelled along the corridor for help. Within seconds, there came the sound of approaching, running feet.

'Fabulous,' Ian said painfully. 'I am so sorry. That was meant for me.'

'Then it is better that I should be its recipient, is it not?' asked the old librarian as he coughed, placed a bloodied hand to Ian's cheek, and died.

Drusus, Gemellus, Tobias and others, including armed guards, were all approaching from different directions now. But for a moment, all Ian could do was hold his fallen friend.

'Who sent you on this errand of betrayal?' Erastus asked his still-struggling captive. 'Upon whose orders do you murder in the *Villa Praefectus*?'

The guard shook his head. A spine-shaking punch in the face by Erastus brought only a statement that he would rather cut out his own tongue than betray his master.

'That might well be arranged,' said Drusus as he helped Erastus to haul the man to his feet, leaving Ian alone on the corridor floor staring silently into space.

To Barbara, observing the bewildering kaleidoscope of nationalities and cultures that were present in Byzantium, this was in itself an education. For two days she wandered around the city, soaking up as much information as she could that would help her to remain alive and at liberty. On the first night she stayed with a Jewish family who treated her with respectful silence, as though mindful of Hieronymous's edict about her. Careful not to overstay her welcome, Barbara left early the following morning and found herself in the Arab quarter where, much to her surprise, she befriended a Greek woman named Cressida in the twisting bazaars of the old city.

It was only after she had accepted an invitation to stay at Cressida's home for a second night that a casual conversation about the tragedy in the market-place a fortnight ago brought a startling revelation from the Greek woman.

'Yes,' she remembered, 'I saw a young girl on her own in the market-place that day. And an old man with white hair. I couldn't, in all honesty, tell you what happened to him, but the little girl was rescued from the crowd by a Greek. A kindly man whose mother named him Georgiadis. I believe that she is still there.'

Tomorrow, Barbara decided, trying hard not to leap up and kiss the woman just in case she got completely the wrong idea. Tomorrow, I will find her.

Having completed, to his total satisfaction, his work with the scribes, guiding them in the direction that he thought they wanted to go, the Doctor returned to the cave in which James and Judith and the other Christians were still sheltering. There was sadness on the Doctor's return when he was told of the death the previous evening of Hebron.

It was rare for the death of one that he had met so briefly to affect the Doctor. After all, he mused briefly, people die all the time. Compared to his own lifespan, that of humans was like a dragonfly compared to a redwood tree. But still, something deep within the Doctor was upset by the news of Hebron's demise.

There was a new arrival within the cave whom the Doctor did not recognise. Another ancient man with white hair and a face shaped by the ravages of time. James broke off from telling the Doctor the sad news when he saw that the Doctor's attention had been caught by the newcomer.

'Let me introduce yet another friend,' James explained quickly. 'A Greek of our acquaintance, Papavasilliou.'

The Doctor shook Papavasilliou's hand, being surprised by the strength of the man despite his wizened and frail-looking limbs.

'I am honoured to meet you,' said Papavasilliou. 'My friend Hebron, now departed, spoke often and with great compliment about you, Doctor.'

The Doctor smiled, genially. 'Any friend of Hebron is, I am happy to say, a friend of mine. Are you also a Christian?'

Papavasilliou shook his head. 'Not as such. Whilst I share many of the aims and hopes of these good people, I have my own beliefs which I share with no other, save, perhaps, the sheep that I tend. *They* know me well, for that is my own way.'

'I approve,' said the Doctor, smirking that James was just out of earshot.

'Nevertheless,' continued Papavasilliou, 'I *do* admire the gentleness and faith of them all.'

'As do I,' the Doctor noted, genuinely.

There was a puzzlement in the face of the old shepherd. 'Your accent,' he said after a moment. 'Your Greek is quite superb for one not of this land. The inflection of your voice indicates that you have travelled far?'

The Doctor gave a dismissive wave of the hand. 'I am from many places and have many homes, and yet no home save that which I carry in my heart.'

Papavasilliou smiled warmly. 'You remind me of a young girl I know. A Briton who speaks with the voice of a sage unique in one so young.'

The old man stopped and wondered if he had said something wrong. He could not understand why the Doctor was dancing gleefully around before him like a child.

Chapter Twenty-Eight
The Passage of Time Leaving Empty Lives Waiting to Be Filled

And at the ninth hour Jesus cried out with a loud voice, saying, É-lö-ï, É-lö-ï, lä-mä sã-bãch-thã-ni?, which is, being interpreted, My God, my God, why hast thou forsaken me?
Mark 15:34

'Who would have thought that a man could shed such blood and still live?' *Praefectus* Maximus noted as Edius Flavia received yet another scream-inducing blow from the *flagellum* across his back. The metal balls dragged chunks of flesh with them as they scudded across Flavia's skin.

'More, *praefectus*?' asked the sergeant. For a moment Maximus was silent. 'Sadly yes, sergeant,' he said as the whip came down again.

Flavia's scream coincided with the entrance of Gaius Calaphilus, accompanying it like some hellish fanfare. The *praefectus* held up his hand both to stop the torture and to welcome the general.

'*Salve*,' he noted, but paused when he saw the grave look on the general's face.

'I bring tidings of great sorrow,' said Calaphilus. 'An attempt has been made within the *Villa Praefectus* upon the life of Ian Chesterton.' He stopped and grabbed the hair of Edius Flavia, pulling him away from the torture stake and making him scream yet again. 'As well you know, you piece of excrement.' He flung the former tribune back against the bare wood and ordered the sergeant to, 'Flay without mercy this despicable excuse for a Roman.'

The sergeant cast a nervous glance at the *praefectus*. After a moment of consideration, Thalius nodded.

'Our young friend is dead?' he asked, sadly.

'Remarkably not,' the general replied. 'But only due to the intervention of Erastus.' The *praefectus* looked relieved. 'Regretfully, however,' continued Gaius, 'I must inform you that the blow intended for Ian took instead the life of Fabulous.'

Thalius broke down and wept, something that just a few days earlier, Calaphilus would have considered an open sign of weakness. Now, he felt like joining in.

'Your plot has failed, wretch,' the general told Flavia as yet another blow landed on his back. 'It has only succeeded in taking the life of an old man who committed you and your worthless allies no trespass. *Non ego tuam empsim vitam vitiosa nuce*. Your life is now forfeit and you shall be scourged unto death with great pleasure.'

For the first time, there was fear as well as determination in Flavia's voice. 'No, mercy,' he cried.

'No mercy indeed,' said Thalius Maximus. 'Tell us the names of your fellow *proditores* or your life shall end this day in *cruciamentum*.'

A final blow seemed to knock all of the stuffing from Edius Flavia. Crushed and broken, he hung limply from the *stauros* by his fingertips.

'Tribune Marcus Lanilla,' he said in an agonised gasp. 'Tribune Fabius Actium. Tribune Honorius Annora. Centurion Didius Domius. Centurion Agressus Comtilius. *Suffecti consul* Marcelinus Gomaus. *Praetor* Gaius Octavian. *Quaestor* Claudius Minimus. *Aediles* Mobius Hartenius. Senator's wife Antonia Vinicius. Tribune's wife Agrinella Lanilla.'

And so it went on, in bursts of agonised confession. Finally, almost on the point of collapse, Flavia finished the list of the names of his co-conspirators.

'Is that all?' asked the general.

There was no reply. The *praefectus* knelt beside the tortured man and then stood up shaking his head. 'He has expired, the unworthy wretch.'

'We have the names,' Calaphilus noted. 'And we know how high the conspiracy goes. Three of the surviving five tribunes. Judges. Supplementary consuls, the city treasurer.... The list is phenomenal.'

'It could have been much worse,' noted the *praefectus*. 'Either your name or mine could have been spoken here.'

'I shall enjoy, greatly, arresting Marcus Lanilla,' noted the general with a triumphant smile on his face. 'I suspect you would wish that your former wife be left unto you?'

Thalius bit his lip. 'I should wish that it had not been mentioned at all,' he said. 'And I should appreciate it if it were to remain that way. I shall deal with Antonia in my own way.'

Two horses trotted with no obvious haste through the barrack gates, and salutes were given and received.

'Stand easy, legionnaire,' said tribune Fabius Actium as the forged iron gates closed behind him and Marcus Lanilla. When they were clear of the barracks approach, the two men spurred their horses to break into a gallop.

'The situation is rapidly deteriorating,' noted Marcus as he reined in his charging stallion at the entrance to the Jewish quarter. 'The time has clearly come for action.'

'What have you heard?' Fabius asked, nervously.

'Nothing but rumours. Yet.'

'Edius would not betray us, even unto death,' said Fabius confidently.

Marcus gave him a quizzical glance which asked, 'Are you sure?' 'Perhaps,' was the limit of his own assurances. 'Nevertheless, we should be more secure in my mind if we act to recover the situation to our own advantage.'

'You have a plan?' asked Fabius.

'I *always* have a plan,' replied Marcus, testily. 'And we shall have need of one, for the accusations will arrive, whether Edius Flavia talks or otherwise.'

Fabius slowed his horse to a trot and withdrew his riding crop, waving it angrily in Lanilla's face. 'Let them make their charges, tribune. I shall defend my honour from all of those dwarves. Bring them on, and let them say their piece.'

Marcus pushed the crop away and grabbed hold of Fabius's reigns. 'You still fail to understand the seriousness of the situation. Any charges, no matter how unfounded, will do us damage. We can deny everything but we shall always be tainted with the mark of suspicion.'

'Then we are undone,' Fabius wailed.

'Not so. What is the one thing that will appease *all* accusations, however base and unproven they may be?'

'I know not,' Fabius confessed.

Marcus smiled at his friend's intellectual discomfort. 'Only the death of the Zealot leader will appease Rome. If we can parade Basellas's head on a spike through the streets then nothing either Calaphilus or Maximus can say or do will prevent us from achieving all that we desire.'

The representatives of the guards of those centurions still loyal to Gaius Calaphilus, and that was most of them, poured through the doors of the Lanilla household and burst into the lightly guarded *triclinium*, overpowering with almost no resistance those few private auxiliaries and *cohors* who were employed by Marcus Lanilla and his family.

With the hallways secured, Calaphilus swaggered into the villa of his hated enemy. How long he had waited for this moment?

The anticipation was lessened slightly as he strode into the *triclinium* only to find Agrinella, her hands on her hips, shouting at the sergeant of the guard.

Her eyes fixed on the general. 'What is the meaning of this

outrage, Calaphilus?' she yelled. But there was something in her voice that told Gaius that she knew.

'Articles of impeachment have been raised against your husband, madam,' he said, with a relish in his voice. Revenge, clearly, being a dish best served... any time one has the ability to serve it. 'A confession by a conspiring insurgent has implicated tribune Marcus Lanilla in numerous and vile treasons against the *praefectus*, the state and the emperor. I am bid, by the powers that be, to bring your husband hence that he might answer such charges as are laid. Your name has also been mentioned.'

'No,' cried Agrinella. 'This cannot be.' It was not the defiant anger of an innocent woman, falsely accused, but the anguished wail of one *in flagrante delicto*.

That pleased Gaius even more.

'Where is your husband, woman?' he asked.

There was no reply as Agrinella stared, dazed and confused, around the room at a sea of impassive and blank military faces. Then, as if realising that all was lost, she threw herself to the floor in front of the general.

'Gaius,' she said, her voice quivering. 'I implore you. Whatsoever my husband may, or may not have done, I know nothing. *Nothing*,' she repeated.

'Get up,' Calaphilus replied, contemptuously. 'Get off your knees, woman, and face your end like a Roman.'

'I can name the names,' she said, quickly and desperately. 'Honorius Annora, Marcelinus, Octavian, Antonia the *praefectus*'s former wife...' Her voice trailed away.

Calaphilus shook his head. 'These names are known to us already, traitor. Take her away,' he told the guards, two of whom reached down for the weeping woman. 'Letters have been sent to your father, the legate, informing him of your crimes. Should he be of a mind to save you, and endanger his own lofty position in Rome, then that will be his choice. My own belief is that he will surrender you to dance on the end of a *gladius* for your treachery.'

'Gaius,' Agrinella said, shaking free of the hands of the two soldiers and struggling to compose herself as the general held up a hand to his men to let her speak. 'I am not a simpering courtesan like Maximus's wife. Neither am I bragging *moecha* like Antonia. I am a noblewoman, the daughter of a legate, the granddaughter of a consul.' She stopped, seeing the hardening face above her. 'I do not beg for my life before you, Gaius, because I know that you will take delight in my death and that of my beloved. I *do* beseech you, however, to allow me to take my own life.'

Calaphilus reached down and gently wiped a tear from Agrinella's porcelain-like cheek. 'No,' he said simply. 'I think not.'

At the same time, a large phalanx of the praetorian guard were accompanying a similarly brutal entry into the house of Antonia Vinicius.

Thalius Maximus arrived at the villa of his former wife a few moments after the guards had stormed the place and fought a brief, yet bloody, battle with the personal guard of Senator Germanicus. Four men lay dead in the corridor along with two of Thalius's soldiers. The *praefectus* expressed his condolences for the losses to his loyal captain as he entered the great hall. Even from a distance he could clearly make out Antonia's shrill voice.

'Oh, you are in trouble now, my dove,' he said as Antonia ceased squabbling with her weeping handmaiden.

Astonishingly, given the circumstances, she began to laugh. Softly at first but then, encouraged by Thalius returning her smile, more raucously. 'You have waited for an age, Thalius, to get me in such a compromising position. I trust that you shall sleep stiffly and long this night.'

It was typical, thought Thalius, that even in his moment of absolute triumph and her moment of total defeat, that his ex-wife could still get the better of him with her vicious and piercing words.

'I give you a choice, Antonia,' he said flatly, and with no delight in his voice. 'Your crimes are uncovered. Face the senate with your treachery, bring your husband down by association, and still end your days with a public execution...'

'Or?' asked Antonia with a wry smile.

'Take your own life. Die with dignity in your own home.'

Antonia hesitated, perhaps still believing for a moment that her husband's position would save her.

'That will not be the case,' Thalius said, reading her thoughts. 'The senator will disown you, to save himself. You know that, do you not?'

'I suspected as much,' Antonia said, recovering her sense of humour as the situation demanded. 'He is a man, after all, and all men are worms, Thalius. You know this.'

'Perhaps, my sweet,' said Thalius and then, in a moment of uncharacteristic weakness, he kissed his former wife on the forehead. 'I loved you once. I would have given you the sun and the stars if they were mine to give...' He shook his head and handed a small, razor-sharp knife to Antonia. 'The guards will return within the hour to arrest you for treason. Goodbye, Antonia.'

'We live in troubled times,' the Pharisee said. 'Such times require order from the chaos.'

Marcus Lanilla smiled and nodded his agreement whilst Fabius merely looked nervous and fidgeted constantly.

'May I ask, Titus, why you have agreed to help us when others within your brethren, notably your leader, have met our entreaties with disdain and contempt?'

Titus had an answer ready almost before the words had left Marcus's lips. 'The Jewish people stand at a crossroads,' he noted. 'We face the choice of dealing with the realities of the Roman world, and flourishing within it, or denying them, and perishing along with all of the other ignorant savages for whom reality is an overrated pastime.'

'But you wish for freedom, surely?' asked Fabius.

'It is my experience that one should be careful what one wishes for,' noted Titus. 'For what is a man to do if he should get exactly what he wants?'

Marcus liked this clever and dangerous little man. The ambitious Titus, it was known, craved Hieronymous's position and, according to rumour, had attempted to use a recent incident of alleged indiscretion with a gentile woman to compromise the old man. Now, seemingly, he was happy that the Romans had finally decided to crack down on the Zealot problem, and to help them behind Hieronymous's back. His implications that Hieronymous himself secretly supported the insurgents was just the kind of poison that Marcus would need when control of the city was his.

Still, Fabius seemed edgy and mistrustful. 'What we really need,' he interjected, 'is the location of Basellas's base.'

'Nothing could be simpler,' Titus told the Romans. 'I shall provide you with that, if I have your solemn guarantee that you will remember my help when the purges begin.'

Chapter Twenty-Nine
One Man Clapping

Watch ye and pray, lest ye enter into temptation.
The spirit truly is ready but the flesh is weak.
Mark 14:38

The tap on the solid wooden door was nervous and timid, almost apologetic.

'Who goes there? What do you want with us?' asked a woman's voice through the door.

'Hello,' said Barbara, looking quickly around in the cobbled streets of the Greek quarter. She prayed that she had found the right house at last, after three previous attempts and various confused directions had stolen most of the day from her. 'I wonder if you could let me in, please, I'm not comfortable with talking to wood.'

The door swung open and Barbara found herself facing a man and woman, both of them with badly bruised faces and worried expressions. In the corner behind them, half-hidden in the shadows, cowered a young, anaemic-looking girl. 'I hope you can help me,' said Barbara. 'I've been told that you have a child staying with you. A Briton.'

'You were misinformed,' snapped the man and moved to close the door on her. Barbara put her foot in the way like a pushy vacuum-cleaner saleswoman and tried a different approach. 'Look,' she said, 'I'll have you know that I've had a very trying day. Where is she?'

'There is no one here such as you describe,' the woman told her. 'Now please leave before you are observed.'

Barbara looked to her right, to the several Roman soldiers entering a neighbouring house. The couple followed her gaze and shrank back into their home, pulling Barbara with them. The man closed and barred the door and, for a second, Barbara was unsure of what to say next. 'You are Georgiadis and Evangeline, yes?' she asked, suddenly realising that she might just have come to the wrong house yet again.

'We are,' answered the woman, to Barbara's relief. 'And what business is our identity to you?'

'I've already told you,' Barbara replied. 'I'm interested in the girl that you rescued.'

'What girl?' asked the man, throwing his arms wide. 'We know of no girl save our own fair daughter...'

Barbara looked at the timid teenager poking out her head from behind an upturned chair. Glancing around the room, she also noticed various pieces of broken furniture and a general disorder that seemed incongruous with the house-proud nature of most of the Greek dwellings that she had seen.

'You've had visitors?' Barbara asked. 'People who would not take "no" for an answer, seemingly?'

Evangeline gave her husband a tired look. 'We wish for nothing more than to be left alone to get on with our lives,' she said. 'One act of kindness and this is our reward.'

The couple and their daughter were clearly terrified and hesitant to speak to strangers after their bruising encounter with authority. And, outside, the place was crawling with just such authority.

'What's their game?' Barbara asked, changing the subject.

'Our neighbours were murdered in their beds last eve,' Georgiadis told her. 'No one is safe from tyranny and foul deeds.'

'Well, it's obvious Vicki isn't here,' Barbara said in resignation, giving the home a final once-over. 'If you do see her again, tell her that Barbara is looking for her.'

There was a momentary pause and then Barbara turned and headed for the door.

'Are you Barbara?' asked Evangeline, as Barbara prepared to step back into the street.

Yes. Barbara rested her head on the door, smiled, and mouthed a silent thank you to the God of timely interventions. 'Yes,' she said, turning around. 'I'm Barbara Wright.'

'And what is Vicki to you?'

'Family,' said Barbara, simply.

'Sit down,' Evangeline said, after a nod from her husband. 'We have a story to tell you that may interest you greatly.'

The praetorian guards returned to the Vinicius villa with expectation. Many of them knew Antonia from the time that she was married to the *praefectus*.

A few of them knew her *well*.

Antonia Vinicius's reputation in this corner of the empire was second to none. A remarkable woman of great beauty and cunning, her insatiable appetite for men was equally celebrated and discussed in the taverns and trattorias of Byzantium and beyond.

The nervous among the guards crept along at the back of the column, hoping that Antonia would not notice, or remember, them and what they'd got up to in her bedchamber. Those to whom Antonia was merely a legend in her own lifetime, a notorious trollop whom they would brag to their grandchildren of having arrested and forced treasonous confessions from, strode on ahead.

They were met on the steps of the villa by the senator's head of household, Redecius.

'Stand aside, freedman,' ordered the praetorian captain, Cicero.

'Tread softly, citizen, as you enter the hall of my lady.'

'You know why we are here?' asked the captain.

'I do,' replied Redecius, 'and my lady stands ready for her fate. Follow me.'

He led a small delegation of guards into the outer bath chamber. A few of the guards exchanged knowing glances as Redecius threw open the double doors to the pool room and knelt beside the door in silent prayer as the captain took a couple of paces into the steamy, humid atmosphere.

Antonia floated, naked and on her back, in the crimson waters, her wrists slit by the knife that lay at the bottom of the gently lapping pool. The blood had seeped into the very fabric of the bath tiles, staining the entire surrounding area.

Antonia, the captain noticed, had a smile of satisfaction on her silent, dead face.

'This thing is done,' he told the still-kneeling Redecius. 'Inform thy master that his wife has taken her own life before the praetorian guard could do it for her.'

Redecius reacted angrily. 'Speak not ill of the dead, disrespectful, vulgar and ignorant man,' he said in a paroxysm of rage. 'My lady does not deserve that, or this.' He pointed into the room.

There was a scornful edge to the captain's voice as he replied while turning and walking away from Redecius. 'Think yourself, and your master, lucky that we had not arrived sooner. It is only through the *praefectus*'s grace and favour that thy profligate mistress's head is not adorning the spikes on the golden gates.'

'Is there anything wrong with him?' James asked, with genuine concern.

In the mouth of the Christian cave, the Doctor was continuing to dance a merry little jig, and mutter happily to himself.

'He has received news of great significance,' Papavasilliou noted. 'I am greatly pleased that it should have been *I* who imparted this news to him.'

'This concerns his lost family, perhaps?' asked Daniel.

'It would seem so.'

The Doctor saw the three men and headed towards them with a jubilant smile, as though all of the troubles of the previous weeks had been lifted from his shoulders. 'My friend,' he said, shaking Papavasilliou warmly by the hand. 'It is *so* good to see you again after the glad tidings of great joy that you brought to me yesterday.'

The old Greek's smile dropped a fraction and, sensing

something was wrong, the Doctor's face followed suit. 'Further to that,' James began, somewhat embarrassed.

For a moment none of the men seemed able to speak, then Papavasilliou blurted out an almost incoherent babble of words. 'I'm sorry,' the Doctor interrupted, 'could you slow down, my hearing's not what it was, do you see?'

The shepherd's eyes betrayed everything that he was about to tell the Doctor. 'When I returned to the Greek quarter yesterday evening,' he began in a more measured tone, 'I was given the dreadful news that Roman soldiers have taken Vicki from the family who were trying to protect her from just such a dreadful occurrence.'

There was more, of course. A couple had been murdered in their beds, seemingly, but the Doctor had lost interest in what the old man was saying. The horror of imagining what the Romans were doing to little Vicki at this moment was simply too great.

Chapter Thirty
Coping

What have I to do with thee, Jesus, thou son of the most high God? I adjure thee by God, that thou torment me not.
Mark 5:7

Death is *never* something that you become accustomed to, Ian Chesterton reflected, as the funeral pyre of Fabulous was ignited by Erastus.

'I shall miss him,' noted Drusus sadly, watching the cremation begin and the fire take hold.

'A good man,' added Gemellus, wrapping his cloak tightly around his neck as a chill wind blew through the gardens of remembrance. A cloud chose that moment to pass in front of the sun and the sudden darkness and cold seemed to say something profound to all of those present about mortality and their relationship to it.

'Would you like to say something, Ian?' Drusus asked, poignantly.

'I knew him for such a short time,' Ian confessed. Nevertheless, he accepted the opportunity and stepped forward. 'We are gathered here today, not to mourn a death but to celebrate a life,' he said. 'Fabulous once told me that history would never die so long as the knowledge of it was carried within the hearts of men. That is true, also, of our memories of the departed.'

There was a smattering of applause as Ian stepped down from the plinth and watched with misty and smoke-filled eyes, as the burning continued.

'All things are changing rapidly,' said Gemellus. 'Arrests continue apace and, with reinforcements to the legion, there are so many comings and goings within the *Villa Praefectus* that I am lost in a sea of confusion.'

'I know what you mean,' Drusus added. 'Only an hour ago,

I ran into yet another of the waifs and strays that we seem to be collecting by the dozen.'

Gemellus clearly sympathised. 'Another of the reinforcements?' he asked.

'Actually, no,' Drusus replied. 'It was a young Briton. A girl who was found within the Greek quarter by Crispianus Dolavia and his men, acting on information received. Efforts are being made to find the youth a suitable family with whom she can live until a husband is found for her.'

It was such a casual conversation that Ian, lost in his own thoughts, almost missed it. On another day, perhaps, he would have done.

Luckily, the important words carried themselves to him.

'British, did you say?' he asked. 'A young girl?'

'Yes,' said Drusus. 'Perhaps *you* could marry her?'

Ian Chesterton began to rock with unexpected laughter, quite oblivious to the funeral proceedings still going on around him. Fabulous, he was absolutely certain, would not have minded in the slightest.

Vicki was walking in the dark again.

Literally as well as metaphorically.

It was becoming a familiar part of each day.

There was a narrow annex corridor that ran from her room in the guest quarters of the legion's barracks through the Roman complex to a door at the base of the mezzanine behind the servants' rooms in the *Villa Praefectus*.

Bored by a day spent watching the massed ranks of legionnaires outside practising stabbing straw opponents with their swords (it had been fun for ten minutes, but there was a limit to even Vicki's tolerance for sweaty bodies and taut, rippling muscles), Vicki had gone off exploring. She immediately found herself in the villa and was quickly spotted and chased by one of Drusus's minions, before being cornered and dragged (complaining) into the kitchens for questioning by the master of the household.

She was getting used to interrogation, almost looking forward to each day's new adventure in the field.

Once Drusus had discovered her position of being under army protection and her status as a citizen and not a slave, he seemed to lose all interest in Vicki herself, simply telling her not to get in the way if she intended to hang around with the slaves.

Vicki liked that idea. The slaves she met were friendly and, when they weren't rushing around carrying out mind-numbingly mundane tasks, they treated her like an equal; they were just about the first people in Byzantium to do that. Of course, being the equal of a slave didn't actually mean much, particularly to the Romans themselves, but Vicki, if nothing else, appreciated the distinction between the *Villa Praefectus* and life in the barracks.

She spent a day sitting in the kitchens, nibbling at the numerous leftovers that the Greek cook, Denisius, kept insisting that she help him finish off. He was a huge and jolly man with a ruddy complexion beneath his thick greying beard, and a bellowing laugh that was heard more and more as the day progressed and the level in the bottle of wine beside his stove sank lower and lower.

In the kitchens, too, she met Dorcas, the beautiful young housemaid, who combed Vicki's tangled and dirty hair between scampering off to run errands, and talked to Vicki about the year she spent with the master and the mistress in Gaul before coming to Byzantium. There was Tobias, too, the huge and bronzed North African Adonis, his bald head and smooth, ebony skin reminding Vicki of a man on the ship to Dido. Tobias didn't say much and smiled even less frequently, but Dorcas adored him and the feeling seemed to be mutual.

There were others, too, that she encountered. Friendly and cheerful house boys and valets. Cocksure and stunningly beautiful handmaidens. Food servants and domestics. And there was Praelius, the studious Thracian scribe who taught the classics to Jocelyn's two daughters by her previous marriage.

This morning, however, the kitchens were all but deserted,

except for one glum-looking woman whom Vicki had not met the previous day.

'Hello,' said Vicki brightly. 'I should introduce myself...'

'I know who you are,' said the woman. 'The talk of the halls has been of little else since your arrival.'

Nice to develop a reputation without trying, Vicki reflected.

'My name is Felicia,' she said. 'Handmaiden to the *praefectus*'s wives. Or at least, I *was*.'

'Why?' asked Vicki, noting the past tense. 'What happened?'

'I did a favour for a general. Take the advice of one who has bitter experience in life and remember never to do favours for anyone, young Briton,' Felicia said woefully and then explained the awful events to which she had been party.

'I'm sure Jocelyn will forget it all eventually,' Vicki argued.

'I do not worry about my lady's displeasure,' Felicia said. 'The *praefectus*'s wife is foolish and empty-headed. She is not the problem.'

'Then who?'

Felicia began to cry. 'You are not wise in the ways of Byzantium, Vicki,' she said. 'General Gaius Calaphilus used me to further his own position. Like a simpleton, and for the wicked love of money, I allowed myself to be so used.'

'So, what's the problem?' asked Vicki.

'Simply that I am likely to become the next victim of the general's purges.'

Vicki didn't quite follow the logic of this, but she was in no position to argue with Felicia.

'Already, rumours are rife about a terror like the wrath of the gods to be unfolded upon the enemies of the state this night. And I shall be amongst the victims of them... Woe, woe and thrice woe,' she wailed, helplessly. 'Who shall save the little people and give them their deliverance from the vengeance of powerful and ambitious men?'

For once in her life, Vicki was completely stumped for an answer.

Fortunately, however, as the two young women looked at each other in anguish, a passionate voice reached out to them across the kitchens.

'Deliverance is a state of mind,' said Dorcas, stepping from the shadows, having clearly overheard much of the girls' conversation. 'Yet it is also an attainable goal.'

As if Vicki hadn't had enough surprises in the last few days, this was an unexpected turn of events. 'How so?'

'Through escape,' Dorcas replied. 'I have a cunning plan to leave this benighted place. I have a route. I have friends who will help and I have a destination whereupon to travel. What I need are two willing accomplices. Are you with me?'

Neither Vicki nor Felicia needed to be asked twice.

Chapter Thirty-One
The Culture Bunker, Part Eight — Just Another Greek Tragedy

And he said unto them, Go ye into all the world,
and preach the gospel to every creature.
Mark 16:15

Dorcas's plan had a relatively straightforward first phase. Flee the compound.

'That's it?' asked Vicki, surprised. She had expected something more complicated with maps and diversionary tactics and suchlike.

'We only have to get past the gatehouse,' Felicia told her. 'I have done it many times before.'

'Greater dangers will present themselves once we are outside,' Dorcas continued as the three girls reached the wall of the barracks, just across the parade ground from the exit.

'Now what?' whispered Vicki.

'We wait until the coast is clear,' said Felicia just as a huge battery of soldiers arrived, cutting off the only escape route available to them.

'Today has been, as t'were, a momentous climax to events of recent times,' general Gaius Calaphilus noted to the massed ranks of his legion.

'We undertake this night, to put down the obscenity which blights our fair Byzantium. To erase, for all eternity, the putrid stench of rebellion within our own ranks. And make it known throughout the empire, from the isles of Britannia to the citadel of Rome itself, that this thing shall not stand.'

There was a huge cheer from the assembled men, many of whom banged their shields loudly with their swords. Others raised their weapons in the air and shook them at the night sky.

'But first,' Calaphilus announced to his troops, 'it is beholden on me to reward those whose bravery and loyalty in the face of threats and menaces has deserved recognition. Step forward loyal centurion Crispianus Dolavia, whom we do now, and with great emotion, promote to the noble rank of tribune in the service of his most divine and awesome majesty, the Emperor Lucius Nero.'

Calaphilus pinned the tribune's regalia to the lapel of Crispianus's tunic and kissed his brother-in-arms on both cheeks. 'May you always have good fortune and triumph in battle, and do unto your enemies great murder.'

There were other pieces of backslapping promotion to be handed out, too. Captain Drusus Felinistius replaced Crispianus Dolavia as centurion, whilst Marinus Topignius, to the men of the legion's hastily expressed approval, was honoured with a captaincy. There was no doubt in anyone's mind that the general had promoted wisely and with an eye on gaining the total support of his men. They would probably have followed him to the brink of death anyway, but with one of their own like Marinus now within the officer rank, it was a foregone conclusion.

This was, in fact, exactly what Calaphilus had in mind. Earlier, he had told Ian Chesterton that he intended surrounding himself with loyal, if unspectacular, men. 'Promoted men are grateful men,' he had noted.

'Our task, this night,' Calaphilus told the men when the changes in rank were completed, 'is to ruthlessly put down the rebellion that is upon us. No quarter should be asked, or given. Your orders are to find Fabius Actium, Marcus Lanilla, Honorius Annora and those others who attempt to usurp the power of Rome, and to end their treasons. Let us march upon the hour, and woe betide the villains who stand in our way.'

'What's going on?' asked Vicki, straining to hear.

'I think they are hunting traitors,' Dorcas whispered. 'We had best wait until they have gone before we attempt to leave.'

So, they shrank back into the shadows, and waited.

A night of terror was erupting around Byzantium as the advanced ranks of the Roman soldiers and their praetorian colleagues took a merciless revenge on treasonous colleagues.

In the forum, a group of soldiers loyal to the dishonoured tribunes had seen their retreat from the city blocked in a swift movement by an ambitious young captain with an eye on a centurion's post. Calaphilus had been sent for and arrived on horseback, with Dolavia at his side, to find twenty or so men cowering in the centre of the market square, surrounded by those troops loyal to the general and the *praefectus*.

'You men,' said Calaphilus, angrily. 'Your lives are forfeit. Die with honour, at the point of a sword, or shamed by the torments of crucifixion.'

There were a series of pathetic cries for mercy from the gathered men. Calaphilus turned to the captain and gave his order.

'Have your men make plain the displeasure of the empire,' he said. 'Get thee in amongst them like crazed dogs and leave not one man standing to spread his odious poison in my sight.'

Then he turned his horse away and headed towards more important matters as the first blow was struck against the traitors.

Zealots, too, were being rounded up and slaughtered.

It was as if the city had finally decided, *en masse*, just exactly whose side it was on.

Barbara dodged through the streets, keeping to the shadows. She saw terrible things as she crept from doorway to doorway towards the barracks where, she had been assured, Vicki was known to be.

She passed the summary execution of a Jew, a Zealot presumably, caught at the rim of the Jewish quarter by a group of angry, shouting legionnaires. He tried to sprint for his life but was skewered on the end of a *gladius*, then dropped to the ground and was hacked to death in an obscene orgy of violence.

Putting a hand over her mouth to stop herself from screaming or being sick, or both, Barbara raced across the now-deserted market square, barely paying any heed whatsoever to the dozens of blood-soaked bodies lying strewn around the forum. She turned left at the temple walls, remembering how she had stumbled in there, afraid for her life, what seemed like a decade ago, but which had actually been just sixteen days.

She circumnavigated the walls of the compound and arrived at the barracks gates to find two lone sentries barring her way. She shrank back into the shadows, waiting for them to make the next move just as, behind them, she saw the movement of three figures, dull and indistinct against the torch light of the barracks frontage.

After a moment, the sentries moved out of sight, leaving the way into the gates clear. But still Barbara waited, knowing that someone inside the barracks would be coming her way soon.

When they did, and it proved to be Vicki, running low to the ground in a zigzag pattern to minimise the chances of being seen, Barbara almost let out of yell of delight, but she caught her breath until Vicki and her companions were actually out of the gates. Then, she leapt from the shadows and called out Vicki's name.

'Crikey!' said Vicki, angrily. 'Give me a heart attack, why don't you?' Then she threw herself into Barbara's arms for a joyous reunion, much to the obvious discomfort of the two young women with her.

'Far be it from me to interrupt this... whatever it is,' began Dorcas.

'This is Barbara,' whispered Vicki. 'She's a friend. I thought you were dead.'

'And I, you,' answered Barbara drawing Vicki and her friends into the shadows from where she had come. 'I found the place where you stayed in the Greek quarter.'

'Georgiadis, and Evangeline, and Iola?' asked Vicki, quickly.

'They're all right,' Barbara told her. 'It might be an idea to try and get back to them, actually. At least that's one friendly shelter in this city. Judging by the things I've seen, we could use one.'

'It is the reckoning,' Felicia told them with a look of horror. 'We are all doomed. *Doomed*.'

For some reason, this made Vicki smile. 'Not if I can help it,' she said. 'Come on, I know a short-cut to the Greek quarter. Then we can figure out what to do next.'

They crossed into the forum again, Vicki letting out a brief, but high-pitched scream as she saw the bodies of the executed traitors up close.

'My God,' she said, 'who could have done this?'

'Honourable men,' noted Barbara sadly. 'They are *all* honourable men, apparently.'

Dorcas looked quickly around her and then motioned for the terrified Felicia to keep up with them. 'We have not far to travel,' she said, reassuringly. 'Once we can get a message to my people, we shall leave this town far behind us.'

Barbara gave her a suspicious look. 'My people?' she asked.

'The Christians,' replied Dorcas.

'Oh,' Barbara noted. 'That's all right then, I thought we might be about to meet some real religious maniacs.'

At the entrance to the Greek quarter, finally, their luck ran out. As they rounded a corner, their way was barred by the terrifying sight of one of the Zealots, wild-eyed, his coat soaked in blood. Roman blood.

'Stand,' he shouted loudly. 'Who goes there?'

'We mean you no harm,' Barbara pleaded. 'We have to get off the streets.'

The Zealot laughed, chillingly. 'Sister, we should be *on* the streets, putting to death the filthy dogs that rape our land.' He removed a knife as smooth and shining as a shark's tooth and held it glinting in the light. 'They say unto me, "Yewhe," they say. "Go forth into the streets and find those who collaborate with the dogs of Rome. And put them to the blade."'

'We are no collaborators,' Barbara replied. 'We are in as much danger as you from the Romans. Please, you must let us past.'

'Must?' cried Yewhe. 'Must? I must do only God's will, sister. And He, through His servant on Earth, Matthew, has commanded me to slay those who do evil in his sight.'

They were trapped. They could not turn around and go back the way that they had come for that would almost certainly lead to them running into one of the Roman patrols that were, even now, meting out justice to most of Yewhe's kind.

'Who do you plan to start with?' Dorcas asked Yewhe, trying to engage the clearly mad individual in conversation.

'Why, those within the compound,' he replied.

'That would be suicide,' noted Barbara with genuine concern. 'You'd be killed before you got fifty yards into the place, it's crawling with Romans.'

'Then I shall die, as I have lived, magnificently fighting the scourge of my people. Yes, they shall kill me, but before I ascend to heaven, I shall send an indeterminate number of those heathen scum straight to hell. I shall become a martyr to my people and will inspire them to rise up and throw off the yoke of Roman oppression that has choked us for too long.'

Barbara had heard this kind of fanaticism before, and she shook her head. 'Yewhe,' she replied, softly. 'That would be pointless. The Romans will be mostly gone from this land in another fifty years and your killing a few of them, and then getting yourself killed,' she paused, 'or, for that matter, threatening a group of terrified little girls like us, will not affect any of this. I have seen the future, Yewhe, and what you seek will come to pass. It will just take time.'

Yewhe thought about this for a moment. 'Fifty years?' he asked.

'Yes,' replied Barbara. 'Then Thrace shall be free.'

It was a lie, of course, and Barbara crossed her fingers as she said it.

'Too long,' replied Yewhe as he advanced on Barbara, Vicki, Felicia and Dorcas.

He raised his dagger above his head and Vicki choked down a scream as she saw the madness in his eyes.

And then he slumped dead at her feet, Ian Chesterton standing behind him with blood dripping from a Roman *gladius* and a bemused expression on his face.

'Perhaps one of you could tell me just exactly what is going on here?' he asked. He saw the equally dumbfounded looks that Barbara and Vicki returned to him and shook his head. 'Seemingly not,' he continued.

'How on earth...?' began Barbara.

'Long story,' said Ian. 'Ridiculously long, if truth be told. I'll explain everything, but I think it would be wise if we find somewhere safe first. If there is such a place in Byzantium.'

Such a place did exist. It was the Georgiadis house, and they reached it without further incident and found the Greek family about to barricade themselves into their home.

'So, you are not Vicki's aunt and uncle then?' Evangeline asked, curiously, as Barbara sat and tried to recollect her thoughts and explain the adventures that she had experienced since leaving the Greek quarter earlier in the evening.

'In a manner of speaking, I suppose,' Barbara told her. 'We're all the other has.'

This seemed to satisfy the Greek woman who was busy feeding her tired guests as best she could.

Ian, meanwhile, was still trying to clean the blood from the sword, explaining to Dorcas and Felicia that it was this gift from the *praefectus* that had saved all of their lives. 'Ironic, really, since it was Thalius and the general's keenness to put their own house in order that's causing chaos for everyone else.'

'I am sure that the madness will pass,' said Dorcas. 'But in the meantime, we must use whatever means are available to us to find our own paths in life.'

'And, with it, a chance to walk and admire the distance we can put between us and the past,' Felicia added.

'So, feel up to explaining how you found us in the nick of time?' Barbara asked.

'I was told Vicki was alive earlier today,' Ian noted, putting down his sword. 'I spent hours trying to find her in the *Villa*. When I couldn't, I figured she might have tried to get back to this place, so I got the location from one of the soldiers who abducted her and, well, the rest you know. Finding *you* was a bit of a bonus, though!'

Iola was delighted to see Vicki again. 'I thought they would have killed you,' she told her friend.

'No,' Vicki replied, 'though I think they had something even more horrible in mind for me. Marriage.'

'Oh, that's not so bad,' Iola told her, confidentially. 'In fact, I think that Mother and Father have got someone in mind for me for next year when I shall be of age to wed.'

'Don't you find that at all outrageous?' Vicki asked.

'No,' replied the girl. 'It is our way.'

Vicki left it at that, but couldn't resist asking Ian and Barbara what they should all do next.

'Help is on the way,' said Dorcas, enigmatically, and as she finished speaking, there was a hammering on the Georgiadis door.

'Let me in,' came a voice from outside.

'Who is it?' asked Georgiadis.

'A friend,' Dorcas told him, rushing to the door and removing the bar.

Tobias dived into the house and hugged Dorcas in his well-muscled arms. 'You followed as you said that you would,' she noted.

'By the trail of your dead,' replied the Egyptian, giving Ian an impressed glance.

'He wouldn't listen to reason,' noted Ian, still cleaning his *gladius*. 'But he got the point. Eventually.'

Dorcas turned and smiled at her assembled friends. 'Now is the time to reveal to you that I have sent word via courier to our brother Christians in the hills. If you will allow us to shelter here this night, then tomorrow we shall be able to smuggle ourselves outside the city walls, whilst the rest of the town is still distracted with the full horrors of the bloody events of tonight.'

Georgiadis looked at his wife and then nodded. 'Stay as long as you wish,' he said, kindly. 'Our home is your home.'

'We shall leave at first light,' Tobias noted and Ian nodded his agreement.

'I should like to stay,' Felicia told them. 'I do not think I could face another step.'

'You are welcome to remain here for as long as you wish,' Evangeline told her.

Dorcas gave her friend a hug. 'You would face grave danger by staying within the city,' she noted.

'No greater, surely, than you shall face in the hills, being hunted by Roman death-squads. I admire your bravery and resourcefulness, Dorcas,' Felicia replied, 'but that is not the life that I wish to lead.'

'And what of us?' Barbara said. 'Without the Doctor, what are we to do?'

'Ah,' Ian said. 'You know, I've been giving that a lot of thought in the last couple of days. I can't say for certain that I saw the Doctor die. Can any of you?'

Vicki and Barbara both shook their heads.

'Whatever the truth,' Ian continued, 'our only option is to head for the TARDIS and hope that the Doctor is waiting there for us. Let's get the hell out of this city.'

The Doctor had been foolish, he knew, to leave the relative safety of the Christians' camp and come into the city on his own, but he still harboured hopes of finding Vicki alive. Yet now he found himself, instead, in the midst of his worst nightmare imaginable, once again in the market square where the horror of the last two weeks had begun, as, around him, the night air was filled with the screams of the dying.

And the blank staring eyes of the dead.

Chapter Thirty-Two
A New Dawn Fades

What manner of man is this, that even the wind and the sea obey him?
Mark 4:41

As the pale light of dawn broke through a heavy and overcast sky, Georgiadis lifted the bar from the back of the door and ushered Tobias and Dorcas outside. Ian and Barbara followed but Vicki lingered for a second in the doorway.

'I'll miss you all,' she said before she kissed Evangeline and Iola. 'Look after Felicia. I think you'll find her slightly less of a handful than your last guest.'

'If not a tenth as alive,' Evangeline said, holding Vicki to her. 'Remember us, little one, for we shall most assuredly remember you.'

Iola didn't speak, but ran back inside, her eyes filled with tears. 'Tell her that I'm not keen on goodbyes either,' said Vicki, as both Barbarà and Ian indicated that they should move quickly. ' I will remember you,' she told Georgiadis and his wife and then turned and ran to Ian and Barbara, trying to fight back her own tears.

'Come on,' Ian said, as the three of them crouched low on the corner and looked both ways for signs of movement. 'Take me to the river, we've got to see a man about a TARDIS.'

The Doctor moved slowly out of yet another blind alley. His entire night seemed to have been taken up running in and out of them, and avoiding the shouts and the cries that seemed to have always been happening just around the next corner.

He was tired and lost and he still didn't have the faintest idea of what he was going to say when he did finally find the Roman barracks. It wasn't the sort of place where you march up to the gates and demand to see whoever was in charge.

Just then, in the middle-distance, he finally saw the full horror of this night in Byzantium. A young man, seemingly a Roman, stripped of his clothes, was being chased by a gang of legionnaires. A hundred yards from the Doctor, the soldiers caught the man, threw him to the ground and then bludgeoned him into oblivion with staves and sword butts.

The Doctor wanted to turn and run but his eyes were transfixed with an insane need to see what they were doing to their unarmed victim. A need to be witness to a tiny fragment of history that would never be recorded in any of the books that Barbara Wright so diligently read for their accuracy.

Here was less than a footnote. But for one man, it was the final paragraph and the ultimate full stop.

A prickling sensation in his back told the Doctor that he was not alone. Turning to one side, he saw a couple of passing strangers, a man and a woman who looked at him curiously. He must, the Doctor reflected, have stuck out like a sore thumb in the ravages of Byzantium.

'Good morning,' he managed to say, feeling ridiculous as he did so. Then he quickly glanced back in the direction of the Roman soldiers. But they were gone.

'You seem to be lost,' the man told the Doctor. 'Allow us to show you the way.'

At Basellas's base, the Zealot leader found himself alone.

They had all deserted him during the night. Even Ephraim, whose toadying had been broken by the noise of the massacre going on in the streets.

He had fled, as they had all fled, denying Matthew Basellas in his hour of need.

Just as the scriptures had predicted.

It was something he had thought about much in recent

days, but now the answer was so blindingly obvious. *He* was the predicted messiah of the Jews.

The enormity of the task that lay ahead of him, to reunite his people, scared Basellas slightly. As he pondered on what to do first in his quest, the door to the safe house burst open and Hieronymous stood in the doorway. He was still, even despite the ravages of age, an impressive figure.

'I was told that I would find you here,' he noted.

'Who...?' began the Zealot.

'Phasaei. A man of limited intelligence. If one is to trust another with secrets of such deadly import as locations like this, it is wise not to tell greedy and deceitful wretches such as he.'

'I shall kill him,' said Basellas, with a manic laugh.

'You are too late,' noted Hieronymous. 'He has proved unworthy.'

Hieronymous sat in Basellas's chair whilst the Zealot watched him closely as he circled the room, catlike. 'Why have you come to this place, old man?' asked Basellas. 'For you must surely know that I will put you to death.'

The old Pharisee shrugged. 'Once, such a threat would have chilled me to the marrow,' he noted. 'But no longer. For I was once like you, Matthew, hot-headed and full of piss and hatred.' He paused and was amused by the scowl on the Zealot's face. 'But I learned to follow the scriptures, and follow them diligently.'

'You can only go so far in life on the Torah alone, Pharisee,' Basellas told him. 'The Torah does not teach us how to fight the Roman occupiers. It does not reveal how the Christians shall be slain in their great multitude.'

Hieronymous shook his mane of greying hair. 'I no longer see a threat in the followers of the Nazarene,' he told Basellas. 'Their ways are not our ways, but they are *good* ways. Maybe He was the Christ, after all?'

'Blasphemies from you, old man?' asked Basellas. 'This truly is a day for signs and wonders.'

'Indeed it is,' said Marcus Lanilla as he and Fabius Actium

stepped through the opened doorway. Basellas turned, but he was dead before he could properly face his Roman adversaries. Marcus thrust forward, expertly, with his sword which sank into Basellas's chest just below the breastbone. A quick and brutal twist of the *gladius* finished him off.

'Not like this,' Basellas cried – his final words as he slumped to the floor, bleeding his life away.

'That was murder,' said Hieronymous, angrily, standing. 'He was unarmed.'

'So is this,' replied Fabius, with a savage slash of his own sword that killed Hieronymous instantly. 'But who shall be witness to such capital crimes?'

Marcus stood cleaning his sword with patience and care. 'And so, in one fell swoop, we have solved the Jews' internal disagreements for them.'

'Truly, we should be honoured by them,' replied Fabius, laughing. 'But we shall not be, for they are ungrateful swine, ready for slaughter.'

As the two centurions loudly celebrated their achievement, Calaphilus and his men arrived.

For a moment there was a strange and silent stand-off as the general looked at the bodies of Basellas and the old Pharisee. This, he had to admit, was an unexpected turn of events. He had to act quickly to wrestle the initiative back from his dangerous opponents.

'See here, Gaius,' Marcus Lanilla said, proudly displaying the dead body of their hated enemy, Basellas. 'This has been a great day for Rome. A *great* day.'

'It shall only be so when all of the treasons of the night are exposed,' said Calaphilus dryly, and he removed his sword. The column of twenty men behind him did likewise. 'Your treachery shall not go unpunished, snake.'

For the first time, there was genuine doubt in Marcus Lanilla's mind. He gave Fabius a glance and saw that his friend was also nervous. Marcus wasn't entirely sure what he had expected when the general arrived to find them standing over the body of the most wanted man in all Thrace, but having a sword drawn on him certainly wasn't at the top of the list.

'You dare not insult or injure us, Calaphilus,' Marcus said angrily.

Fabius put down his own sword, quickly. 'We are unarmed,' he continued, in a nervous, high-pitched voice. 'We make no threats and state no grievances against the empire.'

'You dare not execute us, either, you mad old fool,' Marcus noted. 'We shall be popular heroes in Rome for having ended the rebellion of the Byzantine Zealots. Something neither you nor that thing we call a *praefectus*, with his buttocks clenched on the fence of indolence, were able to do.'

It was true. They had ended, in a single blow, the rebellion that Calaphilus had struggled for five years to put down. If such evidence was presented in Rome then Marcus's friends in the senate would use this to whip up the support of the people and charges of treason would be lost amidst the deafening sound of triumph.

'I appeal to you men,' Marcus said, suddenly, looking past the general to the soldiers behind. To captain Marinus Topignius and his men. 'Who would you prefer to follow? A weak leader like Calaphilus, or younger, braver officers like those that stand before you, rudely cast as traitors by the lies of dishonest men?'

Calaphilus stood his ground. 'Captain,' he said, slowly. 'Have your men execute these *proditores*. These... traitors.'

Which they did, blindly, and with little fuss, much to the astonishment of Marcus and Fabius.

As they lay dead from their multiple stab wounds to the stomach, Calaphilus stepped from behind the murderous assault of his men and loomed over the pair of traitors.

'Rank is still the most important thing to a soldier of Rome,' he told the corpses. 'Something that young pups like you never seem to understand.'

He turned to his men. 'This thing is done,' he said, ending the matter once and for all.

Chapter Thirty-Three
Here's Where The Story Ends

And ye shall be hated of all men for my name's sake:
but he that shall endure unto the end,
the same shall be saved.
Mark 13:13

When Ian, Vicki and Barbara finally arrived back at the place where they believed that the TARDIS had crash-landed, they found nothing.

Ian stood scratching his head for a moment and looking rather stupidly around. 'We must have got the wrong hill. Or something,' he said.

'I'm fairly positive it was this one,' Barbara replied, comforting Vicki as best she could. 'The Doctor wouldn't have just gone off without us,' she continued, firmly, seeing the question that Ian was just about to ask. 'There must be another explanation.'

'There is,' said Ian, pointing into the distance. 'Look...'

From out of the sand of the desert, a series of hazy and shimmering shapes appeared, walking towards the group.

'There they are,' Dorcas told the delighted Doctor as Ian, Barbara and Vicki came into view, waving from half a mile away.

'Your friends are all safe?' James asked, and the Doctor nodded wordlessly, out of breath from being rushed back to the Christians' camp and then out to this distant location.

'I am glad,' Daniel told him, patting him on the back.

'I also,' continued James.

'You can never know the gladness in my heart,' the Doctor told them as they reached the top of a steep incline that led down into the gully where Ian, Barbara and Vicki waited.

***

The Doctor was apologetic to his friends, but there was little he could say. The TARDIS was gone.

James told them that he had learned from a source that the strange blue chariot found in this location over two weeks ago had been taken by the Roman senator Germanicus Vinicius and transported, apparently, to his villa near Rome.

'Unless we want to spend the rest of their lives in this time,' the Doctor noted, 'then we must go in search of it.'

'Walk to Rome?' Ian asked incredulously. 'But it's *miles*!'

The understatement could have been amusing in different circumstances. But not today. 'You have a better idea, hmm?' snapped the Doctor.

Barbara, meanwhile, was pleased to see Dorcas and Tobias with the group of Christians who had accompanied the Doctor.

'We wish you every success in that which you seek,' Dorcas told her as the Doctor said his goodbyes to James and Daniel.

Barbara merely repeated what Ian had told Dorcas and Tobias some days earlier: that the Christians would be free one day.

'If anyone else had stated such opinion as fact, I should have laughed in their face,' Dorcas said with a wry smile. 'But with you, I sense that what you say is preordained. It *shall* come to pass.'

They left their Christian friends and began the long walk to the desert road, and the next town on the Via Egnatia. 'All roads lead to Rome, they say,' the Doctor told his friends. 'That is probably not true, but *this* one certainly does.'

After they had walked for several miles, and the waving figures of James, Daniel, Dorcas and Tobias were distant specks against the horizon, Ian felt compelled to ask the Doctor a question. 'Do you think that we have left Byzantium a better or a worse place?' He paused and tried to put into words a feeling that he had been unable to shake. 'Is it just me, or didn't we *solve* anything?'

'Who knows?' asked the Doctor at last, as they headed out into the desert. 'Not every story has a happy ending you know...'

Chapter Thirty-Four
... And Miles to Go Before We Sleep

And they went forth, and preached every where, the Lord working with them, and confirming the word with signs following.
Mark 16:20

'I had a really freaky dream last night,' Ian Chesterton said, as he poked the embers of the smouldering fire with his stick and made the sparks from it leap into the chilly night air. 'It was all mixed-up confusion, you know? I owned a Ford Anglia which is, in itself, ridiculous because I'd never buy Ford again after the last time. And I drove us all the way to Rome. But we crashed when we got there and I hurt my head. And we met a lion tamer. Then, afterwards, I went to a party in South Kensington with Keith Joseph and Sir Alec Douglas-Home and the Beatles. Alma Cogan was doing the twist on top of the piano with Brian Epstein. And then there was this annoying little pip-squeak I used to go to school with, called Perryman or something, who asked me what I'd done with my life. He said he worked as a book reviewer on some provincial rag. Proud of it, he was. So, I said, "Well I get to travel in time, you pleb." Then I woke up in a cold sweat.'

There was a momentary silence around the fire. No one quite knew what to say next.

The sparks of flame thrown up from the fire briefly joined the light of the stars over the desert before their moment of dazzling brilliance was over and they perished and died.

'Our life in microcosm,' Barbara finally added, pithily. Ian wasn't certain if she was talking about the dream or the fire.

'The party sounds rather good,' said Vicki. 'I wish I'd been invited. Who's Alma Cogan by the way?'

As the Doctor's friends fell about laughing and the rest of the tribesmen with them scratched their heads and wondered what their strange new travelling companions were talking about, he remained silent, a grim and determined expression on his face. What the future held for them all, now, was an unsolved mystery. Their destiny was no longer to be found in the stars, to be sought by the light of distant and magical suns. Rather, it lay along a dusty and ramrod-straight road, the Egnatian Way, guided by a single sun and moon. Earth's sun. Earth's moon. One led them far across the barren, sandy desert by day. The other kept a safe watch over them during the bone-chilling nights.

The TARDIS crew were three days into their journey. Ahead of them lay another one thousand miles of potential treachery and danger, without even the certainty that the TARDIS would be there waiting for them when they finally arrived in Rome.

It was turning into quite an unpredictable adventure and it would get a good deal more strange and dangerous before it was finally over, the Doctor was certain of that.

'Regrets?' Barbara asked him, sensing that the answer would reveal much about this mysterious old man.

Because, if the truth were told, while both Ian and Barbara had travelled with the Doctor for what seemed like a lifetime, neither really knew him. They never knew how he was reacting inside to the things that they saw and the people that they met.

And, she thought, it's unlikely that we ever will.

'No, not really,' replied the Doctor. 'Oh, I'm certain that if we had never come here, we would have found somewhere equally complicated and dangerous to visit. Somewhere for Chessington to get himself into a positive heap of trouble. Isn't that what being a nomad is all about? Ask these people,' the Doctor continued, sweeping an arm towards their new companions. 'I'm sure they will tell you a thing or two about what it is like to have no fixed or permanent abode. To travel only by the position of the stars and to be constantly searching for a place to call your "home".'

They sat around a camp fire in the Thracian twilight with the Bedouin who had allowed the former TARDIS crew to join them as they trekked across the vast open spaces of the northern Mediterranean. Towards Rome.

Towards destiny.

The Bedouin were interesting people with an insular view of the world and a fierce loyalty to each other and to the concept of 'family'. They spoke seldom, and then only in short, monosyllabic bursts. But they shared their food and their tents with the Doctor and his companions and asked only that they share the stories of their lives with them.

History and destiny were important to these people, clearly.

Now it was Ian's turn: '... so, there I was, stuck in the *praefectus*'s villa, surrounded by enemies. I couldn't relax for a single moment. I was a pawn in a game.'

'Oh, I know the feeling, believe me,' Barbara told him. 'And what of Vicki?'

By the light of the fire, it was difficult to tell if the girl's face was really as red as it appeared to be. She didn't speak for a long time. Just as she hadn't said more than five words about her time in Byzantium, since they'd left the city.

'Vicki...?'

'I was thinking about those poor people,' she told her companions. 'All of them. It's a rotten life they've got, isn't it? And what rewards do they get at the end of it?'

'That,' replied the Doctor, 'is a question to which none of us know the answer. More's the pity.'

Vicki stood up suddenly and, without a word, ran from the fireside and into the desert. Barbara moved to follow her but the Doctor placed a hand on her shoulder.

'Let the girl go, my dear. She's been through a lot. What she doesn't need right now is a lot of fussing and faffing about. She'll return soon enough.'

'She might get lost,' Barbara said, worriedly.

'The light of the fire will guide her back. It will be seen for miles. Let her be, Barbara. I'm afraid she's discovered a painful lesson about life.'

'Which is?' asked Ian.

'That growing up is a hard and lonely business,' said the Doctor as though he was speaking from personal experience. 'What are you looking at?' he chided Ian. 'Think I don't know what it's like, hmm? I've forgotten more than you'll ever know.'

'I don't doubt it,' replied Ian.

The long shadows of night crossed the Doctor as the fire flickered, stirred briefly by a gust of wind that rippled across the face of the desert. 'I never thought that I would see you all again,' he told his friends suddenly. 'I just wanted to tell you both, and young Vicki too when she comes back, that even if we are marooned in this era for good, then I'm pleased that we are at least together.'

Ian and Barbara didn't say anything.

There was nothing to say.

'My only regret,' Ian ventured, 'is that I didn't say goodbye to Gemellus and Thalius and the general. They were honourable men, even if their methods were questionable.'

'I think we may try to get some sleep now,' the Doctor continued, a gentle smile of relief on his face as, in the half-distance, he could see the figure of Vicki emerging from the desert and walking back towards them.

'It'll be all right, Doctor,' said Ian, brightly. 'You'll see.'

'We have a long journey ahead,' the Doctor continued. 'And, at the end of it, a carriage to the stars awaits us.'

Epilogue
Two Thousand Light Years from Home

And these signs shall follow them that believe
Mark 16:17

London, England: 1973

Ian could hear snatches of Barbara's conversation with Julia as he stared at another glass case on the far side of the hall.

'You must look us up if you're ever in Redborough,' the woman was saying, handing Barbara a slip of paper with her address hastily scribbled on it. 'We're right next to Robert Lee's bookshop. If you get lost, just ask Mr Ameobi in the newsagents where the Franklins live.'

Ian Chesterton gulped at the prospect and kept his attention firmly focused on the short stabbing sword in the case in front of him. He caught a glimpse of his own reflection in the glass and instantly regretted his choice of orange shirt and purple kipper tie, bought on the recommendation of Greg Sutton from John Collier of Bond Street. 'Johnny,' he called, as his son stopped his frantic chasing of an imaginary friend and ran to his father's side.

'Look,' Ian said, pointing to the sword. 'What do you think of *that*, eh?'

'It's so cool,' said Johnny, his jaw dropping as the light glinted on the sword's sharp edge. 'Can I have one, Dad?'

'Maybe when you're older,' said Ian, absent-mindedly as something on the sword's hilt caught his attention.

Two letters, carved into the metal, almost worn away by the passing of time.

IC.

Ian read the display caption aloud, for his own benefit as much as that of his son.

A GLADIUS, the highly effective short sword used by Roman legionnaires in combat. The very unusual carved inscription identifies the weapon as belonging to a soldier of the 99th Legion, who occupied Biythria and Thrace (including much of modern Turkey). It almost certainly dates from the end of the first century AD.

Ian placed his hand on the glass that separated the sword from the outside world, as though he were waving a greeting to an old friend.

'Come on,' he told his son. 'Let's get back to your mother before we both end up in the doghouse.'

'End of the first century AD?' Ian mused. 'It's nice to know something that they don't, for once, isn't it?'

'How's that, Dad?' asked Johnny.

Ian smiled. 'It's actually thirty-five years older than that.'

Every Day I Write the Book...

I think it was Kingsley Amis who said, 'There's little point in writing if you can't annoy someone with it'. The author would, as ever, like to thank many friends and colleagues for their invaluable help, encouragement and inspiration: the always-reliable Ian Abrahams (whose impressive feminist critique of *The King of Terror* has, I hope, been addressed here), Jinny Algar, Greg Bakun, Ness Bishop (for a couple of brilliant chapter title suggestions), Wendy and Paul Comeau, Neil Connor (who fixed my knackered floppy disc-drive), Chris Cornwell, Andy Cowper, Martin Day (honest and appreciated advice as always), Rob Francis, Robert Franks, Jeff Hart (who named all the stars), Tony and Jane Kenealy, Theresa Lambert, Mike Lee and the rest of the Minneapolis *CONvergence* possé, Mr Kimblew of Cambridge, Davie and Lesley McIntee, John McLaughlin, Ingrid Oliansky, Lars Pearson, Mark Phippen, Tammy Potash (just *lurv* that name), my editor Justin Richards and Sarah Lavelle at the BBC, Camilla Rockwood, Paul Simpson, Victoria Sorel (at least I can *spell* 'Tegan', sweetie!), Kathy Sullivan, Suzie Tiller (a *diamond* of a proof-reader), my brother Colin Topping ('O' level expert), Jason Tucker, everyone at *Gallifrey One* (and especially my wonderful 'voodoo sisters', Suze Campagna and Diana Dougherty) and *The Neutral Zone* and my family (whose occasional, half-interested questions on how the novel was progressing led, more often than not, to blood-curdling if historically accurate descriptions of torture and crucifixion). I would, however, like to assure readers that, despite the evidence of bits of my last two novels, I'm not *that* interested in graphic and sadistic cruelty...

Not forgetting, of course, Paul and Steady Eddie. *Inspirational* figures, both.

Research, inevitably, played a role in the writing of this novel. I would particularly draw readers' attention to several source works that helped to provide copious period detail: *A History of Britain* (Simon Schama, London, 2000), *An Aid to Bible Understanding* (International Bible Students Assoc., New York, 1969), *Atlas of the Bible and Christianity* (Tim Dowley [ed], London, 1999), *Backgrounds of Early Christianity* (Everett Ferguson, Michigan, 1993), *Byzantium, the Empire of the New Rome* (Cyril A. Mango, London, 1980), *Everyday Life in Byzantium* (Tamara Talbot Rice, New York, 1967), *Goddesses, Wives, Whores and Slaves: The Role of Women in Classical Antiquity* (Sarah B. Pomeroy, New York, 1975), *Istanbul, the Imperial City* (John Freely, London, 1998), *Jesus and the Zealots* (S.G. Brandon, Manchester, 1967), *Sexual Life in Ancient Greece* (Hans Licht, London, 1949), *The Dionysiac Mysteries of the Hellenistic and Roman Age* (M.P. Nilsson, Lund, 1957) and *The Roman Imperial Army of the First and Second Centuries AD* (G. Webster, London, 1969). Plus the *invaluable* Discovery and History Channels and the gratefully acknowledged inspiration of *Time Team*, Robert Graves, Dennis Potter and Messrs Chapman, Cleese, Gilliam, Jones, Idle and Palin. And Copey, whose 'Use Me' is the best-ever song about Christianity. Check it out, *drudes*.

All quotations from *The Gospel According to St. Mark* are taken from the *Authorised King James Version* (first published 1611), which may not be the most accurately translated Bible ever printed (that's kind of the whole point), but it *is* the one that most readers will be familiar with and it's certainly one that anyone with an interest in the language of Shakespeare and Marlowe should read at least once in their lives.

Keith Topping
Pons Aelii
Britannia
April 2001 (CE)

About the Author

Dandy highwayman, *bon vivant*, raconteur and dotcom-pauper, Keith Topping continues his ill-starred love affair with Tyneside by continuing to live there when he should have escaped years ago. His life often resembles scenes from *Get Carter*... and that's on a *good* day. Nasty geographical considerations conspire to keep him and his very understanding girlfriend, Suzie, on separate continents. Sad, but true.

Sadly, everything that Keith likes in life is either illegal, immoral or fattening. And his personal motto is, 'Why be difficult when, with a bit of effort, you can be *bloody impossible*?'

Since his last novel, *The King of Terror*, Keith has written several programme guides for Virgin on TV series such as *Buffy the Vampire Slayer* (including the best-selling French title *Tueuse de Vampires*), *Angel* and a forthcoming volume on *Roswell High*. He was also a contributor to the BBC television series *I ♥ the 70s*, albeit wearing a particularly nasty green shirt, for which he wholeheartedly apologises to viewers. He continues to hold down a part-time day job while bemoaning the fact that there are only twenty-four hours in a day and sleep takes up at least six of them. Occasionally more.

Byzantium! is Keith's fourth novel and his sixteenth book.

ALSO AVAILABLE

DOCTOR WHO: THE NOVEL OF THE FILM by Gary Russell ISBN 0 563 38000 4
THE EIGHT DOCTORS by Terrance Dicks ISBN 0 563 40563 5
VAMPIRE SCIENCE by Jonathan Blum and Kate Orman ISBN 0 563 40566 X
THE BODYSNATCHERS by Mark Morris ISBN 0 563 40568 6
GENOCIDE by Paul Leonard ISBN 0 563 40572 4
WAR OF THE DALEKS by John Peel ISBN 0 563 40573 2
ALIEN BODIES by Lawrence Miles ISBN 0 563 40577 5
KURSAAL by Peter Anghelides ISBN 0 563 40578 3
OPTION LOCK by Justin Richards ISBN 0 563 40583 X
LONGEST DAY by Michael Collier ISBN 0 563 40581 3
LEGACY OF THE DALEKS by John Peel ISBN 0 563 40574 0
DREAMSTONE MOON by Paul Leonard ISBN 0 563 40585 6
SEEING I by Jonathan Blum and Kate Orman ISBN 0 563 40586 4
PLACEBO EFFECT by Gary Russell ISBN 0 563 40587 2
VANDERDEKEN'S CHILDREN by Christopher Bulis ISBN 0 563 40590 2
THE SCARLET EMPRESS by Paul Magrs ISBN 0 563 40595 3
THE JANUS CONJUNCTION by Trevor Baxendale ISBN 0 563 40599 6
BELTEMPEST by Jim Mortimore ISBN 0 563 40593 7
THE FACE EATER by Simon Messingham ISBN 0 563 55569 6
THE TAINT by Michael Collier ISBN 0 563 55568 8
DEMONTAGE by Justin Richards ISBN 0 563 55572 6
REVOLUTION MAN by Paul Leonard ISBN 0 563 55570 X
DOMINION by Nick Walters ISBN 0 563 55574 2
UNNATURAL HISTORY by Jonathan Blum and Kate Orman ISBN 0 563 55576 9
AUTUMN MIST by David A. McIntee ISBN 0 563 55583 1
INTERFERENCE: BOOK ONE by Lawrence Miles ISBN 0 563 55580 7
INTERFERENCE: BOOK TWO by Lawrence Miles ISBN 0 563 55582 3

THE BLUE ANGEL by Paul Magrs and Jeremy Hoad ISBN 0 563 55581 5
THE TAKING OF PLANET 5 by Simon Bucher-Jones and Mark Clapham ISBN 0 563 55585 8
FRONTIER WORLDS by Peter Anghelides ISBN 0 563 55589 0
PARALLEL 59 by Natalie Dallaire and Stephen Cole ISBN 0 563 555904
THE SHADOWS OF AVALON by Paul Cornell ISBN 0 563 555882
THE FALL OF YQUATINE by Nick Walters ISBN 0 563 55594 7
COLDHEART by Trevor Baxendale ISBN 0 563 55595 5
THE SPACE AGE by Steve Lyons ISBN 0 563 53800 7
THE BANQUO LEGACY by Andy Lane and Justin Richards ISBN 0 563 53808 2
THE ANCESTOR CELL by Peter Anghelides and Stephen Cole ISBN 0 563 53809 0
THE BURNING by Justin Richards ISBN 0 563 53812 0
CASUALTIES OF WAR by Steve Emmerson ISBN 0 563 53805 8
THE TURING TEST by Paul Leonard ISBN 0 563 53806 6
ENDGAME by Terrance Dicks ISBN 0 563 53802 3
FATHER TIME by Lance Parkin ISBN 0 563 53810 4
ESCAPE VELOCITY by Colin Brake ISBN 0 563 53825 2
EARTHWORLD by Jacqueline Rayner ISBN 0 563 53827 9 (March '01)
VANISHING POINT by Stephen Cole ISBN 0 563 53829 5 (April '01)
EATER OF WASPS by Trevor Baxendale ISBN 0 563 53832 5 (May '01)
THE YEAR OF INTELLIGENT TIGERS by Kate Orman ISBN 0 563 53831 7 (June '01)
THE DEVIL GOBLINS FROM NEPTUNE by Keith Topping and Martin Day ISBN 0 563 40564 3
THE MURDER GAME by Steve Lyons ISBN 0 563 40565 1
THE ULTIMATE TREASURE by Christopher Bulis ISBN 0 563 40571 6
BUSINESS UNUSUAL by Gary Russell ISBN 0 563 40575 9

ILLEGAL ALIEN by Mike Tucker and Robert Perry ISBN 0 563 40570 8
THE ROUNDHEADS by Mark Gatiss ISBN 0 563 40576 7
THE FACE OF THE ENEMY by David McIntee ISBN 0 563 40580 5
EYE OF HEAVEN by Jim Mortimore ISBN 0 563 40567 8
THE WITCH HUNTERS by Steve Lyons ISBN 0 563 40579 1
THE HOLLOW MEN by Keith Topping and Martin Day ISBN 0 563 40582 1
CATASTROPHEA by Terrance Dicks ISBN 0 563 40584 8
MISSION: IMPRACTICAL by David A. McIntee ISBN 0 563 40592 9
ZETA MAJOR by Simon Messingham ISBN 0 563 40597 X
DREAMS OF EMPIRE by Justin Richards ISBN 0 563 40598 8
LAST MAN RUNNING by Chris Boucher ISBN 0 563 40594 5
MATRIX by Robert Perry and Mike Tucker ISBN 0 563 40596 1
THE INFINITY DOCTORS by Lance Parkin ISBN 0 563 40591 0
SALVATION by Steve Lyons ISBN 0 563 55566 1
THE WAGES OF SIN by David A. McIntee ISBN 0 563 55567 X
DEEP BLUE by Mark Morris ISBN 0 563 55571 8
PLAYERS by Terrance Dicks ISBN 0 563 55573 4
MILLENNIUM SHOCK by Justin Richards ISBN 0 563 55586 6
STORM HARVEST by Robert Perry and Mike Tucker ISBN 0 563 55577 7
THE FINAL SANCTION by Steve Lyons ISBN 0 563 55584 X
CITY AT WORLD'S END by Christopher Bulis ISBN 0 563 55579 3
DIVIDED LOYALTIES by Gary Russell ISBN 0 563 55578 5
CORPSE MARKER by Chris Boucher ISBN 0 563 55575 0
LAST OF THE GADERENE by Mark Gatiss ISBN 0 563 55587 4
TOMB OF VALDEMAR by Simon Messingham ISBN 0 563 55591 2
VERDIGRIS by Paul Magrs ISBN 0 563 55592 0
GRAVE MATTER by Justin Richards ISBN 0 563 55598 X
HEART OF TARDIS by Dave Stone ISBN 0 563 55596 3
PRIME TIME by Mike Tucker ISBN 0 563 55597 1
IMPERIAL MOON by Christopher Bulis ISBN 0 563 53801 5
FESTIVAL OF DEATH by Jonathan Morris ISBN 0 563 53803 1
INDEPENDENCE DAY by Peter Darvill-Evans ISBN 0 563 53804 X

THE KING OF TERROR by Keith Topping ISBN 0 563 53802 3
QUANTUM ARCHANGEL by Craig Hinton ISBN 0 563 53824 4
BUNKER SOLDIERS by Martin Day ISBN 0 563 53819 8
RAGS by Mick Lewis ISBN 0 563 53826 0 (March '01)
THE SHADOW IN THE GLASS by Justin Richards and Stephen Cole ISBN 0 563 53838 4 (April '01)
ASYLUM by Peter Darvill-Evans ISBN 0 563 53833 3 (May '01)
SUPERIOR BEINGS by Nick Walters ISBN 0 563 53830 9 (June '01)
SHORT TRIPS ed. Stephen Cole ISBN 0 563 40560 0
MORE SHORT TRIPS ed. Stephen Cole ISBN 0 563 55565 3
SHORT TRIPS AND SIDE STEPS ed. Stephen Cole and Jacqueline Rayner ISBN 0 563 55599 8